OVERFLOW WITH HOPE

ALSO BY E. C. JACKSON

OVERFLOW WITH HOPE

a novel

E.C. JACKSON

ISBN 978-1-7329592-3-1

The Write Way – A Real Slice of Life
Website: hopebooks.faith
Author Page: facebook.com/ecjacksonauthor

Editor: Amber Barry (amberbarryeditor.com)
Proofreader: Martha Rasmussen (bookaholicspress@gmail.com)
Cover design: formattingexperts.com
Typesetting: formattingexperts.com

Acknowledgments

My fifth and final book of the hope-themed series is finally complete. Once again, the scripture *"against all hope, Abraham in hope believed"* sustained me the entire time.

My family and friends supported me with prayers and encouragement during the three-year process that was difficult on many levels. A huge thank you goes to my editors, book formatter and cover designer.

I thank God for surrounding me with people who care about me and my books.

May God, the source of hope, fill you completely with joy and *shalom* as you continue trusting, so that by the power of the *Ruach HaKodesh* you may overflow with hope.

Romans 15:13

Complete Jewish Bible

(*Ruach HaKodesh* means Holy Spirit in Hebrew.)

Chapter One

After installing HVAC systems at a new apartment complex, twenty-eight-year-old Cory Sanders should've headed home, eaten a sandwich, and stretched his five-foot-eleven-inch frame onto his king-sized bed. But today he sought diversions at a friend's pool hall. The short trek across the parking lot led him inside a large yet cozy space teeming with some of his favorite folks. As his eyes adjusted to dim lighting, he stepped up to the counter of the juice and coffee bar.

Glancing at Cory, a middle-aged woman, brown eyes alert, paused her conversation with a customer. "Wait till I tell Dan who stopped by on a late Friday afternoon," she said to Cory. "Of course, neither he nor our sons will believe me."

Miss Laura's husband, Dan, had been Cory's father's best friend since their HVAC training program days. He and his youngest son worked for Cory's father's heating and cooling business, while his wife helped their oldest son, Scott, run his pool hall.

"Keep our secret, Miss Laura, or someone will demand I show up more often."

She winked as she laughed. "If anyone asks me, I'll say you were just winding down from a tough workday."

Cory chuckled. "Sounds like the perfect plan," he said. "One pomegranate slush, please. And Miss Laura, let your son know adding slushes to the juice menu was an excellent idea. If he asks, tell him to add grilled cheese, hamburgers, and hot sausage sandwiches."

"More approval will swell his head. Thank God, he won't inquire."

"I bet you he'd consider those suggestions if he did."

"Serving food ain't happening on my watch. This mama has enough tasks without piling on more. We'll hold off on a food menu until Scott quits his day job."

As Cory left the counter, Miss Laura snuck in, "See you next Friday."

While sipping his slush, Cory peered around the cavernous room and took in the lively atmosphere. Ten pool tables were strategically set up to maximize solo and group play. Walking across the space, he passed a group of men ribbing each other. A fifty-something man pocketed a ball then spotted Cory. "Lookee here. Grab a pool stick, son."

Cory sat on a seat close to the action and pointed at the bald, clean-shaven man. "Not today. I just came to watch you masters clean the table."

"Take notes," another man said. "Stu left this little boy hanging in the pocket."

With that, Cory realized he had chosen the correct diversion after all. His bed and sandwich could wait until later that evening. These lively antics might delete a tiresome woman from his mind. Last year, he had purged her from his heart, but no matter how hard he tried, he could never seem to evict her from his mind. He hoped that changing his long-established habits might help.

* * *

An inner battle that had begun the previous day woke up twenty-three-year-old Tempia Wade from a disturbed sleep. On her drive home from work yesterday, Tempia's dream of magically meeting up with Cory had lost steam. Before climbing into bed, dejection had plunged her into an emotional tailspin. This morning, as reality further hit, her hopes of their celebrating the one-year anniversary of her divorce from Quince died. Many unfulfilled dreams perished at the same time. Cory, the man who had held her future in his hands, had banished Tempia from his life fourteen months ago. She couldn't understand why he had rejected her, but it was evident that leaving an emotionally abusive husband hadn't been enough.

For endless months, she had prayed they would cement a lifelong relationship. Vivid recollections of Cory's constant support before his defection still provided comfort and relief.

If only she and Cory could reconnect on a personal level.

Tempia rubbed her achy forehead. Old disastrous decisions and misjudgments pummeled her psyche full force. Her ex-husband's grievous subterfuge played through her mind again and again.

Locked on the war inside her head, Tempia squirmed on the bed until she broke the silence with her own loud sniffling sounds. Abundant teardrops streamed over her cheeks.

She squeezed her eyes shut and pursed her lips into a single line. Her hands balled into tight fists. How could fourteen months spent rebuilding her life on a solid foundation amount to nothing? Pulling tissues from a box on the floor beside the bed, she reassessed yesterday's wish that Cory would call her.

She didn't know what to do to help herself in that moment. She might as well lick her wounds. "Let it go. He won't call." She stared at the ceiling. "It is what it is. I single-handedly wrecked my own life."

Tempia's cell phone rang as she buried her head underneath the covers.

"Rise and shine," a laughing voice suggested. "Hibernating while I get ready for work is shameful. I adore having sunny days in early March. We could have gone shopping this afternoon if you'd told me before last night that you were taking today off."

Tempia sat up in bed, listening to a shower spraying water in the background of the phone call. Her lifesaving best friend Gabby had struck again. This morning, the habitual late sleeper had awoken earlier than the birds just to lend support.

Tempia cleared her throat, striving to strike the proper tone. "Thank you, ma'am. I needed a wake-up call."

Gabby laughed outright. "Why? If you were getting pessimistic, stop it this minute."

More tears rolled down Tempia's soaked cheeks. "I just can't get over how badly I messed up by marrying Quince and missing my chance with Cory. But don't mind me. Jump into the shower and stop wasting hot water." Tempia shook her head when she heard the water shut off.

"Hope my water-conscious husband is still asleep. Temp, what person hasn't made mistakes? We all, err, learn our lessons, then continue living."

At some point in her existence, Tempia had thought so too. That is, until she discovered some errors last forever and won't ever be forgiven. "Yeah, but we don't all wreck our lives during the process and stunt future growth."

"And neither did you, my special friend. Listen. You corrected each miscalculation. You were formally divorced one year ago today, and dating Cory isn't a lost cause. So, get over yourself. Celebrate a great success."

"You have a special knack for making life sound better than it is."

"Aw, pooh. I simply discovered back in junior high how to forgive my shortcomings. Now, forget the ex. No man is worth any woman living with depression. If the degenerate does come to mind, dwell on how you kicked his butt to the curb and regained your independence."

Tempia's shallow breaths subsided. A weight lifted off her overburdened shoulders, even though depression hovered just above its favorite resting spot. Once again, Gabrielle Stephens proved herself to be the best person anyone could call a friend. "The best friend in the world deserves a free lunch. Can you come over around noon?"

Laughter bubbled deep within Gabby's throat. "Noonish it is. Until then, don't forget that you won the victory in an overdue battle last year."

"I love you, Gabby."

"I love you more," Gabby replied, ending the call.

Tempia practically hugged herself and sprang out of the bed. "Thank you, Lord. I needed a shot in the arm." Her gaze lit upon a painting of a Parisian café that hung on a wall in the living area. She glanced at the alarm clock on the end table, then crawled back underneath the covers.

Despite Gabby's encouraging speech, past regrets immediately stole Tempia's positive thoughts away from her considerable progress. However, she reminded herself that Gabby had made good points about her progress. After living through five pain-filled months, Tempia had launched a new beginning and risen above depression, remorse, and foolish mistakes. Yet, this morning, she couldn't shake re-examining the life highlighted by an ill-fated courtship and marriage. Her hands gripped her beet-red blanket.

On a January evening two years ago, Gabby's fiancé had called while Gabby and Tempia were taking in an antiques show. Lifelong friends, they undertook weekly shopping expeditions, keeping at the forefront of each other's lives. Tempia ogled a vintage curio cabinet as Gabby removed a pealing cell phone from her purse.

"Rob said he'd brought enough work home to steal his entire weekend. He must be taking a break." Her lips curving into a wide grin, Gabby took the call. The smile vanished. She turned around and faced the opposite direction. "Did I hear you correctly? ... You're right. The invitation is a huge surprise ... Well, for one thing, you rarely redirect your evenings on short notice. Plus ... Okay. I won't go on. Tempia is standing beside me. I'll ask her." Muting the cell phone, she studied her friend. "Rob invited friends over for a game night. Wanna head over there?"

Tempia had barely stopped her hands from clapping. "Are you serious? Yes. I'd love to go." Even though Gabby and Rob had dated for three years, none of Gabby's friends had been invited to his house. She'd often wondered why they hadn't met any of his buddies. Also, three of her closest friends were engaged, and most of her other pals had steady dates. Tempia was the only single person in their group. Perhaps a likely candidate would attend Rob's party. She just had to keep up hope that a good opportunity would arise—and maybe even bring a favorable outcome.

An hour later, Gabby parked across the street from her fiancé's house, sprang out of the car, and strolled to the passenger door to wait for Tempia. Casually dressed in black-washed jeans, an aquamarine sweater, suede ankle boots, and a black leather jacket, the five-foot-six-inch beauty looked terrific.

Her hands wringing, Tempia frowned at her own shoes and clothes. Tan flats topped off the beige skinny-leg pants, navy-and-white sweater, and down jacket. The individual pieces numbered among her favorite clothes, but she wasn't sure the total package was right for a get-together among strangers. A soft moan escaped through her parted lips until her head hung.

The women crossed the street, climbed several steep stairs, and stepped onto the porch of the A-frame house.

Gabby eyed her. "What's wrong, Temp? If the dominoes are already in use, there are loads of other games we can play." She frowned when Tempia remained silent. "Listen. At least pretend you're happy about being here. Come on, girl. You enjoy playing games."

She certainly did—but only when secure within her safety net. "Not among people I've never met." Tempia stared longingly at Gabby's SUV.

Gabby laughed. "You can't pray to meet new people on a lark. God not only hears our prayers, He also answers them. Capisce?"

"Kinda, sorta. Did Rob say why he planned a party instead of clearing out his workload?"

"He only said, 'You can thank me later.' Whatever that cryptic remark implies."

Tempia searched her brain for any obvious reasons, then she grinned. "I've got it. He planned a special surprise for his soon-to-be bride."

"At any rate, I'm half-starved. Let's hope he catered his fiancée's favorite foods."

Tempia's lips puckered as Gabby edged toward the door. She truly did want to meet new people, but trepidation was rearing its ugly head. Excitement wrestled anxiety in an uneven match. Rooted to the spot, she inspected her shoes one foot at a time before her lips turned downward.

"How do people dress at game parties? I should have gone home and changed outfits."

Gabby's mouth gaped. "Why? Saturdays are our days to keep it simple. I'm dressed in jeans and a sweater."

"But we're at your fiancé's house. You've probably met all or most of the people inside. Besides, you look good in everything. And your color combinations are fantastic."

"Coming from you, the comment is hilarious. Unless you're admitting I'm a fashion icon." Laughter trilled from Gabby's lips.

Tempia glared. "Have I ever stated a different opinion?"

"Yes. Numerous times. I'll overlook your brain-freeze moment, but I will recall each word on our next shopping binge."

"Quit skimping on accolades. Glowing reviews require nothing less than two thumbs-up."

Gabby was sidling closer to the door, but now she spun around. "Thank you much. The compliment is long overdue. Ready? It's now or never."

Tempia slung her purse strap onto her right shoulder. "All right. Bring on the introductions."

The door easily opened when Gabby twisted the doorknob. She smiled at Tempia, then she strolled inside the house.

After another glance at her shoes, Tempia fell in step behind her friend. Loud guffaws and enthusiastic conversations met the women inside the foyer. She sneaked a quick peek at her unperturbed friend. Tempia managed to calm down when Gabby's eyes twinkled behind her blue-rimmed glasses.

Gabby's silent reassurance relaxed Tempia's grip on her purse strap. She reminded herself that people let extra loose on the weekends when free from job restrictions, and she needed to keep her shunning of unrestrained behavior in check. Or ... perhaps she should have eaten a good meal and gone home. As her ears acclimated to the constant noise, Tempia commanded her body to relax and scanned the crowd.

Probably fifteen people were spread throughout two adjacent rooms. Wherever Tempia looked, people were laughing. Suddenly, she felt like someone was watching her. Her gaze swept the room, and there he sat. The lone exception to the noise. A good-looking man dressed in camel chinos and a smoke-gray T-shirt observed her from a corner chair. It seemed his gaze had pinpointed her arrival from the moment she entered the house. Could she get a closer inspection without outright staring? Somehow, he looked vaguely familiar. A fleeting glimpse of a face she couldn't recapture came to mind. His seemingly low-key persona immediately attracted her.

Was accepting Rob's invitation the correct choice after all? Years of dating partygoers had compelled Tempia to reject gadabouts. She would rather be alone than coddling scoundrels and wasting her precious time. She turned away from the man to avoid his intense observation yet felt his gaze upon her back as she walked down the hallway.

She caught up to Gabby, who dropped her jacket onto a bench in the hallway and entered the kitchen. Tempia followed suit. Once inside the room, Gabby uncovered all the platters on the table and heaped deli food onto a plate. "Not my first choice, but at least there's food."

"I would have chosen a deli restaurant after we left the antiques show." Her plate in hand, Tempia drew up beside Gabby. Her greatest dilemma was gathering information about the attractive man without voicing interest. "Did you recognize the guy wearing chinos and a gray T-shirt?"

Please say yes. And that he is single. Available. And a perfect fit for me.

Alertness highlighted her friend's gaze. "Quick work. I'm impressed. Hold on while I check this fellow out."

Gabby scurried toward the living room door then stood in the doorway with her hands on her hips. A quizzical expression highlighted her features once she re-entered the kitchen. "Well, his being here is a huge surprise." Studying her friend's face, she hesitated. "Hold on, we just arrived, so you could have only gotten a brief glance. Are you interested in meeting Cory?"

Gabby's perplexed reaction to Rob's friend surprised Tempia. "Um ... I was until your bewilderment raised a few doubts. Do you personally know him?" She continued when Gabby nodded. "Do you like him? Does he have a girl-friend?"

"Ignore my initial reaction. Cory is Rob's cousin and one of my favorite people. He's single and a great catch. Last month, he came alone to his aunt's thirty-fifth wedding anniversary." She picked up her overstuffed plate. "And get this: you and he share similar idiosyncrasies."

Tempia glanced up while splashing dressing on her salad. "It's too early in the evening for personality wisecracks. I am not an eccentric person. Oops." Blue-cheese dressing flowed across her plate. In one smooth motion, she piled additional lettuce on top to help sop it up.

Gabby passed her extra napkins. "Yeah. You are. Luckily, Cory shares some of your quirks. Stop frowning. Frowners have fine lines etched into their skin before fifty."

"Oh hush." Tempia rolled her eyes.

Gabby giggled. "You know, Rob throwing this party was definitely a surprise. However, Cory's joining us is an even greater one. I still can't believe he came."

"Why not? You said Cory and Rob are cousins."

Gabby shrugged. "Let's just agree that the reason for our unexpected summons has become clear. Who knows. We might rack up a fun night."

Tempia licked her lips. "I pray to God we do, Gab. Time is running out for me."

"Sheer baloney. Whoever heard of a twenty-one-year-old spinster?" Gabby's objective gaze flitted over her friend. "Adorable as ever. Let's hit the romance trail. Chin up, please. Look forward to your grand entrance." Gabby scooted across the floor.

Oh boy. Tempia hadn't gone on any dates since moving out of her parents' house. *Here's to the next phase in my suspended life. Hope it's more than I expected.*

She matched her friend's steady gait, and the women retraced their steps down the hallway. Inside the living room doorway, Gabby lowered her head, speaking in a soft voice. "Interesting. Your potential man changed his seat closer to Rob, plus he's eyeing you. Get ready for a sweet introduction." Her teasing grin lit upon her friend. "Here we go, superstar. This will only take a moment."

As Tempia padded across the floor, she could feel Cory's gaze upon her. She stole a quick peek. Right as ever. Cory observed her progress the entire way. Halfway across the room, she skidded on objects scattered across the floor. The balancing act to stay upright ended when she careened onto the sofa where he sat. Her salad-filled plate spilled onto his lap. Vegetables drenched in blue-cheese dressing hit his pants and ran down onto his shoes.

The sudden silence in the room spoke volumes. Tempia struggled to regain her composure. Apology ready, she hesitated.

The couple sitting on the love seat snickered in her face. "What a neat trick," the man said.

The woman holding his hand shook her head. "What will you do for an encore? Jump up and down on one foot?"

Tempia's legs wobbled while her heartbeat quickened. A glance around the space increased her angst. Several people playing a board game had stood up to watch. A group in the next room visibly gawked. Everyone who scrutinized her performance seemed to move around in slow motion.

The dressing-covered man directed a crushing glance at the snarky couple, making everyone go silent.

Tears welled up in Tempia's eyes. Brushing fingers across her mouth, her hands splayed on each cheek. "I am so sorry. Please don't hold this accident against me." She scanned the floor behind her, identifying her trip hazard. She then looked at the man's twinkling eyes. While Cory smiled at her, she pointed behind her back. "I tripped on those scattered dominoes."

His mouth broke into a wide grin. "Hey, no biggie. Relax." The seemingly composed man dumped food back onto the disposable plate.

"Bravo," an auburn-haired man remarked. "Great response, Cory. Keep the goal in focus, man."

As several people agreed with his glowing assessment, Tempia squashed tears and glanced at Gabby.

Perched on the seat beside Rob, Gabby's eyelids fluttered. Since their childhood days, the friends had used rapid blinking as their steadfast support. "Cory Sanders, meet my best bud, Tempia Wade. Temp, Cory is Rob's cousin." Her regularly low-pitched voice raised an octave. "Momentum is on our side, folks. I dare any of you to top our grand entrance."

Once again, Gabby made an incredible ally. Tempia refocused on Cory, stammering through another apology.

Cory winked. "The first apology was accepted but unnecessary. I'm certain you would rather chat with me than drop food onto my lap."

He dumped more salad pieces onto the plate, then he set the plate on a side table. When he finished, the blonde beauty sitting beside him cleaned up the floor with wet wipes. More food had landed on Cory than on the tile.

"Thanks, Tina," Cory said. "Do you always carry those things around?"

"Of course. With two small children, I keep wet wipes handy for quick clean-up jobs."

Rising from the sofa, Cory touched Tempia's arms. A sympathetic gaze studied her eyes, which held back fresh tears. "Don't sweat small stuff. We're fine. I'll clean myself up while you fix yourself another plate."

Tempia's body quivered. Small bumps appeared on each arm. His soothing grin and gentle speech had won her heart. She was anchored on the pathway to a promising new adventure.

Before she could respond, an attractive man dressed in a black-and-gold jogging suit appeared by Tempia's side, giving her elbow a slight jerk.

Cory's gaze remained upon her face. "Think positive thoughts about me until I can speak for myself. I'll quickly clean myself up and then sit with you while you eat."

At that exact moment, Tempia completely fell for Rob's cousin. *He is handsome, nice, and still interested in me. Yay!* Blushes that had overtaken her body diminished. Thank God she had accepted Rob's invitation. "You're a nice man, Cory. But I promise on this trip I won't choose salad."

Soft laugh lines appeared around his mouth. "Eat whatever makes you happy." Eyeing the man glued to Tempia's side, Cory exited the living room.

While Tempia watched Cory's departure, the stranger's strong grip left her elbow and fastened onto her hand. He gave a brief bow. "Quince Hightower Jones. An amiable helper at your service."

Tempia stared at him through misty eyes. "Tempia Wade. Gabby's clumsy friend."

Sparkles lit his dark-brown eyes. "Sweet, honest, and delectable. I can feel the heat rising between us."

"Didn't you use that same tired line in high school?" said the man who had complimented Cory.

Quince glared at him.

"Sounds more like it's from junior high," the wet-wipe lady quipped.

Quince sneered. "Ignore the echo chamber. I'll escort you to the kitchen, Gabby's friend. Glad we came."

Who was the "we" he referred to? Were other guests going on a food run with them? Tempia glanced as far as she could around both rooms, then gazed at the man who boldly studied her. His expression posed an undefinable question.

"We? Who are you referring to?" she asked.

A low chuckle rumbled forth from deep within his throat. "I adore naivety in women. Us, sweetheart. Tempia and Quince." Squeezing her fingers, Quince led her out of the room.

Chapter Two

Like an automaton, she allowed herself to be escorted back into the kitchen. Thoughts of Cory's soiled clothes made her settle for a sandwich. It hardly mattered what she ate. Surely she would spend more time talking than eating. But disappointment rocked her composure. The talkative man led her to a card table and two folding chairs crammed into a hallway. Tempia decided to sit down with him when a man dressed in khakis, a checkerboard T-shirt, and white flip-flops shook his head and laughed. Tempia hated being laughed at, even in jest. She decided she would rather hide out there for a while than be laughed at some more.

Quince's smooth witticisms and flippant convictions confirmed his gadabout status. It didn't matter anyway; her mind was on the man she should be eating dinner with. Her accident hadn't appeared to have turned him off. He had lightly touched her arm and smiled before he left her.

Moments later, she realized she had missed the moment when the conversation had become one-sided. Dislike of the stranger's bold approach kept her silent. Tempia attempted to wind him down several times. When he kept speaking, politeness kept her sitting there. He had rescued her from an awkward situation, after all.

But antsy thoughts about Rob's cousin forced her to push her plate aside. Cory had said he and she would chat while she ate. Good thing the night was far from over. Tempia could hardly wait for their one-on-one conversation. She pondered extracting herself from Quince just as Gabby questioned someone in a rather loud voice.

His head cocked to the side, Quince paused.

"Why are you leaving so early?" her friend asked.

Tempia failed to decipher the low-volume reply. Was Cory leaving? Was Gabby sounding a tip-off alarm? She craned her neck but still couldn't see inside the living room.

Seconds later, Cory headed toward the front door. In two swift motions, the door opened and closed behind him.

Her heart sank. She hadn't reacted fast enough to Gabby's warning. *Should I run after Cory? Should I take Gabby along to smooth troubled waters?* She scooted off her chair.

Quince grasped her hand before she left the table. "He's already taken. His girlfriend is the jealous type. He can't stay long at parties she doesn't attend."

Gabby had assured Tempia that Cory was unattached. Had he begun seeing someone after his aunt's anniversary party the previous month? Her friend must have been mistaken or ignorant of his current relationship status.

Tempia eased her hand from Quince's grip. "I have to get up early for church tomorrow morning. My ride and I are leaving shortly."

Quince's man-about-town demeanor turned sober. "Stay a little longer. I've enjoyed our conversation."

After another glance at the door, Tempia retook her seat, wishing she had responded faster to Cory's leaving. Maybe Cory and his girlfriend had broken up. At any rate, she had agreed that Cory could sit with her while she ate. Did the broken promise cause his departure? Had her fear of people's reactions wrecked a potential relationship?

While the reality of her missed adventure dawned, Tempia noticed Quince had intensified his charm. He proceeded to list off his good points and previously unmentioned godly pursuits. Ten minutes later, he slowed down, offering her a ride home.

The offer caught Tempia off guard. Could she last through a thirty-minute drive with him? But she also didn't want to spoil Gabby's fun. She should let Quince drive her home and lick her wounds in private. But what if Cory was coming back?

Quince must be right. If Cory didn't have a girlfriend, why would he leave me hanging? Better tell Gabby that Quince is driving me home.

Her bottom lip secured between even white teeth, Tempia nodded. Almost in a dazed state, she walked toward the living room entrance. Gabby and Rob were playing an animated word game with the bravo man and wet-wipe lady. Gabby spotted Tempia standing just outside the doorway. Gabby appeared frustrated when Quince draped an arm across Tempia's shoulder. When Gabby gazed at her fiancé, Tempia's quick glance revealed an angry man. Affable Rob was about to erupt. It seemed her friend concurred with that assessment. Gabby patted his arm, glanced at Tempia, then pointed across the room.

Tempia wanted to talk to her friend privately, yet she shook her head and placed her palm in Quince's outstretched hand. His half grin made her gulp a deep breath, but Tempia pursed her lips, waved at Gabby, and followed the attentive man outside. Although Cory's departure still rankled, the letdown eased during the ride home. Quince lived a few neighborhoods away from her apartment complex and displayed a quieter disposition than earlier shown. Maybe she had misread his character. Since Cory no longer seemed to be an option, she scheduled a next-day dinner and movie date with Quince.

* * *

The couple's first outing set the pace for a whirlwind courtship. She never experienced goosebumps when Quince touched her as she had with Cory, but Quince was an attractive and devoted man. He called Tempia each morning before she left for work and sent her text messages throughout the workday. Their evenings were spent together, and Quince often visited until midnight. The couple spent Saturday and Sunday afternoons and evenings together.

Nonetheless, in numerous ways, her life became fragmented early in the unexpected association. No one enthused over her burgeoning relationship. Tempia's family and close friends, especially Gabby, even attacked her connection with Quince. One pertinent conversation still haunted Tempia. The friends were eating lunch at their favorite bistro when Tempia mentioned Cory was the only friend of Quince's she had met. And that she hadn't seen Cory since Rob's get-together.

Gabby laughed. "Does Quince have any friends? No one at the get-together who knew Quince likes him. I'm thinking he showed up uninvited. Rob said Quince is a shady and disruptive man."

Tempia quietly fumed as she listened. "May I get a word in, please? Quince said he and Cory had a close relationship, which is why he's surprised Cory won't double date with us."

"Listen, according to Rob, Cory and Quince have never been friends. Quince sporadically calls Cory if the mood hits him, and Cory responds cordially. Cory often goes years without hearing from his old schoolmate." Gabby paused, then continued. "Don't shake your head at me. Do yourself a favor. Pay attention to what I'm telling you."

Tempia rolled her eyes and made a big deal out of yawning.

"On the day of the party, Quince happened to call Cory early that afternoon about hanging out. Rob invited his cousin to the party while Cory and Quince were shooting pool. Cory accepted the invitation and Quince tagged along. Cory and Quince are not friends."

"Then Cory could have upped his game and gone on a double date with us. We want to double date with him and the girlfriend you don't think he has."

"I give up," Gabby said, and she changed the subject.

* * *

Quince laughed when Tempia relayed Gabby's version of his and Cory's association. "Someone fed your friend a bunch of lies. I've hung out with Cory since junior high. I never liked Rob, but I do get along with other people there I knew that night. Please trust me," Quince said as her head hung. He lifted her chin with one finger and smiled into her eyes. "Those slurs came from Rob and not his cousin. Your friend is batting zero with her misinformation garbage. She might get it straight someday."

Tempia nestled into the arm he wrapped around her shoulder. Just like with the "girlfriend" thing, Gabby had been mistaken. Each dire warning about Quince's duplicity never cracked her optimism.

* * *

Tempia was Gabby's maid of honor at Gabby and Rob's June wedding. She was thrilled she would see Cory again, but she hadn't anticipated her body's extreme reaction. Her nerve endings tingled, then her world stood still as the man she had liked at first sight entered the sanctuary. It seemed, though, the feelings were one-sided. Best-man Cory kept a cordial detachment throughout the two-day wedding celebration. He never sought her out for a chat and glanced away each time she made eye contact.

On Saturday afternoon, Tempia preceded Gabby down the aisle on the white carpet. Before reaching the altar, her joy fled. A furious Rob and his bleak-faced best man ignored her approach. Instead, Rob glared daggers at Quince, who sat in the second row. Then the friction vanished as the groom focused on his fiancée gliding down the aisle.

Those off-key moments didn't derail Tempia's spirit on her bestie's momentous day. Only a few low points had given her pause. As with the day before, Cory had given her a wide berth but remained amiable in her presence. She also came face-to-face with Rob's get-together crowd. No one made snide remarks or laughed at Tempia. Each person acted as if they were seeing her for the first time. Even the rude couple who had taunted Tempia smiled her way.

However, Quince's detachment from Rob's core circle had been a great surprise. She had dismissed Gabby's claim that Quince and Cory seldom saw each other—and that no one who attended the get-together could tolerate Quince. She figured Rob had criticized Quince because Quince was dating her instead of his cousin when Rob thought Cory should be.

When Quince proposed marriage the following Monday, Tempia suppressed a negative gut feeling and began planning a July wedding. Her family and friends' hostility toward her fiancé forced her to reject offers of a bridal shower and the rehearsal dinner. She settled for a scaled-back wedding celebration with about sixty people in attendance. Quince's side of the guest list included only four people: the couple who employed him; their son, Quince's best man; and Cory.

On the wedding day, the bridegroom's guests energized the gloomy reception. While the best man guzzled wine at the reception, Cory stood, clinked a spoon on a glass, and toasted the newlyweds.

"May this day of intertwining two lives represent that the best of your marriage is just ahead. God bless your love, friendship, and relationship forever. Repeat these sacred vows on your fiftieth wedding anniversary. I look forward to the celebration."

Those heartwarming words he had spoken still haunted her today. Although the honeymoon fulfilled each item on her wish list, Tempia's fixation on her husband ended the night the couple arrived home.

That night, she discovered she and Quince lived different lifestyles. Those facts had never presented themselves during the six months the couple dated. Until the beginning of their married life, Quince had championed her choices and welcomed her pursuits. He even attended her church service on Sunday mornings. The attentive man she had dated disappeared during the first week the couple blended their lives together inside Quince's home.

How many times had her parents warned Tempia that first impressions mattered? Her husband was a life-of-the-party type guy. His regular companions, whom she had never met, were disrespectful, vulgar, and socially unacceptable. Each night, he and a different mate hung out until the early morning. Thank God, his buddies usually gathered in the backyard utility building Quince had revamped into his party haven. Tempia either stayed in her bedroom or left home if any of them ventured inside the house. The woman who avoided drama at all costs had married a flashy, unapologetic man. His one saving grace was having a strong work ethic. Regardless of his late-night partying, Quince never missed one day of work.

His rejecting marriage counseling had her utilizing diverse marriage-saving tactics. Grievances against her husband's repulsive behavior mounted daily. Massive marriage problems ran rampant.

One late afternoon, Tempia visited her grandparents after going grocery shopping. Her front tire blew out on the drive home. It was dark outside. Her parents had taken her brothers on a weekend trip, and Gabby and Rob were also out of town, so she couldn't call any of them. She texted and called her husband for thirty minutes straight. An hour after the original call had been made, Cory's SUV pulled up behind her car. Quince had forwarded her text messages. Cory had cared enough to help out.

With no conversation, Cory methodically removed the tire, placed it in his trunk, put his spare in its place, and followed Tempia home. A new tire was on her car the next morning. Cory had gotten up early to come put it on for her. Quince was still snoring in their bed. Tempia dropped off a thank-you card for Cory at Gabby's house.

On a Friday afternoon two weeks later, Tempia experienced a walnut-allergy reaction while at work. She had never been plagued by allergies before. Her supervisor rushed her to urgent care and called her husband. Three hours later, suffering from a swollen face and eyelids and an itchy throat, she fell into a crying mess. Cory Sanders sat alone inside the waiting room.

Jumping off the seat, he rushed to her side. "Your husband couldn't leave work. I offered to pick you up and drive you home." His squinted eyes observed her face. "The swelling looks painful, Tempia. Do we need to stop by the pharmacy?"

"No. And thank God my throat didn't swell." But she had stomach pain and nausea. "Please drop me off at work so I can get my car."

One eyebrow rose. "No, ma'am. I don't think driving with swollen eyelids is a good idea. Is anyone at your parents' house?"

Facing her family would make her feel worse than she already felt. Although her father and stepmother wouldn't say "we told you so," they had tried to warn her about Quince.

Clearing her throat, she tried to smile. "I appreciate your consideration, but it's best I get my car and go home."

Cory shook his head and walked her to his vehicle. "Humor me. Where do your folks live?"

Ensconced in the passenger seat, Tempia leaned the seat back for maximum comfort. Brilliant sunlight blinded her inflamed eyes, but she stopped adjusting the useless sun visor.

"Are you comfortable?" Cory asked, starting the engine.

"I'm comfortable sitting here, but my body's unhappy."

"I thank God you are still alive, Tempia. Allergic reactions aren't anything to play around with. Which is why I need those directions to your parents' house."

Why act stubborn over a reasonable request? Holing up in her old bedroom was a better option than returning to a house where the other occupant didn't care whether she lived or died. Had her stepmother been told about Tempia's allergic reaction, Blanche would have reached the emergency room before even her stepdaughter arrived.

Squeezing her eyelids shut kept teardrops from falling. After supplying the address, Tempia faced the passenger window. While her mind tried to focus on his funny job anecdotes, teardrops leaked from her eyes. Cory's light banter—and just his being there—underscored her horrific mistake: marrying a man she hardly knew. She pursed her lips as agony slipped from her lips in moans.

"Hang in there; we're minutes away," Cory said.

Tempia liked that he thought it was her illness and not complete self-disgust that caused her angst. In a vow to herself to not to make another sound, she pressed three fingers over her mouth.

"We're here," Cory announced five minutes later. "I'll help you out of the car."

The front door opened as Cory led Tempia toward the house. Her stepmother rushed outside, her hands covering her mouth as she studied her stepdaughter's face. "What happened, Tempia? Did you have a car accident?"

In less than two minutes, Cory explained the situation, then left his passenger in her stepmother's care. An hour later, he dropped off a fresh flower bouquet and an encouraging get-well card.

With Tempia settled into bed, Blanche read her the get-well card, placed the flower-filled vase on the nightstand, then smoothed the already-straightened quilt. She kept her face blank, hiding her thoughts. "He's an admirable young man, Tempie." She smiled. "Now, when the kids get home from school, they will cheer you up while Sam and I bring your car back here. Also, Sam and I are concerned about your health, so we'd like to keep an eye on you. Please stay overnight."

Tempia hated the idea of returning to Quince's emotional-torture-chamber house, and staying at her parents' house was a viable option. "What about my husband?" she asked. Then she almost choked on her next words, but she felt obligated to defend an indifferent spouse. "Quince might rest better if I sleep beside him. Why cause him needless worry?"

Blanche swallowed hard before speaking. "He's welcome to visit you here if he chooses to come. Although you're out of danger, being waited on will do a lot for your recovery. Consider this an official daughter-pampering day." When Tempia didn't respond, Blanche headed to the door, which she left open on her way out. Tempia's stepmother didn't voice what they both knew: Quince couldn't care less how well his wife rested.

Thankful she had spent the night, Tempia woke up the next morning in her old bedroom, ate a hearty breakfast, and ended up hanging out for the weekend. On her drive home from church service, Quince called her for the first time since the allergic reaction.

That weekend had summed up her marriage in a nutshell: Quince shirking his responsibilities and Cory standing in the gap.

Too many unpleasant remembrances plagued her in quiet moments. Especially the twenty-second-birthday celebration that had almost broken her spirit. Quince had thrown the event together that morning while Tempia fumed in silence. None of her friends had been invited to her birthday party. Cory had declined the invitation but rang the doorbell before the rowdy crowd descended on Quince's house. Upon their arrival, no one acknowledged her presence. Each person bypassed the house and streamed toward the utility building in the backyard. Grinding her teeth, Tempia left the safe space of the house and entered the hostile gathering. None of those posers cared one squat about her. Despising their phony congratulations, she bit her tongue and left the party. Did the guests even notice the guest of honor went AWOL?

An hour later, she strolled toward the kitchen on a hunt for bottled water. Before she got there, she heard distant voices on the other side of the house. She continued toward the kitchen until her husband's amused tone raised her curiosity.

Although his pitch was low and steady, anger tinged the other voice she heard. Did the man ever quit? Who was Quince goading on this occasion?

Tempia switched directions, stopping short of the den's half-opened door, and she listened in on the private discussion. Seconds later, she felt her nails digging into her palm. Teardrops trickled down each cheek.

Quince's smug voice penetrated her horrendous agony.

"Man, Tempia was the perfect woman for me to marry. I was her first serious relationship, and I'm destined to become the last one. Branded women are ruined for any other guys." Quince cracked up over his own repugnant comments.

She leaned closer to the doorway to get a glimpse of who he was speaking to. Cory. He raised his hands in a what-are-you-thinking pose, started to speak, then shook his head.

Tempia observed their interaction as both of her feet trembled. Her shaky hands massaged her arms. Her ungracious husband had just disparaged their marriage in a humiliating manner. Gutted, she almost turned around and ran away.

Quince snorted. "No spiffy comeback, eh? I expected my wife's 'savior' to throw the gauntlet down."

Cory's steely gaze bore through Quince. "That cup contains more than coffee or you are a pitiful excuse for a husband. Either way, those nefarious comments say more about you than your wife."

She knew her teetotaler husband was sober. Quince barely sipped wine even at their wedding reception. He had only consumed enough wine to affirm Cory's toast.

The coffee cup poised at his lips, Quince snickered. "Ah, the man who is everyone's conscience is appalled."

"It's pathetic that you're not. You married a sweet, loyal, and family-oriented woman. Your wife is worth the finesse it will require to keep her."

Quince's grin vanished. He stood ramrod straight. Liquid sloshed over the sides of the cup he plopped onto the desk. He shoved a hand deep into each pocket. "Even finesse from you?"

"Tempia captured my regard the first day I saw her. Her falling for your snake oil ended my pursuit." Cory turned toward the door.

Quince gripped Cory's upper arm. "You're not running out on me before I finish."

Cory shook off the hold. "Don't make me choose between your wife and the snake she married. Tempia occupies my soft spot. I guarantee you will lose."

"No. You lost. My wife chose me over you." His eyes glowing, Quince's mouth quirked. "You fell for Tempia when she entered Rob's house. You never hid your desperation."

Tempia gripped the doorframe when her husband laughed in Cory's face. The man was the only true friend Quince had. How did she get herself into this mess? For once in their relationship, she accepted circumstances for what they were and recoiled at her husband's next words.

"I remember your contentment as if the scene occurred today. You resembled a fat cat sipping cream. I almost lost it when you caressed her arms and gazed into her eyes. Man, you had the knight-in-shining armor routine down pat."

"Don't let your mind play tricks on your memory," Cory said, partially relaxing on the desk.

Quince snorted. "Even though you truly wanted Tempia, her clumsiness and your gallantry let me keep her for myself. I stole the woman you chose in a split second. How do those facts grab you?"

Cory's fingers massaged the bridge of his nose. He sighed, meeting the other man's direct gaze. "You befriended and betrayed an innocent woman simply because you thought I wanted her?"

"The six-month trial marriage ends in January," sneered Quince. "And then you may have her ... if Tempia ever gets over being with me. I hear I am a hard act to follow."

Chapter Three

The hallway spun around Tempia as she sagged against the wall. Her body swayed, but her grasp on the doorframe kept her standing upright. It hit her like a ton of bricks that her husband planned to leave the relationship one year after the couple met.

Did he hate Cory enough to eradicate someone else's life just to get at Cory? Gabby had spoken the truth all along. Cory and Quince had never been friends. Cory really had been just being nice.

The entire marriage was a sham. On Tempia's wedding day, her father and stepmother had tried reasoning with her in Pastor Freeman's study. Their sad faces flickered in her mind's eye.

Sam had held his daughter's hands gently in his large palms. "We're at the eleventh hour. In less than ten minutes, you will own this madness. Be kind to yourself, Tempie. End the association. Now. Let ... him ... go. The right man will know our daughter is a treasure worth finding."

Treasure. *Even though I had belittled his advice, Dad considered me a special prize, even on my ill-fated wedding day.*

Now five months too late, her father's wisdom generated a catharsis against unmitigated anguish. Like a dammed river, tears stopped flowing. Although she had lost ground, Tempia disallowed losing one centimeter more. Pulling a tissue out of her pocket, she swished it across her damp face. Deep breathing increased her flagging courage. The first day of the rest of her life would start now.

In a few steps, she stood framed in the doorway, clutched fingers behind her back. "Please include me in all conversations involving me. Especially if my failed marriage is the topic."

Quince's pinched expression proved priceless. His gaze flicked upward. For once, she'd caught the vile man off guard.

Tempia leaned on the door, harnessing strength she didn't know she possessed. Her focus on the room's other occupant provided much-needed solace. "Cory, you would choose me over someone posing as a friend?"

The silent man studied Tempia, his pain-filled features revealing regret. Was he sorry she had overheard her husband's low regard for his own wife? Or that the ruthless bomb thrower she had married proved beneath contempt?

Her jaw muscles slacked once her unbridled emotions engaged her brain. *Oh ... my ... goodness.* Was Quince's assertion on target? Did Cory harbor feelings for her?

Gazing at her husband brought an avalanche of sadness warring against staunch determination.

When Cory remained silent, Quince's arms crossed over his rigid chest. An insulting gleam infused his gaze. Was he prepared to fight a winless battle? Tempia must regain her self-respect and prevail against what her husband really wanted: his wife's complete destruction.

Back straightened, she prepared for the fight of her life. "Leave, Quince. Take those sorry excuses you call friends and go."

A sneer twisted his lips into an almost comical position. Quince gingerly rocked the coffee cup between his fingers. "Unbelievable. Take my word for it, babe. Cory loves you. As you love saying, imagine that." His gaze moved between Tempia and Cory. When the pair remained silent, Quince tipped his cup, left the room, and rejoined the party.

Cory gazed at Tempia after Quince left the room. "Look ... you moved into your husband's house, not the other way around. He won't leave his home to make you happy. Quince isn't wired that way. Tell me your next step."

She had no plan. Only sorrow occupied her numb brain. Tempia shrugged, blinking back tears.

"Doesn't your father own a truck?"

"He does."

"Call him. Explain what happened. Ask him to bring his truck. Between his truck, your stepmother's car, and both of our vehicles, your personal items can be removed in one trip."

A man in love will fight your battles on every side. Did Cory truly love her yet couldn't show interest in a married woman? This hapless sensation must be what a free fall into the abyss felt like.

Cory handed Tempia his cell phone. She called her father, hoping he would answer an unknown number.

22

Sam answered on the final ring before the call went to voicemail. "How may I help you?"

"Dad, it's me. You and Mom called it right. My marriage is over. I don't ever want to walk into this house again."

"Noah! Turn down that noise. Your sister's in trouble. Tempie, where is Quince?"

"He and his so-called friends are in the backyard not even pretending to celebrate my birthday. Cory and I are inside the house. I'm using his cell phone. Will you and Mom please—"

"Pack your things," Sam interrupted. "We're on our way. Ask the young man to keep you company until we get there."

Tempia studied Cory, who was staring at her. She couldn't decipher his expression. What was he thinking? From his tough-set features, it seemed like nothing good. She cleared her throat when her father said her name. "I don't have to ask, Dad. He will do it."

"I pray he does." Sam hung up as he began calling his wife's name.

Fresh tears streamed down Tempia's face. Where did she go from here to redeem her lost dignity? No tangible answer filled her mind. Wishful thinking never changed lives.

"Quince will hate you helping me."

"Some men despise anything they can't control. On my side, the problem gets rectified before the night ends. Don't ask."

Tempia's lips had parted. Now she closed her mouth.

"Start packing. Leaving once your family arrives is your best option. Do you disagree?" he asked when Tempia moaned.

"Not really. I ... I don't like running away as if I did something wrong. Quince is the culprit, not me."

"I understand," Cory replied, and then he left the den.

Back inside the bedroom, Tempia placed opened suitcases on the bed. Gathering her possessions through tears, she thought back to her and Cory's instant harmony at Rob's get-together. Almost a year later, she and her protector were on the same page. Cory proved he operated on a higher plane, still assisting her without a reason. Yet too many wrong moves separated him and her. Did he still like her? Or did their first false start create an irreparable loss she couldn't redeem? He had witnessed the dissolution of her marriage firsthand. What might have been between her and Cory would probably never be.

Cory appeared in the doorway. "Are you taking your furniture pieces and pictures?"

"I'm taking all of my things. I didn't bring much. Guess I saw this day coming."

His eyebrows raised as fresh tears rolled down her cheeks. He glanced away and then looked back at her. "Life happens to everyone. Winners keep going through each success and trial. Hang in there. Your family will arrive shortly." Cory backed up and left the room.

Forty-five minutes later, Tempia was wrapping her mother's paintings in sheets. Her family had arrived carrying large packing boxes and assorted crates. Blanche walked throughout the house removing items her stepdaughter had overlooked while Sam and Tempia's brothers helped Cory pack the vehicles. Quince never appeared. He chose hanging out in the utility building over reclaiming their marriage. Making amends wasn't in the cards. His absence proved he didn't care whether Tempia stayed or left.

An emptiness engulfed her soul. Her wrecked marriage was all her fault. Except for Quince, there wasn't anyone else Tempia could blame. Stubbornness had fragmented her life beyond repair. Everyone she knew had tried to tell her he was an abominable man.

Feeling defeated, Tempia trotted to her car until her father headed toward the backyard.

Oh no. What now? We just need to leave so I can make a fresh start.

"Dad, please don't confront Quince," Tempia pleaded.

Sam ignored his daughter and disappeared along the side of the house.

Tempia, Cory, and her family watched his progress down the side yard to the back gate. Once Sam unbolted the latch, he faced his daughter, who was inching her way behind him. "Tempie, wait inside your car. This won't take long." He walked into the yard and shut the gate.

* * *

Tempia didn't see Quince after her twenty-second birthday. Despite not seeing him, Quince made the divorce process extra difficult with ludicrous demands until Tempia contacted him via his employer. Her husband sought her destruction for the same reason he had requested the first date: Cory. He craved one-upmanship over the one person who treated him fairly.

Despite Quince's manipulative shenanigans, the divorce decree came within two months.

This day marked the one-year anniversary of her divorce. The ache of playing a consummate fool had lessened during the past year. Divorce had been a blessing in disguise.

Despite that the morning had been dominated by compulsive self-reflection, Tempia felt secure. The worst episode in her adult saga had ended. Her present and future demanded a personal relationship with God and accepting wise counsel. Her mind centered on the valuable man who had supported her during an atrocious marriage. Tempia hadn't seen Cory since the night she left Quince's house. Every fiber of her being desired an everlasting relationship with him, not just fond reminiscences. Several times she had called the cell phone number Gabby had provided. Cory never answered or returned one call.

A loud groan escaped the lips she clenched. Wringing her hands together, Tempia stood up. At this stage in the game, neither positive nor negative Cory-nostalgia counted for much.

* * *

Having driven the work van off the company's parking lot, Cory maneuvered the vehicle through morning rush-hour traffic. As he drove, his mind reflected on his simple MO: avoiding failure on all levels. Yesterday's bombardment of Tempia-nostalgia in his mind had almost set him back to desiring a romantic relationship with her. Memories of Tempia had beset him the entire evening at the pool hall and far into the night. She even featured in a now-forgotten dream. He wondered what the bad penny was up to today.

Cory chuckled. Bad penny was a misnomer. Tempia was a likable if gullible lady who had married the wrong man. Could he have staged an intervention before the "I do's" took place? Cory axed that impractical thought. If her family and friends' efforts had failed, his as a then-newcomer would have too. His best option now was moving on with his life.

* * *

Instead of dwelling further on her past faults, Tempia considered the long day that lay ahead. Gabby's unparalleled encouragement and goodwill demanded an appropriate response, so Tempia would whip up her favorite foods.

Tempia's gaze drifted to the microwave clock on the kitchen counter. Nine-thirty. "Come on," she cajoled herself. "Inaction is depression's best friend. Get out of bed." She dangled one leg from underneath the quilt. "There you go. Cook your guest a marvelous feast."

Dressed in white-denim jeans, camel ankle boots, a gray tank top, and a light-beige cardigan, Tempia entered the kitchen nook some thirty minutes later. Though it was too early to cook lunch, doing some prep work would facilitate the process later. She placed fish filets in a cold pot of water and set the cutting board and filet knife on the counter. Something was missing.

Tempia scoured the room until her gaze alighted upon a glass cabinet. "Mom's china will set a beautiful table."

Still with time to fill, she paced throughout the tiny space. After making several tracks practically in circles, she stopped midstep. "Take a seat. Don't wear a hole in the rug." She lounged on the love seat, setting her cell phone alarm for eleven o'clock. As soon as she settled and silence took over, an egregious Quince returned to the forefront of her thoughts.

* * *

Cory's second job assignment could not end soon enough. He should have completed this task in less than ninety minutes, but his brain and hands wouldn't cooperate. His thoughts kept returning to Tempia. He couldn't get her smiling face and caring nature off of his mind. Nor could he vanquish memories of the night her marriage sailed through turbulent waters and over the cliff.

He decided that a short break from work might help. He left the house and drove around the neighborhood in circles. Distraction turned a short drive into a safety hazard. He drove into a grocery store parking lot, reclined the seat, and let his mind roll.

Cory had often prayed the woman who stole his heart would make appropriate life choices. Once she had become engaged, he prayed the couple's marriage would last. Although she had rejected him in front of his friends, he owned those prayers and attended the wedding celebration on the groom's invitation. The couple's marriage didn't follow a clear road map. Their harmony deteriorated on various levels before the journey even began. Quince resumed his self-indulgent lifestyle on the same day the newlyweds arrived home from their honeymoon.

For five unsettling months, Cory's sideline view showed Tempia's constant struggles to preserve a marriage her husband was sabotaging. Quince ranted against her supporting her favorite ministry. He forbade her to attend church and castigated her family and friends. All the while, Quince partied from evening until dawn most nights. Nevertheless, Tempia reaffirmed her commitment to the ministry, spent many evenings and weekends with family and close friends, and attended church service on Sunday mornings.

Soon, Quince's flagrant disrespect and neglect depleted Tempia's self-confidence. His abandonment in dire circumstances shattered her spirit. In less than two months, Tempia's life had spiraled into a raging-hot mess.

Although Tempia had spurned Cory and accepted a rogue, Cory knew firsthand that Tempia possessed a benevolent, if capricious, nature. Her marriage had turned her life upside down. He couldn't understand how the person he'd met would choose to marry someone like Quince. Her time with Quince was so out of character that she appeared to have developed what he called "erratic personality disorder" during those months. Tempia seemingly went back to being herself once her marriage was over.

That her compassionate nature prevailed had earned Cory's respect. He had even admired her loyalty to her missing-in-action husband. His cousin's wife, Gabby, had also proclaimed Tempia guided her life on solid ground these days. She re-established contact with a host of good friends and reliable associates. But now that she was out from under Quince, she no longer required Cory's assistance. However, Cory thought that she might be ready to try a relationship with him. She was just who he was looking for in many respects, yet some of her previous decisions did give him pause. She had made a huge mistake marrying the likes of Quince, so Cory couldn't help but question her ability to make good lifelong choices. He could not minimize or discount her poor decisions made about life-altering situations.

On the night Tempia left Quince, Cory streamlined his own life. Self-preservation became his main objective. He worked hard at keeping a physical distance from Tempia so as to keep memories of her from lodging within his soul. However, their emotional connection had ensnared Cory to her since admiring her at first sight.

Nonetheless, his dilemma regarding her true personality still smoldered. Who was the real Tempia Wade?

His mindset rebalanced, Cory returned to work and wrapped up the job in less than fifteen minutes.

* * *

Tempia stopped her cell phone alarm and rose off the love seat, singing a song she and her mother had often sung together. She entered the kitchen nook and placed cooking utensils upon the counter. Humming a different upbeat tune, she trimmed potatoes.

Fifteen minutes later, she studied her handiwork. Potato strips were ready to pan-fry. She peered inside the refrigerator. "Radishes. Onions. Celery. Cucumber. Red leaf lettuce. Oops. No salad dressing. Better whip up a tangy vinaigrette and choose dessert."

Gliding across the small space, she dropped her load onto the counter, stooping to pick up two runaway radishes. She chopped and mixed the salad and salad dressing. Then she pulled out two rolls of frozen cookie dough her step-mother had given her last month. She sliced up cookies and stuck them in the oven. A few minutes later, the smell of baking cookies enveloped the kitchen.

Even as she worked, thoughts of her ex-husband infiltrated her mind. "Ugh! Stay out of my brain." She tapped the side of her head. No matter how grievous her past mistakes were, she wouldn't dwell on them or anyone else's blunders.

Unclenching a balled fist, she dipped bite-size cod nuggets into cornmeal batter. A quick glance at the microwave clock had Tempia redoubling her efforts.

Sometime later, she popped a fry into her mouth. "Mmm. Crispy and delicious."

Kissing her knuckles, she raised her fist into the air. "All done. Minutes to spare."

The doorbell rang as she placed a slightly wilted lily bouquet in the center of the small, round rustic table.

Tempia pasted a happy grin on her face and swung open the front door.

Gabby's unique outfit engaged her imagination. The perfect blend of bright and subdued colors enhanced the woman's laid-back personality.

"Come in. It's good to see you, Gab."

Four inches taller than Tempia, Gabby's willowy body glided into the room. "This conversation will last longer than our usual thirty-minute lunch dates. That's right, number one friend, I took off extra time to share our meal." She laughed and tapped Tempia's shoulder. "Hope you made something delicious."

Tempia was grateful to have more time to communicate with someone other than herself. As always, her consummate-planner friend remained one step ahead of everyone else's effort. In elementary school, Gabby's mother had dubbed the girls "the ever-ready twosome."

They grinned at each other until Gabby's gurgling stomach broke the silence. The amused woman stroked her belly. "Oh hush. Guess my stomach got the message that my nose smelled fried fish and fries." She walked across the room, pulled out a chair, and draped a teal sweater across the back. "Did I guess correctly?"

28

Giggles flowed through Tempia's parted lips. "Not quite. You didn't mention the tossed green salad."

"Aw, shucks. I can't smell raw vegetables."

Tempia chuckled and brought their food to the table.

Gabby clapped and picked up a fry.

Tempia pointed to the sweets platter. "I baked your favorite cookies. Lemon and coconut supreme." Before pulling out a chair across the table, she snapped her fingers. "Oh! Almost forgot our drinks that are in the refrigerator." She placed a pitcher filled with apple-spice tea on a copper coaster and took her seat.

The women heaped on food until fries spilled over Gabby's plate rim. "Remember how my mother demanded we take second helpings instead of overloading our plates?"

"Sure do. She said it practically every day," Tempia said. "Those were definitely my good and better ole days."

"During the heartbreak of losing your mom, we amassed a treasure trove of joyful memories." Gabby inhaled a deep breath and glanced at her friend. "What's on your itinerary for today?"

Tempia gave a weak smile. "Acquiring a guilt-free life will make a good beginning. I had a distressing, thought-provoking morning." She lowered her head then lifted her chin. "My brain *will* eliminate an unscrupulous man from my thoughts. I should have gotten past that last year."

"Great trauma merits longer grace periods. Go easy on yourself." Gabby munched a fry, bit into a fish nugget, studied Tempia, and smiled. "The food is terrific. You outdid yourself—again. I should have paid better attention in those cooking classes I paid a small fortune to attend."

"You paid attention but skimped on the homework assignments. I told you—"

Gabby cut off Tempia's critique. "I remember what you said: 'Home projects are an essential practicum in perfecting any craft.' Next time, provide word definitions alongside the free advice."

Tempia's lips resisted their customary grin. Tears filled her eyes. Doubt accompanied by remorse assaulted her tranquility again. Picking up a lemon wedge, she squeezed the juice into the iced tea.

Her friend's furtive glances notwithstanding, the guest and hostess ate their meal in total silence until Gabby tapped her friend's wrist.

"You zoned out on me for far too long. More Quince thoughts?"

Chapter Four

Tears refilled Tempia's sad eyes. "Thank God the marriage ended when it did. I just can't excuse my indefensible bad judgment. I hate living a stalemated life. Give me a moment."

"I came to encourage you." After Gabby ate her last fry, she reached for the cookie platter. "Talk if you want to, or not at all. You may eat in silence, but don't punish yourself with seclusion."

Those heartfelt words were a balm on Tempia's psyche. The best friends were closer than sisters. As a child, minus the evenings Tempia had sat by her mother's bedside, she had practically lived across the street. Gabby's family's house became her second home while her mother languished with cancer. Hospice care helped her father survive those sorrowful last days.

Tempia placed fingers on her thin lips. "Our talks helped me steer through a difficult year. I rushed into marriage and missed the mark by miles."

"True. But you found the right track when it most counted. Not many people admit their missteps and adjust their life choices."

"No one can deny truth that smacks you in the face. Walking away proved easier than remaining inside a hostile environment. Which ... leads to my greatest blunder."

Gabby leaned back on the chair cushion, nibbling a coconut cookie. "Is there a bigger miscalculation than marrying the wrong man?"

Tempia nodded. "There was for me."

"Huh. Okay. Let's hear it. I'm all ears."

"I gave up on Cory. Hindsight can't erase that error nor make it easier to comprehend." Looking at her plate, Tempia pasted a grin on her mouth that quickly vanished. "I liked the man on sight, Gab. Why did I give in to Quince's advances? Even after you tried to talk me down, I gave in to Quince without a fight."

Gabby leaned back in her seat. Her half-eaten cookie arced in the air as her arm pushed forward. "I can tick off several reasons. The scoundrel handed you a stream of lies. Mia and Jasmine announced their engagements one week prior to Rob's party. Plus, I was getting married in five months. And how did being around Quince make you feel?"

Tempia well remembered the heady sensation of having an attractive male think she was someone special. She mulled over her disconnected thoughts for a moment before speaking. "It ... felt like my life finally matched that of my closest friends. As for Quince, I enjoyed sharing full evenings and our weekends together. I thought he was falling in love with me."

"The gadabout created the perfect storm. You hadn't dated any man since leaving your parents' house."

"Perhaps the right men were in places I didn't know about. Yet I played the fool and ignored friendly warnings. I believed ..." Hesitating, she glanced at Gabby. "I ... I can't fully grasp what I was thinking."

Gabby bit into a cookie as she studied her friend's face. "Those thoughts don't matter anymore. Past mistakes won't define us unless we repeat them. So, begin where you are. Enjoy your life."

Tempia gazed at the confident face. "How? Cory is denying me the opportunity to redeem my past behavior. I can't correct his perceptions about me unless we communicate."

"Tempie—"

"Wait. Let me finish giving my side first. The divorce was final twelve months ago, and Cory still hasn't contacted me. I had high hopes that our relationship would take off now."

"What relationship are you referring to?" Gabby asked. "Cory helped you when your ex wouldn't. That sums up your and Cory's association." She paused when Tempia glanced across the room. "Listen. Cory never made declarations of love. Your ex accused him of loving you. You can't hold the man to your ex's assumptions." Gabby stuffed the cookie into her mouth.

Tempia stared at her. "For once, consider the situation from my standpoint, please. Cory didn't deny what Quince said. He supported me until my family arrived."

"That's squirrelly thinking, friend. Why should Cory address the subject at all? The burden of proof belonged to Quince." She hesitated, studying another lemon cookie. "You and Cory shared a special moment at a party. And the next day, you started dating a man he knew, married that man within six months, and divorced him five months later." Gabby gave Tempia a weak smile. "It was quite the roller-coaster ride."

Tempia's chin hung to her chest. Gabby had made a valid point even though Tempia wished she hadn't.

Gabby scooted her chair closer to Tempia. "Against all odds, you've managed a well-balanced life in a short time period. Let Cory come to terms with the overall positive results."

Tempia sighed and cleared her throat. "How can he view me in a favorable light if we don't communicate? See there? His actions don't add up." Her elbow on the table, she put her forehead on her open palms. Cory had assisted her during five chaotic months. And then, nothing. Did he lose interest in her? She raised her head and stared at Gabby. "He supported me through severe trials yet disappeared after the separation. Why would he snub me once we were given a rare second chance?"

"Cory probably sees things differently. You both deserve the right to make the best decision for your individual well-being. Go back to the beginning. Against Rob's wishes, I gave you Cory's cell phone number after the game party. Talking to him then would have nullified Quince's lies, eliminating the second date."

Tempia evaded the direct gaze. "It would have been a tough call. I had already blown any chance of our pursuing a normal relationship." Leaning her head on the seat cushion, she stared into space. "Would you respect a man who shared a special moment with you then dated your friend the next day?"

"Even though you let Quince redirect your purpose, you've adjusted your circumstances and regained your independence."

"You didn't answer the question, because the answer would be no." Tempia slouched in her chair.

Gabby sighed. "My best advice is to allow each other to heal. You need time, Tempie," she said as her friend groaned. "Every good thing needs time to develop. In my opinion, Cory is worth the fight."

"He is an honorable guy. He kept our conversations on an acquaintance level during my marriage. Personal questions weren't asked, nor allowed."

"I clearly hear and feel you." Standing up, Gabby removed a napkin off the table and cleaned her eyeglass lenses. "I need to get back to work."

Tempia stood and handed a small bag of cookies to her friend. "Thanks for the wake-up call and coming by to hold my hand."

Gabby held up the treat bag. "My favorite meal and dessert proved the perfect reward." Her lips bowed up into a slight grin. "Even when people are making positive changes in their lives, people can hold onto bad memories. You'll be fine, Tempie."

At the front door, Tempia wrapped her arms around Gabby in a tight hug. "Understanding I'm loved helps a bunch."

"You have many people who love you. And trust the God who never fails." Gabby opened the door then faced her friend. "See you tomorrow, Shooting Star. Lunch is on me before shopping. Capris. Noonish."

Tempia's eyes opened wide. "You're on. Whoever arrives late will buy dessert on the next two outings." Her lips curved into a lopsided grin.

Rolling her eyes, Gabby walked outside. "Cashing in on my habitual tardiness is shameful." She shook a finger at her friend and closed the door behind her.

Tempia listened to Gabby's heels click along the pavement. Then she snapped the lock and ran fingers through her close-cropped hair. Now she would need more distractions.

* * *

Even though Cory's tiredness was the result of an overactive mind, exhaustion demanded he reassess his afternoon work schedule. In nine years, Cory had never left assignments incomplete. He counted the pros and cons of an early sign-out, then retrieved his cell phone, identifying the last three job assignments. With evaluations made, he called each of their long-standing customers one by one. The twice-a-year seasonal maintenance check, filter change, and condenser hose wash down would keep until Monday.

He turned the van in the opposite direction and maintained a steady pace until pulling into A1 Heating and Cooling's parking lot. The senior Sanders had founded the company some twenty-odd years ago. Cory had apprenticed at his father's company during his teen years, obtained his license early on, and now worked as an HVAC technician. His uncle, two cousins, his father's best friend, and the best friend's son completed the small workforce.

Cory parked his van in the lot and drove off in his SUV. As he drove, he thought about how an active social life might help busy his mind when he'd like to stop thinking about Tempia.

This past year, he had tried dating several women, but they never panned out. His eyes were on the finish line. He was looking for enduring love, empathy, and tenacity.

Last week, his bowling league had met at a local pizza joint. As the group dispersed in the parking lot, one of the women stuffed a receipt into his jacket pocket. Her phone number was written on the back. He now opened the glove compartment, recovering the crumpled wad. Cory studied the number, visualizing the beautiful woman who enjoyed mesmerizing men.

He laughed and shredded the flimsy paper into tiny pieces. "Not a good idea. I pass."

* * *

Sprawled on the love seat, Tempia picked up her ringing cell phone. She sat upright. "Hi, Dad. What's up?"

A firm voice sounded across the line. "Checking on my number one daughter. How goes it with you?"

Tempia laughed. "Only daughter. You and Mom have two sons."

"A lack of another daughter still makes you my number one. Did you get outside of the house today? Or did you play a couch potato?"

A lazy person proved an accurate description. Except for Gabby's visit, this had been an uneventful day. Long, boring, and noneffective. Nothing had been resolved during those annoying trips down memory lane. Better to not divulge those facts. Her father wanted to fix whatever hurt her.

Tempia laughed. "A couch potato fits close enough."

"Good for you. What about the weekend? Any plans there?"

"Earlier, Gabby came by for lunch, then she headed back to work. We're going shopping tomorrow. She's buying Rob a work-anniversary present. This evening, I'm eating dinner and watching movies at your house."

"Which means the rest of your afternoon is free for some you-and-me time. Raspberry ripple ice cream and a walk might jumpstart our evening. Your old man could use something sweet and some exercise. We can head home after leaving the park."

His company closed out the books at month end in March, so she knew he was busy, yet he was willing to leave work and hold her hand. *Being loved feels extra wonderful on a stress-filled day. I love you enough not to let you do it. I won't embroil you in my problems.* "Nice try, Dad. This morning Mom discussed your busy work schedule. She tried to buy me breakfast, but I let her off the hook, too."

"We love you, sweetheart. I blame myself that Quince gained a stronghold before Blanche and I became involved. I could tell he was no good."

"Since I made the mistakes, I accept all blame. You and Mom spotted his deceptive personality in less than five minutes. Curt and Noah detested Quince. It took me eight months to admit the truth. Quince was pure riffraff through and through." Wiping her eyes and nose, Tempia hesitated. "Anyway, you and Mom bear no blame. No person can micromanage two households. Family values have been a pillar of my life since childhood. I betrayed my own belief system."

"Supportive loved ones can ease emotional letdowns." Sam gave an audible sigh.

Tempia hated dumping those same loved ones in the center of her blowups. She had the most caring family in all the world.

"Let's catch up. Are you dating anyone or reacquainting with the real you?"

Straightforward and to the point as usual. Cory Sanders came to mind. She shook her head. No. No, no. Why dump her hapless love life onto her dad's shoulders?

"No, sir. I sorta like hanging out by myself these days. But I promise to keep you posted."

"Be picky. Wait until the right man comes along. Remember, you have an open invitation to come back home."

Tempia wiped away stray teardrops. "This morning, Mom said the same thing. Don't worry. Your only daughter is doing fine." Teardrops slid down both cheeks. She must get her father off the phone. "See you later. Get back to work on your bulging workload."

"Will you consider spending the night, Tempie? You can make us a grand breakfast tomorrow morning."

Tempia laughed through flowing tears. "You just want my from-scratch buttermilk biscuits. Yes, sir. I will. Mom asked me to spend the weekend on her earlier call." If mothers could be perfect, Blanche was close to the mark. "Thank God my family is always there for me. Bye-bye. See you later."

Tempia blinked back tears, holding the cell phone to her ear until her father hung up. Setting the cell phone on a cushion, she tucked her legs underneath her body.

Her father was CFO at an investment firm. He met her accountant stepmother on the job. These days, his wife declared herself a certified homemaker. Sam had married Blanche two years after his wife lost her battle with terminal cancer. The wedding ceremony took place one month after his daughter's ninth birthday. On the day Blanche moved into Sam's house, she treated Tempia like a special friend; she had since become a much-loved daughter.

The thriving couple had two boys thirteen months apart. Curt was now thirteen and Noah, twelve. Tempia loved her rowdy younger brothers.

Despite the age difference, the siblings shared quality time together. They had more things in common than sharing one parent. Thoughts concerning the boys brought her pleasure.

Her sharp gaze perused the love seat and two small armchairs outfitting the living area. Four aligned end tables served as a single cocktail table. The floor lamp in the right corner completed the decorations. A chest of drawers, an occasional table, and a full-size bed occupied the bedroom alcove. Whenever the boys slept over, Tempia would curl up on the love seat and let her brothers share the bed. Pictures of her family lined the end tables. A framed picture of Tempia and her mother was set upon the chest of drawers.

Nowhere near the square footage of her old one-bedroom apartment, she had grown to appreciate her tiny space. Minus the few pieces she had taken to Quince's house, her previous furniture had been donated to families she met at an urban ministry. The pieces she had reclaimed from her ex's house remained stored in her parents' basement. Her present place had been leased and decorated according to her downsized dreams.

Prior to meeting Quince, she had enjoyed an active social life. Dating and marrying a chameleon had obscured her identity. What were her likes? Her dislikes? What activities made her feel alive and connected? Re-examining her current needs and expectations, she was gradually regaining a disciplined, self-controlled existence. These discoveries took time, however. But the resulting information helped reaffirm key points and dismantle misconceptions.

Tempia had moved into her first apartment due to her parents' stifling house rules. Plus, her father took exception to most of the men she dated. Out on her own, she never invited men to her apartment like the ones he had rejected. She finally understood the benefits of men understanding that her family cared about her welfare. Temperamental and partying men had been eliminated from her sphere. The best decision she had ever made was maintaining her self-respect. She hadn't gone on any dates until she met Quince—and he broke all of her rules.

These days, she prized quality time dedicated to family, friends, and people who attended Community Ministries. She also welcomed quiet walks, attending baseball games, and checking out various neighborhoods' curb appeal. Last year, she read to preschoolers at the local library one day a month, enrolled in a conversational Spanish class, and studied acrylic painting. Her current life convictions mitigated every frustration she endured during two disappointing years.

Unable to sit still, she darted off the love seat and stood in the center of the room. Still feeling at odds with herself, she entered the bathroom, leaned against the sink, and studied her features in the vanity mirror. Her deepening scowl almost made her eyebrows touch. Some days, she did not recognize herself. Eyes squinted, she breathed into cupped hands.

Sleepless nights had left shadows underneath her dark-brown eyes. Two months ago, Tempia had resumed her long-practiced beauty regimen. Her old hairstylist welcomed her back, supplying a free manicure and pedicure. Overjoyed by the welcome, Tempia prescheduled weekly Saturday morning appointments.

She tilted her head side to side. The short haircut emphasized a strong jawline. Far more than her physical appearance had suffered neglect, but her health was improving. Her energy increased daily. Mental and emotional depression was no longer a huge issue.

"I'm still weak, Father. Please carry me until I reach familiar terrain." Fighting back tears, she lay upon her bed. Suddenly, she sat up halfway, grinning. "I made it through the worst two years of my life. Way to go, God!" Her exuberance quickly depleted. Tempia had chosen Quince, the gift wrapped inside pretty paper. Cory was the unwrapped box that had been left upon the table.

Nevertheless, once the heartbreak with herself truly ended, one indisputable fact would survive: Cory had implied that he loved her. Quince had been convinced that Cory did. True love couldn't evaporate into thin air. A man who cherished a woman likely wouldn't give up on her even when she'd acted a fool.

Hope that he still had a soft spot for her was prominent in her daily prayers. Either way, it was crucial to rebuild her bankrupt life. She couldn't waste momentum on self-incrimination.

Tempia grabbed her cell phone off the nightstand only to set it back down. Gabby had insisted Tempia lay low, even though her friend sought ways to facilitate a reunion. On their last brainstorming chitchat, Rob had advised that if the relationship was meant to be, it would happen on its own accord.

Yet, a life committed to fate was easier said than done. At lunch, Gabby's words indicated she had succumbed to her husband's advice. Could an uncertain existence become Tempia's destiny?

Snatching her purse and keys off the table, Tempia headed toward the door. Any destination would serve her better than staying home alone.

So much for distracting myself with a new location, Tempia thought, ambling across Crescent Park. She had decided to get the walk and raspberry ripple ice cream her father had suggested, but it didn't jumpstart her afternoon. His presence alongside her might have produced the stress-free environment her private reflections had denied.

Tempia spun in the opposite direction, chucked the half-eaten ice cream cone into the nearest receptacle, and returned to her car. Only shopping made her feel better.

* * *

Inside Rob's garage, Cory belted out a loud chortle. Tears sprang into his eyes. "That was a good one. Twenty-eight years is a long wait, but you accomplished your goal. Good job."

Rob rose to his feet, laughing. "It was an original Rob Stephens joke. Your positive response will have me making up more."

Before he finished speaking, a shadow obstructed sunlight at the garage entrance. Their laughter ended with a quick glance over their shoulders.

Cory adjusted his squatting position beside Rob's car and eyed his cousin's wife. "Almost done. You will have your husband to yourself in a jiffy. I'm fastening on the last lug."

"Welcome home, babe," Rob said. "We're winding down the job."

Gabby slowly inched closer and brushed a finger across her lips. "No rush. We'll grab dinner out a little later. I had a home-cooked lunch with Tempia today." She ignored the pointed look when her husband frowned. "So I'm not hungry for dinner yet anyway." Swinging the cookie sack she carried, Gabby hesitated. "If Tempia wasn't spending the weekend at her folks' house, I would've invited her to hang with us this evening."

Rob studied his wife for a long second, then jerked his head toward his cousin. "What are our plans this evening? Is my nephews' preseason baseball game still on?"

Cory noted the quick topic switch. How long would Rob's wife play along?

Gabby nodded. "They haven't called it off. The field must be dry enough." She stole a peek at Cory as he observed the couple. She turned back to Rob. "Don't forget, Tempia and I will spend tomorrow shopping."

Rob's mouth broke into a broad grin. "Is buying a high-power cordless drill on your shopping list? A special man will consider it a superb work-anniversary gift. Hint, hint."

"Um, maybe." Her teeth nipped her bottom lip. "Why don't we pick up a carry-out meal on the drive to the park? How's chicken? I ate fish at lunch."

Rob shook his head. "A beef au jus baked potato and side salad would hit the spot. The Potato Joynt?"

"Works for me," Gabby agreed. "I love their coconut cream pie."

Rob glanced at Cory. "If you don't have plans, join us. We'll bring your favorite overstuffed potato and cherry pie."

The back of Cory's hand brushed across his forehead. "That's okay. A light meal, hot shower, and bed are on my immediate agenda. This has been one challenging day. It's taken me ten minutes to screw on five lugs."

"Any particular reason why your fingers won't cooperate?" Gabby asked.

Rob supplied a simple response. "Gabrielle ..."

Giving her husband an eye roll, she refocused on his cousin. "The morning was rough going for me as well, but Tempia's magnificent lunch improved my attitude. When I returned to the job, the workday fell into a steady rhythm."

Cory chuckled to himself.

When the men remained silent, Gabby coughed a few times. Her questioning gaze speared Cory. "Let's bring the skeleton out of the closet," she began. "Tempia's divorce became final one year ago today. So, at lunch, although we didn't eat cake and blow horns, we did celebrate her freedom from a louse." Pausing, she steadily gazed in Cory's direction. "Call her, Cory. Support is best served by people who understand the entire problem. You know Quince tormented her."

It seemed that assisting Rob with work on his Boss Mustang hadn't been Cory's best choice. He should have headed home after dropping off the work van. As if on autopilot, his car had driven him straight to Rob's house. He set aside the wrench, eyeing Gabby. Subtlety had taken a vacation. He hoped it wasn't a lengthy trip.

During the past year, an unknown number had called Cory several times. He knew it had been Tempia without being told. Would Gabby admit to giving out his cell phone number?

Gabby's right foot tapped the pavement. "Calling her will promote the friendship you haven't shown lately. Listen. A one-year divorce anniversary is a momentous day for any person, but especially for a woman who suffered miserably because of someone's hatred for you."

So Tempia marrying a vengeful man is all my fault? I beg to differ. Quince used her against me, but a person's bad decisions affect more lives than just their own.

"Your friend has a superb support system already in place," he said. "She can opt to call me or not. Her choice."

Gabby ignored her husband as Rob spoke her name again. "Yeah, well, she's tried. It's difficult to contact a person who ignores you. You treated Tempia like a friend but dropped her once she left Quince."

Cory refused to supply the response Gabby didn't deserve. Still, what she said had two purposes. Gabby sought to advance her friend's cause, plus pinpoint Cory's vulnerable spot. Too bad her fishing expedition featured Tempia and Quince's prior relationship. The concessions he had made for those two would last him a lifetime.

"Did you miss the first part?" He grabbed a wet-wipe container off the bench, cleaning his greasy fingers.

Gabby eyed him up and down. "You mean your comment that Tempia can call you?"

"So, you are listening." He glanced at his cousin. "Call me when you're ready to do a test drive. Can hardly wait until you put the pedal to the metal at the speedway strip."

Rob stroked his wife's arm, hugging her close before he answered. "Minus unforeseen distractions, I plan to race her around the track at Kelley's this Tuesday."

"Getting her completely done by Tuesday will be tight," Cory said. He took keys from his hip pocket, then watched his cousin nod at him and then shake his head at his wife.

Her lips pursed into a thin line, Gabby headed toward the garage entrance but stopped short of exiting. With tiny steps, she ambled back toward the men. "Come on, Cory. Play fair. You still talk to Quince."

The lady was persistent if nothing else. "We talk a few seconds if I'm available when he calls."

Gabby's eyebrows arched as a lone finger tapped her top lip. "You and Quince are no longer occasional friends?"

"Friendships require equally committed individuals being on the same page." Shrugging into his hoodie, he awaited her reply.

Gabby gave him side-eye but didn't speak.

Cory tossed his keys into the air and caught them behind his back.

"Listen," said Gabby. "Tempia's well-being is serious business. I understand you dismissing Quince. However, you liked Tempia the first night you saw her at Rob's get-together. Why play hardball about a relationship that's worth pursuing?"

"Who's playing? My actions speak for themselves." His shoe touched Rob's boot. "See you both at the speedway. Looking forward to the call." Cory strode toward his SUV, glad he was leaving.

Gabby called his name then waited until he faced her. "My husband just lectured me on appropriate social etiquette. Butting into your personal business was wrong."

Right. Respect his preset boundaries. Tempia discussions exceeded his comfort zone. Cory threw up one hand in a brief wave, slid into his car, and drove away.

Regardless of his cousin's wife's opinion, he refused to sweep aside her friend marrying a man she barely knew. Good judgment and sound character were kinsmen. Both qualities were required in successful relationships. Gabby maintained Tempia had put her life back on the proper track, yet Gabby was the same person who had believed Tempia would cancel the ceremony until the couple said "I do" at their wedding ceremony. Today, Gabby angled to rebalance his opinion of her best friend.

"You liked Tempia the first night you saw her at Rob's get-together."

He couldn't disagree that he was instantly fascinated with her. Only, he had first seen Tempia three weeks before Rob's party.

On the night Tempia left her husband, Cory pinpointed Quince's ambiguous plan to crush Cory any way he could. What did it matter if his own wife suffered in the process? That upshot had infuriated Cory. In the end, he almost regretted chastising Rob each time his cousin had decked Quince. Cory left Quince unscathed the evening Tempia left him. Not once had Cory asked himself, "What would Jesus do?" Only God had kept both men safe.

His cell phone buzzed against the dashboard. Quince Jones's phone number lit up on the caller ID screen.

Too bad Quince had run into Cory's eighth unreachable moment that day.

Chapter Five

In the early evening, Tempia parked her car behind her father's truck and grabbed items off the back seat: a bouquet, iced lemon crumb cake, and numerous bags and boxes. Her stepmother would adore the large-eared stuffed baby elephant hidden inside the bag.

She climbed the steps and placed what would fit on a glider; the rest she dropped onto the gray-slate porch. Removing the key ring from her pocket, Tempia unlocked the front door and poked her head into the foyer. Muted voices were heard from somewhere near the kitchen.

"Curt, Noah," she called. "I need some help."

Her brothers' footsteps sounded in the hallway as if they had challenged each other to a foot race. Tempia's head shook at their competitive spirit. She shut the storm door and eyed the items on the glider. The trek through the mall had produced unrestrained buying. Tempia should have continued the quiet walk through the neighborhood park.

Noah beat his older brother to the door. His eyes open wide; he froze in place. His gaze searched the porch. "Wow! Packages and boxes are everywhere." He called over his shoulder into the house. "She's moving in, Mom. Come see all the stuff she brought over here."

Tempia thumped her brother's arm. "Ha, ha. Very funny. You'll thank me later."

The storm door opened and closed. "Whoa!" Curt shook his head, laughing. "I think Noah got it right." Reopening the storm door, he poked his head inside. "Hey, you guys. Your daughter's moving back home."

"Two comics in one family are two too many." Tempia nudged both boys toward the steps. "Leaving the video games and movies inside the car for now means you will carry fewer items."

"Nix that," Noah said. "Get real, Tempie. Why would we leave them inside the car? You bought these gifts for us."

"Are you a comedian posing as a bossy sister?" Curt asked.

Tempia propped the door open with her right foot and retrieved the gifts off the glider.

"Lock up my car when you're done. And if you fail to lock it up, next Saturday you both will treat me to lunch at Cubbies."

"What's your payment to us when we do lock the car doors?" Curt questioned.

"A matinee movie at Midday Theater and playing games at Scooter's Arcade."

Tempia handed the flowers to her stepmother, who was standing halfway down the hallway.

"Save your pennies. Your sons will lose their bet, bigly."

"I heard. They had better lock all four car doors."

Blanche smelled the blooms as the women strolled into the kitchen. She set the red vase of yellow irises on the buffet. When Blanche walked toward the cabinet, she spotted the bag hanging on Tempia's arm. "And what's that?"

Tempia set the dessert box on the table and propped the sack on the counter. "Add this little guy to your collection. Mom, do not peek until tonight. Be surprised about which stuffed animal you're getting."

Blanche sighed. "Your command is a mighty tall order."

Sam entered the kitchen from the laundry room, sat at the table, and opened the newspaper. Before speaking, he grunted at the headline. "There isn't enough room in our house to add more cuddly toys. Make that gift the last one."

Tempia laughed. Muttered words sounded behind her back. Curt's hip bumped into his sister as he passed her.

"Ouch!" She rubbed her lower side. "That was intentional. Say sorry."

"I was just playing," he said, grinning.

Noah followed his brother into the kitchen, dropping the parcels he carried onto the table.

Tempia lunged forward and reached for the top package as it toppled sideways.

Kerplunk!

The box landed on the floor.

Blanche jumped while carrying a pot of boiling water to the sink. Hot water splashed her hands and the tile. She glared at her son, set the pan on the stovetop, and ran cold water over her hands. "Be careful, Noah. Stop making so much commotion." She wiped her hands on a dry towel, watching Tempia grab the mop.

Noah set the box upright. "Fragile isn't stamped on the package."

His newspaper lowered, Sam surveyed his youngest son. "Does that mean you can be careless?"

"No, sir. It does not. I'll be careful. Sorry, Mom."

Blanche set a bowl of spaghetti and meatballs on the table. "Tone it down, boys. Don't make your sister regret spending the weekend."

"She threatened us outside," Noah said.

Blanche set breadsticks nestled in a wicker basket on the tabletop. "How? I didn't hear any threats."

"Tempie told us to leave the gifts she bought us inside the car," Curt complained.

"Are the gifts still inside her car?" his father asked.

Both boys' mouths hung open. They looked from their father to their mother, then back to their father.

"She didn't mean it, Dad. Right, Tempie?" they said in unison.

Her brothers speaking in flawless synchrony always tickled her. Unable to speak, she laughed instead.

* * *

Cory turned right at the corner of a tree-lined street, parked his SUV at the curb, and drummed his fingers on the steering wheel. "It is what it is. No second guesses. Walk a straight course."

He got out of the vehicle and headed toward the gangway beside the brick house. Jogging down six steps inside the backyard, he opened the door that led into the living room. Three years ago, he had wised up, moved back home, and renovated his parents' house for their thirtieth wedding anniversary. The main floor was designed according to their precise specifications.

Renovations included the lower-level basement where Cory dwelled. The previously seldom-used space had been transformed into a three-bedroom apartment featuring a separate laundry room and eat-in kitchen.

He also built an expansive patio underneath the double-tiered deck. Since neither Lillie nor Timothy were outdoorsy people, Cory had the backyard to himself.

There were three ways he could access the upstairs portion of the house. Although the front porch and back deck provided easy access, he preferred going up the basement stairs. For all intents and purposes, he lived alone. It made little sense to buy a house elsewhere. Cory loved his St. Louis city home.

As his friends had done, he had initially moved out of his family house. But ten months later, he roamed around his one-bedroom apartment thinking about what living situation he would prefer. It did not include being surrounded by parking lots, strangers, and limited recreation space. The swimming pool and spa on the other side of the apartment complex proved insufficient. Cory enjoyed outdoor activities and sitting outside whenever possible.

He realized he'd made a major miscalculation in moving from the family home. It was perfect for him. From that experience, he learned to choose the proper road for himself, even if it meant walking alone.

He tossed keys onto the nightstand and headed into the bathroom. A hot shower was at the forefront of his mind. Soon, the rainfall showerhead's pulsating massage soothed taut muscles he discovered he had today.

Forty minutes later, he sprawled on the couch dressed in light-gray denim jeans and a dark-gray crewneck sweatshirt. The oversized sandwich he had eaten had hit the spot.

Cory was drifting to sleep when the doorbell rang twice. He turned down the music volume. His parents rarely entertained guests on Friday evenings. Any person visiting him called in advance and came down the gangway to his front door. The ringer pealed two more times in succession. Needless noise. People had the right to ignore ringing doorbells. But his parents never had. Cory jogged up the basement steps. From the hallway, he noticed his mother peeking out a living room window.

"It's Quince again," Lillie told her husband. "He stopped by earlier today, but I ignored the doorbell. Cory's downstairs. I should've told him when he came home that Quince had stopped by."

Cory entered the living room, making his presence known. "As usual with our visitor, selfishness overrode decorum. To Quince, this day might hold significant meaning."

"In what way?" Lillie snapped her fingers. "Oh. Yes. The divorce. Has it been one year already?"

Timothy brought his recliner upright. "A failed marriage doesn't deserve feedback or celebratory rights. His problem is the young lady let him off too easily. His cruelty demanded adequate compensation she let slide."

His mother parted the drapes a half inch and peeked through the window. "He's still standing on the porch."

The doorbell buzzed off and on. Quince appeared adamant about whatever he wished to say.

After a while, Lillie closed the curtain and sat beside her husband. "Cory, he thinks you're home because your car is parked out front." She hesitated when the doorbell rang again. "We haven't seen Quince in ten years. Does he know you live in the basement and don't accept callers from the first floor?"

"No, ma'am. I only volunteer necessary information in our limited conversations."

Lillie glanced at Tim. "I guess the apple didn't fall far from the tree after all. Remember, guys, openness can produce abundant rewards."

"Plus, numerous pitfalls no one anticipated," her husband said, studying his son. "What's prompted Quince's visit?"

Cory shrugged. "Who knows."

Tim nodded. "Do you want us to go into the kitchen?"

"You two stay put. Quince isn't welcome inside our home."

In the foyer, Cory opened the front door, stepped outside the house, and shut the door behind him. Leaning on the handrail, he watched Quince bounce on his feet like a trained boxer. Since Quince paid the visit, Cory let him have the floor.

No longer bouncing in place, Quince resembled a tiger ready to pounce.

Cory took a forward step, grinning. "This is an unplanned visit. What's up?"

The silent man's narrowed eyes resembled slits. "Not the expected welcome. Did ... you ... anticipate seeing me today?"

The men hadn't seen each other since the night Quince and his wife separated. They had never frequented the same places, nor shared common friends. Still, Cory had made himself available whenever Quince called. "Is there a specific reason why I should? We haven't seen each other in ages. Next time, call first. Don't drop by my house unannounced."

Quince snorted. "I haven't seen you since the night you took Tempia away."

"Reframe your loose accusation," Cory said. His head tilted.

Quince pulled a cord on his jacket. "I came to clear the air, not pick a fight. Man, you ghosted me like our friendship meant nothing."

"Right. I decided to avoid one-sided associations."

Quince's hands flexed at his side. "That sounds like an indictment against my character. What changed? We have always kept in touch."

"We did until the connection severed. I don't rebuild burnt bridges."

"This discussion isn't about your self-interest." Anger filled Quince's eyes as he surveyed Cory. "You plan to shelve our friendship after I endured unlimited garbage through the years. Hanging out despite your friends' insults."

46

"You saw my friends at Rob's party. No one insulted you there."

"You must have a short-term memory issue. Did you forget the after-thought comment?"

A classmate had taken a dig at Quince in their sophomore year at Madison High.

"You're by yourself today," she told Cory and everyone else who listened. "Did the afterthought get lost?"

"Look. That was twelve years ago. Get over it."

"No sympathy for the poor maligned man?" His nostrils flaring, Quince repeatedly flexed his fingers. "Don't dismiss how I felt around your crowd. What the cheerleader said wasn't an isolated incident."

"You heard me set each person straight. Self-doubting people make hateful comments. I control *my* actions."

"Lose the God complex. *You* ... defending me couldn't erase ... *their* contempt."

"But it should've earned me your respect. Instead of viewing me as a buddy, you upped the garbage that caused your problems."

Quince took several deep breaths, glaring at Cory. "Get off the fence. Let's get to the real issue. Still sniffing behind my ex-wife?" His cheeks pulsated as his top lip curled.

Cory gauged Quince's shifting body language. Inner battles often proved the worst sort. "Keep talking. You won't get a second shot."

"I think you hoodwinked me and stole Tempia from me to pay me back for taking her away from you." Quince's head jerked sideways when he snorted. "I told Tempia you were dating a jealous woman, so she jumped at the chance to date me. But old news doesn't matter."

One lie had ruined what Cory believed was a promising beginning. Tempia had changed direction because of one false statement. Quince undermined the man who never blew him off. His deceit cut the last thread in the men's fractured link. However, the revelation implicated Cory's cousin in the deception. Cory had never heard about the jealous-woman lie. *Rob!*

He reached behind his back and gripped the doorknob.

"Walking out on me? What happened to that revered Sanders compassion?"

Cory dropped his hand. His stance widened. "If you are trying to convince me that talking to you is worth the effort, you failed."

Mixed emotions contorted Quince's face. "People considered you the main player and me a misfit. Just once, I wanted to rub your face in my pain of getting rejected. Some quality Tempia possessed drew you to her, man.

Your winning streak couldn't last forever. Tempia became the pawn in my game. I knew her dating me would turn you off."

"You revamped your lifestyle to punish me? I figured the man who maligned relationships had fallen in love."

Quince laughed. "My class act confounded the one person who knew me best. Interesting ... Blame yourself for the lengthy dating period. Your disinterest raised the stakes."

Cory understood why his cousin had repeatedly decked the idiot years ago. Quince would never own his bad behavior. "It's my fault you betrayed an innocent woman? Invent an excuse worth hearing."

"Because you failed to confront me about stealing Tempia, I morphed into her dream man, abandoning my preferred lifestyle."

"Don't gloat about your shameful character flaws," Cory said. "No person can justify despicable behavior. Why did you propose marriage?"

"I knew you would reject her if she and I slept together. I just miscalculated her antiquated beliefs. Her view of no sex outside of marriage snuffed my plan to sleep with her and move on. Yet freeing her to date you did not work for me." Quince massaged his chin then laughed. "Trust that marriage became the last resort. You would cold-shoulder any woman I married."

Cory chuckled. "Ya think?"

Quince glanced away for the first time, then he cleared his throat, eyeing Cory up and down. "Lose the righteous attitude," he snapped. "You played it straight until you took advantage of my slipup. Explain how a supposedly upright man eclipsed my game and disrespected our friendship."

Cory should have gone back downstairs and continued his nap instead of engaging a remorseless man. Quince's main goal was trumping whatever comment Cory made. "Why come here? You could have raised fictitious accusations and bragged about your creep status in a text message."

Quince sneered until his lips broke into a grin. "I expected an apology. Not fallacious hogwash. Man, while dating Tempia, I suffered through six sex-free months. Yeah," he said when Cory's head shook. "I abhor cheaters and always play a straight hand."

Quince wouldn't cheat on his girlfriend or wife but would ruin their life? Until this moment, Cory had failed to comprehend the depths of Quince's mental deficiencies. One truth remained: Quince possessed serious emotional problems.

His shoulders back, Cory's stance widened. "Okay. Let's get to the point of your visit."

The grin on Quince's face never reached his eyes. "I want a friendship restart. No more speedy or unanswered phone calls." He stuck out his hand. "Still friends?"

The question didn't warrant a response, but Cory searched for a reply that wouldn't haunt him later. "Friendship escaped us in junior high. Be kind to yourself. Seek professional counseling."

"Are you questioning my mental health? Am I not acting normal enough for you? Last year, I lost my wife and my best friend in one day."

Cory shrugged. "Mental and emotional stability fosters clear thinking."

"Get over yourself. You branding me crazy doesn't affect my life. Have you ever walked in my shoes?" Quince asked through clenched teeth.

"Thank God they don't fit. Look—"

"You ... look ... man. Your glaring disrespect and defection have been endless." Flinty eyes fixed onto Cory. "*You* ignored her because she chose me instead of you. *You* knew marrying Tempia was the highest point in my life. *You* became her benefactor. My wife filed for divorce because of your interference."

"We both remember the truth regarding your ex-wife and you."

Quince's one step placed him and Cory nose-to-nose. "Belittling me at this point is useless. I've already reached rock bottom."

Cory couldn't remedy someone else's self-delusion. He removed his hands from his pockets and shoved the agitated man backwards. "Don't kid yourself. Look down. There's plenty of room below."

He stepped across the threshold and locked the door on the man who he'd prayed would excel in life. The men's final discussion exposed Quince's irrefutable mental crisis. Two combustible ingredients had wreaked havoc inside a volatile mind. Pure resentment, plus low self-regard, had driven an unbalanced man near the edge.

What about Tempia Antoinette Wade? Even her middle name had etched itself upon his brain. Cory had maintained decorum in all dealings with her. Perhaps he'd misjudged Tempia's eating her meal with Quince. Would the outcome be any different had he remained at Rob's party? Cory had rolled onto his back and played dead. He almost blamed himself for the troubling results.

His mother's favorite catchphrase came to mind. Upon completing a burdensome task, Lillie would brush her palms together, wink her eye, and say, "Spick and span. The old is out. The new is in."

Valuable time had been wasted on a man still courting self-destruction. Years ago, the two men had charted divergent courses. No more playing a lame duck to an unrepentant man, tying up his own hands.

Cory's peaceful night had hit obstacles at every crossroad. He put a grin on his face and entered the living room. "Quince won't be back. Count on it. He hasn't earned any slack."

Lillie and Timothy glanced at each other, and then they refocused on their son.

Cory pushed the ottoman aside and eased onto the settee. "He has serious emotional issues. Eons ago, I should have sent his calls to voicemail."

"You never would. You're an empathetic man. You treated Quince better than he treats himself. Quince lacked a firm hand while growing up. Despite their failing health, his grandparents raised him the best they could after his mother passed away. Pray his life changes for the better."

Timothy nodded. "He was dealt a harsh hand. You tried to level the odds. Good will might escort people to the building, but it can't propel anyone beyond the entrance. Everyone must take their own next step."

Which proves inertia is the wrong reaction to life's challenges. I allowed stagnation far too long. "Thanks. I appreciate the food for thought."

Lillie called to her son as he headed toward the door. "What about Tempia? You talked up your mystery lady until seeing her at Rob's house."

"Quince just admitted he told Tempia I was already taken. He arranged a date for the next day."

"He knew you would step aside if he did," his father said. "I'm proud my son has a conscience."

"Where does his confession leave you and Tempia?" his mother questioned. "Although we haven't met her, she seemed like a nice lady at Rob's wedding reception."

"Our moment has passed," he said. "Tempia is a burnt bridge I won't rebuild."

Lillie sighed. "Someone else lit the match, son."

"Tempia failed to blow it out," his father reminded. "She gave Quince permission to pretend he was the man she wanted him to be. Lillie, you're overly concerned about a person you've never met. There are plenty of godly women our son can date."

Apparently, they all have done an excellent job of going into hiding. I haven't met any woman I've wanted to see more than once.

"I'm just saying, Cory liked Tempia. He gave us a fantastic report until Rob's party."

"Sometimes conjecture is proven wrong once an actual introduction takes place," her husband replied.

"Then why did he help her during her marriage? Rob told us the entire story. Our son saw her again at the wedding rehearsal. What if they had been properly introduced at your nephew's party?"

"Rob's wife introduced them on the spot. Tempia opted not to further their acquaintance."

"If Quince fed her lies, I'm sure she had sound reasons," his wife said.

Tim grunted. "Only God knows the future and understands the past and present. I thank the Father that He spared our son needless humiliations."

Cory leaned on the wall once the discussion stagnated. His folks' assessments appeared realistic. Although both positions could be wrong, Cory believed one of their perspectives was correct. Indecision prevailed until the bottom line seized his mind: Quince had set up Tempia for failure. He used an innocent woman to get back at a man he should have valued like a friend.

Cory hadn't dated anyone for several months before he officially met Tempia at Rob's party. He felt sure Tempia had shared with Gabby Quince's lies about Cory having a girlfriend. And no doubt Gabby would have set her straight and told his cousin. Why would Rob and Gabby deprive Cory of those pertinent facts?

If Tempia had been deceived, could he ignore she should have known better?

No. He couldn't. Not unless she had a good reason for believing it. He needed to speak to Rob. Who knew what other relevant details Cory hadn't been told.

"Rob's nephews have a preseason baseball game at Crossfield Park. I'm headed out," Cory said, but he paused, sifting through his thoughts inside the doorway. His mind made up, Cory waved a hand and left the room.

Chapter Six

On the drive to Crossfield Park, Cory conceded that Quince's deception did not pardon Tempia's blunder. She had to have known the difference between a lie and the bitter truth. His thoughts waffled back and forth as he parked his car in the sparsely filled parking lot. He recognized that final decisions should wait until full facts have been analyzed. Quince's account was suspect, but Cory's cousin would tell the unvarnished truth.

Cory stepped onto the bleachers, greeted several relatives, and kissed his aunt's cheek. He slid down the row and stood by Rob.

Gabby's hands clasped her chest. "Glad you joined us. We could've picked you up a meal from The Potato Joynt. Or at least a slice of cherry pie."

"I ate earlier but need Rob's ear a moment." Cory sat beside his cousin and spoke in a low voice. "Quince just left my house. We need to talk." He rose, retraced his steps, and waited beside his SUV.

Born two days apart, Rob and Cory had been best friends since rolling over each other inside their baby cribs. Their genuine trust and affection had flourished until this day.

The men spent the next twenty minutes talking over each other.

"Be reasonable," Rob said. "I can't undo past actions. I can adjust how I handle the Tempia situation going forward."

"But sharing the truth from the beginning might have stopped a disastrous marriage from ever taking place."

Suspicion appeared in Rob's eyes. "Your supposition may be correct, and if so, I apologize. But is the Tempia connection severed? Will you lay the past to rest and date other women?"

"That's not what we're talking about here. My trust in you is on the table."

Rob stepped backwards. "Why? Because I was concerned about your well-being? Is loving someone a crime these days?"

Cory glared. "Caring about me is synonymous with telling me the truth.

Which you clearly did not do."

"That's cold, man. Consider circumstances from my viewpoint. You leaving the party meant Tempia's desertion had devastated you. The man I know would have ignored Quince's slight and stuck around. He wouldn't have rolled over and played dead."

Cory counted to fifty and calmed himself down. He wouldn't voice words that could not be taken back.

A glance over Rob's shoulder showed Gabby strolling their way.

"*You* credited God for your providential party idea after I revealed she was my mystery lady," Cory retorted.

"I did until she disrespected your benevolence and spent forty minutes talking to a reprobate."

"Tempia's behavior doesn't matter in a discussion about you and me. If you were concerned, you should have voiced that. That is how best friends treat each other."

Rob's eyes appeared transfixed as his right hand rubbed his left shoulder. "One mistake in twenty-eight years and you question my allegiance? Is that your position?"

"You've been living out the lie for two years."

"You've cast me as the villain instead of Quince? Would you prefer I apologize to Tempia?" Eyes narrowed, he paused, apparently waiting for an answer.

Giving his cousin his best "you can't be serious" look, Cory remained silent.

"Are you going by Tempia's apartment?" Rob asked.

"Why would I visit her apartment? Remember, your wife told us in the garage Tempia was spending the weekend at her parents' house."

"Stop getting testy. It slipped my mind that she's holed up at her parents' place."

Cory's raised hands framed his face then dropped to his side. "There you go. The words 'holed up' suggest something nefarious occurred and Tempia's hidden herself away. She and her family are celebrating her one-year divorce anniversary." Cory clocked Gabby as fewer than forty steps away. "We're done. Your wife is waiting on you."

While rolling up his shirt sleeves, Rob stared at his cousin. "You come here, dump on me, and leave? Sure you want to travel down that road? Are you leaving to talk to Tempia?"

"Gabby is walking up behind you. Five. Four. Three."

Rob turned sideways and spotted his wife. "Is the game over, honey?"

Two steps later, Gabby reached her husband. "You and Cory have talked long enough. Is there a problem involving Tempia?"

"Your husband can relay the story," Cory said. "See you guys." Cory waved his hand in a brief salute and drove off, debating his next move.

Tempia was front and center in his head. Was contacting her today a wise step? Making a phone call felt like it would fall flat. He must see her facial expressions and body language during their discussion.

* * *

Laughter filled the Wade family's living room when the bank robber made a getaway in an electric bumper car. Even though he hated spoofs, Tempia's father laughed throughout the movie. The ending had given her stepmother a laughing fit.

"Okay, Noah. I had my doubts, but the movie was quite funny." Blanche picked up two DVD jackets and read the movie summaries. "We'll watch Tempie's tearjerker first and Curt's bowling comedy last."

"Smart move," Sam agreed. "No one should fall asleep right after viewing one of Tempie's heart-wrenching tales."

"Stop questioning my impeccable movie tastes. To make amends, you and Mom can make a fast-food run if you both enjoy the movie. The boys and I will be starving after the second movie ends. Agreed?"

"No," Sam and Blanche spoke together.

"Tempie loves for other people to make concessions for her," Curt said with a laugh.

Noah chortled. "My brother learned a new word. Clap, everyone." Noah jumped off the couch, dodging multiple pillows Curt threw at him, which instead knocked over a table lamp.

Curt scuttled across the floor and set the lamp upright, then headed back to his chair. "The lamp didn't break, Mama."

"But it could have been broken. Keep the horseplay outside," his father said. "I would send you both to your bedrooms, but the best punishment is making you watch the movie your sister chose."

The others laughed—but not at her expense. Genuine affection tinged the air. Everyone sat in the living room watching movies because they loved her, Tempia Wade.

"Group hug," Curt said, rushing to her side. When the group surrounded her chair, everyone pecked her cheek and hugged her neck. Noah whispered in her ear, "You're the best sister any boy could have."

Blanche broke away from the group, blinking back tears. "Movie time. Take your seats and enjoy the show."

"I hope Tempie made a good choice," Sam said. "If not, guess she'll head to Ginger Pop before Curt's movie begins."

"Of course I will," Tempia said, burrowing deeper into her chair. "The boys and I can also make an ice cream run."

* * *

An hour later, heartbroken over an emotional burial scene, Tempia ignored the cell phone ringing on the end table. Seconds later, it rang again. Busy brushing teardrops off her cheeks, she let the call go to voicemail. When it rang a third time, she picked it up, glancing at the caller ID. Gabby. Perhaps she should take the call.

"Hold on," Tempia spoke into the receiver. She muted the phone, left the sofa, and headed for the door. She turned toward her family. "Gabby keeps trying to call. Continue watching the movie. This won't take long."

Blanche reached for the remote control. "We'll wait. Hope everything is all right."

"I'm sure it is." Tempia unmuted the cell phone in the hallway. "What's up, Gab?"

"We only have a few minutes," Gabby spoke in a breathy voice. "Rob thinks Cory may be on his way over there."

Tempia and Gabby's earlier conversation popped into her mind. Her spread fingers pressed across her mouth. "What happened? Why is Cory coming here?"

"When I came home from work, he and Rob were working on the Mustang in the garage. We talked briefly. But he showed up at the ballgame an hour ago. He and Rob held a discussion without me. Rob just supplied the focal point. Listen. Cory hasn't seen your ex-husband since the night you and Quince separated. Although Quince has called Cory, today he paid a visit, exposing the jealous-girlfriend lies."

Tempia stared at the cell phone, then placed it back against her ear. Even if Quince had admitted his deception, why would Cory seek out Rob? Old facts weren't newsworthy, unless ... a new twist had developed. A sharp pain hit the head she shook. "Why is his admitting the truth today important? Cory already knew about Quince's crusade to spread misinformation."

Gabby gave a long, hard sigh. "Neither Rob nor I told Cory about Quince's lies. We just kept them to ourselves."

Whoa! Cory's noncommunication had convinced Tempia that Quince's story about Cory having a girlfriend had been the truth. Why else would Cory, who had shown an interest in her, not correct the lie? Why had Gabby and Rob withheld the information from Cory about Quince making up the story? Her nostrils flared. Sweat dotted upon her forehead. *Gabby Stephens, Cory's outing Quince's lie might've saved my heart from breaking. You had better have a brilliant explanation for not telling him about it.*

Her teeth gritting, Tempia modulated her voice. "I'm lost. Why didn't someone tell Cory his friend couldn't be trusted?"

"He may not have known Quince lied about the girlfriend thing, but Cory isn't stupid. He knows Quince can be dishonest in general." She paused, taking an audible breath. "Listen. Rob disliked the way you handled the incident at his house. Tempie, you ghosted a man who returned your interest—and you did so all because of a silly accident. Rob reasoned that Cory's favorable reaction to the situation should have heightened your attraction for Cory."

My goodness. She wasn't an idiot. "It certainly did. Cory's great response saved me from being completely humiliated."

"But you and Quince laughed and talked for a full forty minutes—"

"I was embarrassed! On my way back to the living room, a man on his way to the bathroom looked at me, shook his head, and laughed."

"Forty minutes, Temp. Instead of approaching me, you believed Quince's lies and let him drive you home. I had already said Cory didn't have a girlfriend. Setting up a date without verifying facts was reckless." There was a long pause while Gabby sniffled.

Still fuming, Tempia gritted her teeth until Gabby continued.

"It's the way you handled everything. You hadn't dated anyone in months, so why wouldn't you tell your best friend you planned a date with a man you had just met? Especially when you met him at my fiancé's house. I learned about the date only after you returned home."

Tempia had improperly handled the incident, but so had Gabby. Their two wrong reactions had almost ruined her life. "When was I supposed to contact you? I spent the day at my grandparents' house and met Quince at Dragon King.

We ate dinner, took in a movie, and ate dessert at Kylie's. I got home at 10:30."

"A brief phone call would have sufficed," continued Gabby. "I interceded on your behalf, but Rob gave me two choices: either I mind my own business or he would inform Cory that I had told you Cory was unattached *before* Quince lied."

Tempia rested her head on her hand. What else could go wrong? Bad news normally came in threes.

"Rob just told Cory I had told you Cory didn't have a girlfriend before Quince lied."

Tempia dropped onto the staircase step. "What did Rob say? That I believed a stranger and not my best friend of over twenty years? I'm surprised Cory's coming by my house at all."

"Well, despite all that's happened, Rob should have let *you* tell Cory that I had told you he was unattached before you talked to Quince. Instead, he spilled the beans. Sorry all this drama happened on your celebration day."

"Dating Quince is my fault," Tempia said. "I apologize that my stupid actions put you and Rob in a difficult position." Hesitating, Tempia squeezed her eyelids shut. "Gab, it took me a moment to realize, but I think you and Rob staying out of it was the correct choice."

"Rob thinks so too. For me, the issue is still debatable."

"It shouldn't be." Tempia blotted teardrops off her cheeks.

"Humph. Well, anyway, we're about to leave the baseball game. Just wanted to let you know that Cory was on his way over there."

Tempia moaned. Her restless fingers stroked her hair. "Bet you he isn't bringing glad tidings."

"Stay positive. Fight for him. Trust the God who never fails." Hesitating, she sighed. "I'll wring Rob and Cory's entire conversation from my husband in the car. Ugh! What an incredibly difficult day."

Outside noise snagged Tempia's attention. "Hold on. A car just pulled up across the street." She crossed the hallway and peeked out a side window. "Yep. He's here. Cory in the flesh. Oh boy."

"Rob's coming," Gabby whispered in a low voice. "Tomorrow will bring a brighter day. Call me."

"Nope. We'll discuss everything at Capris. Celebrate this night with your spouse. Sorry I caused problems between you and Rob."

"Nonsense. We don't require anyone's help to make problems. We do a terrific job on our own."

Cory sat inside the vehicle drumming his fingers on the steering wheel. Tempia watched with mixed emotions. She both wanted him with her and to go home. Would he forgive her foolishness and declare his love? What was he thinking? Had he changed his mind? Was he coming inside to bridge the gulf that separated him and her as a couple? Her brain wouldn't stop racing.

The vehicle door opened. Cory stood beside his SUV. Tempia scurried down the hall, poking her head inside the living room. The silence in the room surprised her. Her family waited for an explanation. Simplicity might best serve her purpose.

"Gabby's call was a heads-up. Cory just parked across the street."

Concern rose in Blanche's eyes. "Do you know why he's coming?"

Sam stood. "Is his visit good or bad?"

"Dad, please sit down. Mom, his purpose for stopping by is anyone's guess." Her raised hands dropped at her side. "I'll let you know after he leaves."

Blanche grasped her husband's arm, patted his side, then held his hand. Her gaze never left her stepdaughter's face. "Should we step in if he invites you outside?"

"No, ma'am. Cory will always behave like the gentleman he is." *Father, from my mouth to your ear. Please! Make it so. Give Cory and me a fresh beginning.* She glanced behind her as the doorbell rang. Her lips trembling in a tight smile, she faced her father. "It's okay. I'll let him in."

Tempia inhaled a steadying breath, then opened the front door. She and Cory stood there, staring at each other. She couldn't think. Not even a simple hello crossed her mind. She tried deciphering his noncommittal expression.

No matter what he was thinking, seeing Cory after such a long hiatus replenished her hope reservoir. She scanned him from head to toe. The past year had treated him well.

Her fingers rubbing together, Tempia whispered, "We're watching a movie in the living room. Would you like to join us?"

Cory's lips broke into a fulsome grin. Still holding onto the storm door, he backed up. "How about we talk privately outside? It's a long-overdue discussion."

Tempia preferred welcoming him inside her parents' home, but she exited the house and settled on the two-seater glider.

Cory bypassed the empty spot next to her and chose a wicker chair facing her direction. The easy grin he wore brushed her heart. Life-altering circumstances seldom marred his calm facade. Composure fit him like a second layer of skin. Until the night Tempia left Quince, dubious conditions had never fazed him. How would she feel if the shoe was on the other foot? Would she have visited him this evening? She probably would have kept her distance and stayed far away. Why had he come?

Tempia twiddled her thumbs and shifted positions on the cushion.

Cory clasped his hands behind his head. The easy grin vanished. "Sorry I dropped by unannounced. Did Gabby call?"

"A little earlier." Tempia cleared her throat, attempting an even-keeled tone.

Hooded eyes bore into her soul. "Since she gave you a heads up, I'll dig right in." He hesitated, studying her outfit. "By the way, your outfit reminds me of what you wore the first day I saw you—three weeks before Rob's get-together." A teasing flicker lit his gaze. "You wear that style well."

Her breathing constricted. She suddenly realized what Cory's comment indicated.

Three weeks before the night of Rob's party? Where? How?

Tempia absolutely would not have overlooked Cory Sanders. But clearly, she had. Her gaze swept across the porch. "Wait ... at Rob's house, you did look vaguely familiar. Did you really see me somewhere else?"

"Sure did." His gaze observed shadows in a living room window. Two pairs of silhouettes on each end had shifted their positions. "Your family loves you. Let them know I come in peace. You will always be safe around me."

Her soundless lips moved until she cleared her throat again. "My stepmother labeled you as my special guardian. You've always assisted me wherever needed. They know you're safe, but I'll remind them."

Cory remained silent while Tempia slid off the glider and slipped inside the house.

Moments later, she stood in the living room doorway.

Her family turned around together. Sam stood beside Blanche. Curt and Noah flanked their sides.

"Cory saw your shadows in the window. He said he comes in peace and that I will always be safe around him."

Her parents' glances met until they quietly studied their oldest child.

"It's late," Sam said. "You didn't invite him over here. Did Gabby explain why he was paying an unexpected visit?"

"Sorta. Just pray Cory and I will end today on friendly terms. I'm fine, sir."

"Talk to your young man," her stepmother replied. "We'll hold the movie until you're ready." Blanche linked her husband's arm and shooed her boys across the room.

Once her family settled down, Tempia scooted back outside, stealing a glance at the shadowless window.

Cory waited until she reclaimed her seat on the glider. "Thanks for vouching for me. I can explain my visit, but it will help if I start by giving some background."

Tempia bit off a fingernail. Chill out, she told herself. You prayed fourteen months for a heartfelt conversation with the man you love. God brought Cory over. Be thankful.

Cory stretched his legs until his shoes stopped near Tempia's sneakered feet. "My parents' longtime friends, the Pearsons, run Community Ministries. I love the assistance they provide in their neighborhood. Since the Pearsons couldn't afford to replace the HVAC system at the ministry right when they needed to, I provided free patch-up jobs as needed. I was inside the utility closet on your initial visit."

Tempia's world flipped upside down. Chrissy and Lester Pearson! She loved how their ministry helped so many people. Did the couple realize she knew Cory? Had they heard details concerning her marriage and divorce? She had only spoken briefly about both events.

Tempia digested the unexpected revelation. Hmm ... Cory had seen her before his cousin's party. He had known she supported the ministry he loved. Why had he held back this information that would have annihilated Quince? She glanced at the man studying her. His silence must mean he was assessing her reaction. He'd done that a lot since he'd arrived. It seemed Tempia wasn't the one who had wasted valuable time. Had Cory been upfront with her, they might have been married by now. She dampened her disappointment and hid the turmoil ripping her soul apart.

Why hadn't Gabby warned her that Cory knew the Pearsons?

Chapter Seven

"Imagine, your parents being the Pearsons' friends," Tempia said. "My brothers and I visit their ministry once a month."

His glowing eyes squinted. "Miss Chrissy said the Wade family renewed her hope in teens and young adults. And last year, your family's unequaled enthusiasm developed into a real-life commitment. In the long term, few folks fulfill their obligations or make pledges. By the way, that compliment from her was almost verbatim."

Tempia had supported the ministry before and during her personal crisis. Assisting families at Community Ministries had given her something else to focus on. Praying for other people who were going through difficulties kept her own faith alive. She wanted to repay those cathartic experiences.

Tempia hesitated. Why had Cory kept quiet about the ministry connection? She watched an elderly couple walk around the neighborhood. "I'm confused why, in all this time, you didn't share that information. It would have brought us closer. Why did you keep our ministry connection a secret?"

When Cory didn't answer, she gazed at him and noticed his composure hadn't shifted one bit.

"I planned to tell you while you ate, but I ended up not getting a chance that night," he explained. "And those details became irrelevant after you began dating Quince—and especially once you married him. Still, I can't undo your initial impression when I first saw you at the ministry."

"If you already had a favorable opinion of me, why not at least tell me about all of this after hearing about the first date? You knew Quince was a bad actor. You didn't consider he might have been using me?"

"His motivations for dating and marrying you are appalling. Even though hindsight is twenty-twenty, I stand behind my decision not to contact you when you were dating Quince. Unless my perspective changes during this visit."

Hope rose within her. Would Cory alter his perception of her behavior?

Besides, his moral code wouldn't have allowed her ex to intentionally dupe her. He would have outed the liar had the agenda been recognized.

Tempia schooled her features to match her visitor's nonchalance. "So, how did I make a favorable impression at the ministry? Many folks drop off food donations."

Cory leaned forward, then reclined his back on the chair cushion. "Most people drop off their donation and hurry out the door. Your family sat down multiple times and befriended families."

He truly cares about the place and its people. Our small donation and respect for the families impressed the man who was working there for free on his day off. Imagine that.

Tempia smiled. "On the previous Sunday, our pastor had told us the ministry provided families in need with social activities seven days a week. That Saturday, my stepmother and I baked five dozen cupcakes. The next day, the Wade siblings sprang into action." Eyes squinted, she paused. "You could see us from where you worked inside the utility closet?"

"A clear line of sight. What sold you on the Pearsons' dream?"

Tempia remembered the children's drawn faces as she and her brothers set the cupcakes on a bottled-water-filled table. The younger children were whiny, the slightly older ones acted rebellious, and the preteens and teenagers suffered boredom while their parents' shoulders appeared heavy. "The ministry offers life-changing alternatives many families require. Particularly the after-school tutoring programs." Those worthy causes required dedication Tempia had never previously achieved. Community Ministries grew her up. "It wasn't just single moms or dads. Both parents were present in most cases."

Cory nodded. "The Pearsons' benevolence is boundless. Each donation is appreciated."

"Any service that people offer will help in some measure. Even supplying cupcakes and conversation."

"Exactly. Knowing other people care can lessen loads." He glanced toward the window where her family had been standing. "I considered you my 'mystery lady.' It took restraint not to bombard the Pearsons for an introduction. I strategized meeting you on my fourth visit there, but that one never came."

What? Tempia had missed Cory three times? He couldn't be serious. Perhaps there had been one account where she hadn't seen him. But how could she have missed him two more times? Tempia held up three shaky fingers. "I don't remember any of those."

"One time, I was driving off when your family returned. The boys were carrying a television, so it caught my attention. Miss Chrissy said you and the older children had watched *The Chronicles of Narnia* while your brothers occupied the younger children by playing games. Then, the following Saturday, you provided a home-cooked meal. I left while you, your brothers, and the families ate breakfast. I hear the Wade siblings still bring Saturday breakfast once a month. Kudos to you."

The best man in all the world had been close enough to speak to on three separate occasions. He could have taken Tempia to Rob's party instead of seeing her there. *I guess it's all water under the bridge I missed traveling on.*

"On all three occasions, you and your brothers operated as a team. You three must spend quality time together."

"For the last four years, my brothers and I have spent the last weekend of each month together." She thought back to all the times they'd shared.

"Tempia? Did you hear my comment?" Cory asked.

She shook her inner self, withdrawing from private thoughts. "Sorry. I was having a flashback."

"I was saying that your family values intrigue me." Cory studied her face while shifting positions. "This is where the Rob factor figures in. For three years straight, he tried hooking me up with you."

Her gaping mouth formed a perfect circle.

"You obviously made an impression on the man. He was relentless with his requests."

"I'm happy to hear that," Tempia said, laughing. "Although, I bet he hasn't made that suggestion since his party."

Cory's eyebrows rose. "What do you mean? Does a problem exist between you and Rob?"

Stick to relevant facts. Do not get lost on endless trails that won't matter.

Tempia nibbled her bottom lip. "Where is this conversation headed?"

Cory grinned. "Remember, I come in peace. On the day of his get-together, Quince and I were shooting pool when Rob called. Rob had set up a games get-together to help you and me get to know each other. I didn't expect Quince to trail behind me."

"Does he typically attend parties without an invitation?"

"At my cousin's house? No way. Quince normally gives Rob a wide berth. Once there, I sat alone second-guessing myself. The fog cleared when you strolled into the house. After the salad incident, I thought that your expression and your remark about not holding the accident against you meant you had seen me at the ministry and wanted an introduction." Cory paused.

Did he expect a response? He had submerged her into a haze surpassing his obviously now-cleared fog. Tempia focused on the Bradford pear tree in the neighbor's yard. Questions nagged her scattered thoughts. Gabby had never mentioned Tempia meeting Cory. Did Rob tell Gabby why he'd hosted the party? Or had he kept his fiancée in the dark?

At the antiques show, Gabby had turned away from Tempia while she and Rob talked. But then she expressed surprise at Cory being at the party. Had she known her fiancé had invited his cousin? Or did Rob keep the Cory invitation a secret from Gabby?

Cory's voice sifted through her ragged emotions. Tempia searched his face, seeking answers to her unasked questions.

"So, I'm confused about how we left things. I felt we had an instant connection. In my mind, the dropped food heightened the suspense. So why did you then sit with Quince instead of me and accept a date with him for the next day?"

The truth would make Cory run back to his SUV. How could she explain the unwise decision that almost destroyed her life? Would the simple truth suffice?

She sighed. "It was because you left me there and I was told you had a jealous girlfriend. I accepted the date after Quince drove me home. It felt like eons had passed since the party first began." Hesitating, Tempia shrugged. "Since I thought dating you wouldn't happen, going on a date with Quince seemed like a good idea."

She looked down at her shoes. How could she make Cory understand an indefensible position? She raised her head and eyed Cory. "I was embarrassed, Cory. People laughed at me. That, plus the other people's teasing remarks, hurt my pride. Quince's nonsensical high opinion of himself entertained me while I ate. After you left the party, I wanted to run after you, but Quince stopped me with the jealous girlfriend lie."

Cory's mouth curved downward. Did her defense stamp "dope" on her forehead?

Tempia's pulse fluttered. Cory's sharp surveillance seemed to last forever.

"Why ... Tempia ... why did you believe a stranger's word without checking out the facts, at least with Gabby?"

"An excellent question I asked myself throughout my marriage. I made a horde of inadequate assumptions and figured your pal knew about your social life." Gathering her reflections, she licked her lips. "I hoped you would contact me. When you didn't, I thought my reputation had been sullied beyond repair. Gabby said you never mentioned me. Your silence seemed to stamp 'the end' on our short story."

Compassion filled his steady gaze. "This evening, Quince confessed his duplicity and Rob admitted the coverup." Cory shook his head, laughing. "Perhaps 'coverup' is a tad of an exaggeration. Let's just say my cousin never disclosed facts I should have been told."

Cory rehashed highlights from his discussions with Quince and Rob, observing Tempia's reactions the entire time. Since she remained quiet after he wound down, Cory continued speaking. "You disbelieved Gabby, yet you knew Quince might have been lying."

Tempia's head shook. "You make what happened sound simpler than it was."

"No, ma'am. Rob kept me in the dark, but I accepted his explanation. He also said Gabby gave you my cell phone number way back then. She wanted you to verify Quince's claims since you doubted her word."

Her shoulders drooped. "I just thought Gabby had either been mistaken or your dating status had changed."

"Gabby ignored Rob's preference and provided my cell phone number. After the get-together, you could have substantiated Quince's assertions instead of digging yourself into a deeper pit."

Tempia closed her eyes to keep teardrops from falling down her cheeks. When her eyes reopened, tears welled in her eyes as she studied Cory's controlled features. "If a man and I had shared a special moment, then he asked my friend out, I wouldn't have given him a second thought."

Tempia scooted to the edge of her seat as Cory considered her response for an extra-long moment. "Communication is crucial to me," he finally said. "Stubbornness without communication can wreck lives."

Was he for real? The critical indictment against her character couldn't go unchallenged. "In theory, yes. Unless ... the object of someone's affection had already walked away."

"People should discuss important matters ASAP." His voice lowered. "Your initial date with Quince can be branded a mistake. Subsequent dates were obvious choices."

Tempia squirmed in her seat. "Quince's steadfast pursuit and charm helped me feel less lonely. He caught me off guard."

Cory rested his chin on bridged fingers and resumed a stretched-legs position. "You dated Quince despite receiving initial warnings, and then even deepened the relationship. I want to understand why you didn't verify facts."

Until after their engagement, she had truly believed Quince had spoken the truth. By then, it was too late to change course. Her assumptions had been wrong but defensible. "I wasn't sure Rob's information was accurate—especially since he didn't really talk to Quince."

"You had just met Quince. Why doubt Rob's word?"

"At first, I truly believed Quince had told the truth. And then, justifying his deception became easier than admitting he had lied. Quince had pulled out all the stops and won me over."

Deep in thought, Cory studied the Japanese maple tree by the neighbor's fence. His silence confirmed that he was taking in each word Tempia had spoken. Did he consider the stakes too high and wouldn't take a chance on a relationship? Had she pled her case hard enough?

"Cory ..." She cleared her throat several times.

Cory's head dipped in a slight nod.

The gesture compelled Tempia to continue speaking. "I ... apologize for entangling myself in Quince's scam against us. As inadequate as my explanation sounds, I appreciate you listening to my side. I understand your character better now." Tempia's hands rubbed across her pants.

Cory dangled a leg over his thigh. "In what way? Hope I didn't come across like a prosecutor."

Tempia hoped a bright smile would cheer up her teary face. "You kept a difficult conversation on track. Thanks for making our frank discussion easier to have than it might have been. You're kind. You are," she added when a question entered his gaze. "You stood aside regarding a woman you were interested in for a frenemy." *See there, I can discern good character when required.*

"It was your right to choose Quince over me." A self-mocking chuckle began in his throat. "Besides, when Quince saw you every day, it curtailed his nightly partying, and he attended church. You did a lot of good for him."

"Yeah, well, Quince eventually morphed into an evil caricature of his former self. The husband I thought I married never existed. The man is a grand manipulator. When he and I were dating, he and my brothers played video games when they came over to my place for the weekend. Can you believe my brothers were unwelcomed in Quince's house after we married?"

"Unfortunately, I can. The night you left Quince, both boys kept silent, worked fast, and watched their sister. They seemed anxious about your safety."

Pride filled her heart in an instant. "They are two staunch allies."

"Those same awesome family values snared me on the spot. I liked the way you treated your brothers and people you hadn't met."

"My family offers each other continuous support. I ignored some suggestions and wise counsel. Marriage presented a sharper picture, though."

"Had your parents warned you off Quince before the wedding?"

"We had been dating for three months before they met Quince at Gabby's wedding reception. My stepmother insisted I bring him by their house the next day. So, my parents spent time with Quince on Sunday, and Quince proposed on Monday, the following day." Sighing, Tempia clasped her hands beneath her chin. "I ignored my parents' considerable objections throughout the engagement. The truth was unveiled early in the marriage. Every one of Quince's character detractors were proven right."

"Your family is close-knit. Why did it take you three months to introduce Quince?"

"I doubted they would like him, and they didn't. Their apprehension intensified during the house visit."

Cory frowned. "Your parents didn't insist on meeting a man you were dating seriously?"

"Mom and Dad were preoccupied with something else." Falling silent, her head hung.

Not moving an inch, Cory remained silent.

"My whole life was off-kilter before meeting Quince. Earlier that year, my stepmother had suffered serious health issues. Due to my mother's premature death, Dad fully concentrated on my stepmother's healing. She made a complete recovery just before Gabby's wedding."

"That explains the lapse in scrutiny. During your stepmother's illness, your father probably wrestled with your mother's premature death." Pausing, he smiled. "Let's tie up a loose end. Until today's visit, I last saw Quince the night you left him."

Tempia had rejected the awesome man God had sent, and then she settled for crumbs. Unconvinced all had been forgiven, she wondered why Cory had come. "Thanks for caring enough to stop by and clear the air." Tempia blinked back unshed tears.

"As with all control addicts, Quince often projected false strength to make him feel like he'd won. Over time, chicanery loses its hold."

Tempia still couldn't comprehend why Cory had aided her while she was with Quince yet dropped her after she became a free woman. "That Saturday afternoon ... you had declined Quince's invitation to the party on my birthday. So why did you end up coming?"

"I changed plans after Rob said that he and Gabby hadn't been invited. I wanted to ensure you would be okay."

So here we are. And all because I rejected the advice of people who love me.

After Tempia filed divorce papers, Rob had said, "Cory doesn't backtrack in relationships." This evening, she accepted that her dreams had been unsustainable at the onset. Tempia set the glider into motion. "Do you still patch up the HVAC system at Community Ministries?"

Cory chuckled. "They got a new unit, so they don't need me now." Cory's eyes lit up. "I have an empty tomorrow." He switched seats to the one beside Tempia. "Would you like to share a meal?"

Tempia's stomach flipped-flopped twice. The pulse point behind each ear twitched.

But a dinner invitation does not necessarily imply romance. Might as well ask for clarification. "Are you suggesting we become romantically involved?"

The smoldering look in Cory's eyes made her stomach quiver. The man honestly liked her.

"Let's see how one date goes. Then we'll see if a relationship can survive the long haul. Here's to baby steps." He touched her hand.

Tempia rested her other hand upon his. "Meaning ... you will let me beyond your guardrails?"

Cory grasped her hand and squeezed her fingers. "That is the plan, Tempia. May I pick you up tomorrow at five o'clock? Do you have any food preferences for a Saturday dinner?"

"Anything with you is fine with me. I've missed you, Cory. Please surprise me. I will be ready on the dot." Tempia brushed away the single tear rolling down her cheek. "I love the way you handle difficult situations. You walk a straight line on each occasion. I pray our relationship will last forever."

"I pray we cross the finish line holding hands." Cory rose to his feet. "I've kept you from your movie long enough. May I ... tell your family goodnight before leaving?"

Tempia slid off the glider and grabbed his outstretched hand.

The couple entered the house together and continued down the hallway as they listened to Curt's animated voice. Thank God her brother was discussing his bowling league and not their guest. Still holding hands, they reached the doorway.

His lips curving into a broad grin, Cory glanced at each person. "Hello, Miss Blanche, Mr. Sam, Curt, Noah. My unannounced visit interrupted your movie night. Please accept my apology." His forward motion propelled him and Tempia into the room. He focused on her father.

Sam never broke eye contact. "Hello, young man. We haven't seen you in quite awhile."

Blanche elbowed her husband. "Hi, Cory. Tempia's friends are always welcome inside our home. We can restart the movie if you enjoy sad stories."

"The main character is terminally ill," Noah said.

"Tempie chose a good tearjerker on this go-round," Curt added.

Cory winked at her then refocused on her family. "I'll let you all enjoy the movie without me this time. But I may see you all this weekend. Tempia and I have a dinner date tomorrow evening. Goodnight, all."

As the couple exited the living room, pride for her family purged the last doubt from Tempia's heart. Her family had handled their shock well.

When she opened the front door, Cory stepped onto the porch. "Your parents' hospitality ended the evening on a high note. It's great that your family shares a strong bond."

"My parents are great about giving me what I need in various situations."

Cory's hand moved in a brief wave as he headed to his SUV. "I'll see you soon."

Tempia locked the storm door, her fingers moving up and down the glass. "Tomorrow is a heartbeat away. See you soon. Drive safe."

"Safety is a priority." Cory trekked down the steps, waving again before entering the SUV.

Tempia observed his progress until the car left the curb, then she sat on the steps leading upstairs.

She and Cory were going on a bona fide date just because he liked her. Her happy place loomed ahead. Enthralled beyond reason, she rethought the unexpected dinner invitation. What had prompted his unpredictable request after fourteen silent months? Cory had criticized Tempia's judgments and behavior. His demeanor hadn't indicated an offer was in the making. He had popped the dinner invitation just as her hope indicator had bottomed out.

Chapter Eight

Tempia's stepmother spotted her entrance into the living room before the other family members did. "Tempie's here. Wind down the conversation, boys." Blanche restarted the movie.

A second later, Sam's anger-filled eyes speared his daughter. "When will you secure your well-being? Don't interrupt me," he barked as Tempia's lips parted. "Going on a date implies you're at that man's beck and call."

The blatant derision and personal attack seared her soul. Tempia stuttered a few incoherent words then fell silent. Her father had been a staunch supporter, even when she married Quince against his sound advice. How could dating a decent man merit instant wrath? Her shocked gaze fixated on her stepmother.

In one fluid motion, Blanche snatched the remote control off the cocktail table. The movie paused. "We can't hold the young man accountable for our daughter's error. It's commendable that Cory accommodated an old school mate who wasn't a true friend."

"Still—"

"Still, nothing. Give Cory and Tempie the benefit of your doubts. Cory saw more of Quince during her marriage than he had in ten years. Why? He was protecting our daughter the best he could. I can't blow him off."

"He could've contacted Tempie despite believing she had chosen Quince over him ... but I concede your point," Sam agreed. "Those sad consequences weren't his fault. But Tempie can't live a life fueled by low self-esteem. I refuse to let another man bankrupt my daughter's soul." Steely eyes fastened onto Tempia. "Self-respect must ignite somewhere in your attitude toward this man."

How could Tempia convince her father that dating Cory was more than a reflex? "I understand your concern, Dad. But Cory coming here tonight is an answer to my prayers."

"Maybe. Maybe not. Today you saw him for the first time in over a year. What is the mad rush for getting involved on a personal level? Consider consequences before accepting future dates."

"Sam!" Blanche spoke in the sternest tone Tempia had ever heard her stepmother use. "Our daughter lives a dignified lifestyle. When Tempie moved away from home, she stopped dating nonserious men."

"How did that poor excuse for a husband slip in?"

"My illness caused us to lose focus on our daughter's welfare."

"Which is why we're paying better attention starting now. Even twenty-three-year-old women can commit dating errors."

Blanche stroked her husband's knee. "Tempia's ex-husband misstep shouldn't erase her prior and subsequent good judgments." Hitting the play button, Blanche ended Sam's rebuttal.

* * *

The next morning, Tempia's stepmother smiled as she and her husband entered the kitchen. "Tomorrow we're treating your grandparents to lunch. Feel free to join us," Blanche said.

Kneading biscuit dough, Tempia peeked at her quiet father. "I'll pass. I plan to head home and vegetate."

"Today your brothers are having a video-game marathon. Your father and I will relax upstairs."

Tempia laughed. "Great minds still think alike."

"Oh, do they? Let's see if they still think alike at the end of our discussion," Sam said.

Her mind alert, Tempia cooked their meal and listened to her father's newest tirade. The countless accusations wreaked havoc on her otherwise happy day. Sam recounted each dating talking point he had ever dished out. Once his sons entered the kitchen, he immediately dropped the topic.

Where had her father hidden his grievous condemnation? His attitude brought an ominous sea change into their relationship. Sam wouldn't redirect his outright obstinance against Tempia's decision. How could she convince her father that she was on the appropriate track?

Blanche took advantage of the respite. She sidled beside Tempia at the stovetop, whispering into her stepdaughter's ear. "Keep the communication lines open with Sam and me, but assess each situation using your own best judgment. We have faith in you, Tempie. Pray long and hard, and listen."

After hugging her stepmother, Tempia sat beside Curt and snuck a peek at her father. He and the boys were busy discussing Noah's next speech meeting.

Feeling buried beneath endless turmoil, Tempia ate a tasteless meal and crept upstairs while her family finished eating breakfast. There was nothing left to do but bide her time. She lay across the bed counting down the minutes until it was time to leave the house for lunch and face Gabby.

* * *

Fully dressed, Tempia closed the bedroom door behind her. Curt exited the living room on her descent down the stairs. He made small talk and escorted her down the hallway. Outside on the porch, he fell into step beside her. The siblings walked together in companionable silence. Once Tempia reached her car, Curt opened the door and let her slip inside the vehicle. He beamed her an endearing grin.

Caught off guard by his sincere behavior, Tempia returned the smile. "Thanks for keeping me company. I've been a little off-kilter this morning."

Curt closed the car door and motioned for her to lower the window. He leaned on the automobile. "Tempie, on the day you left Quince, Cory's sad eyes watched every step you took. Last night, he looked at you with happy eyes." Leaning inside the window, Curt hugged her. "I think he really likes you."

Her brother's observations touched Tempia's burdened heart. His astute insight helped balance their father's negative estimations.

"Thanks, Curt. I value your opinions. Pray for me," she called behind the boy who was retracing their steps.

Pulling away from the curb, Tempia prayed Cory had achieved a peaceful night, along with an uplifting day.

What's he doing? Wonder if he's thinking love thoughts about me.

* * *

Cory sprawled on the back-deck lounge chair sipping sparkling water. Every so often, he checked his watch. Last night's enthusiasm mired him down today in second thoughts. He reassessed his premature request for a dinner date and pinpointed the chink in his thinking.

He'd overreached. A belated frank discussion had spiraled into a spontaneous date request. Cory should have waited and contacted Tempia next week, if at all.

Too late, he realized Tempia was a weakness he hadn't overcome. That weakness showed itself differently now from when she was married. On Friday morning, Cory had accepted a Tempia-free existence. By evening, he had proposed a Saturday-evening meal. Had his brain taken a vacation while his lips talked?

He found himself wishing he hadn't dropped by the baseball game, which is when his actions seemed to spiral out of control. Either that, or he should have faced Gabby and Rob at the same time. Gabby's input would have championed her friend's cause, but Gabby understood the lady better than anyone else he knew. Their honest dialogue might have revealed invaluable insight. Armed with information from two vital discussions, he could have spent time considering what he'd learned. Then he could have contacted Tempia if personal interaction seemed warranted. But, the opposite had occurred. Quince's odious behavior and Rob's self-justification deterred Cory's rational thought process. Two separate discussions had culminated into a hasty evaluation and snappy judgments.

All in all, Tempia's well-being had reigned above his own welfare. He should've chosen better.

Cory set the drink on the mosaic accent table. He realized correct timing topped his main concerns in pursuing Tempia.

"Hello, neighbor," a voice called from the next yard. "Tell Miss Lillie and Mr. Tim that I baked an old-fashioned caramel cake."

At the property fence, Cory greeted his sister's childhood friend. Four years older than Cory, Evelyn had lived in an adjacent state for twelve years and returned last year after her divorce. She had moved into the vacant duplex her parents owned. The senior Watkinses occupied the other side.

While Cory and Evelyn chatted, her youngest son and daughter splashed water in an above-ground swimming pool.

Evelyn glanced at her older children when the patio door opened and closed. "How's the dating life going? Meet any interesting prospects?"

"My schedule can't accommodate a dating lifestyle."

"Why not?"

"I work in a demanding, turbulent field. Plus, my evenings and weekends are overtaken by four rambunctious kids. No pushing," she told her daughter, who had elbowed her older brother in her rush toward the pool. Moments later, the gangly lad jumped feet first into shallow water. "Troy, behave yourself," Evelyn advised the boy who missed hearing her sound advice. Tired eyes studied Cory. "See there? There isn't any strength left for dating."

"Unlike a lot of single mothers, you have capable and willing babysitters at your disposal. Take advantage of my and your parents' free offer. You can always hire a babysitter if we're unavailable when one is needed."

"Wish logistics were that simple," Evelyn said. "Although I dream of dating, most eligible men back off when they learn I have four children. Of course, my ex-husband got remarried five months after our divorce."

"He left you for another woman, but you got the better deal: full custody of four irreplaceable kids."

"At least the ruling let us relocate to friendlier territory. Will didn't object to my requesting full custody of our children. Marrying the wrong man was my fault. Too bad truth doesn't make the repercussions more bearable. Each day, forgiving oneself is an uphill climb."

His neighbor's predicament was real-life drama that couldn't be swept aside. Having a ready-made family was a tall order but not an unsolvable problem. The right man would come well-equipped. Cory listened as Evelyn simultaneously watched her children and poured out her melancholy heart.

Empathy heightened as Tempia's face superimposed itself upon Evelyn's features. It appeared that his quagmire followed Cory wherever he went.

"Mama, make him stop hitting me! Leave me alone!"

The squeaky command broke Cory's contemplations.

Her hands on her hips, Evelyn spun around. "The next person who gets reprimanded will make everyone go back inside the house and read a book."

Cory's nieces and nephew seldom misbehaved, yet Evelyn's children required constant discipline. Maybe he should rethink his wish of having six children. "You have your hands full. We'll talk more later."

As the small-statured woman loped across the yard, Cory headed toward the deck, evaluating their conversation.

* * *

Once Tempia arrived at Capris, she chose her and Gabby's favorite table near the live entertainment. Years ago, the restaurant had hired a pianist to play old show tunes, jingles, and sitcom themes on Saturday afternoons. Her favorite piece was from a 1977 candy commercial.

She glanced at the entrance when the main door opened. Four teenage girls moseyed into the lobby as they yakked in loud voices. The hostess met the group and led them across the diner. Tempia laughed. That same phenomenon had occurred when she and her girlfriends frequented restaurants in their teen years.

While she clocked their progress, Gabby ambled across the room, pointing at the centerpiece clock that hung above the bar. A smirk spread across her lips. "Broken speed limits put me here on your dot. No free desserts for you. So there."

Tempia's soft voice gurgled forth in giggles. Her friend disliked losing Tempia's impromptu bets.

Gabby leaned on the back cushion. "Okay, girl. Take me on the journey. Plot the entire Cory saga."

Gabby behaved as if she hadn't committed a huge offense. Withholding information had been a major violation. Tempia had expected a passionate on-the-spot apology. Her shoulders slumped. "Most people greet their friends and then pry into their personal business."

"Thank God I am an above-average person." When Gabby's head shifted positions, sunlight reflected off her eyeglasses. "Quit stalling. Tell me every detail."

Tempia set her glass on the table. "This is a full-circle moment, Gab. I have multiple questions for you."

Gabby's eyes widened. "Is there a problem involving me?" She paused as their favorite server approached the table.

"The usual?" the grinning man inquired.

Laughing, the women made small talk with him then watched him slip away. Gabby leaned her back on the chair while Tempia watched. What was the most amicable way to begin an inquisition? Her bestie must explain the communication breach.

"Talk to me," Gabby said. "Don't search for soft words. If you do hurt my feelings, I bounce back."

No-nonsense Gabby struck again. The woman seldom skirted important issues, and neither would Tempia. "Did you realize your husband wanted Cory and me to meet?"

Gabby sat upright. "Sure did. *But* I didn't volunteer the information to you in case his cousin wouldn't cooperate. Did Cory tell you he declined the offer for three years straight?" She sipped water when Tempia nodded and then continued. "It boggles the mind that the man attended Rob's party. Especially since he and Quince were together and a mystery lady had captured his fancy."

"That would be me. Cory's mystery lady in the flesh." Tempia observed her friend's reaction.

"What? You?" Gabby shuffled in her seat.

Her wide eyes and gaping mouth released Tempia's knotted shoulders. Thankfully, her friend was surprised by the news.

Gabby brushed her lips with her fingers. "Talk about keeping secrets. Cory withheld that nugget during his discussion with Rob last night."

"Either your husband had facts beforehand or Cory returned the favor to your secret-keeping husband."

"Show kindness. Rob and I will have major problems if Cory told him before today that you were his mystery lady because Rob didn't tell me." She picked up her water glass. "I am astonished. Cory operates within certain norms. His being there surprised me due to the mystery lady factor. I bet Cory was shocked when you walked inside the house."

"He was pleasantly surprised. Why would your husband extend the invitation if he thought his cousin liked someone else?"

"My exact question after the party ended. Rob said he was tired of Cory mooning over a woman he hadn't made inroads in meeting."

"Then Rob invited me as a diversion." Tempia laughed. "I can imagine your response."

"Rob should have stayed out of Cory's love life. At the very least, he could have clued me in on his plan. I'm stumped. Why did Cory finally agree to meet you? He hadn't in the past."

"Maybe meeting me was more palatable than spending extra time with Quince. Their pool game had ended, but Quince didn't take the hint and followed behind Cory."

"That's another mindblower. Rob said he and Quince were sworn enemies."

"Really?" If they were sworn enemies, no wonder Quince had left the house before Rob kicked him out. As the picture became clearer, Tempia retold an abbreviated version of her and Cory's discussion. The shadow that fell across the tablecloth halted the narration. She paused mid-sentence, letting the server place their food on the table and saunter off.

Gabby poured dressing on her salad. "Carry on. I'm lining up your version and Rob's account. Sequence wise," she added when Tempia frowned.

"Smart move. Are the stories adding up?"

Gabby nodded. "So far, so good. Tell me more."

Tempia summarized her and Cory's conversation.

Gabby asked pertinent questions along the way.

Some time later, she lost steam and sipped iced cranberry tea. Deep in thought, she set aside the glass. "Here's the real kicker, Gab. This Saturday is booked up. I'm eating dinner with Cory tonight."

Gabby choked on her drink. She coughed in succession and covered her mouth with a napkin.

"Are you okay? Should I pat your back?" Tempia scooted back her chair, watching her friend struggle for air.

Gabby shook her head, drank water, and signaled for Tempia to finish her account.

"You would've been proud of me had you been there. I said a simple 'yes' instead of jumping up and down and doing cartwheels across the porch." She sipped her drink. A quiet Gabby did not bode well. "Share your thoughts, please."

"I'm ... the idea is growing on me." Gabby fiddled with her wedding band until she smiled. "I agree. You're right. The dinner date represents a full-circle moment. Set up a few double dates so Rob and I can join in on the resurrection. Seeing you both together might ease Rob's angst somewhat."

"Double dates, huh? So, you want to show Rob that Cory has accepted the real me."

"Something like that. Rob and I discussed the situation regarding the party throughout the night."

"And?"

"Rob staged the party without my knowledge. I would've alerted you had I known Cory was coming."

"I believe you. But advance warning wouldn't have changed the outcome."

"Maybe. Rob doesn't love his cousin any more than I love you. I liked the idea of you and Cory meeting, but I kept his plan secret from you for your protection. Cory had roadblocked each introduction approach Rob made until then."

"So ... you ... truly found out I was Cory's mystery lady today like I did yesterday?"

"Yes. And it's a pity I didn't put the ministry connection together. I never figured you were 'the woman.' I hope Rob doesn't know you were the lady Cory pined over. Because if he did and didn't tell me ... ugh! I will cross that bridge if I reach it."

Tempia wringed her fingers underneath the table. "Either way, let it go. When you arrive home, love on your husband."

"Fat chance that will happen. It's a big deal if he found out the truth before yesterday but kept it a secret. Then there's the fact that he might have discovered the truth at the park but didn't inform me. Both aspects are frustrating."

"Gabby—"

"My point is, had you known about the Community Ministries connection, you would have contacted Cory and upended Quince's profuse lies."

Tempia nodded. Perhaps ... just maybe ... Cory might have believed her explanation and given Tempia a second chance.

"No one can redirect the narrative at this point. However, Rob should have told me if he knew."

"Whoa, girl. Quit theorizing. Tell your husband how you feel."

"Rob and I should have told Cory that Quince fed you lies after I had already given you the facts. And that you believed Quince's account instead of believing me and let him decide how to go from there. Rob and I made a mess of the situation."

"I do feel uneasy that your husband treated me the same way he always had, yet he had this hidden dislike of me because of Quince. Does he hate me?"

"Heck no. Rob likes you. He's guilt-ridden. Blaming himself that his cousin got swept into Quince's grand scheme."

Unshed tears filled Tempia's eyes. "Me too. Cory deserved better."

"You both did. Listen. Cory's an adult. Rob must get over himself." Gabby scooted back her chair, snatching her purse off the table. "If we don't go shopping soon, I might reconsider purchasing the cordless drill he requested."

* * *

That afternoon, Cory surprised his mother and father by buying them lunch at a neighborhood deli. In the semi-crowded restaurant, they splurged on soups, subs, and homestyle desserts.

"What time are you picking up Tempia?" Lillie asked.

Cory brushed cake crumbs off his mouth. "Five o'clock. Our reservation is set for six."

Lillie swallowed the sticky toffee pudding. "Lying low during Tempia's separation and divorce was the right call. Why have you avoided communication with her and not Quince?"

"Whatever affects Tempia can influence my decisions. Quince's circumstances won't move me one inch. Unless the situation involves his ex-wife."

"For your emotional health, leave the woman alone altogether." Tim's orange drop cookie arced in the air as he joined the discussion. "You've done it once. Do it again. This time, make a permanent break."

Cory faltered here and there, but godly principles modeled his life

78

choices. Lillie and Tim's diametrically opposed viewpoints confounded his decision-making process. Lillie believed dropping Tempia was wrong. Tim thought restoring communication was amiss. Cory's principal advisers' positions could not be any further apart.

His mother's spoon hovered beside her lips. "Tim, let me clarify one point. Tempia earned our son's respect throughout her five-month marriage."

Grunting, Tim set his cookie on a saucer. "Did you reach that conclusion on your own, or did you consult our son?"

"Actions speak louder than words ever could. No matter what occupied Cory, he dropped everything whenever Tempia needed help." Lillie reached across the table, placing her palm upon her husband's clenched fist. She beamed as Tim clasped their hands together. "Cory is still keen on this woman. Like and respect might develop into an awesome love match. We know Rob's wife agrees."

"Best friends usually do. My nephew isn't impressed by his wife's friend."

Lillie squeezed his fingers. "I want Cory to be happy and enjoy his life. Because he shielded Tempia, she may have developed tender feelings regarding him. Let them test the waters and find out."

"Happiness isn't found in other people. Cory wisely dropped Quince's ex. Rushed judgments wreck too many lives."

"Tim—"

"No, no, Lil. What's the hurry? Safeguarding his own life should be Cory's top priority."

Their lengthy discussion summed up Cory's conundrum. His wisest confidants each provided credible rationalizations for their polarized opinions.

On the short drive home, Cory revived a conversation about his parents' greatest joy. Lillie and Tim doted on their grandchildren.

Chapter Nine

Tempia and Gabby spent an hour shopping, then stopped by a hardware store. Their shopping completed, the women stood beside their cars near the plants for sale.

Gabby's grievance against her husband had smoldered throughout the day. While the women shopped, Tempia tried calming the couple's troubled waters. Now, she gave the problem another shot. "Gab, I'm glad you bought the gift Rob requested. I would have felt terrible had you settled on the powder-blue bathrobe." She giggled when her friend's lips pursed into a thin line. "I do agree the sale was awesome, though."

"Almost free is always a good deal. Even though my disappointed husband would've claimed it was a spite purchase."

"And we both know you would verbally attack Rob if he did."

Sighing loudly, Gabby shrugged. "The man is a loyal friend, but so am I. Safeguarding his cousin handicapped my protecting you."

Her hip on the car door, Tempia scratched her head. "I've thought about that possibility all afternoon. There's no guarantee more knowledge would have achieved different results."

"Well, your second date occurred because Rob and I didn't out the liar, so I think things would have turned out differently."

So much for my stint as peacemaker. I riled Gabby up again just as she was headed home. Poor Rob.

"That is a true statement. But—"

"No buts or excuses will change my mind," Gabby interrupted. "His poor behavior hasn't earned a pardon."

"Gabby Stephens. You don't know how much Rob knows. Go home and ask him."

"He knew Quince lied. Do us both a favor. Listen for a change." Gabby's right shoe tapped the ground. "Sorry I didn't press Cory about dating his mystery lady. He didn't disclose meeting her had fizzled until I asked."

Her fingers tapping on her nose, Tempia considered her next words. "Last night, I saw Cory in a different light."

If Cory had recognized her embarrassment and Quince's lies, perhaps he might have excused the forty-minute conversation and Sunday date. But what-ifs and daydreams never solved real-life problems. Despite her marrying a loser, the man she loved was escorting her on a dinner date. She needed to focus on positive results for once. She checked her watch, then placed a hand on Gabby's shoulder. "Running late. Gotta go. I only have two hours to do my three-hour beauty regimen. Go easy on Rob. Promise?"

"We'll see," Gabby said in a subdued voice. She opened the car door, grinning. "Can't wait for the date report. Call me tonight."

The women gave each other strong hugs, entered their vehicles, and drove away.

Tempia eyed the dashboard clock, then maneuvered her car through the crowded parking lot, joining other vehicles that sped by. When a police patrol car pulled up beside her, she drove the speed limit down the road and hummed her favorite tune. She rounded the corner, parked behind her father's truck, grabbed her bags off the back seat, and rushed inside the house.

"I'm here," she yelled into the silent air.

"So are we," Curt replied. "Watch us play City Builders. You can take the next turn."

Tempia poked her head inside the living room. Her brothers were playing a video game.

She glowered at their backs. "Does anyone care enough to welcome me back?"

"I did," Curt replied, steadily playing the game. "I said you can have the next turn."

She slouched against the wall, rustling the shopping bags.

Noah eyed the large sack and protruding smaller bags. "Tempie, did you blow our weekend-retreat money on new clothes?"

She laughed out loud. "Sure did. I spent all my pin money on me."

"Ah man! Stop buying clothes. You have a jammed closet upstairs and another one at your apartment."

"Which is none of your business. Save your allowance." Her laughter flowed as she headed into the kitchen.

Blanche met her stepdaughter by the door. "You came home late for a person going on a big date in less than two hours. What are you wearing?"

Tempia spread three pairs of pants and loose-fitting tops on the table. "I chose clothes like the style I wore yesterday. I was wearing something similar on the day Cory saw me at Community Ministries."

Blanche picked up a maroon-and-white shirt and matched it against gray ankle leggings. "Excellent. This combination works well."

Tempia nodded. "Smoke-gray ankle boots and a multicolored blazer will set it off."

Her stepmother slid the clothes back inside the shopping bag. "Sam and I were discussing Cory seeing you at Community Ministries. These pesky preliminaries would be completed if Quince hadn't interfered."

"Which could be good or bad. The jury is still out on that verdict," Sam said.

Blanche laughed. "Meaning himself. Your father is the judge and jury where our children are concerned."

Tempia spun around inside the doorway. "Relax, Dad. Cory is a sincere person if nothing else." Leaving the kitchen, she skipped upstairs. Inside her bedroom, she spread the clothes on her full-size bed, studying the individual pieces. Why had Cory liked the outfits she'd worn both at Community Ministries and yesterday? Was it the color schemes? The individual pieces? Or a combination of both?

She reminded herself that stressing over another person's opinions is a primary reason people should dress to please themselves.

Tempia flung open the closet door, removed a gray midi wrap dress, and headed into the bathroom.

Thirty minutes later, she sashayed in front of the mirror, hoping she'd achieved the style Cory had complimented yesterday.

Her finger weaved through soft, springy curls. She wondered if Gabby and Rob were behaving themselves. They had dated for two years and were engaged for one. It was strange she hadn't met Rob's friends until the game-night party. Even now, Tempia had only met a few relatives and buddies. Were any of those friends and kin shared by Cory? Thus far, she hadn't seen anyone who had attended the get-together since Rob and Gabby's wedding reception.

The doorbell rang while Tempia prayed for Gabby's marriage. Her thoughts about the trouble raging inside the Stephens household must wait until tonight. Tempia took a final glance in the bathroom mirror, breathed into cupped hands, and exited the bedroom mouthing short prayers.

Cory held open the storm door as Tempia exited the house. His appreciative glance focused on her face. "Lovely as ever. Thanks for accepting my dinner invitation."

Her confidence level ticked up additional notches. Her disinterested ex-husband had shredded her self-esteem, sparking an emotional collapse. Cory thinking her lovely warmed every void point in her soul. She locked the front door and faced the attentive man grinning at her.

"Ready?" He crooked his arm.

Tempia placed her hand above Cory's elbow and fell into step beside him. Could he feel her body shake? Seconds later, she stumbled on damp leaves scattered on the sidewalk. Her feet moved in opposite directions. Her arms flailing, Tempia jockeyed upright. Her entire body quivered. "Whoa! Almost fell flat on my face!"

"You're still standing. The SUV is just ahead."

Tempia matched her steps to Cory's sure gait. Heat infused her mortified body.

"I'm not usually this clumsy. You must think I'm one big klutz."

"Or just head over heels for me," he said, laughing.

A quick glance revealed a teasing gleam in Cory's gaze. "We've known each other two years. Going on a date shouldn't generate stress," Tempia said.

Cory made eye contact before glancing ahead. "Despite that, it will take some hard work to catch up with each other after all this time. Though I still feel well connected to you."

Tempia tucked those encouraging words deep within her soul. "We are. Despite my derailing our promising beginning. Thank God for second chances."

Cory stopped beside the SUV, opened the passenger door, and stepped aside. "Let's agree that you simply took us on a slight detour from whatever our purpose is."

"Most people won't forget I missed the target by a mile."

"Who cares? You won't make the same mistake twice."

Her eyes shielded against the setting sun, she settled into her seat. Tempia's composure soared. Cory's statement indicated he believed she possessed a strong character and would make good decisions. His faith in her emotional stability strengthened her resolve to justify his good opinion. She waited to continue the conversation until he slid inside the car. "Will you tell me where we're headed, or is it a surprise destination?"

"Primers Steakhouse and Seafood. I've always fancied a five-star restaurant experience. Have you dined there?"

Primers was a reservation-only restaurant. The five-star eatery anchored in Chicago one century ago. Its second location opened in downtown St. Louis last year. Primers had garnered rave reviews since the day it opened.

Tempia shook her head. "Never thought I would dine there."

"I live by the motto, never say never. Blessings come every day."

"Well, I am super impressed. Primers doesn't have any reservations for months. How did you reserve a short-notice table for a Saturday evening?"

He started the engine. "Our company installed the HVAC system. Last night, I accepted the open invitation extended to my parents."

"Ah. Being the boss's son has its perks, huh?"

"No complaints here. My sister and her husband booked a table for next week."

Finally, she thought, he's sharing some private family information. Tempia restrained herself from asking questions and rubbing her hands together. She must vet the Sanders clan without appearing nosy. Cory had always evaded personal queries. Could she open him up then keep him from shutting down? How should she begin? Then she realized Cory had provided the perfect lead-in.

"Gabby told me you had an older sister. Does she work in the family business?"

"Cathy is four years older than me, and she's a stay-at-home mom with four children under nine. My three nieces are ages eight, six, and four. My only nephew is fourteen months old."

Tempia stored the data in her Cory Sanders file. What question should she ask next? The children. His eyes had gleamed while revealing their ages. "Cathy spaced out her children well. My brothers are only thirteen months apart. How often do you see the little ones?"

"At least once a week. My parents host our Sunday family dinner. The tradition started years ago."

Hmm … "Do you like children? Are four kids three too many?"

"Nah, I want six." He laughed when she inhaled a deep breath. "But I would settle for five."

His happy banter about children inspired hope. Could she keep the positive vibes alive? "Five children are a bit much for me. My everyday performance excels when I function under overload capacity."

Cory chuckled. "An excellent comeback. I'm adding word wizard to your list of accomplishments."

The verbal communication buoyed her inquisitive spirit. "Cory, I know you're thoughtful, but I know little else about you. Gabby said you live in the city with your parents. North, south, or midtown?"

"In the hub of everything worth doing. Central West End. I love my urban neighborhood—even the traffic." Cory winked.

Tempia winked back even though he didn't see it. "Smack in the middle of all the city has to offer. I frequently truck down Highway 70 and watch the Cardinals ball games. The team is fantastic."

"Complete with extended losing streaks. Hope you make the trip downtown on their winning nights."

Cory was trashing her favorite ball team. Had she heard him correctly? "The Cardinals have won eleven World Series championships, nineteen National League pennants, and eleven Central Division titles."

"What an amazing memory! Their management should compensate you for the free advertisement. Have they done anything beyond 2000?"

"I just restrained myself from sticking out my tongue. Did you catch the eye roll?"

Cory chuckled. "I'm glad you attend events in the city. Except for business reasons, I rarely visit any suburb."

Tempia dismissed his limitations. Crossing her fingers, she glanced at him. "Would you ever consider suburb-living in the future?"

"People should live where their hearts dictate. The suburbs aren't really for me, but I won't say I'd never live there."

Tempia giggled. "Almost all of my friends live in the suburbs. Gabby is the lone exception."

"Besides visiting Gabby and the Cardinals, is there anything else you like about the city? Or urban life in general?"

"I love the Central West End area. Years ago, on Sundays, my father would drive us through some of the urban neighborhoods. In the back seat, my mother sketched renaissance revival houses. Mother was a talented watercolor painter."

Cory glanced in the rearview mirror, then changed lanes. "Did your father keep her paintings?"

"My mother had a huge clientele and sold everything except her and Dad's favorites. There are four large and several medium-size paintings stored in his basement. The ones I brought from Quince's house hang in my bedroom at my parents' house. Her smaller canvases spruce up my apartment. Her artwork will decorate my house someday."

"The paintings displayed at Quince's house were beautiful. I would have complimented her work had I identified the artist."

Cory would appreciate the paintings Quince had scorned. Curiosity grabbed her. Rob had bought a house and so had Quince. Why hadn't Cory spread his wings?

"Have you always lived with your parents, or did you move out and back in?"

When a speeding driver cut him off, Cory waved. "Some people should lose their driver's license. As for living at home, out and back in. I renovated the house Cathy and I will inherit. Her family lives close by."

"You are one hundred percent vested into an urban lifestyle."

"It is my top preference. Is living in the burbs high on your wish list?"

Not anymore. City dwelling is looking better. "Not at all. I can be happy living just about anywhere with the right person. Plus, Busch Stadium and the best baseball team in the country are in the city."

"Perhaps the best baseball team in the country will notch up a few wins this current season."

Tempia resisted the urge to thump his thigh. "Every team experiences a slump here and there. The Cardinals will be just fine." She brought him up to speed on the Wade clan, including losing her mother two days after her seventh birthday. "Your turn. Introduce your family one by one. Include minor details, please."

"I can sum up the Sanderses in one word: bland." His straight features didn't crack a grin.

"Hmm ... a lack of distinction? Or projecting a smooth and soothing image?"

"Does your brain have a built-in dictionary and thesaurus?"

"No. It does not. But I do pay attention to what people say to me."

"Then I had better choose my words wisely," Cory said, pausing. "I've never critiqued the Sanders family. My parents are nondescript people who greet sunrises each morning. In late spring and summer months, they miss streetlights coming on. Cathy and her husband, Eric, aren't much more interesting. Their children do provide entertainment, though."

Throughout the next ten minutes, Cory provided humorous accounts of the Sanderses' lifestyles.

Tempia massaged her left side. "I've been laughing so hard my side hurts."

"Then I won't describe what happened the day an alligator chased my father through the swamp."

Tempia's hand dropped off her side onto her lap. "An alligator? Which swamp? When? *How?*"

"In the Everglades, Dad hooked a gator instead of a fish. We thought he was a goner until he slid down an embankment into quicksand."

Her eyes opened wider. "An alligator? Quicksand? But your father is alive ... isn't he?"

Cory nodded. "The gator backtracked. Guess he didn't think my father was worth the extra exertion."

Tempia shook her head clear of over-thinking cobwebs. The account sounded like a tall tale. She studied the driver looking straight ahead. "Is this a true story, Cory?"

Flecks of light twinkled in Cory's eyes when he glanced at her. "Those events really happened."

"Huh ... well ... how did your father escape certain death?"

"No-drama Dad pulled himself out of quicksand using a tree branch. Which is a slight exaggeration of what occurred," he admitted when she gasped. "But it's an amusing version nonetheless."

The account presented a unique twist on what Tempia had believed to be a serious-minded man. What other character traits had the man suppressed? Did Tempia prefer his softer side? The troubleshooter had made her feel safe and protected. Would the man who readily laughed at life fare better? Unmistakably, he was a kindhearted problem solver and an unabashed teaser. Which unidentified trait balanced both sides?

Chapter Ten

Two miles down the road, Cory exited the highway onto Tucker Boulevard and proceeded east toward Laclede's Landing in the heart of downtown St. Louis. The nine-block area was once the manufacturing, warehousing, and shipping hub of St. Louis. Today, the landing housed historic buildings, restaurants, clubs, and attractions.

At the district's entrance, cobblestone streets led the way to a vintage brick-and-cast-iron building. A warehouse had been renovated into a luxury restaurant. The eatery's original charm had been maintained throughout restorations, as evidenced by its 1800s design. Once inside, the host's courteous greeting delivered an unparalleled welcome.

The trimmed beard host picked up two menus off the podium. "Good evening. My name is Pete. Welcome to our little oasis."

The couple shook the host's extended hand. "This is our first visit," Cory said.

"May this evening be the first of many more," Pete replied. He led the couple across polished-concrete floors into a cavernous space that included numerous tables and a circular bar. Located behind twenty equally spaced floor-to-ceiling glass room dividers, several banquettes occupied the building's east wall. Servers passed in and out the kitchen area located behind a frosted-glass panel on the building's west side.

Pete pushed Tempia and the chair she occupied underneath the table's edge.

Tempia beamed a wide smile. "Ah, thanks."

The cheery man gave a slight bow. Seconds later, a twenty-something woman with dreadlocks stopped beside him. Pete placed the menus in her hand. "I'll leave you both in Camille's excellent care. Please let us know if there's anything you need."

"Thank you," Cory told the host's retreating back.

"Hello, Camille." Tempia gave her a bright smile.

The smiling Camille passed both guests menus. "This evening's special is prime rib with cremini mushrooms. Take your time perusing the options."

Tempia looked over the one-page menu. "Mmm. Each dish sounds terrific."

"Hard choice," Cory agreed.

After a few moments, they gave their orders to Camille.

"Primers has an awesome layout," Tempia noted once Camille left the table. "Think I found my happy spot. I appreciate you bringing me here." She surveyed the layout and gushed over floating tea candles situated on each table.

A quartz waterwall extended along the rear wall. The distinct sound of rippling water added to the peaceful ambiance.

Tempia touched Cory's arm. "Primers's waterfall is breathtaking. And so unusual for an indoor space."

Cory then went on to describe various natural waterfalls he'd visited, making Tempia want to visit each one.

The robust conversation wound down when their server approached the table.

"You chose my favorite dish," the grinning woman told Tempia. "Hope you enjoy it as much as I do."

Tempia unfolded her napkin onto her lap. "I'm sure I will. It wasn't an easy decision, though. Everything sounded so delicious."

Camille set their feast upon the table, and Tempia savored her filet mignon and roasted beetroot while Cory devoured his herb-marinated ahi tuna and charred tomatoes.

Tempia's warehouse facilitator job at Midwest Freight Solutions consumed the couple's conversation while they ate.

"One co-worker entered incorrect shipping information on a stat order. He shipped a 60-gallon air compressor and accessories and other construction tools and equipment to Montpelier, France, instead of Montpelier, Vermont. The transaction cost our company a substantial amount."

Cory chuckled. "That's quite a blunder. Somewhere in the process he should have noticed, if nothing else, the considerable freight cost and logistics."

"The finance manager made the same argument. Especially since Jess's counterpart told the manager that he had advised Jess to recheck the order before shipment. Jess had rejected the suggestion out of hand, just because he could. The next day, Jess was demoted to the warehouse division. He quit the company less than two weeks later."

"Demotion is a huge step downward for one incident. Were there other occurrences of the same nature?"

"It was the only mishap that affected finances. The CFO has a low money-loss threshold."

Tempia joined Cory's laughter and ogled sweets on the dessert cart the server rolled beside their table. Her gaze roved over mouthwatering sweets until she gave the patient woman an apologetic grin. "No, thank you. I can't eat another bite."

"I'll provide a take-home bag if you can squeeze in a small taste," Camille offered.

Tempia inspected the desserts display for several seconds. Chocolate sauce cascading down the marble-cheesecake brownie to the saucer's rim almost made her reconsider. "I almost relented, but no thank you. I am stuffed."

The server pinpointed Cory with a dazzling grin. "How about a scrumptious dessert and take-home bag if needed?"

Cory chuckled. "It's tempting, but I agree with my lovely lady. Dessert on our next visit, Tempia?"

Tempia's heart thumped in her chest. She scoured her brain to add a clever piggyback behind Cory's compliment. Nothing. A trembly smile split her lips. "Definitely. Looking forward to coming back here."

"Next time, then. See you soon."

Camille placed the bill presenter on the table, then she pushed her dessert cart across the room.

Tempia smiled deep within her spirit. My ... lovely ... lady. A bright future dotted the landscape, and the evening hadn't even ended.

Cory pushed back his chair and left money in the bill presenter. "Which dessert caught your eye?"

"The marble-cheesecake brownie smothered in chocolate sauce."

"Since the evening is still young, let's take a stroll along the river park. You game?"

Tempia tried to keep her excitement from showing on her face. "My grandmother often says, 'The evening is still young' whenever I'm about to leave their house," she told Cory.

"Believe it or not, my great-grandmother says the same thing. The feisty matriarch celebrated her ninety-fourth birthday a few months back."

"God is blessing her with a long life." She placed her hand in Cory's and fell into step beside him. The couple left the restaurant and, walking side by side, headed east toward the riverfront.

Tempia's entire body vibrated at Cory's unspoken words indicating he wanted to stay together longer. His desire and her mind frame agreed. Too bad they couldn't talk together through early morning and beyond forever.

Cory squeezed Tempia's fingers while the couple walked along Riverfront Trail. The twelve-mile paved route along the Mississippi River began at the Gateway Arch. On the east side of the trail, the Mississippi River flowed north to south. Visitors to the area could immerse themselves in local history and view the Lewis and Clark statue adjacent to the trail. Multiple other activities existed, from riverboat rides to helicopter tours.

She hadn't visited the area since the riverfront's major renovation. Except for Busch Stadium trips, she never ventured downtown. This updated version of the landscape inspired Tempia. The graffiti wall along the left side of the trail dazzled with its artwork and dramatic colors.

Looking around him, Cory slowed their pace. "I haven't ventured downtown in over ten years. I've missed a treat."

Tempia basked in the serene atmosphere and swung their clasped hands. "The fantastic artwork weaves a story of hope and persistence. Artists put their souls into these paintings." She stopped in front of a mural that depicted an African American family crossing into freedom. The vivid imagery inspired self-reflection. "This is a powerful reminder that people lived in those sorrowful conditions."

Farther down the trail, Cory lingered in front of another poignant painting. A towheaded family toiled in a soybean field. The children ranged in age from a few years old to around eleven.

"Each mural showcases a proud heritage passed down through multiple decades," Cory added. "Families in pursuit of better lives met the tasks head-on with hard work plus determination." He squeezed Tempia's fingers. "Your mother's paintings also demonstrate keen insight. Her work would have fit in well here."

Tempia had been thinking those precise thoughts. How did he always speak the right words? "Mom believed some artists' very souls signed their paintings." She beamed as Cory grinned.

"Going north, the trail ends at Old Chain of Rocks Bridge. I think your brothers would like checking it out."

Tempia rubbed goosebumps running alongside her arms. "We can make the walk one Saturday on their weekend visit."

"We'll pack a picnic lunch and take the entire day." He glanced at banners blowing in the breeze. "It's getting cooler. Better head back."

Unlike the short walk to the riverfront, it took the couple twenty minutes to make the return trip. Tempia kept her phone camera busy shooting pictures every few steps.

Before rounding the corner, she videoed the well-lit riverfront area. A riverboat caught her gaze. "Have you eaten dinner on a river cruise?"

"No, but the glow in your eyes suggests an excursion is in our near future."

When they reached the Primers parking lot, Cory tucked Tempia inside the SUV and slid into the driver's seat, facing the smiling woman. Green flecks flickered in his dark-brown eyes. "Is there somewhere else you would like to go? I hate wrapping up our evening this early."

Me too, Tempia thought. More conversations might reinforce their young, yet promising relationship. Her father's stagnation in upset mode eliminated her parents' house. In two seconds, she nixed her apartment, Cory's home, and a darkened movie theater. Gabby and Rob sprang into her mind. Was a drop-by visit worth the gamble during their tiff? A house call might prove a risky but necessary gambit.

"Gabby and Rob's house? Maybe I can redeem myself and regain your cousin's trust."

Cory's slow gaze roved across her face. "You're serious, aren't you?" His eyes narrowed when she nodded. "Does a problem exist between you and Rob? If so, explain what happened."

Oh boy. Cory was unaware that Rob wouldn't sanction a personal relationship between him and her. How could she articulate his cousin and best friend's current attitude without placing blame? Land mines lay ahead. Here goes everything.

Tempia's hands folded and unfolded on her lap. "Gabby and Rob reached a stalemate concerning us. Don't get me wrong. Your cousin doesn't treat me any differently than he always has." Her body shifted positions on the car seat, fully facing the curious man. "But I doubt he's eager about our dating."

Cory leaned back, thinking private thoughts. "That wasn't my impression after we spoke yesterday. Besides, only two people will vote on our relationship. Rob isn't one." He turned the key in the ignition. "An unannounced visit is an excellent suggestion."

"I hope this goes well. If nothing else, we will remember this visit." Nibbling her bottom lip, Tempia secured her seat belt.

Cory maneuvered the vehicle onto the streetlight-illuminated road, then began a rambling monologue until he parked across the street from his cousin's house. Both Stephenses' vehicles were parked out front. "Seems like they both are home."

Once the couple climbed the steps, Tempia rang the doorbell. "Lights are off in the living room. Won't they be surprised."

Through a side window, the couple watched a lone silhouette approach the door. Seconds later, Gabby called to her husband. "Rob, you won't believe who our visitors are!"

Gabby swung open the door wearing a huge grin. At the end of the hall, Rob leaned on the bedroom doorframe.

Tempia entered the house, waved at Rob, and embraced her friend. "Did our coming by unannounced disrupt your evening plans?" she whispered in Gabby's ear.

"This visit is a lifesaver," Gabby whispered back, giving her friend a double hug. She broke the hold and spoke in a normal voice. "Just finished the kitchen cleanup. The living room was my next stop."

Tempia glanced from Gabby to Rob, then studied her friend a bit more. Friction crackled in the air despite the couple standing a house-length apart. Discord had gained a solid foothold.

When Cory massaged Tempia's shoulders in circular motions, she relaxed against his strong frame. "I have a five-star restaurant review to share. All of the claims that Primers is awesome ring true."

Approval entered Gabby's eyes. "Primers? On short notice? Impressive, Mr. Sanders."

"We're going back soon," Tempia said. "We agree the scrumptious-looking desserts deserve a genuine taste test."

While they talked in the foyer, Rob sauntered down the hallway and entered the living room. Gabby followed her husband inside the recently redecorated space. Tempia and Cory shadowed behind her and watched the couple from their post inside the doorway.

Rob studied his guests longer than etiquette dictated, and then his outreached hand extended toward his wife. Her motionless response declined his offer. Her curved lips resembled a grimace rather than a smile. He sent a gaze of longing to his visibly unmoved wife.

Tempia's heart broke. She held her breath until Gabby accepted her husband's hand.

Rob pressed his wife's fingers to his lips and led her to the love seat.

Tempia's compassion toward the under-fire man proved short-lived. He chose the cozy love seat, which forced their visitors to settle on a thirteen-foot-long sofa. Was Rob distancing Tempia from Cory or simply sitting closer to his wife? When Tempia practically sat in Cory's lap, Rob's fervent gaze remained on Gabby.

Rob rubbed his forehead on Gabby's forehead then glanced away. "Sounds like someone pulled out all the stops. Is it true Primers is a tranquil oasis?" The lilting tone belied his pointed gaze.

"That description might be a little over the top," Cory said.

Gabby sighed. "Despite the rave reviews, Rob hasn't been sold on the restaurant."

Rob placed his arm around his wife's shoulder. "I'll book us a table for their earliest opening. I would be happy eating a meal inside a desert hut if you were my companion." He tucked a strand of hair behind his wife's ear, then he kissed her cheek.

Tempia almost clapped her hands. Gabby didn't wipe off the smooch.

Rob snuggled closer to Gabby. "So, tell us more."

"The waterfall display saved us an unnecessary Reedy River Falls visit. South Carolina can become a future vacation spot." Cory nudged Tempia's side. "A painter's daughter will appreciate Liberty Bridge's peaceful community vibes."

Gabby gave her first grin of the evening. "Aw. Already planning vacations together. Rob and I might join in on a few."

Tempia beamed. "Please do. We talked about how Cory's family had traveled to all fifty states by the time he graduated high school. We learned a lot about each other over dinner."

"I'm glad you were both so open. Disclosure is important to relationships."

"I divulged more about family events this evening than I've spewed across ten years," Cory said.

"Good for you. Communication will always win the day. Now, I'm curious, Primers placed my cousin on a month-long waiting list. How did you book a table with a day's notice?" Gabby asked.

Cory's eyebrows wiggled. "Either I switched dates last night or I am a well-connected man."

"My uncle installed their HVAC system," Rob said. "It seems service providers possess more clout than attorneys."

Silence filled the room. What broke up their lively discussion? "Does your law firm handle the restaurant's legal affairs?" Tempia asked.

"Becker and Steed represented the proprietor's interest before they chose the Laclede Landing location."

Once Rob finished speaking, a longer silence filled the space. What upended their free-flowing dialogue? *Come on, Gabby, help me out.* "Did you recommend your uncle's heating and cooling company to the restaurant?" Tempia probed.

Rob nodded. "I give family shout-outs wherever possible."

"Great. Families should stick together." Tempia nudged her pump on Cory's shoe.

He leaned closer. "You and Rob are doing fine. Carry on."

"I hear a partnership is on the horizon for you," Tempia told Rob.

His arm draped across his wife's shoulders, Rob sat ramrod straight. "A partnership might not be the correct career course. These days, going solo looks better than ever."

"Sounds like you chose to leave the company since the last time we talked about it," Cory said. "Your wife being a first-rate legal assistant will speed up the transition period."

"It will if Gabby decides to join me. After her internship, she turned down Becker and Steed's generous job offer."

"Yet the remarkable lady accepted you. Which in my opinion provided a win-win situation for two deserving people." Cory's unflinching gaze pierced Rob's startled demeanor. "May Tempia's and my connection fare as well. How can an admirable woman and a commendable man lose in a personal relationship?"

Rob's fixated gaze riveted on his cousin's face. His parted lips never uttered a sound.

"Did you guys have dessert at the restaurant, Temp?" Gabby questioned.

Tempia noticed the sudden topic change and realized she had already stated the couple didn't eat dessert. And then, she understood. Her friend just demanded a private consultation.

"I was stuffed and couldn't eat another bite. Breathing became easier after walking on the riverfront."

"Glad to hear it. Well, I hope you're hungry by now. I have some dessert to share. Help me bring it out." Gabby headed toward the hallway. "I made your favorite shortcake, Cory. Cherry almond."

"Can't wait," Cory said.

Gabby preceded Tempia in their wordless trek into the kitchen.

Gabby entered the kitchen, removed a storage container off the refrigerator, and planted it on the countertop. She opened a cabinet and drawers, grabbing saucers, spoons, and a large serving spoon. Laying it all on the counter, she faced Tempia. "Those pieces look good worn together."

Tempia looked down at her outfit and beamed a bright smile.

"Don't grin. You told Cory that Rob is antsy about you and Cory dating."

Was Rob's opposition a guarded secret? Cory had clearly stated that contacting him before she dated Quince would have refuted Quince's lies. Communication was crucial to him, so she couldn't imagine not telling Cory about Rob's true feelings about her. "I admitted Rob doesn't like me but emphasized he treats me like he always has."

"I'll say it again: Rob likes you. You keep comparing Rob's behavior toward you before and after his party. Why does it matter that you didn't know he thought you snubbed Cory?"

"It's deceptive. His behavior toward me should represent his true feelings about me."

Gabby scooped dessert onto four saucers. "Rob treats you like you're my best friend."

"If you say so. What made you think I told Cory?"

"You share comparable quirks. His 'two deserving people' speech was a warning to stand down. He's making a substantial investment in your relationship. He won't accept failure without a fight." Gabby entered the pantry, then re-entered the kitchen carrying napkins. "Cory likes you, Temp. He wants a true alliance. With you."

"Then why not cut through needless red tape?"

"By proposing a quickie marriage? You've already had one of those. Wasn't one enough?"

"No sane person desires a bad relationship or a drawn-out courtship."

"I get that, but would you accept a reckless marriage proposal from Cory?"

"I would be hard pressed not to. I love him. Cory Sanders is a godsend who lives by solid family values."

"You need to be sure this time. Love is a strong emotion that warrants full test results." Gabby's shifting gaze indicated she sought the right words. Sighing, she returned the shortcake container to the refrigerator top.

The deep sigh caught Tempia's attention. Procrastination rarely featured in Gabby's conversations. Tempia braced herself for more straight talk.

Gabby faced Tempia. "Listen. You and Cory shared an instant attraction, and he supported you during a turbulent marriage. Neither of those attributes equal his being a perfect man. Like everyone, Cory has plenty of annoying faults."

"According to you, he's one of your favorite people."

"So are you and me—and sometimes we're hard to live with. Listen. I like a lot of people you wouldn't marry."

"Um ... good point. Enough about me and Cory. What's going on between you and Rob? Tension was flowing fast when we entered the house. A butter knife could have cut the strife."

"We're working through some things. But we'll get there. I'm trusting the God who never fails." She paused. "And sorry, Temp. Cory told Rob you were his mystery lady during the party."

Rob's obstinate attitude against Tempia became clearer. That night, he'd realized Quince's talking to her had deeply wounded his cousin. Especially since they both had had favorable impressions of each other and a real conversation hadn't taken place.

Tempia shrugged. "I somewhat thought he had. Rob's knowing Cory had been interested in me explains his strong reaction against my dating Quince. Rob probably slowly boiled while a man he despised and the woman his cousin liked made small talk in the hallway."

"Which means all Quince's schemes would have failed had I been told."

"Hop off the merry-go-round going nowhere. Those facts do not make one iota of a difference. Pardon Rob. Move on."

"Oh, pooh. I've already forgiven him. But his self-righteous attitude is bothersome. Rob handicapped my helping you. He must own that fact just as I admitted that not telling Cory the truth was negligent." Gabby picked up two dessert dishes and headed toward the door. "Come on. Those two have argued long enough."

Chapter Eleven

Tempia removed the remaining shortcakes off the counter. With thoughts of what would happen next, she trailed behind her friend. The women walked inside a tension-infused room. Unresolved conflict crackled in the air. The men's annoyed gazes were locked together.

Their stare down was broken when Rob accepted the dessert as his wife settled beside him. "Smells delicious, love. I bet it tastes even better than it looks." He set the saucer on an end table. His squinting gaze pinpointed Tempia as he watched her sit beside Cory. "Hey lady, I realize you and my wife are friends for life. You're dating a man I love and respect ..."

The opening passed muster. Why did Rob hesitate? Was there a "but" coming?

Tempia viewed Cory in her peripheral vision. His countenance had shifted since she had walked into the room. His bland facial expression hid his thoughts.

"Tempia ... I thought you and Cory would become a splendid match on the first day you and I met. For three years, he wouldn't even meet you. It felt strange setting up the game party, because meeting a specific lady was his preference. His ready acceptance stunned me. I hurriedly invited people over to my house. Thank God most of our closest friends were available. I calmed down once you accepted my invitation."

"Rob felt he'd made the correct choice from his soul. All systems were go," his wife added.

"I sat in amazement after your mishap almost landed you in Cory's lap," said Rob. "The accident, your guileless response, plus my cousin's obvious delight, vindicated the party idea. I could feel that a topnotch match was in the making."

"I was horribly embarrassed when I dropped my food, Rob," Tempia said. "My reaction might have been better had I known your guests."

"That's probably true," Rob said. "Even though both your and Cory's initial responses amazed me, your reactions made sense after Gabby whispered that you had noticed him while walking through the front door and Cory's mouthing the words, 'That's her' when he came into the living room after cleaning up. Those verifications convinced me the entire good deed had God's approval."

Gabby rested her head on Rob's shoulder. "The evening ending in a fiasco doesn't mean a meeting between you two wasn't preordained."

Rob fingered her hair in gentle strokes. "I laughed at Quince's classic pickup line," Rob confessed. "The woman I know would have dismissed his drivel, but instead, you fell for his smooth talk. Your naivete needlessly hurt my best friend because I interfered in his love life." Grimacing, he shook his head. "You bringing the lowlife to our wedding added salt to the wound. I almost left the altar and popped him in his smug mouth. His inappropriate kisses were slaps in Cory's face. Then you announced your engagement two days after our wedding. After your phone call, my bride sobbed throughout our honeymoon."

When the fork shook in her hand, Tempia placed it onto the saucer. Gabby hadn't revealed that the news had destroyed her and Rob's honeymoon. Tempia shouldn't have interrupted their celebration with a text message about herself. "Rob—"

"Explanations are unnecessary. I understand the situation better than you may think." He hesitated as Tempia brushed teardrops off her cheek. "I hold you in high regard, lady. You are and will always be a welcome guest inside my home. Sometimes good people marry sleazeballs."

A weight lifted off Tempia's shoulders. "Thank God you didn't write me off. Why didn't you invite me to your house and introduce me to your friends before the get-together?"

Rob pointed to his cousin. "Cory and I had a no-interference clause regarding women we dated. I ignored the stipulation after meeting you and kept pushing an introduction. His refusal to give in meant I couldn't invite you to my house or any place he might attend. He would have charged me with subterfuge had he run into you by accident."

Tempia steadied her breath. Rob liked her and had broken his longstanding promise with his favorite cousin and trusted friend. Tempia placed her head on the sofa cushion, reliving the past two years in microseconds. As an inner struggle assaulted her assurance, the room remained comfortably quiet. Whether or not he deserved one, she would give Rob an apology.

"Dating Quince ran me around in too many circles. Everyone I knew was equally unimpressed. I suppose Quince couldn't vanquish his one true friend without marrying a woman he didn't love. Please forgive me for doubting you and Gabby."

A dim light filled Rob's eyes. "No apology was expected or required. Let's do a restart." He scooped shortcake onto a spoon. "How about Gabby and I destroy you both in a dominoes marathon?"

Cory slid a spoonful of his favorite shortcake into his mouth. "Mmm! Scrumptious as usual, Mrs. Stephens. The losers will take the winners on a dinner cruise in June."

Gabby fell over herself laughing. "See there, Temp. You and Cory have lots of things in common. You both scrounge free meals whenever possible."

* * *

Two hours later, Tempia unlocked the front door, pondering if she should invite her date inside the house. While she hemmed and hawed over her next step, Cory handled the sticky point on his own. He followed her into the foyer and closed the door behind him.

Only Tempia heard the sigh that coursed throughout her soul. A goodbye had stuck inside her throat. In a perfect world, their peaceful night would last until tomorrow. The couple's first date had surpassed her wildest expectations. Her redemption plus reaffirmations of Rob's friendly intent inspired courage amid potential failure.

Cory glanced down the darkened hallway. "Is your parents' house always this quiet on weekend nights?"

Tempia nodded. "Regardless of the day, all roads lead upstairs to their bedrooms by nine o'clock."

His gaze trailed up the stairway to the second-floor landing. "Is everyone awake or asleep at this point?"

"Awake. Except for during family celebrations, they bunk down in bedrooms when dusk hits."

His gaze stole back up the stairs. "Preteens who willingly go to bed early on a Saturday night are an anomaly."

"Curt and Noah are not asleep. They are probably playing a board game in one of their bedrooms while Mom and Dad are watching old Westerns in bed." Headed toward the living room, she spun around. "May we converse awhile? I can grab a snack from the kitchen."

100

Cory shook his head and beckoned Tempia to his side. "Since this is your parents' house, I'll head home and call you tomorrow." His half-closed eyes scrutinized her face.

Tempia's lips curved into a full-fledged grin. "Is that a pledge you'll stay later at my place?"

"Yes, ma'am, if I'm allowed." He still studied her in silence. Then his right thumb brushed her forearm. "This evening tossed me into scenarios I have never imagined. In fact ... if you're free tomorrow, will you join our family dinner?"

Tempia's body fizzled and popped all over. She had only thought the evening had surpassed her craziest dreams. She hadn't expected Cory wanting consecutive dates.

I'm meeting Cory's immediate family super-fast. We're on an uphill climb all the way to the top.

"Ooh, I'd love to share your family's Sunday dinner."

"Glad to hear it. Mama will appreciate meeting a good-hearted woman from my past."

Tempia shifted her posture and cleared her throat. "Your past? What do you mean? Am I a relic?"

His low chuckle tickled both her ears. She valued the throaty tone he had adopted all evening.

"What I mean is," Cory said, "you're a woman she has seen but never met. My parents attended Gabby and Rob's wedding ceremony and reception."

Throughout that celebration, Tempia had observed attendees, guessing who his parents were. The sociable man's actions hadn't singled out any one couple, though she had noticed a resemblance between Cory and one of the women. The woman could have been an aunt or some other relative. "I knew they were there and wondered who your parents were. I played guessing games and can't wait to see if I chose the correct couple. Did I make a favorable impression?"

"Mama went home thinking you're lovely; she'll enjoy an introduction."

Cory's nimble fingers, massaging her shoulders, stifled clear thoughts. She might have breathed easier had he referenced both parents, not just his mother. Yet eating crumbs was better than perishing on starvation diets.

Tempia glanced at the man who appeared introspective. Did he seek to accelerate their relationship? Only time would tell. Tempia hoped her smile displayed her increased self-assurance.

"Thanks for accepting the short-notice invite. Should I pick you up here or at your apartment?"

"My apartment is fine. It's just three blocks away. I moved back into the same apartment complex I was in before I lived in Quince's house." Tempia shrugged.

Cory's grin deepened. "It's nice that you're close to your family. Support systems can help us go beyond our comfort zones."

Tempia snapped her fingers. "Before I forget, what dessert should I bring?"

"Mama will have dessert covered. Only your lovely self is required."

His enunciating each word branded the air she breathed. Tempia wobbled on her feet.

Cory brushed two fingers down her right cheek. His lips hovered mere inches above her mouth. Their lips touched. Tempia felt the floor beneath her vanish. Her arms tightened around his neck. Her brain felt like it would explode from happiness. Alive. Secure. Elated. Tempia lost herself inside these intense emotions.

Tempia's God-appointed man—the same man she had thrown away in ignorance and fear—cuddled Tempia lovingly. Their kiss provided an unequaled sensation she hoped would never end.

As Cory's head rose, he studied her facial expression in total silence. An unspoken question lingered in his eyes.

When Tempia released the grip around his neck, weariness spread throughout her body. She had intensified a tender kiss to an unprecedented level. Shame usurped her newfound aplomb. She feared she had missed the mark by miles, and that once again, this special man occupied a ringside seat.

His backing toward the door decreased the charged atmosphere, which Tempia regretted she'd created.

Cory stood still. His curved bottom lip offered a reassuring grin. "Our visit to Gabby and Rob had a good outcome. The hatchet was buried in the past and not inside my cousin."

She shook her head to release cobwebs hindering her thought process. Tempia inhaled a deep breath. "Rob believes I won't willfully hurt you."

"He likes you as more than his wife's closest friend."

"Is it because Rob thinks you and I are a good match?"

"You got it. He loathes your ex-husband but invited me to the get-together while Quince and I were hanging out. Surprisingly, Rob took a chance on me co-operating and Quince not coming along."

"Rob was on point, but like a klutz, I dropped the ball." Tempia's hand brushed through her curls.

Cory didn't defend her prior foolishness. And it made her realize she may have unconsciously hoped he would let her off the hook. *You want an adult relationship. Behave like an adult.* She cleared her throat several times. "On occasion, my inappropriate decisions affect the people I love most. My parents were disillusioned and my error's fallout hit Gabby."

"Ah, but your parents still love you, and your best friend put her best foot forward. Rob is a loyal man. His keeping secrets from me proves how much he adores his wife."

"In doing so, he angered both you and Gabby."

Cory chuckled. "It ended well in any case. Everyone has a better grasp on each other's strengths and weaknesses." He shoved his hands inside his pockets. "Plus, it looks like I'm dating Missouri's domino queen."

Cory excelled at subject changes. He was giving her an easy way out of yet another uncomfortable topic. *Play along. Don't squander his goodwill.* "My father is the reigning domino champ," Tempia whispered as if divulging a state secret. "I learned the game rules when I learned to walk. Gabby and Rob were destined to buy us a Skyline dinner cruise."

Amusement appeared on his face. He reached behind his back and unlocked the front door. "Mama likes to have her Sunday meal in the late afternoon, so how about I pick you up at two-thirty?"

"I will be ready on the dot. Are you sure I shouldn't bring dessert?"

"Mama probably prepared tomorrow's dessert today." Cory stepped onto the porch.

Tempia grasped the doorknob. "Goodnight, Cory. We had a cathartic and fun-filled date."

"In spades. Until tomorrow." Cory stepped outside and closed the door behind him.

Tempia turned the lock, resisting the urge to track his progress across the street. The stairway loomed ahead like a steep mountain peak. Earlier, a hope-filled woman had bounded up those steps with big date plans. Now the climb seemed harrowing. Thank God Cory hadn't rejected her or her improper kiss.

She would just learn from her mistakes. Unless Cory canceled dinner plans, Tempia would see him again tomorrow.

* * *

Feeling unsettled, Cory processed his date's passionate kiss during the drive home. Sexual gratification had remained off the table since Cory had begun dating. He had witnessed numerous instances of couples who shared premature intimacies falling apart emotionally once the relationship died. He wanted to keep himself from the devastation and disillusionment that comes with sexual escapades in unmarried couples.

A growing relationship with God had simplified his life in numerous ways. His priority was to marry a godly woman. Along the way, he had acquired the good sense to slow his roll. Tempia had stolen his heart, and one day, the remarkable woman would enjoy her present life instead of living in past regrets and future aspirations.

But the passionate embrace had caught Cory off guard. Wrapped in his arms, Tempia had pitched him an unhittable curveball. The kiss had descended into an area he had no wish to yet tread. And neither had she, if he'd correctly read her woebegone facial expression and stressed body language.

Despite the awkward situation, his initial attraction remained intact. Tempia was a woman he could cherish. Her Community Ministries devotion proved her high regard for other folks' welfare. Going the extra mile by providing cupcakes and free entertainment underscored her compassion and adaptability. The retained godly principles and an allegiance that her condescending husband didn't deserve depicted a resolute spirit. Those positive characteristics, plus many more, provided a potent magnetism that held Cory captive.

While Tempia's guard was down, powerful emotions had flickered across her face. Cory had affirmed dinner with a woman who dreaded his rejection. Her potential distress demanded he re-examine his previously held position: What if their relationship ended without a marriage proposal? Would their failure as a couple cause Tempia irreparable damage?

Cory laughed out loud. If his sister had heard his inner thoughts, she would mock his reflections. He almost heard her stinging indictment: "Don't think more highly of yourself than you ought. Tempia will find herself a more worthy man."

Laughter spewed from Cory's lips as he exited the highway. He wiped moisture from his eyes while navigating fun seekers walking in the road. Could he secure a Tempia link and not cause disruptions in her life? Her ex-husband had dealt the woman enough sorrow to drain ten people.

Cory couldn't determine what to do. It was too late to cancel their dinner plans. He needed to remember to proceed with caution.

* * *

In church the next morning, Tempia's chin rested on her chest to check her watch during Pastor Freeman's lengthy sermon. Surprisingly, he was running shorter than on previous Sundays. Once the choir sang their last song, she left her seat, full of worry. Her gaze swept around the parking lot until she observed her stepmother. Sam was engaged in conversation with Tempia's grandparents on her mother's side. Her father's second marriage had added an additional set of grandparents to complement the two sets she already had. All her grandparents were alive and doing well.

"Hey!" Tempia squeaked. Curt and Noah had hooked her underneath her arms. She dug in her heels against the pavement as the boys propelled her body toward her grandparents' white automobile.

"I don't need help walking across a parking lot," she said.

Curt's head nudged her hair. "You stood there staring too long. You should have walked over and said hello."

"Yeah," said Noah. "Greet everybody so we can go eat lunch."

Tempia yanked her arms away. "Since I am not going with you, when you eat lunch does not concern me."

Two feet away from Tempia's grandparents, Noah and Curt chorused, "Hi, Gammy. Hi Gramps."

Tempia stopped by the elderly couple and gave them hugs. "Hello, Gammy. How is your hip mending, Gramps?"

"I've been pain-free for five days, which is a nice change after suffering unrelenting agony for seven months. Wanda's finally done caring for me, but she provided excellent care."

"Graham should have gotten the hip surgery last year," his wife said. "Tempie, we're eating lunch at your Aunt Betty's house. She said to tell you that she cooked Thanksgiving dinner in March."

"Aunt Betty makes the best giblet gravy in the world. Ask her if she'd please save me some, and tell her that I'll stop by on Tuesday for lunch."

"Betty and your mother were very close sisters. She'd love to have you visit more often." Gammy slid into the driver's seat. "You kids come by the house for dinner on Thursday. I'll whip up your favorite homemade pizzas."

"We'll be there," Noah and Curt spoke together.

"No, you won't. Noah has a speech meet after school each day this week."

"Can we make it next Thursday?" Curt asked.

"Thursday next week works for us," Gammy said.

Gramps said goodbye, closed the passenger door, and waved until the car left the parking lot.

When the others headed toward Blanche's car, Tempia hung onto her stepmother's arm. "Mom, could I speak with you? We will join you all in a moment, Dad." The boys stopped in their tracks, staring at their sister until Tempia shooed them both away.

"Make it quick," Sam said. "We're meeting your hungry grandparents at Hot Wok for lunch."

Chapter Twelve

Blanche's alert gaze speared Tempia as the others moved on. "You've been droopy all morning and sat alone. What's happened since we left the house?"

Tears filled Tempia's averted gaze. "I gave you all a glowing date recap, but I didn't mention the misstep I made last night." Her loose arms dropped at her side. "Mom, I'm unsure where to begin."

Parishioners heading toward their cars streamed outside. Blanche led Tempia farther away from the crowd until they reached the courtyard filled with bonsai trees. "Start at the beginning and state the simple truth."

Tempia repeatedly cleared her throat. "Um, okay," she said once Blanche's head tilted sideways. "Yesterday revealed some new information and challenges. Even so, I am blessed and there's no doubt about it."

"Go on."

"Yesterday, a wonderful man took me on my dream date. We discussed our families, friends, and jobs. We discussed every imaginable topic. The best part was Cory and I visited Gabby and Rob's house." Tempia hesitated. "Well ... Rob had reservations about Cory and me dating. As always, Gabby is encouraging and supportive."

Blanche frowned. "Her husband isn't? What's the problem?"

"I dated Quince instead of Cory. Rob had been hiding his disdain beneath civility. I didn't realize there was an issue until this weekend."

Blanche's eyebrows quirked. "Disdain is a harsh word. Displeasure, perhaps?"

"Yes. But in spades. My dating Quince caused too many problems for numerous people. Thank God we cleared the air last night."

Clearly framing her next words, her stepmother frowned. "Good. When it comes to your dating issues, Gabby's husband's opinion doesn't count. Tell me what happened between you and Cory."

Tempia shuffled on her feet. "Oh, Mom. I already told you about our restaurant and riverfront experience. Everything except ... I neglected to share our Gabby and Rob visit. And … the goodbye. Last night, I flubbed the farewell."

Tempia relayed the story as if it had just occurred. "See there? I blew up our date by acting rash."

Blanche wore a blank expression. "Perhaps you gave Cory more things to consider, but trust me, his pursuit won't end because you deepened his kiss."

"You had to be there, Mom." Tempia bit down hard. "I keep messing up by making foolish errors." Tempia's open palms spread out beside her face.

Blanche smiled. "As your father loves saying, 'rubbish.' Dating Cory will determine where your relationship will lead. Keep steady, and don't put so much pressure on yourself."

Tempia's head shook involuntarily. Until the disastrous kiss, she had seen light beyond the lengthy tunnel. Now the darkened void appeared endless. "I don't want to suffer a setback and lose momentum. Cory is an awesome man and will make an excellent husband. Despite his thinking I had chosen Quince over him, he supported me during my toughest trials."

"Your father and I thank God the young man assisted you." Smiling, Blanche hesitated. "Don't forget Jesus is our true champion. Only God is in complete control. People aren't." She inched closer. "Tell me when you realized you love Cory."

Tempia's eyebrows wrinkled. "I haven't told you I love Cory."

"Yet your actions and words suggest you do. I agree that you and Cory have a connection worth pursuing. You desire a permanent relationship, and maybe he does as well."

Tempia tried to stifle her anxiety-filled thoughts, but tears stung her eyes. One look at her stepmother's affectionate expression unleashed a storm of tears.

Blanche immediately drew her stepdaughter into a snug embrace. The hold decreased as Tempia's body relaxed against Blanche's chest.

"I realized I loved Cory the night I left Quince. Seventeen, Mom," she said, sniffling. "Cory bailed me out seventeen times during my marriage. But his cutting off communications without an explanation made me feel like my life didn't count. He should have explained why he snubbed me." Pausing, she dried her eyes on wet fingers. "His saying he wants us to cross the finish line together was almost like an informal marriage proposal."

"Not to the young man. Honey, you thinking a marriage proposal will automatically follow his requesting a date is an irrefutable long stretch. It helps to understand other people's behavior and motivation."

"Mom—"

"We only know two facts. You left Quince, and Cory cut off contact. Why did he rekindle communication?"

Tempia opened her mouth and then shrugged. "Cory and Quince had barely spoken except for my ex's few short phone calls. Quince stopped by Cory's house on Friday and relayed the jealous-girlfriend lie. No one had told Cory about that. He and Rob had it out before he visited me."

Blanche's gaze narrowed. "Did Cory fill you in on their discussion?"

"No, ma'am. He only questioned why I believed a man I had just met over my best friend. In the end, he fully accepted my explanation. He wouldn't have asked me out if he hadn't." Her voice lowered. "I think Cory still loves me."

"Tempia—"

"Remember, Quince believed Cory did."

"Quince doesn't get a vote on either of your lives. Distorted thinking creates problems. Learn to realistically evaluate circumstances."

Tempia pursed her lips, sighing. "Gabby voiced practically the same opinion."

"Good. Because it's true. No doubt Cory and Quince's discussion, plus the Rob exchange, instigated Friday's visit. Each man understands the depth of their individual conversations. Only Cory knows what prompted his visit."

A voice sounded behind Tempia's back. She jerked around and faced her father.

Sam's eyebrows were drawn together. Grooves etched around his mouth. "Is there a problem? What's wrong, Tempie? What happened last night?"

Blanche unwrapped her arms from around her stepdaughter's shoulders. "We're done here. Our daughter is accepting that people must live out their lives in real time."

His eyes narrowing, Sam touched Tempia's arm.

Blanche extracted a small tissue case from her purse, passed it to Tempia, then patted her husband's shoulder. "Tempie is fine. I will join you all in a minute, dear."

Blanche remained quiet while her husband retraced his steps, then her gaze focused on her stepdaughter. "Your beautiful idea of living happily alongside Cory is intriguing. It will be interesting to see if those dreams survive life's severe tests."

"I pray they will. I lost myself in a man who didn't love or respect me."

"Hush. That useless critique borders on self-pity. Don't let anyone live rent free inside your head. Kick him out."

"I do. He keeps returning. How do I break depressing mental ties?"

"Don't accommodate Quince thoughts, whether they're good or bad."

"Mom—"

"You must remain steadfast toward your goal in mind and deed. You'll figure it out. However, scripture instructs us to live within the confines of today. Forget about your and Cory's future. You'll see him this afternoon. Now, dating a nice young man may produce positive results. Common goals are reached through hard work and objectivity. A rational mind helps the process." She paused when Tempia groaned. "It's a tall order for any couple. Especially ones who have adverse baggage dotting the trail."

Tempia held her stomach and moaned louder until she sucked in a deep breath and sported a half grin. "It feels like time is running out. Am I asking too much too soon?"

Nodding, Blanche wrapped her arms around her stepdaughter's shoulder, rubbing their cheeks together. "Let me predict my daughter's future. You and Cory will either get married or settle into a comfortable friendship."

Tempia giggled. The practical prediction made their conversation lighter. "Cheater. In other words, we won't wind up hating each other." She broke away, hiccupping. "Excuse me. I guess him not hating me is a hopeful outcome."

Blanche gave her a quick hug. "Just like yours and Gabby's, the right friendships will last forever."

* * *

On the drive home, Blanche's unanticipated prediction mingled in Tempia's mind with her own errant-kiss evaluation. Fewer than five blocks from her apartment, she made a detour onto Highway 70 and headed east. She drove on autopilot and ended the twenty-mile drive on the riverfront. The romance permeating the atmosphere yesterday was absent today. Unlike last night, today the Mississippi River was muddy to its swift-moving core.

Nevertheless, the dinner boat held her gaze as she slowed down her speed. In June, Tempia, Cory, and their best friends would dine on a river excursion. Until last night, neither couple had considered eating dinner on a riverboat. In her mind's eye, she saw the event in living color. She even imagined the Saturday riverfront trail hike she and Cory would take the boys on. Tempia took in the full area until her gaze fixated on the Gateway Arch. It stood alone in all its glory.

Tempia lowered the car speed even more and cruised past the art memorial, making a right turn at the next corner. Her drive ended in Primers's empty parking lot. She relived the momentous drive downtown, her excellent meal, and her and Cory's riverfront excursion. The fortuitous drop by the Stephenses' house surpassed all other parts of the evening. Tempia felt as if she had come of age talking with Rob. She listened to his side of the story without finding fault with either him or herself. She simply accepted Rob's explanation and moved on.

Tempia texted Cory. *Miss you. Cannot wait until you pick me up.*

Cory sent a speedy reply. *Likewise. I might arrive a tad early. See you soon.*

Tempia started the ignition and headed home. Their date is beginning with promise and will end in … the smile disappeared in a flash. Her date would complete the statement on its own accord.

* * *

The phrase "meet adversity head-on" propelled Cory upstairs once the doorbell rang. Preemption would best serve everyone enjoying their Sunday dinner.

Loud shrieks sounded on the porch. Lillie laughed, swinging the door open. "Welcome, family. Come inside."

"Grandma! Grandma!" the girls squealed in hyper voices.

Lillie stooped onto her haunches, hugging her three chatterbox granddaughters. Then she stood upright and tweaked the cheek of the small boy nestled in his father's arms. "Walk, little man. Practice steps make for perfect running."

"Andre always wants Eric to carry him up steps. I don't think he feels confident navigating them on his own." Cathy peered down the hallway. "Where's Cory?"

Cory stepped into the hall. "Heading out. Mama and Dad have a special dinner guest this afternoon."

The curious gazes of Cathy and her husband studied Cory. "Is it Tempia?" Cathy asked. "Didn't you see her yesterday?"

"What do you know about Tempia?" Cory asked.

"This morning at church, Rob updated me on the mess. He tried to make me see things differently, but he failed. It doesn't change that the numbskull woman chose Quince Jones over the obvious better choice."

"There were mitigating circumstances," Cory finally said.

"There usually are when a person prefers snake oil over strong character traits. Oh, by the way, Rob's wife took issue with my response."

He bet Gabby had intervened on her best friend's behalf. "Did you apologize and redeem yourself? Good family relationships and all that."

"I like Gabby. It's her best friend I'm not sure about."

Heat rose so fast within Cory's body that his ear tips singed. "That acerbic comment should be beneath you—"

"We're neither judge nor jury over anyone else's behavior," Lillie broke in. "That one fact alone makes all our opinions useless." Her hands hastened Cory out the door. "Go fetch the young lady I've waited two years to meet."

"Can I go?" four-year-old Bella asked.

"Not on this trip. Next time," Cory promised, closing the door behind him.

Cory's sister was more incensed than he had expected. What had Rob said to her? As if it mattered. Cathy should've rejoiced over Cory's second chance with Tempia.

Cory entered his SUV and pulled the cell phone from his pocket. "Cathy came down on Tempia like a tornado. What did you tell her?" he demanded once Rob answered the call.

"Not much. Two years ago, she questioned me about what happened to your mystery lady. She knew you met the woman and it was a no-go. I told her the woman was interested in Quince. This morning, Tempia told my wife she was sharing your family's Sunday dinner. After church service, I informed Cathy the mystery lady was Gabby's best friend, Tempia. And that Tempia had met you and Quince at a get-together at my house. Jones won her over using subterfuge. Tempia married the lowlife six months later and divorced him five months after that. You and Tempia had your first date yesterday. And that, Gabby and I are delighted about it."

"Well, I'm glad you covered it all with her so I don't have to. However, forewarned is forearmed. Clue me in if there's a next time."

"You were my next call. I've mollified Gabby the entire afternoon."

"Has she forgiven my sister's brutal rebuttal?"

"She's working on it. But not as hard as I would like her to." Rob laughed.

Cory chuckled. "Sounds about right. Think I'll make a quick stop, then I'm off to pick up Tempia."

"She loves gardenias," Rob said just before he hung up.

Cory started the vehicle. His sister's knowledge might make her radioactive. Perhaps politeness would override any annoyance on Cathy's part.

* * *

A car door closed outside her apartment an hour after Tempia had hurried through her front door. The ringing doorbell ripped the silence. Would Cory

112

speak about their first kiss? She unclenched her fingers, swung open the door, and stepped aside.

Cory strolled inside the apartment, dressed in gray denim jeans and a garnet short-sleeve polo shirt. Tempia's arm circled his neck in a quick hug. Her gaze landed on a fluted-glass vase filled with white gardenias and blue baby's breath that spilled over the sides.

Tempia accepted the uplifting gift, taking in the scent of each bloom. "These beautiful blooms smell like a midsummer morning."

"An apt description. And you are both appealing and delightful in every sense."

His soulful eyes mesmerized her.

Tempia set the vase in the center of the small dining table. "My building is tucked away inside this little alcove. Was I hard to find?"

"Not at all. I drove straight here." Cory focused on her beige T-shirt, burnt-copper button-down shirt, and olive-green cargo pants. His eyes lit up when she retrieved a cream blazer off a chair. "You look nice. It's a chic, classic look." He chuckled as her mouth gaped. "I appreciate a thing or two about female fashion. While growing up, the women in our household were shopping addicts."

Tempia folded the blazer over her forearm. "On Saturdays in junior high, Gabby, me, and our mothers would scout clothing shops across four counties."

"Sounds like you and Gabby received huge perks by shopping with your mothers instead of with your girlfriends."

"We did until we ditched our mothers in high school and joined our friends at the local mall. Too bad we were sucked into group-mentality thinking."

"Battling for independence is a typical teenage-girl thing. My sister pulled the same stunt."

"Girl thing?" Tempia's eyebrows raised.

Cory chuckled. "Sorry. I guess my response was a boy thing I picked up years ago." He studied pictures that hung on four walls. "Your mom's?"

Tempia's quiet "yes" brought a smile.

"These are quite different from the ones that were displayed at Quince's house," Cory said. "Mrs. Wade had quite a variety of styles and did outstanding work."

"This tiny place demanded smaller pictures. Mom sold her paintings in local art shows. She had racked up a steady clientele before she passed away."

"I can see why. Your mother was a talented painter. The compositions and color schemes prove she respected her subject matter." His gaze took in the entire space. "Your home is compact and beautifully decorated. Very homey."

Tempia attempted to view the décor using Cory's perspective. Her furniture pieces were modest and functional. Furniture her mother adored was housed in her parents' basement. She hadn't used any in her last apartment or Quince's house.

"Thanks. I've tried to make it mine. My old one-bedroom apartment was occupied by the time I moved out of Quince's house. I lived with my parents for a while. This was one of two units available in the complex when I left their house. I selected the smaller one facing east."

"Great choice. It's the apartment I would have chosen."

Tempia beamed. "I love sunrays hitting my face each morning. Summer is my favorite season."

"Mine as well. I am an outdoorsy guy—except when it comes to camping. That activity hasn't won me over."

"Me neither. I hate bugs, insects, and crawly critters."

The couple headed to the SUV and down the highway, sharing outdoor experiences along the way. Tempia was grateful Cory was acting as if her mishap the night before hadn't occurred.

Thirty minutes later, Cory turned onto a street featuring brick houses. In every respect, it appeared to be a quiet neighborhood. A few cars were parked at the curb. No children played outside their homes.

Cory parked the SUV in front of a brick house. The Sanderses' property absorbed Tempia's full attention. The landscape merited two thumbs up with its meticulous manicure.

"Your home has tremendous curb appeal. The luscious thick lawn is a designer's dream. The layout is ideal."

"Mama's long-term gardener makes biweekly visits. And with compliments like that, Mama will adore you."

Outside the vehicle, Tempia walked a few strides behind Cory. Double blinking, she climbed six steps. Cory rang the doorbell ... but he lived there. Where was his key? A visitor at her parents' house, she never rang the doorbell. Tempia retained a key to each lock.

"Um ... don't you have a door key? Do you always ring the doorbell?"

"I do have a key, but I rarely use it up here. Normally, I enter the house through the basement door and come up the lower-level staircase. My folks might suffer culture shock if I walked through the front door unannounced."

114

Tempia's eyebrows rose. "Seriously? They would be shocked if you used a house key on the front door?"

"Just joking. The elder Sanders are laidback where I'm concerned."

The door opened, and a medium-height woman stood in the doorway. Her dancing light-brown eyes softened her pleasant features and made Tempia smile. A small salt-and-pepper afro emphasized her heart-shaped face. Crinkly skin around her eyes and mouth indicated the lady laughed a lot. Tempia almost performed a victory dance; two years ago, she had chosen the correct couple. Cory was his mom's spitting image. Her sincere gaze instilled trust and conveyed good humor.

"Mama, meet Tempia Wade. Tempia, this is my mother, Lillie." Cory placed an arm around Tempia.

She stepped forward once he squeezed her shoulder. "Hello, Mrs. Sanders. Thank you for accepting me as your Sunday dinner guest."

Lillie shook Tempia's outstretched hand. "The pleasure is ours. Tim and I heard our son's mystery-lady tale two years ago."

Tempia blushed all over. "On Friday, I found out Cory had first seen me at Community Ministries."

"I remember the day well," his mother said. "He arrived home and gave the family a glowing report during dinner. He called you his 'mystery lady.'"

"I wish Cory had truly met me prior to Rob's get-together," Tempia replied.

"Later is much better than not ever," Lillie said. "Lester and Chrissy Pearson have given you paragon status. All commitments to their ministry are appreciated."

Tempia included Cory in her smile. "I enjoy helping however I can."

Lillie smiled. "Dinner is piping hot, but let Tempia meet the family first." His mother retreated down the hallway, disappearing around a corner.

Tempia brushed a hand across her forehead. "Your mother is a blessing. I feel welcomed."

Cory winked his approval. "There's no need to be nervous. Let's go find the family in the living room."

Tempia followed behind him, deep in thought. She felt like this would go well, with no land mines in their foreseeable future. At least she hoped so.

Chapter Thirteen

Together, the couple entered a spacious room. No one smiled or greeted Tempia. She sized up the occupants' cool reaction in a microsecond. A graying older man still dressed in church clothes lounged on a recliner. With his hands linked above his nose, Mr. Sanders studied his guest. A younger woman with cornrows sat on the sofa beside a mustached man. The couple studied Tempia, glanced at each other, and then continued their examination.

What was the issue? Tempia's clothes should fit right in. Cory's sister was casually dressed in blue jeans with side zippers that adorned each leg. A lavender tank top, white utility vest, and open-toed sandals completed the ensemble. *Layers. We dress alike. No wonder Cory had made his "chic, classic look" remark.* The woman's husband wore a multicolored jogging outfit and running shoes. He appeared to be six inches taller than his wife.

Tempia thanked God that her preferred dress style fit the occasion. Her body relaxed until she noted the prolonged silence. Tempia interpreted the unspoken greeting. Cory's father, sister, and brother-in-law knew about her marriage and divorce. Though so did Cory's mother, and she was kindness personified. How much information had been released? The hair on the back of her neck raised. She shuffled on her feet, bumping into Cory.

Cory draped an arm around her shoulder. "A special friend is our dinner guest. Everyone, meet Tempia Wade. My 'mystery lady' is paying a visit."

Two girls playing a card game they obviously enjoyed looked up. Giant cards, the size of a small paperback, were stuffed into their tiny hands. The girls dropped the cards onto the carpet.

"Uncle Cory! Uncle Cory!" the girls screeched.

The two girls and a younger one raced across the space, wrapping their arms around their uncle's legs. Cory stooped and picked up the youngest child.

He winked at Tempia again. "Since the kids usually ignore me, they must expect an introduction."

"We do, Uncle Cory," the oldest girl said. "Hurry so we can all play."

"This lovely lady is Tempia Wade. Tempia, these are my adorable nieces. The oldest is Mali, this is Sophia, and Bella is the youngest girl. The little stinker toddling our way is Andre."

The older two girls giggled and covered their mouths with tiny hands.

Thank God more than one person didn't oppose her visit. No adult in the room had pretended an approachability they apparently didn't feel. Only the children seemed zealous about engaging their uncle's friend.

Tempia quietly cleared her throat. "Hello, everyone," she spoke to the room at large. She then focused on the children. "I was checking out your gigantic card deck. I haven't seen anything like it. What game were you playing?"

"War," Sophia replied, twiddling her thumbs.

"Do you want to play a game?" Mali asked.

"Sure do," Tempia said, laughing.

"Perhaps after dinner," Cory said. He leaned closer, then acknowledged the adults. "I flubbed the introduction with my 'mystery lady' remark. Tempia, meet my father, Tim Sanders. My sister, Cathy. The tall dude is my brother-in-law, Eric."

Tim lowered his hands onto the armrest. "Welcome to our home, young lady. Cory told us this morning he had invited a dinner guest."

Tempia hadn't considered that Cory had sprung the news on his parents just today. No wonder the air was chilly, even though the cook had voiced a natural greeting. Tempia cleared her throat again, striving to rebuild her waning confidence. "Glad I'm here. The delicious-smelling food is making my stomach growl."

"My wife is a fantastic cook," Tim said.

"I concur," Eric added. "I never eat breakfast or lunch on Sundays."

Tempia glanced downward when Andre tapped her knee and lifted his hands.

She immediately cradled the toddler in her arms. Her gaze then lingered on each attentive child.

"My younger brothers would love you guys and your colossal card deck. What other card games do you play?"

"Uh ... Go Fish. And I can almost play Crazy Eights," Sophia said.

Mali clapped her hands together. "Can we see your brothers and go outside and play?"

"Tempia's brothers aren't here right now and are almost babysitting age. They won't become future playmates." Cory lowered Bella to the floor and placed Andre on the carpet beside his sisters.

Tempia scanned their disappointed faces and engineered an appropriate substitute. "I owe my brothers a matinee movie and time at the arcade. We're going this Saturday."

Mali clapped her hands together. "We like watching movies and playing games. Don't we, Soph?"

"Uh-huh," Sophia said. "Everyone does but Andre. He cries a lot."

"I don't cry, and I can play games too," Bella chimed in.

"But you talk through movies," her oldest sister reminded.

"And can only play hide-and-seek," Sophia piped in.

The sisters' lively conversation made Tempia laugh. "That all sounds like the best recipe for family fun. You all can come too."

"Yay!" the girls shrieked together.

Their glee pulled at Tempia's heartstrings. "We can watch a family-friendly movie everyone should enjoy. The more the merrier, as they say."

She beamed at the children until the deafening quiet garnered her attention. Cathy resembled an angry cartoon character. Eric's firm arm kept her seated.

Tempia immediately realized her overreach. *I blew it big time. Of course I should've asked the parents' permission first. I need to apologize.*

She braced herself against hurt feelings. "Cathy—"

"Our children can't accept invitations Eric and I don't first approve," Cathy interrupted. "If there's a next time, consult us first."

Tempia felt Cory's body stiffen. She grabbed onto his hand to keep him quiet. Her lips quivered as she smiled at Cory's sister. "Please excuse the gaffe. My offhand invitation missed the mark by miles. I understand parental protocol better than my offer indicated."

Cathy's brisk nod suggested Tempia's swift agreement had de-escalated the conflict.

Eric studied Tempia's woebegone face. His arm lifted off his wife's shoulder. "I welcome our children's invitation wholeheartedly."

"So did the kids," Cory replied. "Thanks, Eric."

"Cathy and I haven't eaten a peaceful meal in ages. Constant stimulation can wear the nerves thin. Right, Cat?" Eric rose, offering a hand to his glaring wife.

Cathy took his hand, but her lips remained soundless.

Eric focused on his brother-in-law. "If you can help manage this brood, Cathy and I will eat a couple's lunch this Saturday."

Cory studied his sister through half-closed eyes. "I'd be glad to take them out with Tempia. Enjoy a childfree Saturday on us."

"We accept," Eric agreed. "Andre might spend the day with my parents. I'll drop off the girls here around ten."

Cathy's gaze flicked over Tempia, seemingly declining the peace offering. She and her daughters left the room. Eric secured Andre on his shoulder, and they joined the exit parade.

Tim stopped the living room exodus beside the couple. "This household appreciates all kind gestures. The children and I thank you. Now, dinner is ready. Lillie began cooking our meal early this morning. Hope you're hungry."

Tempia flashed a wide grin. "Thank you, Mr. Sanders. I ate only fruit salad for breakfast this morning, so I'm ready to eat."

"Lillie prepared a feast. She even baked my favorite dessert yesterday."

"Pound cake and hot pudding sauce," Cory said. "Mother bakes the world's lightest pound cake."

Tim's head bobbed in agreement. Like his wife had done in the foyer, he unabashedly studied Tempia, then he exited the room.

Tempia hung her head. "I received a D grade in less than ten minutes. Hope my score improves during dinner."

For the first time since the couple met, Cory sighed. "My sister is a better person than the version you just met. My family will jump aboard the Tempia Wade train before you leave."

Cory knew his sister better than Tempia did, so she'd have to believe him. Two thoughts dominated her present mindset: Cathy resented her husband's intervention, and Mr. Sanders now appeared a shade friendlier than he had at first. He seemed to disapprove of his daughter's rude behavior. Tempia would accept whatever crumbs Cory's father offered. Besides, he couldn't be a complete pariah considering the courteous lady he'd married. Despite Mr. Sanders's noticeable misgivings, he had at least belatedly welcomed her into his home.

Tempia accepted Cory's prediction with a few reservations. "I trust your word. You understand your family dynamics better than I do." She smiled.

His eyes narrowed. "About Cathy ... look, it's unsettling seeing another person bullied on my behalf."

Cathy had dismissed her on sight. Her reaction was senseless, unless ...

Tempia eyed the man awaiting her reply. "Did you tell her about my marriage and divorce?"

"My personal business remains private unless the person has the right to know. Cathy did not have that right."

119

"Could Rob have told her?"

"Rob told Cathy and Eric after church today that you and I were dating. She's aware you were my mystery lady, met me and Quince at his party, and then married and divorced Quince within eleven months."

What else was there to say? Tempia hooked her fingers on Cory's crooked elbow. She would speak if addressed and not a single word more. Tempia matched Cory's stride down the hallway. "Let your words be few" repeated nonstop in her mind.

* * *

Inside the dining room, the girls occupied a small green-and-yellow table and chair set. Andre's highchair was situated between his parents at the main table.

Loads of appetizing food was spread across the space. Fried onions and tomatoes garnished a platter filled with cube steak. Smothered garlic-and-sage chicken took up a round dish. Collard greens, turnip bottoms, roasted spring vegetables, and candied sweet potatoes piled up in several serving bowls. Cornbread patties and homemade rolls topped colorful wicker baskets. Tempia prayed her stomach wouldn't demonstrate its huge admiration.

Once Cory and Tempia took their seats, Tim's head bowed in prayer. "Thank you, Father. Today we welcome an honored guest for Sunday dinner. Please bless our food, our day, and our lives each day. Keep us obedient to Your will."

The short prayer enthused Tempia's heart. She joined everyone's "Amen," beamed a cheerful smile, and piled a full course onto her plate. Moments later, her stomach flip-flopped while listening to Cathy's diatribe. In full drama mode, Cory's sister recounted Tempia's invitation to the movie and arcade. "The invite materialized out of nowhere," she told her mother, winding down. "It was a nice gesture and all that, but Eric and I are particular about which movies our children watch."

"Tempia surely possesses that same strict standard regarding her younger brothers," Lillie stated in a quiet voice. "She will choose an age-appropriate movie that will satisfy her parents and you guys."

"Tempia cared for Curt and Noah years before Mali was even born," Cory added. "I have no doubt she will be more than on top of what the children require—and your preferences. Or did you miss her saying she would pick a family-friendly movie everyone should enjoy?"

Tim's glass clanged onto the table. His gaze pinpointed both his son and daughter. "Rain is in the forecast. We haven't experienced a real soaker in three weeks."

Then the tactful hostess redirected their conversation to neutral topics. Mrs. Sanders's steel backbone and jovial determination ensured the dinner dialogue embodied laughter and goodwill. She appeared vested in her guest eating a stress-free meal.

* * *

Two hours later, Cory escorted Tempia on a basement home tour. The bottom level had the same livable square footage as the top floor. The upstairs layout had been reversed downstairs and almost replicated. The eat-in kitchen faced the street, included a center island, and featured a walk-in pantry. The laundry room was situated next door. Wide windows dominated half of the walls in each bedroom. A full-size shower completed the en suite master bathroom. The Jack-and-Jill bathroom, separating two guest bedrooms, could be accessed from the hallway. Two ten-gallon aquariums occupied an alcove in between the kitchen and living room. The living room's back wall featured French doors that led to the patio and deck.

The midcentury décor gave a homey vibe that Tempia adored. Her mind envisioned her keepsakes occupying strategic areas around the place. Her mother's paintings would enhance the comfortable atmosphere. Those masterpieces had clashed with Quince's ultra-modern interior design. The space perfectly fit a place Tempia could call home.

Pleased that she and Cory enjoyed a similar decorating taste, she sank onto the recliner sofa.

Cory sat beside her, stretching out his legs. "You seem tired. Did the girls deplete your energy playing war?"

"Not really. Although I did forget it is an exceptionally long game." Shifting position, she slid closer to Cory. "How do the girls manipulate such large cards in their tiny hands? I felt like an outright klutz."

"They play cards every day, so they've had some practice." He picked up her hand and lightly squeezed each finger. "How did you like my family? I trust my sister's poor performance didn't put you off."

Her gaze averted, Tempia placed her hand on his hand and leaned against the cushion. She had spent an enlightening day among outstanding people. Maybe Cathy Robertson would grow on her in time. To her credit, his sister did behave herself once her parents' strong will shut her down.

"My heart trembled in the living room. I feared getting tongue-tied and fumbling my regrets."

"You're a real trooper for hanging in there. You handled the situation better than I would have. Her boorish attitude begged retribution."

"I didn't have many options, and I made the initial blunder. Thank God Eric took charge." She hesitated. What else could she say without slamming Cory's sister? The woman's outrage escalated beyond Tempia's poor judgment. Tempia prayed for limited confrontations. "Let's change the subject. Your mother made a splendid meal. It was like eating a family Christmas dinner."

Leaning toward Tempia, Cory caressed her fingers in his right hand. "Mama cooked like she does on grand occasions, which must have meant your visit ranked high. Four desserts wouldn't have surprised me."

Double wow. High praise from a man who kept his feelings under wraps. She closed her eyes a moment to abate joy-filled tears. "Each treat would've tasted scrumptious if she had." Super comfy, she drew her legs underneath her body on the couch. "I like your family, Cory. Your mother's kindness soothes hurt feelings."

"Mother has hound-dog instincts where unease is concerned. She sniffs out potential trouble areas. My dad only interferes if someone crosses his predetermined line. And then ... well, the table shook when he slammed down his glass. Thank God it didn't break."

Cory had come to Tempia's defense when his sister misbehaved. Her lips curved into a gentle grin. "Please accept my belated thanks. Your help saved me today." Tempia recalled his usual swift support. "It felt like old times, although the stakes were lower."

"I will support you however I can. Consider me your on-call personal ally."

Tempia liked the word "protector" better. "Do not downplay your kind deeds. You bailed me out again. And because of doing so with your sister, we get to spend Saturday afternoon together."

A light deepened in his glowing eyes. "We can hang out all day if we come back here for a while after the arcade." Cory pointed toward the French doors. "We can grill dinner outside. Four kids live in one of the duplexes next door. The oldest two are around your brothers' ages. The boys can swim in the neighbor's pool. I'll drop my non-swimming nieces off at their house after the arcade. What do you think?"

Did extending their upcoming Saturday together indicate how much he enjoyed Tempia's company and wanted to befriend her brothers? She thought of her ex's sad neglect throughout their marriage. Cory had won the unofficial round once again. "I love the idea and so will my brothers. Should we also provide Gabby and Rob with a domino rematch? They might end up buying us dinner for two months straight."

"I think that might be a bit much for one day, especially with having the kids all day." Cory's sweet kiss silenced Tempia's reply. Raising his head, he stroked her cheek. "What does your upcoming schedule look like?"

The momentum kept increasing for the couple. Tempia hugged Cory's neck and kissed his cheek. "My evenings are free until next Thursday. My brothers and I are eating Gammy's scrumptious homemade pizza. She invited us this morning after church."

"And Gammy is?"

"My mother's mother."

"A generous lady. Does all your extended family attend the same church as you? I chose the same church as the Pearsons, which isn't the one my parents attend."

"Only the Millers, my mother's family, attend our church. My father left our membership there so my mother's family and I could feel connected." Sam had always sought to lessen his daughter's growing pains over losing her mother. Plus, he didn't propose marriage to Blanche until she and Tempia had secured a tight bond. Her father possessed keen insight regarding people in his daughter's sphere. One day he would welcome Tempia having Cory in her life. "Dad, Mom, my grandparents, and my brothers went to Hot Wok for lunch after church."

"Did coming here cost you a free lunch?"

Tempia laughed. "I'd rather eat a free meal with you, though I do enjoy seeing them whenever possible."

"So, what is your work life like?"

"I work seven to four, Monday through Friday, with an hour-long lunch at noon. And yours? Describe a typical workday."

"A normal day begins at eight and ends by five. I take a lunch break after my last morning job and work weekends on established customers' emergencies. Do you and your friends have daily or weekly routines?"

Tempia directed her gaze across the room. She hated disclosing her social life. Or lack thereof. Loneliness filled her nonworking hours. "I lost friendships after dating Quince, though my closest buddies stayed in touch. They're all married and don't have much time to hang out. I'm not a homebody, but I don't go out much."

Cory's eyebrows wrinkled. A quizzical gaze observed her facial expression. "Why did dating Quince cut off everyone but your closest pals? I assume the friendship breach began on your end."

"I hate to admit it, but yes. Quince demanded my complete concentration. No one I knew liked him. My friends since junior high, Mia and Jasmine, hung in there like Gabby did. Quince's snide remarks made his house off limits, though Gabby came and brought your cousin along on each visit. Quince avoided the living room until they left."

"He probably reflected on the beatdowns Rob dealt him in high school."

Tempia's mouth hung open. "Rob and Quince got into fistfights? Neither one ever hinted at physical altercations."

"The most severe occurred in our junior year. Only God knows why Quince attended Rob's get-together. Or why my cousin ignored Quince being there. The pool hall could have been our last contact until the following year."

She was still somewhat clueless about how her ex-husband ticked. His decisions had defied all reason. Perhaps the man sitting beside her had greater insight. "Why do you suppose he tagged along to the party?"

"Who knows. It was a bizarre day in every respect." He leaned closer until their shoulders touched. "Let's hang around here a while longer."

Tempia's feet tapped the floor in a drumming beat. "Your backyard has some great entertainment options. I spotted a basketball goal and a volleyball net. You entertain often?"

"Quite a bit, yet most evenings are spent relaxing on the deck alone."

"I haven't played volleyball since high school. May I beat you in a quick game? And then, after your defeat, may I curl up in your arms and sleep through a good movie?"

"And if you lose?" Cory asked.

"You pick the movie *if* the impossible occurs."

Cory chuckled. "Sounds like a master plan in all respects. I do have one request. I'd like to invite my friends from Rob's games party over here to meet you sometime soon. We can grill burgers and lounge outside. Of course I'd include Gabby and Rob."

Tempia's heart sank. Cory's question was unexpected. She would eventually see those folks anyway but would rather wait until she and Cory had dated for a while. "Will you let me get used to the idea first? I don't know how they will react to me."

"I guarantee everyone will respond courteously. They will probably reach out once told we are dating."

"I'm not totally against the idea, but I need some time to pump myself up for it."

If Cory was disappointed, he hid his displeasure well. Tempia didn't know how to continue the conversation without giving in. Her lips pursed into a thin line, waiting for him to speak.

Popping his knuckles, Cory grinned. "While you're deciding on the proper timing, also think about adding in those friends you let go when you married Quince."

His last suggestion was more palatable than the first request had been. Tempia realized just how much she'd missed those friends.

"Cory, I consider your suggestions extremely important. I'll work on my embarrassment and hard feelings."

"What more could I ask for in light of the situation? Ready?"

Cory held out his hand. Once Tempia placed her hand in his, the couple rose together and headed outside arm in arm.

Instead of peppering the ball over the net in a cooperatively scored game, Tempia insisted on playing a traditional volleyball set. Soon, Cory had her running full court. She fumed when he spiked another ball over the net. His height advantage neutralized her speed.

"That was an unfair spike. I'm standing here. Why spike the ball over there?"

"It's called winning. I'm supporting your boast. You can't beat me if I let you win."

Before Tempia could answer, a lightning bolt pierced the sky, followed by thunderclaps. The sudden downpour soaked the couple on their sprint toward the house.

Inside the living room, Tempia pulled wet, sticky clothes away from her skin. "I can't believe we got soaked in less than two minutes."

"Hold on." Cory disappeared inside his bedroom. On his return, he handed Tempia a dark oversized T-shirt, matching socks, and a white robe.

"Change in the bathroom. Dry towels are in the linen closet."

"Thanks, Cory. Put your wet things on the kitchen island. I'll drop our clothes in the dryer once I'm done."

Cory was sitting on the couch when Tempia left the bathroom. She put their clothes in the dryer. "Will your parents mind us raiding the kitchen while I'm dressed in a T-shirt and robe?"

"No, ma'am. They'll surmise we got soaked outside."

The couple snuck upstairs and grabbed Lillie's scrumptious pound cake off the counter. They heated the pudding sauce for fifteen seconds in the microwave.

"Stop looking over your shoulder. You have on more clothes now than you wore when you first arrived. Your body is respectfully covered."

"It feels weird wearing your stuff in your parents' kitchen. Now ... if we were married."

She laughed when Cory escorted her downstairs.

Once the couple sat on the couch, Cory passed Tempia the remote control. "Did you reach your threshold for tearjerker movies last week?"

Tempia passed the remote control to Cory, then stretched her legs on the recliner sofa, reflecting on dating Cory and her wasted marriage. The oddly symmetrical occurrences in her Quince and Cory datelines proved uncanny. Those parallel circumstances made comparisons between the men an inevitable consequence.

Tempia had met Quince on a Saturday. The couple ate dinner and took in a movie on Sunday and went window shopping Monday after work. Cory had dropped by her house last Friday. He and Tempia ate dinner at Primers and visited Gabby and Rob on Saturday. Today, the couple ate their Sunday dinner with his family. She had seen both men for three consecutive days. Whereas she and Quince had spent alone time, she and Cory shared a date plus visited their families and friends.

Impromptu contrasts between the men's mannerisms and responses surfaced. Quince's zealous courtship had demanded Tempia's equal participation. Cory's low-key approach kept the couple on a steady pace. Quince pursued her like an ardent suitor in love. Cory teased her as a special friend he wanted to know better.

The contrasting styles altered her dating perspective. What constituted genuine wooing? Compatibility, mutual liking, and sheer determination might improve her and Cory's relationship. Her ex's rapt regard had fed insecurities that manipulated her vulnerabilities, whereas Cory's outstretched arms sought closeness while he guarded their personal space. Nonetheless, each tremendous step forward buoyed her "we are a dynamic couple" spirit.

For no apparent reason, Cory glanced her way. A satisfied gleam lit his eyes. Tempia quelled her comparisons and curled up on his chest. She laughed outright during the first scene.

* * *

An hour later, Cory opened the outside basement door, beckoning Tempia outside.

She hung back. She wanted to thank his parents for their kindness in person. The dinner invitation had fulfilled her wildest ambitions.

"Your parents deserve a personal thank you. May I go upstairs and say goodbye?"

Cory's eyes gleamed in the dim lighting. "Sure thing. Keep showing my family the real you."

Chapter Fourteen

On the main level, a light shone inside the living room. While Tempia and Cory waited to be acknowledged, Tempia studied the couple watching television. Cory's character was molded by these people.

Cory mouthed the words, "The floor is yours."

Tempia believed striking the right tone mattered. She sought the proper conversation starter. A simple thank you would best serve her purpose. "Mr. and Mrs. Sanders, I enjoyed the company and home-cooked meal. The collard greens and cornbread are the best I've eaten. Dessert was fantastic."

"A pure labor of love," his mother said. "Thanks for joining us for dinner, Tempia."

What a heart-tugging reply. Tempia's lips trembled. "Cory and I came back to have another helping of your fluffy pound cake and special pudding. No wonder Mr. Sanders said it was his favorite dessert. May I have the recipes?"

Lillie nodded. "Cory will deliver recipe cards this Saturday. And Tempia, it's been so nice that Tim and I can finally match your name and face. Chrissy and Lester will hear we met you."

Mr. Sanders spoke through bridged fingers. "How well do you know the Pearsons?"

Tempia's smile faded. Were the Pearsons aware that Cory knew her ex-husband? Did they have her marriage and divorce details? She'd only disclosed she was getting married and asked for prayers during her divorce.

"We discuss outreach opportunities the last Saturday of each month. Have they mentioned me in conversation?"

"They brag on the wonderful young lady who backs their ministry efforts," Lillie said.

"We haven't discussed you with our friends. Lil and I keep personal business private," Tim added. "It's anyone's guess where relationships might lead. Two years ago, my nephew mentioned you to Lillie and me."

Optimism fled Tempia's soul. Some anonymous obstacle stymied Mr. Sanders from sanctioning his son dating her. Cathy hated the idea as well. What message had Rob conveyed?

Cory took Tempia's elbow between his thumb and finger. "I will tell the Pearsons we're dating. Mama, Dad, see you in a few."

"Tempia, please join our Sunday dinners whenever you like," Lillie said. "It's been a real pleasure meeting you."

"I bet this young lady enjoys a close-knit family who often eat Sunday meals together, so I imagine we won't see her every week," her husband said. Tim turned to Tempia. "The grandchildren can't stop talking about this Saturday. Goodnight, Tempia."

Her lips trembled through her smile. "Goodnight. I had a delightful visit."

She silently walked beside Cory as he led her down the hallway. How could she pose questions without offending him? Fatigue hampered her thought process.

The seldom-used key appeared in Cory's hand. Tempia stood aside and watched him lock the front door until her trembling hand wiped the lips she licked. "What's the verdict? It's evident your mother and father heard how Rob's party ended."

Cory clasped Tempia's hand and led her down the steps. "Verdict regarding which event? We've shared many."

"Your parents know I believed Quince's lies. Have I now redeemed myself in your folks' estimation?"

Cory opened the passenger door and stepped aside. "Pessimism doesn't serve a credible purpose in our relationship. My parents know less than you may imagine."

"Your parents, sister, and brother-in-law seem aware I chose Quince and not you."

"You were coerced into that decision. Manipulation set up a stronghold your ex used against you."

Tempia pulled on each finger until Cory entered the vehicle. "What exactly has your family heard about me?"

Cory started the engine and steered the vehicle down the road. "On Friday, my parents learned you believed the big lie and dated Quince."

"And? What else have they been told?"

"That Quince mistreated you and I assisted where I could. Also, your divorce was final last year. Other than those small tidbits ..."

Which meant they had full knowledge. They had heard everything possible to hear. His family probably thought her an idiot. Cathy's patronizing attitude now made more sense. Tempia wouldn't have allowed an imbecile around her children either.

Her rapid blinking held back tears. "Small tidbits, huh? More like full details. What else is left, Cory?" Her hand raised, squelching his response. "How much information do the Pearsons know?"

"Only what you told them. Remember, Miss Chrissy and Mr. Lester don't know we've met. Just now my father disowned spreading gossip."

"Are you certain no one has mentioned my name to either Pearson?"

"That much I can guarantee. Rob attends a different church, so he didn't tell them like he over shared with Cathy and Eric."

"Oh, please. This situation isn't funny, Cory."

"The Pearsons don't know we are acquainted. Look ... this morning, Cathy and Eric were told who you are, how we met, and that you had married and divorced Quince. Rob is discreet. His only aim was to get us over the hump. Lighten up. All is good," he said when Tempia moaned. "My parents are my go-to sounding boards. Pictures become clearer after hearing their often-contrasting beliefs."

Maybe his mother did like her. But did his father? Oh, boy. "Do their opinions often vary from each other?"

"Sometimes they do. They analyze their separate viewpoints and reach consensus."

"If you say so," Tempia replied.

Overall, Sunday dinner had culminated into a fun-filled experience. She'd been able to confirm aspects of Cory's character. More carefree than she had suspected, he possessed a supreme determination to do the right thing—Cory Sanders style.

And that might handicap her desired outcome concerning the couple's future. Marriage. Children. Mutual respect and everlasting love. No doubt he liked and appreciated her charitable nature, but neither like nor appreciation foretold he would declare "I do" this year.

Would Cory's slow quest reach her coveted destination? A long silent sigh relaxed her entire body.

Cory secured a parking spot by the tennis court and followed Tempia inside her apartment. Unlike last night, she felt more secure in their relationship, yet their vital connection might perish if his father didn't accept her. She faced the man leaning on her closed front door. His relaxed posture denoted contentment, while the bland expression disguised his thoughts. An intense gaze beckoned her closer. Tempia could lose herself in those compassion-filled eyes.

Talk, Cory. Give me feedback, please. Critique our day so I can skip assumptions. "I enjoyed meeting your family," she offered when he remained quiet. Tempia continued when he grinned. "Hope today's family meal won't be my last one."

A frown replaced the grin in an instant. "No way that will happen. Mama offered you an open invitation."

"Which your father didn't second. It's okay. Mr. Sanders smiled when he changed subjects."

"No one can revoke another person's goodwill. Father paid you a humongous compliment." Cory chuckled.

Tempia's lips quirked. "All right. Let's hear it. The spin had better be sound."

"Spin? You've relegated my qualified insight into my father's personality as truth slanting?"

"Qualified insight, huh? You are full of yourself today. I'll play along with your pretense. You might comprehend why your father does whatever it is he does."

Cory wiped moisture off his eyelids. "Quick on the repartee, Ms. Wade. A new conversation technique perhaps?"

At least she had grown a spine in Cory's view. Some progress beat existing in a standstill state or regressing. "Ahem. An explanation would make me sleep better." She tapped her foot on the floor. "Still waiting. Make it good enough to pass the 'keep Tempia from having hurt feelings' test."

Compassion replaced the dancing light in his eyes. His hands clasped her fingers. "Father acknowledged that you value family interaction on its highest level. He realizes the Wade family is no different than his own family."

I truly admire Cory's empathetic nature. Does his helping spirit fill in potholes for every person he meets? Our time together will uncover hidden truths. "Good start," she whispered.

"How about Dad noticing you gave up a free Saturday to bless your brothers—and my nieces who require greater care?"

Tempia blew on her fist then rubbed her knuckles upon her chest. "Since Andre isn't coming Saturday, we won't have toddler limitations. The wearisome part will be Curt and Noah's constant begging for treats I won't buy."

Curiosity dotted Cory's features. "No eating popcorn at the movies or snacking on cotton candy at the arcade?"

"Uh-uh. No treats from me. A matinee movie and limited game play at Scooters will cost $50. A piece. My brothers receive an allowance each Friday. They can eat snacks on their own dimes. Of course, I will purchase your nieces' treats."

"The girls' treats, movie, and game expenses are on me. I will spot your brothers' treats as compensation for interrupting their movie night last Friday."

Tempia's thinned lips turned downward. "No way. Those two self-centered boys should learn to appreciate what they get. They love spending their sister's money."

"Since Curt and Noah are so close to you, I'm stepping up to the plate. Also, I'd like to be included in the Wade siblings' monthly weekend retreats. Let your brothers see good male manners in action."

Tempia bit down hard. Could dating Cory affect her brothers in any negative fashion? Especially if her and Cory's relationship doesn't make the marriage mark? She preferred keeping impressionable boys away from distorted dating notions and actions. Seeing her disastrous marriage proved enough to last Curt and Noah throughout their lifetime. Movies and the arcade this Saturday. A future walk and picnic on Riverfront Trail. And now mention of the weekends at her place. Could his plans be too much, too soon for Curt and Noah? Tempia must limit their involvement for now. An engagement ring would lengthen the leash.

"My brothers will like and respect you like their sister does. However, they've already lived through my mess up regarding Quince. I won't warp their dating concepts any further."

"I disagree with your commendable viewpoint. Dating is a healthy part of the maturing process. Your bad treatment will teach your brothers to respect and honor women. Our relationship will prove beneficial either way, because we will always remain at least good friends."

It wasn't a roaring endorsement, but it was reasonable. "Translation: You and I will remain friends whether we marry or not."

Cory leaned closer. "Count on longevity in our relationship. I believe we will both welcome the same result."

Tempia desired much more than Cory's friendship. Yet having no communication from him at all would be unbearable. "I'm thankful you've intertwined permanency and me together. I don't ever want our friendship dissolved." She took a deep breath, releasing air in spurts. "So, here's a big question. Have we reached boyfriend and girlfriend status?"

He let out a robust laugh. She didn't know whether to feel offended or sad.

"Lady," he finally said after several speaking attempts, "I won't date other women as long as I am dating you." Cory leaned in and gave Tempia a sweet and satisfying goodnight kiss. His muscular frame was reassuringly close.

Raising his head, Cory stared into her eyes. "Goodnight, my first and only girlfriend. Keep in touch." He gave a light wave, exited the apartment, and closed the door behind him.

Keep in touch? That was an odd way to end their conversation when they were in a relationship. Tempia shrugged off the thought and flashed a wide grin. Satisfied, she sat cross-legged on the love seat. First and only girlfriend? How could an exceedingly handsome, hardworking, and fun-loving man reach twenty-eight and never have had a steady girlfriend? Gabby had contended he had sporadically brought dates to family events. She and Rob had double-dated with Cory and various women on a few occasions. But she'd admitted those occurrences happened more than two years ago. Even then, he had never brought the same woman around twice.

Her mind switched from his past dating habits to their present commitment. What takeaways underlined her and Cory's second date? Their yesterday was marvelous, but their most recent outing held an extra-special meaning. Today she had met the people closest to his heart. Visiting his home showcased how Cory relaxed when he was on his own. His peaceful and stable inner sanctum helped produce a well-grounded man.

On the drive to Primers, she had discovered he was a natural-born teaser. She had already known he was a skilled troubleshooter. After those realizations, she had wondered what unidentified characteristic balanced out both sides. Today, the answer had dropped into her lap. Solid family values undoubtedly produced his clearheaded perspective when other people's lives became affected.

Another remarkable exchange had occurred last night. While Tempia and Gabby portioned dessert in the kitchen, Gabby launched an unpredicted complaint against her husband's cousin: "Like everyone, Cory has plenty of annoying faults."

Thus far, Tempia hadn't noticed any worrisome behavior that might doom the couple's restart. With that reassurance, she floated into the bathroom, smiling at her reflection in the mirror. Her cell phone pealed. She scuttled across the floor in a flash to grab it out of her purse on the counter. "Hi, Gabby. Just got home. I'm happy Cory invited me. Mrs. Sanders cooked a Christmas feast."

"That's great, but what about his family?"

"Cory's mother made initial greetings easy. His mom is a gracious hostess. And Mr. Sanders. Hmm … maybe I will grow on Cory's father. The potential is there. Eric was reserved and noncommittal. As for Cathy … well … the children liked me." Tempia relayed her living-room misstep. "I messed up. But the punishment surpassed the crime."

"Cathy and I had a debate about you this morning," Gabby said. "Rob filled her in on your being Cory's mystery lady and my best friend. I like Cathy, but she can't get past her baby brother being overlooked. She's irked you chose a different man than Cory."

"Well, I can't undo what's been done."

"Let her work through it all. Rob believes she will."

"Cathy must be okay if you still like her after an intense challenge. I'm banking on our tendency to like the same people."

"I feel you and hear you. Hang in there, Temp. Gotta go."

"Thank you. Life is looking up."

Tempia moved the cell phone aside. "A night of sound sleep is a sure bet. Thanks, God."

* * *

On his drive home, Cory revisited a recurring idea. While Tempia critiqued her job during their Primers dinner, he had planned a surprise workplace lunch. He must find a nearby restaurant and provide an intimate midday meal.

Cory crept his vehicle into his neighborhood, scouting for a vacant parking space near his house. Their partying neighbor down the road had most of the parking taken by party guests.

A thought seized his mind while walking the one-and-a-half blocks home. He should invest in a carport built in the backyard. More than adequate space existed off the alleyway. Four parking slots could be constructed and maintain restful aesthetics. In the end, a peaceful outside ambiance remained his ultimate goal. He increased his speed, chuckling. Four. He had unconsciously added an additional parking spot beyond the three his family needed.

Upon reaching the house, he jogged up the porch steps. Lights shining through the living room window signaled his parents were still awake. Cory rang the doorbell, unlocked the door, and entered the house, twirling keys on his finger. Measured steps girded his resolve against a possible confrontation. He peered into the living room. His parents were watching an old comedy show.

Tim spotted his son the moment Cory stepped inside the room. "Lenny called. Your aunt had just returned home from visiting your great-grandmother."

Cory froze midstep. He hadn't experienced this sudden sinking feeling since his great-grandfather passed away last year. Braced against another sorrowful death, he eyed his father.

"Barbara said the air conditioner stopped working before she left Granny's house tonight."

"Whew! It is bad news, but better than what I had thought you were going to say."

"If Jake correctly assessed the malfunction, Granny needs a new condenser," Tim said. "We're replacing the HVAC system and air ducts tomorrow. We can't piecemeal the upgrades. Making those mechanical repairs is essential."

Oh boy, here we go. Tomorrow will be an all-day job. The work assignment would sorely test his patience. His loveable great-grandmother was a handful. "In a house Granny's size, replacing air ducts is a two-day job. Does Granny know we're working at her house all day? She hates work zones and any noise she doesn't create herself."

"The final decision was made too late to wake her up."

Cory chuckled. "Gotcha. But you are aware Granny will make us leave once she discovers why we're there?"

"Come on, son. She isn't that bad. But point taken," Tim said when his wife laughed. "Your grandfather will arrive early in the morning. Lenny will work alongside you and Jake. Father will keep his mother company while the job is being done."

"We would finisher sooner if Shawn lent a hand."

"You and Shawn pushed four job orders onto Monday's schedule. Dan, Shawn, Lance, and I will handle the add-ons, plus our regular orders. Everyone will work late tomorrow."

On his mental calendar, Cory revised his work schedule and scratched off Tempia's lunch surprise. His fortifying their relationship remained a major goal. Like Lillie, he agreed that budding relationships required dedication to the blossoms. His girlfriend was a garden worth tending.

Cory bypassed the settee and walked farther into the room. He sat in a wingback chair. "I'm glad you're still up. I wanted to touch base before the night ended."

Her keen gaze upon his face, Lillie muted the television volume.

"Go ahead," his father said.

He hoped his grin was charming his parents. "Please keep an open mind while Tempia and I date. Though vulnerable, she's made huge headway."

"How?"

His father's one-word question spurred Cory on. "Her lifestyle changed after meeting Quince. Her self-discovery is an undertaking I endorse." Cory massaged the bridge of his nose. "I will assist her where I can."

"Tempia is delightful," Lillie said. "Your young lady brightened up our meal. I like her, son."

"She's a good-hearted person who aims to please everyone she meets."

"Her willingness to try captivated you. I find that affable and caring individuals typically win you over. She's witty and winsome ..." Lillie hesitated.

Cory chuckled. "And ..."

"Her timid conversational approach shouts that she lacks confidence. Was she self-assured in the past?"

"She is naturally shy around new people. I believe Tempia asserted herself more in the past. She was inquisitive and super friendly when she and her brothers first arrived at Community Ministries. Quince undermined any self-confidence she may have had."

"Humph," his mother said. "I hate emotional abuse and mistreatment. That young man had better ask the Father for forgiveness and address his troubled life and mental health. I pray Quince acts on your advice to seek professional help."

"Repentance works after salvation," Tim said. "If this discussion also concerns your sister, we addressed Cathy's behavior before she left."

"Her reprimanding any guest won't be tolerated nor repeated," his wife added.

"Will her cooperation extend beyond your house? How will she behave somewhere else?"

His parents nodded. Had they reached a consensus already? It usually took them several days. "Lil and I dealt with the problem," Tim said.

Cathy was made accountable for her actions. He hoped they'd read her the riot act. Rudeness deserved much more than a stern rebuke.

"Had the situation been reversed, she would have castigated me. How did the tyrant defend her actions?"

"Stop the name calling," his mother said. "Your sister mounted the usual defense. She was protecting her gullible younger brother's interest."

Cory looked away, laughing. "She had the gall to pin naivete onto me? Being a decent human being is a problem? Please ..."

"Old habits are addictive. Cathy believes Tempia is an emotional liability. She suggests you slow down the tempo."

"No, ma'am. She wants me to dump Tempia. Period."

"Cathy questioned why Tempia had been attracted to a man like Quince. That relationship is your sister's roadblock."

"Tempia was hoodwinked by a despicable person. Sadly, many people are conned by bad actors."

"Try seeing things from your sister's perspective," Lillie interjected. "You and Quince being polar opposites presents a problem Cathy won't gloss over."

"Meaning? Did Cathy elaborate?"

"She generally questioned how Tempia preferred Quince then transferred her allegiance to you."

"Without knowing the details your mother and I are aware of, Cathy made a reasonable observation," his father said. "Every person except Tempia's family and friends probably asks themselves the same question."

Cory rubbed his chin in slow motion. He couldn't refute his father's argument. "I doubt if even Tempia herself can answer it." Cory chuckled. "I'm happy she likes me."

"You're smitten enough to ignore the apparent problem? Didn't your mother and I raise you better?"

Cory understood his father's reasonable concern. "Dad, an unsavory man spotted an open door with Tempia, taking advantage of the security gap."

"Precisely. You and everyone else realized her husband took advantage of her. Did she ever voice concern about their relationship?"

Tempia never spoke one negative word against her husband to Cory—which earned her an indisputable point in her favor. "I learned Tempia is extremely loyal, even when perhaps she shouldn't be. She kept up a happy marriage facade until the end, even while crumbling inside."

His father grunted. "Either she is a foolish woman or unable to accept reality."

"How about she possessed a fierce fortitude to make her marriage work? Problems will plague everyone who marries. No one will receive a free pass in this life." Lillie focused on their son. "Let us get better acquainted with your lady friend."

"That's the master plan for everyone involved. The stakes are high in dating Tempia but fully worth the risks." He paused, passing his keys back and forth like a juggler. "Twelve years after going on my first date, I have a girlfriend."

Yet he knew full well that knowledge of the pitfalls didn't guarantee final acceptance for either Tempia or himself. Quince's suave courtship created a high bar Cory wouldn't surpass. His personality didn't include stalking prey. The couple must accept each other for who they are and not for who they desired each other to become. The more they learned about each other might torpedo their romance on both sides, but he deeply felt that either way, they'd each gain a lifelong friend.

Chapter Fifteen

On Monday morning, a peaceful Tempia sprang from the bed in one motion. Her first stop was the kitchen nook. She peered through her window, sipping peppermint tea. The entire world appeared brighter than ever for the woman traveling aboard properly connected trains. Debris-sprinkled tracks wouldn't impede her progress.

Minus the habitual doom-and-gloom fantasies, she delighted in her surroundings. When had the courtyard blossomed in such vivid color? African, French and signet marigolds bloomed in the garden bordering her building. Various colored shrubs and trees lined the tennis courts' walkway.

Her mouth gaped. She observed a hummingbird flying backward, hovering in midair above a feeder. The bird dipped his long needlelike beak into the nectar several times and flew away upside down. She observed the unusual flight pattern until the neighboring building blocked the distinguished bird's departure.

Dating a well-balanced man stripped cobwebs and prickly entanglements from her brain, allowing her to absorb the environment in all its glory. Tempia drained her tea and set the rinsed cup inside the dishwasher. She wrapped her arms around her waist, squeezed herself, and sighed. Would Cory call this morning? On his lunch break? Or would he wait until the couple could enjoy a leisurely conversation that evening?

Tempia preferred all three options. A man who requested back-to-back dates might pursue his girlfriend all day.

She headed toward the bathroom, grabbed her cell phone off the table, and checked the ring volume.

"Call, Cory. Do not make us wait until this evening. Call me."

* * *

Cory wiped crumbs from his sticky fingers. The family sat around his great-grandmother's kitchen table eating sugary treats that his grandfather had brought over for breakfast. The company required a work okay from the sharp-witted woman. While the men waited, Cory's cousin, Jake, shared his peculiar dating habits. Why women ran behind this capricious man was a mystery Cory hadn't solved.

Cory's great-grandmother finished eating her favorite old-fashioned cake doughnut and wiped her mouth on a frilly white napkin. Her gaze focused on Jake. "Enough. Don't utter another word. Those girls might put up with your garbage, but I don't have to hear about it."

"Oh, Granny. It's all good." Jake laughed.

Granny shook her head. "Settle down, Jake. One day there won't be any women left for you to date." Her eagle eyes focused on her son. "These boys can get started, Robert. Hopefully work will keep this young'un quiet."

An alert Lenny jumped up. "All systems are go. Let's hit while the iron is hot."

The men quickly left the table and headed toward the basement. Cory's grandfather, Robert, kept his mother sitting down.

Jake chuckled as they descended the basement steps. "My strategy works like clockwork. Granny hates what she calls my glib tongue."

Cory eyed his cousin. Jake was nowhere near cad status. His younger cousin simply enjoyed feminine attention from multiple sources. Rob maintained his younger brother never promised more than he provided. The women appeared satisfied and held on to Jake for dear life.

"First, we'll break down this dinosaur. Dan will drop off the new system this morning," Lenny said. The furnace was situated in the middle of the basement. He tapped the structure with a wrench. "Hope there are no surprises going forward. We need to finish tonight. I don't see Granny letting us work here tomorrow."

Lenny gave orders that his son and nephew followed, then the younger men headed to the attic.

First, his preplanned lunch, and now, his unplanned dinner. Cory kissed seeing Tempia today goodbye. He had underestimated his great-grandmother's ancient furnace. How could they dismantle the monstrosity, put in a completely new system, and install air ducts by dinnertime?

* * *

Tempia drove the highway vacillating between euphoria and wondering why Cory hadn't called. Boyfriends were supposed to call their girlfriend and say hello. Even Quince had contacted Tempia whenever they weren't together. Early morning. Evenings. And throughout the workday.

Those thoughts followed her into the workplace. A quick read through her emails released nonexistent Cory calls from her brain. Her jam-packed morning accelerated until adverse energy reared its toxic head. The order department had made a drastic error.

"Ugh. This mistake is unthinkable. That's it. T. J. Coggins clearly hadn't been thinking." Tempia dashed across the building. Destination: warehouse.

* * *

"Does anyone want lunch?" Robert called into the attic. "Lenny's working straight through."

The cousins glanced at each other then shook their heads.

Cory poked his head through the floor opening. "We'd rather work until the task is completed. I believe the others will head over here, work until four, and then resume the regular schedule. The extra manpower might seal the deal."

Robert nodded. "With four extra men working four hours, we can likely complete the air-duct replacement in one day."

"One can only pray that it happens," Cory said.

* * *

Two hours later, Tempia sent the expediting supervisor an incident report. Her boss walked into her office as the telephone rang. Tempia gave him a finger wave and took the call.

The frantic booming voice on the phone's other end pierced her eardrums. Tempia pulled up his order on the computer. Thank God the problem had been identified before his call. "Yes, sir," she said once the man took a breath. "Mr. Humphries, your company's order was shipped this morning at 9:46 a.m. Express shipments should arrive within 72 hours."

"My company's substantial expenditure deserved more than the standard 'we received your order' email," the man broke in. "Why not describe the process status and expected arrival date? Several messages were left over the weekend. A prompt return call would have allayed our worst fears."

"I understand your concerns," Tempia replied in what she hoped was a soothing tone. "A confirmation email typically goes out on shipping day. But I will alert the scheduling department to your concerns and suggestions. Expect an arrival around noon on Wednesday." Tempia glanced at the quiet man standing beside her desk, then she pointed to the phone. She continued speaking after her boss nodded. "Our operations director, Terrance Briscoe, will also receive notice regarding your concerns. He will contact you this afternoon."

"Let's hope he does. A lackadaisical business approach doesn't work for our company. I trust further calls won't be necessary."

"A repeat call will not occur unless you have unrelated concerns. Our truck driver will contact your company just outside city limits. Midwest Freight Solutions appreciates your patience, Mr. Humphries." She cringed at her choice of words. The man was anything but patient. She thanked the purchasing manager and ended the call.

Tempia leaned her full weight onto the chair cushion, massaging her temples in exaggerated motions. "Although orders dropped the ball *again,* I appreciate you accelerating the delivery process."

"Consider it a good omen that I was attending an expeditor meeting when you called. On to meeting number two." He moved toward the door, then turned around, facing her. "The Cardinals have a doubleheader today. Several team members requested to leave early. It surprised me your name was absent."

"I attended a game last week," Tempia informed his retreating back.

Out of all the frustrating aspects of her job, their top troubleshooter Terrance's upbeat personality paid her untold dividends. She valued working in his department.

Unfortunately, her midmorning optimism tanked thirty minutes later. Worker inefficiencies up and down the spectrum triggered error-based calamities. On top of job-related catastrophes, having not had a call from Cory that morning turned her optimism upside down.

Tempia unzipped her purse and checked her cell phone. No calls had sneaked into voicemail. Not even robocalls or scam calls. Her finger hovered above her contacts, and then she shoved the cell phone back into her purse. She would not call the man who hadn't called her.

Was he thinking about her and her feelings at all? Or was her neediness overtaking good sense? Either way, Tempia's positivity was undone.

* * *

Cory wiped his forehead when feet sounded on the ladder. His father bounded into the attic.

"Good job," Tim told his son and nephew. "It's looking good."

"For want of a better word, the 'calvary' has arrived," Jake said. "Glad you all came."

Lance stepped off the ladder behind Tim. His father, Dan, Shawn, and Lenny followed close behind.

"Shawn and Lance will work on air ducts with you all while Dan and I assist Lenny," Tim said. "We'll help here once we're finished."

Cory grinned. Maybe he and Tempia could hang out later this evening after all.

* * *

The petite woman sitting on the opposite side of the table shoved an over-laden dessert spoon into her mouth. During her pregnancy, Jasmine had developed a ferocious appetite for sweets.

Tempia could no longer hold back her giggles. Her trilling laughter made Jasmine smile.

"I feel guilty eating praline ice cream while you eat plain yogurt," her friend confessed.

Jasmine ate the last scoop of ice cream, set the spoon aside, and swished a napkin across her mouth. "Congratulations on living fourteen solid months without any epic drama."

"Do you understand the meaning of epic drama?" Tempia inquired.

"No. And neither do you." Jasmine snickered.

Tempia burst out laughing. "How long have I known you?"

"Since seventh grade. How fun it is that we are still close friends and work for the same company?"

Tempia ate the final spoonful of yogurt and studied the laughing woman. "Like I told you years ago, we are two peas in dissimilar pods."

"Oh yeah. Your pointing out our differences reminded me: Marcus has a co-worker you should meet. Jeff's unusual personality matches your quirkiness to a T. Plus, he is a terrific guy. Everyone loves him."

"Uh-huh." Tempia rose and dumped her trash on the tray. "Gabby voiced a similar judgment regarding my date on Saturday and Sunday."

"What!" Hurrying around the table, Jasmine stood beside Tempia. "You had a doubleheader last weekend? Who is he? Where did you go?"

"Running late. Call me after you put Chelsea to bed." Just before Tempia reached the exit, she placed her tray on the conveyor belt.

Jasmine cornered her in the hall. "Don't you dare leave me hanging. Fill in the blank spaces. Now, please."

Tempia checked her watch. "Tonight. You will demand the entire story if I feed you tidbits, and I have to get back to work now."

"I sure will want the entire story. He must be a man Gabby knows." Her eyes bulged. "Goodness gracious. Is it Cory? Calling you tonight," she said after Tempia nodded.

Wriggling her fingers in a mock wave, Tempia walked away.

* * *

After work, Tempia drove directly home in case Cory planned a surprise visit. In the kitchen, she whipped up a swift meal on the off chance her desire rang true.

Two hours later, she lounged on the love seat in an apprehensive mood. Heat rose within her body until rapid door knocks had her racing across the carpet. The banging sounded like someone was trapped. No one stood in front of the peephole. On her tiptoes, she looked in both directions. One hand sought the door lock, and her other hand gripped the doorknob.

"Who's there?" she asked in a belligerent voice.

"Open the door and find out," a gruff female voice replied.

That isn't a male voice. "Mia!" Tempia swung open the door. "You and your crazy shenanigans. I should have guessed it was you."

Mia's ponytail bobbed as she sauntered into the room. Hands on her hips, she perused the small space. "You're alone. Good." She kicked off her sandals and sat cross-legged on the love seat Tempia stood behind. "We want to hear what we should have heard before today."

Her friend had an extreme case of entitlement syndrome. Tempia folded her arms across her chest.

Mia patted the space beside her. "Stop digging in. Take a seat, Temp. Jasmine was rocking Chelsea to sleep on my drive over here. She should be asleep by now." Mia ignored her frowning friend and video called Jasmine. She placed the cell phone on an end table.

"Hey, girl. Your godchild is fast asleep. Where's Tempie? There you are," Jasmine said when Tempia sat down.

Mia's body slanted toward her reluctant hostess. "What's happened between you and Cory? Don't skip any details."

Mia's entitlement proclivities were boundless. "How about asking how I'm doing first?"

"Mia has a twenty-minute drive home after we finish talking. Who knows how long our conversation will last, so let's get going."

Tempia leaned forward. "Good point. I feel like I should blow a horn or something. This weekend surpassed my wildest dreams. The story is quite simple, though. Cory paid a surprise visit to my parents' house last Friday and invited me on a dinner date."

"Where to?" the voice emanating from the speaker inquired.

"Primers. His parents were issued an 'always welcome' guest pass. Afterwards, we played dominoes with Gabby and Rob. We're going on a free dinner cruise in June because he and I won."

Mia laughed. "Bet Rob hated the results. Besides his being a cheapskate, the man hates losing."

"Perhaps losing to his cousin made his fate more acceptable," Jasmine mused.

Tempia laughed so hard tears rolled down each cheek. Once she regained her composure, she continued recounting her weekend. "Saturday night, Cory invited me to the Sanderses' Sunday dinner. I like his mom. A lot. She reminds me of my Aunt Betty. Soothing to the nth degree."

Mia and Jasmine high-fived empty space.

"How about those results? You're on the fast track," Mia crooned.

"A special dinner date and meeting the family the next day. Sounds promising," Jasmine agreed.

Tempia nodded. "I think so too. It was an awesome weekend all around."

"Here's the pushback," Jasmine broke in. "Mia declared you're on the fast track. So where are you headed? Did he explain his fourteen-month snub?"

Tempia had accepted Cory's non-explanation. She spoke while nibbling a fingernail. "Not really. He said his absence helped him figure out how to proceed." Her lips pursed when she hesitated. "My Quince escapade had been a bit much on any account."

"I disagree," Mia said. "Sure, other people were affected, yet the major fallout targeted an unwilling victim. You. And do not claim it was all your fault, because it wasn't. No one has the right to abuse someone else."

"Besides," Jasmine began. "Cory was a bystander who performed good deeds when they were needed. He probably championed your cause because he felt guilty about bringing a sleazeball to the party."

Tempia had never considered that angle. "Wait until you truly meet Cory. Plus, there's more information." Tempia relayed the Community Ministries connection. "Cory strategized meeting me without directly involving the Pearsons. He saw me, met me, and lost me in a three-week span. For six months, Cory listened as Quince bragged about dating me ad nauseum. And then Cory spent five months bailing me out of my Quince-made mess. For nearly twelve months, I apparently consumed his waking hours."

"Which is a good enough reason to bide time," Jasmine admitted. "I'm happy you revived your life and moved on."

"Which you've done well," Mia added. "You're more focused than you've been since we met. Junior high happened eons ago." Mia laughed.

Tempia rolled her eyes. "So, I'm in a better head space than I was at age twelve?"

"I would've phrased it differently," Jasmine said. "But I do agree. Since we successfully cleared up that small distraction, take this unsolicited advice."

Tempia's head tilted sideways. She waited for whatever point the woman would make. Jasmine ensconced herself inside a cookie-cutter world she and her husband, Marcus, thrived in. "More Jasmine-isms regarding another person's life?"

"I am selflessly committed to my family and friends. There's plenty of wise advice to spread around."

Tempia groaned. "Make it quick."

"Ignore your intense Cory feelings. Do not rush into a new relationship."

Tempia's lips parted, then her mouth snapped shut.

"No sprints around the garden on this trip," Jasmine continued. "Take a nice long stroll along the winding pathway. Date ... other ... men. I mentioned Marcus's co-worker, Jeff."

Mia gave an exaggerated throat clearing. "I know an overly qualified candidate, too. Tony is the perfect balance between easygoing and uptight. I met him right before meeting Kevin."

Is she serious? Good thing she married Kevin. I am not a fan of any other male she's ever dated.

"No, thank you. Dating someone else's castoffs won't work for me. I'd rather stumble along my own trail."

"Whoever said that we dated? Tony didn't ask me out. His nonchalance bugged me until I met the perfect man. For me, that is."

"Kevin Beauchamp is a fantastic man who married an amazing woman," Tempia replied. "Thank God I already have a boyfriend," she said, laughing. "Cory is an awesome gentleman."

"When will we meet this virtuous person for real?" Jasmine asked.

Mia eyed Tempia and covered her mouth when she yawned. "Home for me," she said, standing. "I have this weekend open. You game?"

Tempia followed behind Mia, providing an edited version of her Saturday plans.

"You, your brothers, Cory, and his nieces. Sounds serious."

"Oh well. We'll plan an outing soon. Goodnight," Jasmine said, ending the video call.

Mia drove off while Tempia waved goodbye. Why hadn't Cory called her? He wasn't the type of a man who would string her along. She picked up her cell phone. "I will not text him, even though he might text back." Tempia tossed the cell phone on the bed, placed her watch in her jewelry tray, and prepared for a sleepless night.

Chapter Sixteen

"Goodnight, Granny. Make sure you lock the door." Cory waited five seconds. "I didn't hear the lock snap."

"I'm waiting for you to reach your car and drive off," a hearty female voice replied behind the closed door.

Was it Cory's exhausted state, or was his loveable great-grandmother developing an uncooperative spirit? All day she had disregarded every idea his Uncle Lenny had suggested. She initially rejected the HVAC system she badly needed. The precious dinosaur she cherished had received meticulous care throughout the years. No one could remedy the manufacturer discontinuing those parts. An upgrade was not only needed, but required—unless she accepted living in a hothouse all summer and an igloo in winter. As a preemptive measure, new air ducts had also been installed.

Seconds later, his uncle and grandfather appeared on the porch.

"Is there some problem?" his grandfather asked.

"Yes, sir. Granny won't lock the door unless I drive off."

His grandfather slid his hand into his pocket, extracting his key ring. "Mom, it's late. Please lock the door. Let your great-grandson go home and go to bed."

"No one is keeping the child here against his will. Leave, Cory. Go home."

While assessing the situation, Cory ignored the cool night breeze tingling the hair on his arms, and he blew out a long breath. *Pretty please, Granny. Don't work against our common goal of getting a good night's sleep. You're keeping me from calling my lady.*

Jake ran up the steps and stood beside his father. "What's the holdup? You okay, Granny?"

His great-grandmother opened the door, squinting at everyone as she rehashed previous concerns about driving her vehicle and moving in with her son and daughter-in-law.

"Mother, we covered each of those points earlier in the day."

"Humph. Not to my satisfaction. I can decide where I live and when to lock my doors."

"Mother—"

"No, no, no, son. I needed a new condenser. But I did not need a new furnace or my air ducts replaced."

Creeping closer to the door, Cory's grandfather massaged the bridge of his nose. "Cook Carol and me buttermilk pancakes for brunch tomorrow. We can eat a splendid meal, plus negotiate our differences. You did say you loved the house renovations."

The older lady covered her yawning mouth and rubbed her eyes.

Love imbued his grandfather's face. He never lost patience during his mother's fierce oppositions for independence. Her obstinance had strengthened since her husband passed away the previous year.

The one look touched Cory's heartstrings, bringing Tempia to his mind. How would she behave at ninety-four? Would he feature in her life to find out?

"Will you unlock the door if I perform the honors on your behalf?" her son asked.

"That would be petty, Robert. Of course not. I appreciate that you all love me. And I thank God for my family." Suddenly, Granny looked plumb tired. She leaned on the closed screen door, eyeing her youngest great-grandson. "It's been an exceedingly long day. Look at Jake. The poor boy will topple over soon. Good night, family. Run along home." She gave a brief wave and closed the front door.

Cory's grandfather turned the key in the lock, denying his mother a chance to change her mind. He spoke through the closed door. "Thanks, Mama. Don't cook breakfast in the morning. Let Carol and me buy you JD's all-you-can-eat brunch. We'll come here and you can drive us to the restaurant in your car."

"Uh-huh ... that's what you say now. Let's see what we actually do tomorrow."

The light inside the foyer dimmed to a soft glow. Pleased by the somewhat fast turnaround, the exhausted men trooped down the steps.

Jake stopped walking when he reached where Lenny and Robert were parked in the driveway. "Goodnight, Dad." He faced his grandfather. "You're letting Granny drive you all to brunch tomorrow? Hope to see you after tonight, Granddad."

Cory chuckled, watching the older men enter their cars. "Next time, folks. See ya."

"Drive safe." The senior relative waved, then shut the car door.

Lenny stretched his arms above his head, rotating his shoulder muscles. "My bed is calling. Since Barbara cooked a light dinner, I'll eat and hop in the sack. Tomorrow will unleash another hectic workday."

The two cousins watched the older men drive off, then they headed to their vehicles.

"Check your messages," Jake said beside his car. "I just read a text Rob sent earlier. There are no available openings tomorrow. He's test-driving the Mustang Thursday."

"He must have worked on the vehicle all weekend," Cory mused.

"More than likely, he didn't eat or sleep. I'm eager to see how she runs. Later, man."

The cousins slid inside their cars. Jake drove off first.

Cory steered the vehicle down the road, braking behind the younger man. His seemingly never-ending workday had ended. The day had been monotonously long. His body demanded a shower, a light meal, and substantial sleep.

How had Tempia occupied her evening? If she was still awake, he would find out in less than one hour.

* * *

Tempia slipped on an ultralight night shirt, padded across the room, and slipped into bed. She wavered between worry that a tragedy had overtaken Cory and seething that his entertainment excluded his girlfriend. "Stop acting silly. You know he isn't on a date or somewhere having fun." Which left ... was Cory harmed in some manner? Nope. The man was fine. But something or someone occupied Cory instead of her. Ten thirty-six. Cory hadn't made one call all day. No wonder he'd instructed her to keep in touch. Evidently, he never intended to contact her. Did he plan to ignore his *girlfriend* until Saturday?

Tempia turned off the lamp and burrowed underneath the quilt.

* * *

Dressed in pajama bottoms, Cory leaned on the refrigerator. A grunt began low in his throat. Wobbly legs took him into the bedroom. Even fixing a simple sandwich had proved too taxing. His mind centered on his weekend's bright spot. All day, thoughts of Tempia had exhilarated his soul. Concentration on a special lady in conjunction with a clear conscience supplied immeasurable gratification.

Cory shoved two pillows behind his back and leaned against the headboard. His growling stomach emphasized its hungry state while the phone on the other end rang.

"Hello," a soft, sleepy voice whispered.

He checked the clock on the nightstand. Eleven-fifteen. "Hey, lady. Did I wake you? I can call you back tomorrow if it's too late now."

"What happened? Is there a problem?" she asked, yawning. "I expected you to call all day. Hope everything is okay."

"Last night, Dad found out my great-grandmother's condenser died. Today, we installed an HVAC system and replaced the air ducts. I started the job at six-thirty this morning and got home only twenty-five minutes ago."

"Oh, Cory. You must be exhausted. Did you do the work alone?"

"Thank God, no. It would have taken three days if I had. The entire workforce worked alongside me at some point throughout the day. Try talking a ninety-four-year-old independent-minded lady into doing anything against her will."

Cory's growling stomach went into overdrive. He rubbed his abdomen, wishing he wasn't exhausted.

"Did you hear that noise?" Tempia asked. "It sounded like a machine gun."

"My stomach's demanding food my body is too tired to provide."

"Aw. Should I bring over a meal so you can eat? Hold on."

His eyebrows narrowed. She would get out of bed and drive thirty minutes to bring him a meal?

Soon, rustling noises emitted from the cell phone. Moments later, it sounded like items were being pushed around. Tempia didn't speak.

"I hear running water. What are you doing?"

"Just packed up leftovers from dinner. Now I'm cleaning up a bit before heading your way."

Cory sprang off the bed and stood on shaky legs. His whole body rebelled against sudden movements. "Let's compromise. Rob is test-driving the Boss Mustang this Thursday at Kelley Speedway. I'll eat a sandwich tonight. If you don't have prior plans, may I pick you up Thursday at six? We can eat what you were bringing tonight and watch him put the Mustang through its paces."

"Are you sure a sandwich will suffice? I don't mind driving down there.

Your great-grandmother needed the work done. It's good that willing family members assisted her today."

"Tempia ..." Cory opened his mouth twice, yet he paused each time. How could anyone adequately compliment her compassionate gesture? Providing a home-cooked meal surpassed what friends normally did for him. He settled on what he could convey. "You are one incredible lady. Go back to sleep. We'll talk again tomorrow."

The water immediately ceased flowing, and rustling noises erupted in the background. Cory pictured the sleep-deprived woman in bed and snuggling underneath a blanket.

"Night-night. I'm glad you called me before tomorrow."

Cory's grin stretched ear to ear. "Good night. Sleep tight."

Night-night. He hadn't heard those words spoken in too many years. Even his nieces no longer uttered that evening salutation. Tempia was a woman he could cherish forever. Cory switched off the lamp, laughing. Hook. Line. Sinker. Had he fallen back underneath her spell in just three days?

* * *

Adjusting his phone-call tendencies, Cory called Tempia each evening before he fell onto his bed. He was working late most nights because it seemed April's heatwave had agitated antsy customers seeking cooler temperatures.

Tempia imagined his grinning face as he fell asleep. For her part, she had begun periodically texting Cory scripture, first with Matthew 11:28–30. *"Come to me all of you who are tired from the heavy burden you have been forced to carry. I will give you rest. Accept my teaching. Learn from me. I am gentle and humble in spirit. And you will be able to get some rest. Yes, the teaching that I ask you to accept is easy. The load I give you to carry is light."*

Cory texted back. *Just read the entire chapter. Thanks for sending.*

The scripture-sending process was repeated several days in a row. On each occasion, Cory sent correlated scriptures. The couple settled into a satisfying routine.

* * *

That Thursday afternoon, Tempia left work two hours early, excited that she and Cory would spend the evening together. She rushed inside the house, busying herself inside the kitchen nook. The leftovers she offered Cory on Monday night had supplied an exceptional Wednesday lunch. She made a fresh meal for the speedway. Rob's spending long months laboring over the vehicle he restored deserved nothing less than her classic picnic meal.

Finished cooking, Tempia fanned a paper towel over her face, then wiped a light sheen of sweat off her forehead. She dropped the makeshift fan into the waste can, surveying the counter.

"Just need to pack the basket."

Potato salad, grilled zucchini and yellow squash, fresh kaiser rolls, and fried chicken were meticulously packed inside the wicker basket. Next in were watermelon wedges and red seedless grapes. She then poured home-made lemonade into a one-gallon insulated jug.

Tempia rubbed her hands together, eyeing her collection. She picked up paper cups, paper plates, napkins, and a wet-wipe container off the counter. "Is something missing?" She tapped her lips with one finger. "Nothing. Can't think of one single thing."

She quickly packed the nonfood items into a carryall. Nibbling on her bottom lip, Tempia glanced around the kitchen nook again. "Can't shake the feeling something's been overlooked. What did I leave out?"

Tempia rechecked the basket and carryall one item at a time. "All the food is packed. Paper cups to drink lemonade. Paper plates to hold our food. Napkins to clean our mouths. Wet wipes to clean sticky fingers." She leaned against the wall, laughing. "Ah, yes." She opened a drawer, removed a plastic utensil bag, dropped it into the sack, and pulled the drawstring closed.

Her gaze lit upon the microwave clock. "Get going, lady. The prompt man will arrive in twenty-three minutes."

* * *

When the doorbell rang, Tempia opened the door holding the wicker basket in one hand and the insulated jug in the other. Her purse was slung upon her shoulder. The carryall dangled off her wrist.

"Think you're bringing enough food?" Cory asked. He lifted the jug and picnic basket from her fingers.

"Hope so. I wondered if Jake is bringing a date. Is he?"

"He's sure to. Plus, my cousin Shawn, who works for Dad, is coming. He and another co-worker, Lance, are bringing their wives."

Her hands free, Tempia took a jacket off the doorknob and locked the door. "How are you and Shawn related?"

"Our mothers are sisters. Lance's father is Dad's best friend. He and

Mr. Cooper round out our work staff."

"Sounds like a regular family-and-friends affair. It's terrific you all work and play well together."

When Cory crooked an elbow, Tempia hung on. The intimate gesture seemed as natural as breathing. Her mind drifted back two days to when Cory had called her special. The word fulfilled a high-school longing: dating a man she respected and who considered her worthy of pursuit.

Forever the gentleman, Cory opened and closed Tempia's car door. The couple rehashed their uneventful workdays on the short highway drive. The conversation shifted at the halfway mark. Tempia described the marvelous meal she had eaten at her aunt's house on Tuesday. After the revelation, Cory's dialogue centered upon her extended family on all three sides. He mentioned the Wade siblings eating her grandmother's homemade pizza the following Thursday and accepted an invitation when Tempia invited him along.

In her humble opinion, the heightened interest in her family core spoke volumes. Did Cory contemplate combining two distinct families into a unique familial unit?

Tempia and Cory chatted as Kelley Speedway silhouetted upon the horizon. It was less than fourteen miles from her apartment, yet Tempia had never noticed the place existed. Cory exited the highway and followed four cars to an ample parking lot.

Tempia thought the building and surrounding grounds resembled a posh resort. The connecting A-frame timber and beige-stucco structures took up a small portion of the huge lot and resembled a ski lodge. Small trees, plants, flowers, and shrubs presented a cozy setting.

She alighted the vehicle on her own and waited until Cory reached her side. Activity bustled everywhere. Long lines queued beside two food trucks parked in the west parking lot. People were spread throughout the grounds. They either sat in the stands or on blankets on the lawn.

Once the couple moved beyond the gate, a large transparent fence and wide pavement separated the track and spectators. The track surrounded a canopied area containing multiple stations and small structures.

Tempia studied the large crowd, guessing no one was leaving soon. Everyone appeared vested in the event until the end. She touched Cory. "Since car restorers strut their stuff on both Tuesdays and Thursdays, I expected fewer people here. Every place I look, people are eating and socializing."

"This crowd is light compared to the hundreds who come every weekend.

Just spotted Gabby and Candace sitting on blankets beside the bleachers."
The couple headed their way.

Sure enough, her friend had spread two king-size purple blankets side by side. Gabby sat cross-legged talking to a woman Tempia hadn't met.

Tempia came up beside the blanket. "We're here. Where's Rob?"

Gabby pointed behind her back. "Signing up for the test drive. Shawn is there as well. Candace and I are expecting updates from Shawn soon."

Candace and Tempia said hello at the same time then burst into laughter.

"I'm Shawn's wife," Candace said. "I'll introduce you to my husband once he joins us."

"Looking forward to meeting him," Tempia replied. She left two feet in between herself and Gabby and motioned for Cory to sit beside her.

He peered in the direction her friend had pointed out. "I'll join Rob and Shawn under the canopy. Be back soon."

Tempia felt a little nervous and wanted Cory by her side a bit longer.

"The others have arrived," Cory said.

Two casually dressed couples stood near the blanket's edge. The well-groomed younger man's incessant gaze caught Tempia's face. Thank God his smiling eyes and lazy grin projected a harmless spirit. In an instant, her uneasiness upped a notch. The man continued staring.

Whoa, boy. He must be Rob's younger brother, Jake. Here we go.

"You're here earlier than expected," Cory said. "What time did you complete the Harris job?"

Jake grinned. "Three-thirty. The dirty filter hadn't been changed since we installed her furnace last year."

A woman dressed in a white button-up shirt and beige khakis sat across from Candace. Lance claimed the spot beside his wife.

"Was it 'the furnace only runs three months a year' argument?" Lance asked.

Still studying Tempia, Jake chuckled. "The very one. I suppose having an outside condenser confuses people."

"No reason why it should." Cory observed the woman clinging onto his cousin's arm. "Introduce your friend so I can present my leading lady and join your brother."

Jake's amused gaze switched from Tempia to Cory. "Excuse me for detaining you. Hey folks, Melody and I attended the same concert last weekend." He turned a megawatt smile on the woman. "My cousin Cory wants to introduce his date, then leave us."

Cory squatted beside Tempia and draped an arm around her shoulders. He hugged her closely and kissed her cheek. "Tempia, meet Melody, Diana, Lance, and Jake. Hope everyone is hungry. Tempia cooked us a dinner feast." He pointed toward Gabby. "And Gabby brought an unknown dessert."

"Tempia's beautiful blush indicates the relationship is new. I like her bashful smile," Candace said, facing Gabby. "Does 'unknown' mean that you didn't reveal what you were bringing, or that it's an original recipe?"

"Both. I tested the recipe on my brother, Mac. He absolutely loved it." Watching Tempia and Cory snuggling closer, Gabby smiled. "My best friend's remarkable personality tops off the shy smile. It's nice feeling secure, wrapped inside protective arms."

"Oh. How long have you two been dating?" Candace asked. "Shawn hasn't leaked one word. I bet Cory gave him details before now."

"We didn't start dating until recently, but we met more than two years ago at a get-together at Rob's," Tempia provided.

"Lance didn't tell me Cory had a girlfriend," Diana said. "I would've stopped running my friends by the man had I known." She playfully punched her husband's arm.

Tempia's stomach jumped into her chest hoping the women would choose a different topic besides her. Her body shakes subsided once Lance grinned and took the hit in stride.

"I hate feeling left out," Diana continued. "What's wrong with men?"

"Plenty," said Gabby. "Now, about dessert. Rave reviews are required before any of you can leave."

Cory stood, pulling Tempia up with him. He walked her away from the group. "Did Jake's staring gaze make you nervous?"

"Initially it did. I thought he might bring up my ex."

"I doubt if he knows anything about Quince. Jake is newsy but doesn't gossip."

"You're sure he doesn't possess darker motives? Like wondering why you're dating me?"

"He's harmless, and only you and I will decide about our relation-ship. I trust that outsiders won't influence your decision."

Right as ever. Nothing or no one would ever keep her heart from saying yes.

Tempia ceased walking. "Get the lowdown from Rob while I go back and mingle."

Jake claimed the spot beside Tempia on her return, settling the still-clingy

Melody on his other side. Conversations among the group flowed freely. All discussions ceased once the evening's car parade began.

Each participant gave a brief renovated-vehicle history, their desired outcome, then demonstrated the car's velocity and endurance in a race around the track. Tempia had assumed the owners were displaying their "babies" for other car enthusiasts' accolades and admiration. Eight of the eleven contributors wanted their vehicles purchased that evening. Rob and two other men professed full restoration had been their sole goal.

Once the demonstration ended, the guarded automobiles were displayed behind a chain-link fence while professional mechanics answered potential buyers' questions. Spectators roamed back and forth between the automobiles and individual groups. A huge picnic vibe charged the atmosphere.

Cory, Shawn, and Rob joined the group after the main event ended. Cory nudged Jake and Melody over and slid his body in between Tempia and his cousin. Shawn opened the picnic basket, then claimed the seat beside his wife.

An exhilarated Rob announced he'd received several offers right after his test run. Happier than Tempia had ever seen the man other than on his wedding day, Rob took the empty spot beside his wife. While heaping food onto his plate, he recounted verbatim each unanticipated offer, then he ate his meal in silence.

Chapter Seventeen

"Will you sell your baby?" The question Diana asked was on everyone's mind. She called Rob's name twice when he didn't answer.

Each time, the bright-eyed man remained silent.

Gabby tapped her husband's hand. "Earth to Rob. Diana asked a question."

The bemused man lowered the fork. "Sorry. I didn't hear you. My mind is processing those insane purchase offers."

Rob's known miser status made everyone laugh. The scrimper had considered selling his most prized possession. In the end, love for the vehicle overruled the dollar signs in his eyes.

While Lance and Shawn provided humorous shop talk, Jake made Tempia's personal affairs his and her main topic. He should have left her alone and concentrated on the obviously smitten woman vying for his attention. After the fifth query, Cory quizzed Jake on inconceivable life questions in between bites. The relentless inquiries ceased Jake's nosiness, hopefully forever.

"We have thirty minutes left before they close the joint. Where's dessert?" Shawn asked, wiping his hands with wet wipes.

Gabby extracted a dessert tin and a sealed bowl from an insulated sack.

Diana passed plastic bowls and spoons around the circle.

Everyone consumed the scrumptious treat in total silence. Only lip smacking could be heard until Candace patted a napkin across her mouth. "Mmm ... simply delicious. I've had a similar recipe that includes pecans."

Gabby nodded. "It typically does. One day, Tempia experienced a scary allergic reaction to a walnut. I've banned tree nuts from all recipes I feed her. I added several different ingredients than the recipe required. Glad you liked it."

"See an allergist," Melody advised. "Find out what foods you're allergic to."

"My stepmother made that demand the following week. The doctor said I was allergic to all tree nuts and nothing else."

For the next ten minutes, the group relayed allergic-reaction horror stories. Tempia listened, thanking God she hadn't died.

The voice speaking on the microphone interrupted her musing. The speaker requested the car owners retrieve their vehicles.

Once the couples headed toward the parking lot, Jake whispered in Tempia's ear. "I can tell my cousin met a woman he adores. See you at my grandparents' fifty-fifth wedding anniversary in October."

"These are early days. I haven't been invited," Tempia whispered back.

"Just remember I told you so. See you there." Jake patted her back, then he and Melody strolled away.

Cory had correctly called his cousin's personality. The man was neither rude, crude, gossipy, nor slanderous. Gabby's ease as Tempia and her brother-in-law talked had underscored Cory's earlier assertion: Jake's curiosity overrode his discretion.

On their trek across the parking lot, Shawn slowed his car beside Tempia and Cory. Candace lowered the passenger window. "Each year, we have a cookout the last weekend in July. Mark your calendars."

I'm in, Tempia thought. Relief is what success felt like. "Sure will. Sounds fun."

"Let's take in a movie or go shopping one day soon," Candace said. "I'll get your cell phone number from Cory."

"Looking forward to it," Tempia replied.

Diana blew the horn as she and Lance passed by. Tempia waved until the car disappeared. Unlike at Sunday dinner, here, she had been accepted as Cory's girlfriend.

She no longer felt like she was on pins and needles when meeting Cory's relatives and friends. But then again, how would she fare among Rob's get-together group? Each one had avoided Tempia and Quince during Gabby's wedding reception. Would she find acceptance within a Quince-bashing crowd?

She waited until Cory slid into the SUV. "I like both cousins, your friend Lance, and their wives," she told him. "Somehow, I don't think I'll see Melody again."

Cory chuckled. "Correcto. Jake enjoys playing the field."

"I thought as much. Yet it seems he's genuinely people-oriented ... and likes their personal business too much. His personality is lightyears away from Rob's. I liked their two older sisters when I met them at Gabby's wedding."

Cory nodded. "Jake is the spoiled rotten baby." He started the car, joined the queue, and exited the parking lot. "Thanks for providing ample food on short notice. It seems like everyone loved it all. You and Gabby are carrying empty food containers home."

"Empty containers are a great compliment. This has been a fun evening I won't forget."

Their knuckles clanged in an unplanned expression of unity. Gabby had called it. The spontaneous fist bump proved Tempia and Cory shared similar mannerisms.

Instead of rehashing the evening, the couple settled into a restful moonlit drive. Though quiet, Tempia racked her brain determining why she had hit a home run tonight but not on Sunday. How could she bring around a woman who purposely stacked the deck against her? Could Cathy's limited knowledge about Tempia's marriage become a future game changer? How would Cory's sister react if she learned the entire story?

Inside her apartment, Tempia slipped off her sandals while Cory placed the picnic basket, carryall, and jug on the kitchen counter. When he faced her wearing a huge grin, she patted the other cushion. "Can you stay and watch a movie?"

In a few seconds, he claimed the seat beside her. "It's been a long two days, and tomorrow's jobs have piled up. I'll fall asleep if I don't head home."

No clinging. Say a gracious goodnight, and let the man drive home wide awake. Her face was raised for his goodnight kiss.

Cory brushed a light peck across her lips and headed toward the door. Once Tempia reached him, he dropped another kiss upon her lips. "Being with you was the best part of this day. They all enjoyed meeting my girlfriend."

The expressed profound emotion hit its target. "You will always feature in my days. The evening ended on a high note. Cory, I feel accepted on a personal level." She brushed her hand across his chest. "See you soon, boyfriend. Drive safe."

"Goodnight until tomorrow." His head lowered, and he claimed a final, lingering kiss. "Perhaps I should stay inside and close the door," he joked before leaving.

Tempia brushed her fingers across the lips he'd kissed and locked the door he'd closed. Although he seemed invested in being here, Cory had high-tailed it out of the door, making a speedy exit. Quince would have visited past midnight. But then, of course, her ex had probably headed to the nearest party once he left her. Comparisons of authenticity proved noneffective. Cory would drop into the sack as soon as his feet hit the bedroom floor. Plain tiredness had sent him home early.

Tempia suppressed the debate and reflected on her evening. The highlights more than compensated for the few low spots.

The word "boyfriend" brought on a huge smile. Each of her friends, except Jasmine, had had multiple boyfriends in high school and after they graduated. Jasmine and Marcus became a couple in their sophomore year of high school. Tempia went on her first date at sixteen. Her father had maintained strict rules about his daughter's dating life. Sam interrogated any fellow ringing their doorbell. Quince had been the only man she had seriously dated, but neither she nor any friend had called Quince Tempia's boyfriend. Only Cory Sanders had received that honor. Tempia relished calling Cory by his special title.

* * *

The next day, Tempia started her car, then turned on the radio. Her favorite radio station played R&B and soul slow jams on her drive home. The blast from the past made the rush-hour drive tolerable. Thirty minutes into the trip, she exited the highway four cars behind a black Mazda Miata. Quince! Why now? Tempia hadn't spotted him anywhere near her since their divorce. She slowed down her speed. If he was on his way home, he would make a left turn onto Creve Coeur Mills Road, and Tempia would turn right on the same street.

Their favorite oldie came on as Quince entered the left turn lane. When it did, he veered across two lanes and made an immediate right turn. Had the old song he knew Tempia loved brought her across his mind? Or was he simply going on a forgotten errand that might have caused the hastily changed direction? With the same four cars still between them, she followed Quince down the road. At the corner that led to her old apartment, his destination became apparent. Sweat beaded on her forehead. Tempia turned the car around in sheer panic.

She circled around an adjacent parking lot and observed Quince park behind the trash receptacle. He could view her old apartment without her seeing him, had she been inside. Hidden a distance away, she watched him stake out her old home. After watching him for twenty minutes, she called her stepmother, relaying the entire episode.

"Do not go home," Blanche said. "Drive straight over here and park behind my car. If Quince wants to contact you, let him knock on our door."

161

Tempia started the car. "On my way. And Mom, do not tell Dad."

"Sent him a text message while you spoke. He's on his way home. Make sure Quince doesn't see you, Tempie."

Tempia cruised away and soon parked behind her stepmother's sedan. Noah and Curt waited for her arrival outside. The boys stood when she stepped onto the porch.

Curt opened the storm door, waving his sister inside. "Did he see you?"

"I'm sure he didn't. I drove through neighborhoods all the way here. Come inside," Tempia said when Noah remained standing on the porch.

"Dad's home. I'll wait for him."

Tempia and Curt stood in the foyer when Blanche walked downstairs. "We're switching cars," Blanche explained. "Take my extra car key off the rack and leave your key in its place."

"I think that's unnecessary," Tempia began. The opening door captured her attention.

Sam sauntered into the room as if he hadn't a care in the world. Which didn't explain his making a thirty-minute drive home in twenty minutes. "Did your mother ask you to switch cars?" he asked.

Tempia glanced at Blanche and then back at Sam. "Mom told me we're switching cars. Didn't you, Mom?"

"I expect acquiescence without a battle," Blanche replied. "Even though the boys were supposed to spend the weekend with you—"

"Oh, man," Noah and Curt burst in unison.

"We're having a special day tomorrow," Noah continued.

"Tempie lost the bet. We locked her car doors," Curt added.

Blanche's gaze pierced her sons standing side by side. "Hush. Your sister can still drive. No one's stopping your outing tomorrow." She refocused on Tempia. "The perfect solution is for you to stay with us awhile. We've no idea what we're dealing with."

"Yes, you do. I explained that I think Quince made a decision on a whim. I think a strong reaction to the song decided for him."

Sam grunted. "Perhaps. But lie low anyway. Will it hurt you to accommodate us for a month? If so ..."

Don't belabor the point. Compromise whenever feasible. "Easing both your minds is the very least I can do," Tempia agreed. "But I will spend only one weekend, and this is it. But I'm happy to drive around in Mom's Lexus all month instead of my Forte."

"Our daughter has some keen insight. Keep it going by taking breakfast to Community Ministries next week instead of tomorrow," Sam said. "The man has your routine down pat."

"Remember your keen insight," Sam reminded her when she frowned.

Tempia's lips pursed into a thin line. "Then how come I'm surprised you came home instead of confronting Quince?"

Her gaze locked with her father's. Sam stared with minimal blinking. "Possibly on a lark, Quince made a fishing expedition. My showing up would've become a fish in his net. He'll move along once someone other than you enters or leaves that apartment." Sam's cell phone rang. "What's the lowdown?" he asked the caller. "Gotcha. Thanks for checking. I owe you one. Problem solved," he told the group waiting for information. "Your uncle Fred reported that Quince drove off when a middle-aged couple opened the front door using a key."

"Tempia ..." Blanche warned as their daughter's hands clapped.

"I keep my promises," Tempia reminded everyone. "I'm spending the week-end here and driving the Lexus for a month. And we'll eat breakfast with our ministry friends next week instead of tomorrow. Now, is dinner at the usual time? What did you cook?" she asked when her stepmother nodded.

"Your second-favorite meal. Homemade beef stew with baked sweet pota-toes and cornbread patties."

Tempia rubbed her belly. "Yum-yum. I'll serve you and Dad breakfast in bed tomorrow morning." She stepped onto the bottom step. "Heading upstairs. See you in a bit."

In her bedroom, Tempia called Cory and left a short voicemail conveying the Quince incident. After she had showered and changed clothes to white denim jeans and an olive-green crop top, Cory texted his response.

Got my hands full on a long job. I decided against contacting Quince. Any intervention from me will confirm you live somewhere in that complex. Glad you're staying at your folks' place tonight. Provide details when I call later.

Tempia moseyed downstairs and entered the kitchen, claiming her usual seat. "Curt, Noah, you'll receive a special treat tomorrow. Cory and his three little nieces, ages eight, six, and four, will join our movie and arcade visit tomorrow. And then we're hanging out at his place."

"To do what? Watch you two make moony eyes at each other?" Noah inquired.

Tempia rolled her eyes. "Don't be cute. Cory has a volleyball net and a basketball goal in his backyard. His neighbor has an above-ground swimming pool. Two of the children are around your ages. We'll drop off the girls at their house after the arcade, then head to his place. So now I get your happy face," Tempia said when Noah gave an ear-to-ear grin. "We're meeting the others at the movie by ten-thirty sharp. Be ready at ten o'clock."

"Is it wise to include your brothers on your dates with Cory?" Sam asked.

Ease him in a little bit each day. Cory will make Dad the perfect son-in-law. "Yes, sir. Cory and Quince are miles apart in character and integrity." Tempia gave a toned-down account of the story around her invitation to the girls on Sunday.

"Tempie, what were you thinking? Your heart was in the right place, but you overstepped by a mile," Blanche said.

"By miles," her father added. "Never offer perks you wouldn't accept for Curt and Noah."

Blanche nodded. "Decrease the tempo a little. Cory already wants to date you. Enjoy the journey. I'll pray your relationship with his sister quickly mends."

"Gabby likes Cathy. She and Rob believe his sister will come around. In fact—"

"See there, Mama," Noah interrupted. "You should have bought us new swim trunks last month like Curt asked you to."

Her brother's reverting to his old pout brought back long-forgotten memories. He used every trick except sticking out his bottom lip and sucking his thumb. Tempia noted Sam's sharp look and watched Blanche study her youngest son. Her stepmother's lips parted.

"We'll go shopping after dinner for new trunks," Tempia broke in.

Without reprimanding Noah, their parents headed toward the kitchen, talking softly.

Curt laughed, sidling closer to his siblings. "Thank Tempie for the save. Mama almost banned you from leaving the house tomorrow."

"Dad too. I envisioned having added days pile up," Noah agreed. His gaze switched to his sister. "Tempie, let's go to a sporting goods store instead of a clothing shop. Then you won't get tempted to buy more clothes."

"Really. You can always stay home, Noah. Curt and I will leave after dinner."

* * *

After working eight hours at one location, Cory left the work van in the parking lot, undecided about his next move. Decision made, he drove home, took a quick shower, and grabbed a banana off the counter on his way back

164

outside. He didn't think Tempia had been traumatized by Quince's sneakiness, since she blamed the man's stakeout on a song rather than malice. But Cory believed boyfriends should supply support whenever feasible. He massaged his aching lower back and headed to his car.

* * *

Tempia and her brothers visited a mom-and-pop sporting goods shop in their search for swimming trunks. The merchandise selection couldn't match items carried in a big-name retailer, but the store stocked the exact swim trunks the boys required. The cost was nominal and within their weekly allowance's budget. At the counter, Tempia stood behind Curt and Noah, beaming as they purchased swim trunks.

Heading for the exit, Tempia denied Noah's fishing rod request and Curt's tennis racket inquiry. She advised her brothers to tell their parents they were interested in trying new sports. Their task completed, the trio headed home, singing Christmas hymns on their way.

Miles down the road, shocked, Tempia stopped singing as an SUV turned onto her parents' street. Cory! She tried not to jump to hasty conclusions. There was more than one silver Chevrolet Traverse in Missouri. The actual man was either winding down work or heading home.

But then the vehicle parked behind her father's truck. Tempia parked behind him. Cory stepped outside the SUV and headed her way. She sprang from her stepmother's car and rushed into his open arms.

"I can't stay long," he said, wrapping both arms around her elated body. He glanced at her brothers, who openly stared at him.

"Curt, Noah. My nieces are excited about tomorrow. Hopefully, they'll fall asleep in their own beds tonight so they can get some sleep."

"We can't wait to meet your neighbor's children and swim in their pool," Noah said.

"Plus meet your nieces," Curt added. He tapped his brother's shoulder and pointed toward the house.

"After the arcade, we'll drop off the girls at their house, then head to my place," Cory called. "Looking forward to our outing."

"So are we," Curt and Noah spoke together.

Once the boys walked inside the house, Cory grabbed Tempia's hand and escorted her to his vehicle. Reaching into the back seat, Cory pulled out a beige Primers sack. "We won't make it back to Primers before next month. Enjoy the marble-cheesecake brownie smothered in chocolate sauce on me."

He remembered! Feeling squishy inside, Tempia retrieved the sack from his hand. "That's very sweet of you. Thank you."

"Tell me what happened with Quince before I leave."

Tempia explained that Quince probably staked out her old apartment because of an oldie song they both adored.

Cory nodded. "I agree with your assessment. However, Quince has much emotional baggage. His stability on any day is uncertain at best. In other words, be aware of your surroundings and know he could appear at any time."

Tempia frowned as she tried to decipher the message. Did Cory consider Quince a dangerous man?

"I'm borrowing Eric's seven-passenger vehicle tomorrow so we can all ride together," Cory continued. "We'll switch at my house when they drop off the kids. By the way, I think it's an excellent idea to change the ministry breakfast to next week. Then you and your brothers can eat with everyone like you normally do instead of dropping off the meal." He gave a slight bow. "I'll pick you all up at ten o'clock tomorrow morning. Now, please go inside, pretty lady, so I can take off. I need adequate rest for our big day."

Tempia told herself to let Cory's Quince comment go so he could get on home. Something like a reward for considering her safety above his own well-being. "Goodnight, boyfriend. Take your time driving home. Hey, text me once you arrive. Promise?" she asked when Cory nodded.

"Definitely."

Tempia gave him a one-arm hug and walked away despite the pull to stay with him. Facing Cory, she gave a quick wave and stepped inside the house.

A man in love with you will inconvenience himself for your comfort and goodwill.

Tears entered Tempia's blinking eyes. God's favor supplied great mercy, grace, and love. Her stepmother had advised her to enjoy the journey, and she would. Even an erratic ex-husband couldn't abolish her newfound peace.

Chapter Eighteen

After the upstairs doorbell rang, a firm knock sounded on the basement door. Eric's SUV was parked out front. Cory heard the kids' joyful voices on the front porch. And then, he realized: It was Cathy knocking on his door. Cory recognized a peace offering when he heard it. He opened the door and drew his sister into a strong embrace.

Cathy responded like she had the last time Cory had almost given her a bear hug in his late teens. She briefly returned the hug, butted his chest with her forehead, then pushed Cory back. "I love you, little brother."

Those were her exact words during the occurrence that happened years ago. Her mist-filled eyes were dead giveaways that she regretted Sunday's fiasco with Tempia.

The rest of his heart thawed lickety-split. He searched the face of the woman he held in high esteem. "As I do you, older sister. Which makes your having a strong relationship with Tempia paramount."

Her gaze narrowed. "Do you consider your girlfriend and me a package deal? I either love the woman you date or lose our close connection?"

"I can't dictate your behavior any place but inside my home. However, I won't subject Tempia to frivolous ridicule anywhere. One day, my date and I might become a permanent unit. Don't burn bridges you can't rebuild."

"You just said, 'might become.' Are you leaning in that direction?"

"The fact that we're dating confirms I'm interested in a forever relationship. But then again, only our quality time will determine the outcome for either of us."

When Cathy entered the living room, Cory locked the door. Sister and brother faced each other in the middle of the room.

"The woman preferred *Quince Jones* over you. You have nothing in common with the ingrate. It's like ... comparing a hot dog to prime rib."

"Cathy, do me one favor. Analyze your most appalling mistake and the rationale that caused the problem."

Cory relaxed once Cathy's eyes closed. She had made a similar miscalculation equaling Tempia's initial error. Thank God his sister had escaped the dire consequences that Tempia had stumbled upon.

Her eyes gradually reopened. "I love the man you've become, most beloved younger brother." She squeezed his arm, smiling. "Heed a little sisterly advice. Don't rush. Tread lightly. Forever will last a mighty long time."

"Compared to eternity, life on earth is short. I plan to make every second count."

Grabbing his wallet off the counter, Cory ushered Cathy up the basement steps.

* * *

Tempia and her brothers were waiting on the porch as Cory pulled up in his brother-in-law's SUV. At first, Tempia didn't see the girls, and then she spotted four tiny hands waving from the third row. Their voices rang out once Cory opened the passenger door.

"We're here," Mali shouted.

"Andre didn't come," Sophia added in an equally loud voice.

Still strapped into her car seat, Bella leaned sideways, giggling.

"Tamp it down, girls. Always use your best behavior when meeting new people. Lower the boom after you hook them in," Cory spoke above the uproar.

"Wow! Too late for that strategy," Noah whispered to his siblings. "Those itty-bitty girls are too noisy. Mom would say they're boisterous."

Halting beside Cory, Tempia grasped his forearms and rubbed her cheek on his chest. Their gazes met before she turned to greet the girls. Lowering his head, Cory pressed his lips on her mouth and gave her body a light squeeze. The smoochy hug lasted mere seconds, yet goosebumps covered both of her arms once he pulled away. At this stage in their relationship, Tempia hadn't expected a public show of affection from the normally inexpressive man. Her brothers' shocked faces conveyed the significance of the embrace. However, on this occasion, they seemed pleased on some personal level. Curt and Noah had shown irritation whenever Quince touched their sister in any manner.

Tempia glanced toward the upstairs window. Were her parents sneaking a peek from their bedroom?

168

Introductions over, her brothers settled themselves into the second row of the SUV. Their light banter kept Mali and Sophia laughing during the short ride. Cory's nieces' exuberance prompted Cory to join in on the fun. Everyone participated in rambling conversations except a perplexed Tempia.

The group behaved as if they had known each other for many years. Cory engaged them in conversation, which she had not suggested. Tempia glanced at the vehicle's rear occupants just as Curt shifted in his seat and played patty-cake with a wide-eyed Bella. The boys even hyped to the girls the animated film they were all going to see, which the boys had initially lobbied against viewing.

After the movie, the group headed to the arcade. When they arrived, Cory wrapped his arm around Tempia and ushered everyone to the outside café. Food suggestions spiraled out of control until Cory splurged on the tacos and nachos special. Tempia noted how he listened to their ideas but then picked food items that everyone should enjoy, but no one had requested. She considered Primers's high prices last weekend and their movie expenses earlier in the day. Against her wishes, he had been spending so much on everyone and never complained. She hoped he would let her cover the arcade tab.

Inside the mammoth arcade gallery, rows of colorful machines competed for attention with bleeps, bloops, neon lights, breaking glass, and barking dogs. Once again, the proud sister witnessed her favorite lads stepping up. On the boys' recommendation, Curt and Tempia played Skee-Ball and Whack 'N Win with Bella, while Noah and Cory played Spin 'N Win and Tower of Tickets with Mali and Sophia. Later on, to save time, Cory played explosive-gunfire video games with her brothers, and Tempia played racing games with his nieces.

Twenty minutes later, Tempia and the girls stood beside Cory and her brothers as they each played the same game on separate machines. The effortless camaraderie wasn't lost on the woman who had prayed her ex-husband and her brothers would secure a comfortable and loving relationship. Their rocky initial introduction never grew into more than tolerance on either side. Both boys never trusted the man Tempia eventually brought into their family. On her brothers' overnight visits before she got married, they refused to stay in the apartment alone with Quince. The one time Tempia attempted an ice-cream run to a neighborhood shop, Curt and Noah followed her outside the apartment.

When blinking lights and whirring noises indicated the game had ended, the boys semi-demanded to play another round. Chuckling, Cory steered the group outside, where they joined the bumper boats' lengthy measurement line. Tempia's heart lodged in her throat. The unruly shenanigans she could see happening in the pool almost made her wish Bella stood less than thirty-six inches. Darn it. The munchkin was thirty-seven-and-a-half inches tall.

Once their turn for a boat arrived, the attendant let Bella sit in between Curt and Noah in one boat, Cory rode with Sophia, and Tempia teamed up with Mali. Instead of attacking, Tempia and Mali fled from Cory, Tempia's brothers, and a host of strangers bumping Mali and her up, down, and around the large pool. Perhaps the duo should have attacked the other bumpers and not run away in sheer terror, but Mali was as petrified of falling out of the boat as Tempia was.

Exiting the pool area, the water-dampened septet paid a repeat visit to the outside café for ice cream before leaving the arcade. Bella fell asleep on the drive home, a stuffed unicorn dangling from her fingers. From the middle seat, Sophia and her Super Mario hand puppet acted out scenes from the animated movie they had seen earlier. Laughing at her younger sister's playfulness, Mali nuzzled her face on a Pac-Man pillow.

All along the drive to the city, Tempia compared Cory's and Quince's impacts on her life. Her ex's destructive contribution had undermined her self-respect. Excluding his fourteen-month desertion, Cory had shown her high regard. His abandonment when she needed him most couldn't abolish the across-the-board good effect.

Tempia listened as Noah and Curt described their friends and usual pursuits. Cory's insightful questions and informal guidance depicted a genuine interest. Her boyfriend would become a wonderful influence for many years.

After Cory parked his brother-in-law's vehicle in the Robertsons' driveway, Tempia stood beside his SUV, praying for a fast getaway. Her brothers freed Cory's nieces from the back row while Cory held her hand.

Carrying Andre, Cathy opened the front door. Eric stepped onto the porch behind his wife and son. Sophia spotted their parents first, held up her new toy, then joined Mali, who jumped up and down, waving. Their acknowledgement over, the girls chased each other around the front yard.

"Mama, Daddy," Bella said. Slowly ascending the steps, she pulled on her mother's leg, reaching for her little brother.

"I'll hold him while we're standing on the porch," Cathy told their youngest daughter. She took the stuffed animal from Bella's hand. "Go join your sisters in the yard, love."

Eric watched his youngest girl trek down the steps one foot at a time, then studied Tempia. "I ate a serene lunch complete with second helpings. Thank you, ma'am. You can take out the girls again whenever you like."

Tempia glanced at Cathy. "Curt, Noah, and I enjoyed having young female company for a change." Dragging Cory with her, she walked halfway up the steps and held out a rubber duck toward Cathy. "Here's Andre's souvenir. Hope he likes floaty toys."

Her lips parting into a smile, Cathy accepted the gift, set her son on a chair, then handed him the duck. "That's nice of you. Thank you."

Tempia almost fainted on the spot. This was not the same person she'd met at the Sanderses' Sunday dinner. Did Cathy have a change of heart? Was she requesting a restart?

"I only wish he had been old enough to join us," Tempia replied.

Cory winked at her when she glanced up at him. Although he still held onto her hand, the man was unusually quiet. And then she remembered. He had remained silent at Gabby's house while Tempia and Rob negotiated their new relationship last Saturday. Had he and his sister reached an agreement regarding Tempia and Cory dating?

She donned her widest grin. "Providing keepsakes was the least I could do."

Eric pointed to his son, who was sucking on the duck's plastic ear. "Most children would have dropped it on the ground by now."

"Maybe the duck serves dual purposes: teething ring and floaty toy," Tempia mused.

"My wife lures the little rascal into the bathtub using floaties." Eric carried his son down the steps and introduced himself to her brothers. "I referee basketball, and my brother coaches a team in an early-teen league. Are either of you thirteen and interested in playing?"

Curt raised his hand. "Me. Curt. My brother Noah is twelve. We attend a private school that doesn't have athletics."

Turning sideways, Eric included Tempia in the discussion. "The team isn't limited to city dwellers. We have several county players on the roster. Noah can help the assistant coach spot individual players' trouble areas." He faced his wife, who was still standing on the porch. "Hon, will you fetch me a brochure off the console table?"

His wife nodded and entered the house. Back outside, Cathy navigated through the girls and stopped beside Cory's SUV. She passed Tempia a welcome packet. "For four years, I've served as the team mom. If your brother joins the league, we can watch the games together."

Cha-ching! Cathy Robertson had declared a truce. Thank You, Jesus. "My father and brothers are sports fanatics. The boys also do various extracurricular activities. This week, Noah won two speech-meet awards. Dramatic and duo interpretation."

"Congratulations," Cathy told the grinning boy. "We want our children engaged in speaking events. I'd love to get the program schedule."

"I'll send you one," Tempia promised.

Cathy tapped her forehead. "Well, this stay-at-home mom leaves the homebase for two hours on Monday, Wednesday, and Friday evenings. Let's get together one evening ASAP."

Tempia leaned her back against Cory, blinking back tears. Cory folded her into his arms. Peripherally, she noticed her brothers standing beside her. "This Wednesday is free. Call me. Thanks for letting me make amends. I seldom make the same mistake twice."

Curt laughed. "Unless the error is keeping tabs on her brothers' whereabouts. Tempie always finds us no matter where we go."

* * *

When they reached Cory's block, Tempia exited the vehicle sniffing the aroma of grilling meat. Someone close by was barbecuing.

"Cory, may my brothers meet your parents before meeting the neighbor's kids?"

Pleasure spread across his face. The grinning man pulled her into a brief hug. "Easily said and done."

Tempia had anticipated going upstairs from the lower level. But Cory took everyone through the main front door.

His parents were talking in the living room. The couple seemed unfazed that three uninvited guests were interrupting their conversation. Something had changed since Sunday. His father's courteous reception left Tempia feeling comfortable and content. She did for now, at least.

Cory held her hand, waiting for her to speak. She cleared her throat. "Mr. and Mrs. Sanders, these are my brothers, Curt and Noah."

The boys entered the room, rubbed their palms on denim jeans, then shook Mr. Sanders's outstretched hand.

Tim grinned broadly. "Firm grips. Your father taught you young men the

172

proper way to shake hands."

Both boys laughed and hugged his standing wife.

"And to extend proper hugs," Lillie said. "Did you boys enjoy your outing with our grandchildren?"

Her brothers gave a succinct movie and arcade critique and answered each question.

Once his parents thanked Noah and Curt for entertaining the girls, Cory pulled out his cell phone and led the group downstairs.

"The boys are here. We're headed outside ... Of course you'll meet my girlfriend ... Ah. You fired up the grill. I owe you one." Cory followed them outside, then locked the door behind him. "Evelyn is supplying dinner. Let's head right over."

* * *

Around six-thirty, Cory monitored the older kids' safety in the pool while the younger girl and boy knocked croquet balls around the yard. Tempia and Evelyn had made quick work of the outside cleanup. Now the women were inside the house tidying up the kitchen.

Cory checked his watch again. "Everyone should be waterlogged by now. Let's wind the fun down."

Evelyn's oldest son rose in the air then sank back into the water. "Yippee. We can play volleyball in your yard."

His sister treaded water, moving closer to where Cory sat on a purple deck chair. "We usually have five people on each side. We can invite over more kids and make a proper team."

"Ouch! Mama! I got hurt!" The youngest girl sat on the wet grass, peering at her knee.

Cory squatted down beside her for a better view. There were no bruises or broken skin. He gingerly pressed the area, then gave the face staring from the window a thumbs-up.

"It may hurt a little, but you'll be all right. Nothing is broken or bruised. Take your time going inside the house."

The youngest boy bumped into his sister as he zipped by her. Her pain forgotten, she caught up with him at the kitchen door.

"Thank God for healing miracles," the amused man called behind them.

Massaging his neck, Cory vetoed his original idea. He'd supposed the boys would swim next door while he grilled meatball shish kabobs. Then after dinner, all the kids would shoot baskets and play volleyball in his backyard. However, Evelyn's thoughtfulness had altered those preplanned assumptions. He could invite Curt and Noah over on a different weekend.

Cory reviewed their day thus far. On a high note, his nieces requested they all go on another outing together. One anticipated outcome was Cory liking Tempia's brothers on multiple points. The boys were alike and dissimilar in obvious ways. Nowhere near being an introvert, Curt proved more reserved and deliberate than his younger brother. But he possessed a mischievous streak a mile long. No doubt Noah could be a handful, yet his energy and self-interest were balanced by a God-centered upbringing.

Throughout the day, he could tell Tempia had made frequent comparisons between Cory and her ex-husband. He could see her mental wheels spinning whenever Cory's actions brought Quince to her mind.

In a conscious effort, Cory had upped the public show of affection, despite it making him uncomfortable. Would his limited steps suffice or contrast him against a man who didn't possess a moral compass? Might the once-married woman crave further physical contact in private settings?

Dilemmas bounded on every side of the equation. His parents' Sunday meal loomed ahead. Would Tempia expect a dinner invitation for tomorrow? Cory had had firm plans for this day that he'd revised last Sunday with considerable hardship. Friends let him move a male-only surprise birthday brunch and games fest to this Sunday. Those new plans were set in stone. Tomorrow's all-afternoon event would take place at someone else's house.

Tempia sat on Cory's lap and leaned on his chest once she and Evelyn came outside.

In Cory's mind, she'd elevated their connection to greater intimacy. Or had his actions heightened their familiarity in two days? While Tempia and Evelyn held a hassle-free chat, he contemplated any duplicity on his part. Once the minute hand on his watch struck seven-thirty, Cory waited until the women paused for a chance to break in.

"Sorry to interrupt, but it's getting late. Next time, we'll eat meatball shish kabobs in my backyard and let the kids play basketball and volleyball."

"My goodness," Tempia said. "I lost track of time."

"So did I," Evelyn interjected. "So much for my good deed. Tempia, bring the boys again soon. My children and I have had a marvelous time."

"Sure thing. Cory and I will discuss dates and see if you agree."

That night, Tempia lay in her old bedroom reliving the delightful day. Curt and Noah were disappointed they'd swam too long and couldn't play basketball and volleyball this evening. Their entire visit had been spent in Evelyn's backyard.

Tempia yawned, squirming underneath a lightweight blanket. Saturday had been a long, fun-filled day. She especially enjoyed meeting Cory's sister's lifelong friend. Evelyn's expansive welcome eclipsed Tempia's previous experiences. The woman's actions and conversation sustained her warm greeting throughout their visit. In a short time span, Tempia noted her hostess's complex and inconsistent personality. A sadness overshadowed what Tempia perceived was a friendly temperament.

The day's only downside had been her boyfriend's missing invitation for Sunday dinner. Cory's outward fondness in front of everyone had convinced Tempia the couple would spend an additional day together. She'd felt certain a Sunday-dinner invite would follow the warm welcomes from Cathy and Mr. Sanders. Somehow, a sea change had occurred in Evelyn's backyard. By dinner, Cory's affectionate words were measured. After dessert, his actions had completed the distance that his guarded dialogue had implied.

Due to the sweet kisses she'd received throughout the day, Cory's goodnight smack confirmed his disengagement. His mouth skimmed her lips before he said goodnight. No mention had been made regarding the upcoming week. At least he'd already promised to eat pizza at her grandparents' house this Thursday. Besides feeling a trifle rejected about tomorrow, everything else about the outing had been more than satisfactory. The icing on the cake had been his sister's astonishing invitation. How might their first excursion end? If not as friends, she hoped at a minimum they would embark on a comfortable association. Her fingers drumming on her chest, Tempia fell asleep.

* * *

Tempia called Cory after church the following day. As usual, the call went straight to voicemail. Did the man ever answer his cell phone? An hour later, she called again. No returned call. No returned text. Ghosted. As if one Tempia Wade no longer existed. Again. She almost speed-dialed Gabby to complain until acknowledging her friend's probable response.

Come on, girl. Are you really that needy? Cory is being disrespectful if he doesn't hold your hand? You've dated for one week, Temp. Since no one is available to distract you, entertain yourself. You've done it before, now do it again.

Tempia had cleaned up what her friend might have actually said. One thing was certain, though; she wouldn't coddle Tempia. Which made the agitating woman the perfect friend.

Entertain herself. Why not? Her fingers tapped her lips until she grinned.

In seconds, Sistas in Love popped into her mind. Over the past three years, an old friend, Nikki, held a weekly Sunday meeting in her mother's house. At least she had two years ago. Out of touch for far too long, Tempia wasn't sure if the group still existed. The text she sent came back in seconds.

Hello, stranger. Same time. Same place. Will love seeing you!

Nikki was one of the friends Tempia had lost while dating Quince. When Nikki accused him of spinning a web of lies around Tempia, Tempia felt she had two choices. She could either agree with the verdict or back off from the friendship. Nikki's refusal to apologize after publicly dissing Quince forced Tempia to distance herself. In her mind, distancing herself meant pulling back, not abandoning the relationship. In a pleasant meeting between the friends, Nikki and three other buddies agreed to disagree. Nevertheless, each one declined to attend the nuptial celebration or visit her at Quince's house. The four high school buddies stopped contacting Tempia after her honeymoon. All the while, their Gabby, Mia, and Jasmine connections had remained intact.

Which is why each one had known about her marriage separation and sent an encouragement or thinking-of-you card. Tempia had cried while repeatedly reading each reassuring message. Embarrassment had kept her from calling, texting, or sending a thank-you card in return. She'd cried over her asinine behavior instead of accepting the forgiveness the cards had implied they represented. Her affirmation might have reconnected Tempia to the friends she'd discarded for a contemptible man. In her mind, "simpleton" had been branded on her forehead, yet her old pals still wished her well.

Would any of the friends she had forsaken attend the event? If Nikki's reaction reigned supreme, the others had forgiven her defection and betrayal. Disloyalty seized her mind. Nikki had called Quince out as a way to open Tempia's eyes. Tempia, ignoring the accusation, neglected holding his feet to the fire.

After retrieving the thank-you cards she had purchased but had never mailed, Tempia walked outside and drove away.

Chapter Nineteen

Her peace offerings in hand, tears entered Tempia's eyes when Pam opened the basement door. Clearing her throat, Tempia held out the bakery box.

Her old friend's trembling fingers accepted the package. "Hi, Tempie. It's nice to see you. Head back to see everyone. Switch off your cell phone so we're not interrupted."

Blinking back teardrops, Tempia sniffed several times. "Thanks for accepting me, friend."

Misty-eyed, Pam nodded and stepped aside.

Gazing straight ahead, Tempia sat in a folding chair beside Sandra, then she spotted Monica sitting across the room. All four of her old friends were there. Either the other women still attended the weekly meeting or Nikki had spilled the beans that their "sometimey" friend was coming over. No doubt each old friend had come to greet Tempia.

* * *

Late that afternoon, Tempia drove home more relaxed than she'd been in two years. Her guess had been an accurate one. None of the women had been coming to the meeting today, but they changed their plans after Nikki revealed Tempia was attending. Nikki's short discourse on esteeming your self-worth without requiring another person's validation brought on a ninety-minute animated discussion highlighted by true-life stories and prayer. Nikki had started the weekly meetings right after high school, inspired by a frightening encounter Pam had had with someone she'd dated.

Excluding Tempia's four buddies, only three people remained from the original group. Throughout the discussion, the women drank tea and ate the iced oatmeal and chocolate chip cookies Tempia had provided. Although she hadn't met the other five women, she recognized their wisdom had been earned in the school of hard knocks. Tempia listened and nodded during the frank dialogue. Thank God, she fit right in.

After everyone left besides her friends, Tempia gladly received their life updates and happily contributed her own news. Of course the women wanted to meet Cory, just as she wanted to meet Sandra's fiancé and Pam's boyfriend. Monica and Nikki still diligently played the field.

* * *

Back at home, she kicked off her sandals, wondering why Cory hadn't called.

Cell phone! She snapped her fingers, laughing. "Oh yeah. It's still turned off. He might've called multiple times by now." There was a call from an unknown number and … phew. Tempia had missed two of Cory's calls.

She listened to the voicemail then smiled. Cory explained how his friends had switched their hanging-out plans so he could bail her out yesterday. Tempia laughed. "Bail out" was her term and not his. He promised he would call her tonight. She made a speedy decision to keep her reunion with her friends a secret until she could witness Cory's reaction in person. Would reuniting with her buddies remind him of the meet and greet with his friends?

Tempia listened to the next voicemail. The surprise caller was Candace, Cory's cousin Shawn's wife. True to her word, the woman had asked Cory for Tempia's cell phone number. Shawn and Cory were both at the male-only game fest and Candace had wanted her and Tempia to hangout as well. Tempia returned the call pronto. After Tempia explained about her friend's Sunday meetings, Candace agreed to go the following week. Perfect. Tempia could attend the meeting with Candace, then zip to the Sanderses' house for Sunday dinner if invited.

Entering the kitchen, she cooked a light meal while recalling the reunion with long-lost allies. Love and respect for oneself teemed through her brain. While assimilating the inspiring message Nikki had delivered, Tempia vowed she would spread the word, especially regarding the women's group. Her cell phone rang as she ate her meal.

"Hey, Gabby. Candace called. We're getting together next Sunday. Guess what I did this afternoon?"

"Mended fences with four dismissed friends. Glad you healed the breach your stubbornness enacted."

Tempia caught her cell phone as it slipped through her fingers. Even good news traveled fast. "I just left Nikki's mother's house. Everyone was headed to different events. Who could possibly tell you this quickly?"

"Mia did. She and Kevin saw Sandra and her fiancé at the gas station. Nice work. You hit four balls out of the park with one swing. Plus, you tied up next Sunday's loose end. Now all you must do is meet Cory's game-party friends."

Tempia's shoulders slumped. "My actions and the fallout from Rob's get-together are difficult to forget. Did they forget about my actions and the outcome?"

"Cory's judgment is the only one that counts. I like everyone who was there, Tempie—even the couple who laughed. I forgave them, and so will you."

"I don't feel any malice for those people."

"The 'those people' remark belies your assertion. Don't blow off Cory's lone request."

"Every time I think about that night ... I'm working on the proper response. Pray for me."

Tempia ended the call, reassessing her position. Each person who had attended the party knew she had married and divorced a loser in eleven months. Would any of them sanction a marriage between her and their life-long friend?

Decisions. Decisions. Decisions.

Kicking off her shoes, Tempia settled onto the love seat and picked up her book off the end table.

* * *

The following Wednesday, Cory stalled the car in front of Midwest Freight Solutions ten minutes before Tempia's lunch break would begin. He hoped a surprise meal would compensate for his quick phone call the night before. Bone tired, he had dropped into bed late Monday and Tuesday. This had been a light-work morning. However, he had a full afternoon schedule. He extracted his cell phone and hit speed dial.

"Hi, Cory," Tempia said in a super-sweet voice. "On your lunch break? I'm headed to the cafeteria in five minutes."

"How about detouring to the front door. I brought a meal for you to enjoy."

Laughter trickled across the line. "On my way pronto. I'll tell Jasmine she's eating lunch solo today."

Once inside the vehicle, she touched his shoulder and kissed his cheek.

Pulling away from the curb, Cory drove to a small park he had passed on the drive over.

She stole a peek at the sacks on the back seat. "Something smells delicious, yet I can't determine what it is. Are we eating fish?"

"Hopefully this lunch tastes as good as the superb picnic dinner I gorged on at the speedway." He stopped the car in a parking spot within the park, reached into the back seat, and pulled two sacks up front. "Here you go."

Lifting the bags from his hands, Tempia set them at her feet and read the restaurant name on the bag: Home-cooked Meals by Granny Emma. "I've heard of this place. Don't they usually have a line that wraps around the building?"

"I called in my order and beat the crowd."

Tempia removed two black containers from the bag. "Are both meals the same?"

"Yep. Jack salmon, coleslaw, green beans, and hush puppies." Cory nodded at two smaller opaque boxes. "Peach cobbler. Drinks and utensils are in the other bag."

Tempia passed Cory a black container, napkin-wrapped utensils, and a drink.

"Iced tea," he supplied once she glanced at him.

Maximizing their time, the couple silently ate their meal and drank their drinks.

"Fantastic food, Cory. The long lines are well deserved." Tempia threw her napkin and utensils into an empty bag and distributed their desserts. Shoving a spoonful into her mouth, Tempia made short work of the tempting treat.

Finished eating, Cory dumped his trash into the other bag. "Granny Emma is always up to the task. Rumors say all their cooks must fix a full meal, plus dessert, before they're hired."

"Given the food quality, that might be true." Cleaning her hands on a prepackaged wipe, she paused. "Thank you for bringing yourself and lunch. Surprises make me happy. Do you enjoy them as much as I do?"

Cory would never tire of witnessing her shy smile. "On those rare occasions when I'm truly surprised, one size won't fit all. My response will depend on each individual revelation."

Tempia burst into laughter. Her abundant display of joy caught him off guard, and he liked it. It validated his hour-long drive for lunch.

He waited until she wiped her eyes, and he smiled. "Your friend Jasmine is a co-worker? You mentioned her and Mia Friday before last. I remember seeing both of them at your and Gabby's wedding celebrations."

"Jasmine and Mia were besties before they transferred to our school in seventh grade. Jasmine's dad works at Midwest Freight and secured jobs for the four of us. Gabby hated the place, and Mia prefers job hopping."

"These days, long-term friendships are practically unheard of. Too many people exist in transient lifestyles."

"Remember I told you about losing good friends while married to Quince?"

Cory started the engine. "Tell me more while I take you back to work."

Tempia relayed her Sunday of reuniting with Nikki and crew. Then she gave him a synopsis of the group's long-term friendships, hijinks and all.

"Funny stuff," Cory interjected. He exited the vehicle, walked around to the passenger side, and opened the car door. "I like how you admit your shortcomings and willingly make amends, even if other folks might consider the effort too late to bother."

"I took so long because ... in some respects, I chose him over them. None of them attended the wedding."

"That part of your life is over and done with. Finito. Tempia, are you ready to meet my friends who attended Rob's party?"

"It wasn't easy making up with friends I've known for years. The people at Rob's get-together ..."

"Are Rob's and my shared school friends."

"But I don't know them, Cory. I will meet the people closest to you, but considering the circumstances, I need more time for those particular people."

"You understand your comfort zone better than I do. Keep in mind, though, that four of them are in my bowling league, other ones shoot pool or attend other social gatherings that I attend. I won't be able to invite you to those places."

Tempia's lips twitched as she digested the information.

"The last job today will probably end around seven. Are you and Cathy getting together this evening?"

"Bella and Andre were running temperatures yesterday. Cathy's staying home, but we'll reschedule an outing soon. Hope the littles ones feel better today."

"It's nothing serious, or I would've heard by now. I'll call you from home after settling down."

Her dancing eyes glowed as she hugged him. She hurried toward the building and waved before disappearing inside.

I was right, Tempia thought, heading toward her office. Watching Cory's reaction to revealing her connection with her lost friends had been the right call. The pleasure in his gaze displayed his approval. But just as she had suspected, her reuniting with her friends reminded him of his buddies. Until she met his friends from the party, portions of Cory's life were off limits. She'd better get used to the idea soon.

* * *

At ten-forty-five that evening, Cory tumbled onto the couch, eyeing the short hallway leading to his en suite bathroom. A short time ago, he had completed a five-hour job that should have lasted forty minutes. He detested unexpected complications. Massaging his strained shoulder muscles, he pulled out his cell phone and sent Tempia a text message instead of making his anticipated phone call.

Too tired to do anything but vegetate awhile. In a few minutes, I'll shower, eat, and hit the sack. Calling you tomorrow to set up a time to pick up you and your brothers for dinner at your grandparents' house. Sleep tight.

He fell asleep after pushing the send button, but a crick in his neck woke him up four hours later. Slowly rolling his neck from side to side lessened the pain enough to allow gentle shoulder-to-shoulder head rolls. His neck popped, bringing instant relief, but he also had cramped leg muscles. Standing, he stretched his sore muscles and limped toward his bedroom. Thoughts of Tempia entered his mind. Doubling back to the couch, he retrieved his cell phone.

Maneuvering onto the bed, he stretched out flat on his back and positioned his pillow underneath his neck. He flinched as a loud stomach gurgle cramped his abdomen. He hadn't eaten a scrap of food since he and Tempia had had lunch. Once he was almost pain free, he read her reply to his earlier text message. Grunting deep within his throat, Cory tossed the cell phone aside, rolled over, and fell asleep.

* * *

Tempia's eyes popped open at four o'clock that morning. A nightmare about her and Cory's text messages had wrecked her sleep. Even though the man had been exhausted, he hadn't left her hanging, taking the time to tell her he needed rest. Picking up her cell phone, she reread his message.

Too tired to do anything but vegetate awhile. In a few minutes, I'll shower, eat, and hit the sack. Calling you tomorrow to set up a time to pick up you and your brothers for dinner at your grandparents' house. Sleep tight.

Sighing, she read her cringeworthy reply.

Maybe it's just me, but how hard would it have been to place a call after you realized the time? You did that same thing last Monday when you were at your grandmother's house. How hard would it have been to give me an 'I'm out of pocket' update? And today? Who knows? Please don't take me and my liking you for granted.

Her head hung so low that Tempia's chin rested on her chest. What had she been thinking? Clearly, she hadn't been thinking at all.

Just as the thoughts had bombarded her brain last night, Quince and his unrelenting pursuit came to mind. Her ex had wooed her every day and all throughout the night. Contact with Quince had only been a call or text away. So, did she desire a deceptive gamester who massaged her ego or a man who genuinely cared about her well-being? The message from the meeting at Nikki's mother's house hadn't been retained by her namby-pamby mind.

Esteem your self-worth without requiring another person's validation.

"Jesus, please don't let Cory give up on me now. Let him know I'm truly trying. I've come too far to give up on myself."

Since he hadn't answered her text message, would she ever hear from him again?

Tempia held onto Cory's promise to call her about a pickup time today.

* * *

Leaving her apartment, Tempia drove to work that morning without listening to her favorite morning radio show. On pins and needles throughout the thirty-minute drive, her cell phone pinged as she pulled into the parking lot. Racing to her favorite parking spot, she pulled her cell phone from her purse. Cory had sent a long-awaited message. Perhaps she should have apologized before he responded. Saying a quick prayer, she read the text.

You forgot to tell me what time I should pick up you and your brothers. We will discuss your message this evening. Looking forward to meeting your grandparents.

Did his lack of retaliation mean he'd forgiven her rant? She reread the message that failed to reveal his feelings. Hmm ... resting her head on the side window, she sent a reply text.

My last message displayed a lack of understanding and concern. I have both. I am not as needy as I appear to be. Please forgive me. I promise to do better going forward. We'll be ready at five-thirty.

Cory sent a fast response.

We know each other too well in some areas and not enough in other ones. Our personal relationship is in the newbie stage. Anything worth having will take proper time to develop. Our relationship will grow in the correct way. See you later.

Tempia's reply was rapid.

Thanks, Cory. I really do appreciate you!

* * *

The cell phone vibrated as Cory switched to the company van at work. Before driving off, he read Tempia's message, then stuffed the cell phone into his pocket. Every relationship has its ups and downs. So far, the joy of getting to know Tempia better outweighed the needless irrational drama. However, did *liking* him outweigh the apparent trouble spots for her? That question needed answering before he fell into a deep abiding love. Cory realized that Tempia must be comparing him to her ex-husband. Doing so would doom their relationship before reaching his hopeful conclusion. The two men held nothing in common.

Cory wouldn't jump through hoops imitating an irrelevant man.

* * *

On their way to their cars after work, Tempia and Jasmine discussed Jasmine's frustrating workday. On reaching the first row of parking spots, Jasmine said, "Why do you always get super-close parking spots?"

"Because the early bird gets the worm. In our case, a prime parking place."

"Lucky you. Chelsea won't cooperate in the early mornings. She clamps her mouth together, refusing to eat. Try prying tiny gums apart."

"I have. And it wasn't fun."

"Oh yeah. I forgot about your Curt and Noah battles. At least you didn't have prior commitments. A job," she said when Tempia frowned. "You were a preteen and unemployed."

"What about their stubbornness when they got older? Those brats made me late going shopping many a day."

"Keep it real. Your brothers kept you from spending more of your parents' money."

Giving Jasmine side-eye, Tempia waved her off. "Wrong answer."

Jasmine giggled. "Mia and Kevin are coming over to watch the ballgame later. Are you seeing Cory tonight? If so, join us."

Opening the car door, Tempia nodded. "We and my brothers are eating dinner at my grandparents' house."

"Girl, your man and you are off to a great start. Mia's planning an outing so we can all have some Cory time."

Tempia reconsidered her and Cory's early-morning texting. All day, she had resisted the urge to fire off another message begging for forgiveness. Since Cory had never replied to her last text, she must believe he had forgiven her. She flashed Jasmine a fleeting grin. "Your man. Ooh ... I like those words. Tell Mia an outing is the perfect choice. Cory is usually easy to please. Can't wait for him to get to know you guys."

"Have enough fun tonight for both of us." Waving her hand, Jasmine strolled across the parking lot.

Tempia's cell phone pinged as her friend walked away. She slid into the vehicle and read her latest text.

I'm at the floral shop. What are your grandmother's favorite flowers? Looking forward to seeing you.

Tempia brushed teardrops off each cheek, then touched her fingers to her lips. There was no way anyone could fault her boyfriend's class act. She knew her major flaw was comparing Cory's sincere encounters to Quince's bogus courtship.

Lilies. She texted back, vowing to step up to the plate.

* * *

Forty minutes later, Tempia rolled to a stop behind Blanche's car and turned off the engine, seconds before blowing the car horn.

Opening the front door, she stuck her head inside the foyer. "Hi, Mom. I'm here, you guys. We're running late. Let's go."

Blanche walked down the hallway carrying an envelope. Curt ran down the staircase while Noah entered the hallway from the living room.

"Cory's picking us up from my apartment in one hour." Meeting her stepmother by the staircase, Tempia gave her a hearty hug. "We'll drop off Curt and Noah back here after dinner. Tell Dad sorry I missed him. I'll visit this weekend."

"Eat dinner here tomorrow so Sam and I can hear about today's dinner."

Blanche glanced at her sons. "You know your brothers will gloss over details when they come home this evening."

"Dinner sounds great. May I place a bid for zucchini salad, sloppy joes, and poppy-seed buns?" She continued as Blanche nodded. "Perfect. I'll bring dessert. Things got a bit shaky between Cory and me yesterday. By tomorrow, I will have lots of good stuff to share." She paused, considering how much information to reveal now. She squeezed Blanche's free hand with both of her own. "I'm finding out my boyfriend and I make a wonderful couple. He's a team player, but your daughter is catching up."

"Boyfriend?" Her stepmother raised an eyebrow. "It's only been two weeks, my dear. Do not get ahead of yourself. Stay grounded."

"She will, Mama," Curt said, opening the front door. "Dad said, 'all that glitters is not gold.'"

"Tempie doesn't want fool's gold," Noah added. "She isn't stupid."

"Wait until your father hears that his sons do listen on occasion."

Curt laughed. "I just don't think Tempie's new boyfriend will do a switcheroo on us."

"He won't pretend he likes us if he doesn't," Noah added, following his brother outside.

"My brothers are growing up faster than their big sister did," Tempia said. "Curt surprised me last Saturday. And now Noah. Something tells me we will have an interesting night. Bye-bye."

Grinning at her stepmother, Tempia shut the door behind her.

* * *

When the siblings arrived at Tempia's apartment, the boys played dominoes while their sister got dressed. Thirty minutes later, Noah rushed to the window.

"I heard a car door shut. Cory's here." He opened the front door before the doorbell could ring. Grabbing Cory's hand, he pumped it up and down. "Glad you're going to Gammy's and Gramp's house for dinner. I love eating her homemade pizzas."

"Gammy makes the best Italian food," Curt added, stacking dominoes on a miniature rack.

Tempia almost laughed at the look on Cory's face. The stunned man retrieved his hand out of the boy's grasp. "I'm looking forward to trying it." Taking another look at Noah, he closed the door. "Didn't I see you last Satur-

186

day? You just greeted me as if we hadn't seen each other in years."

Tempia reappeared in the bathroom doorway. "It's the same greeting you would have received even if he had seen you yesterday." Beckoning Curt, she lifted her purse off the chair. "Let's go, everybody."

Chapter Twenty

Four vehicles and a truck were parked under the carport at her grandparents' house. Twenty years ago, Gramps had purchased the property next door and extended his yard. He built a carport half the length and width of the previous dwelling. The entire area resembled a small-scale park and picnic area that contained a miniature basketball court. Gammy and Gramp's house was the family gathering place.

Cory stood on the sidewalk holding a blown-glass vase filled with lilies. His squinted gaze studied the spacious property. "Did your grandparents buy an adjoining lot?"

Tempia nodded. "When the Dotson house burned down, the family chose to relocate to the city and not rebuild. Gramps jumped at the prospect of extending his property line. He had a hard battle with the county but prevailed in the end."

Cory's strange expression made her hesitate. He appeared ready to speak, then he paused.

"My grandparents' renovations produced a boomerang effect in the area. More folks purchased the house next door when their neighbor moved out. A short time later, the high price of real estate halted that practice."

Cory had turned his observation from the property onto her.

Tempia turned away, wondering what was on his mind.

The couple joined the boys on the porch. Her cousin Jackie opened the door after Curt rang the doorbell.

Wagging a finger at Tempia, Jackie stepped onto the porch. "We're waiting on two more late arrivals to get here."

"Late, huh? The rest of us don't live across the street. Who all is coming?" Tempia asked.

Jackie ignored her cousin and reached for Cory's hand to shake it. "Overlook my cousin's bad manners. I'm Jackie, the brightest star on the family tree." Laughter twinkled in her dark-brown eyes. "Forget the across-the-street wisecrack. I am on time and happy to meet you."

Shaking the extended hand, Cory chuckled. "Hello, Jackie. I'm Cory."

"He's Tempie's boyfriend," Noah added.

Jackie entered the house, laughing. "Did my young cousin just warn me off?"

A man sporting a buzz cut appeared by her side. "Thanks, man," he said to Noah. "Keep looking out for my interest."

Jackie swiped her husband's shoulder. "I suspect Noah was looking out for his sister."

By the time the group spilled onto the back porch, two additional families were walking through the carport into the backyard.

Gammy must have invited the entire family over for pizza after Tempia asked permission to bring her boyfriend. Stopping beside her grandparents, she wrapped her arm around Cory's waist.

"Gammy, Gramps, this is my boyfriend, Cory Sanders. Cory, these are my mother's parents, Wanda and Graham Miller."

Cory extended the blooms to Wanda, who eagerly accepted them from his hands. "Thanks for letting me barge in on your dinner plans," he said, eyeing the surrounding group. "I've waited a long time to meet Tempia's family. The wedding celebration didn't count."

That single assertion successfully broke the ice. People quickly introduced themselves then moved away. Cory received the bonhomie in stride and chose a spot by the birdbath to eat a quiet meal. Curt and Noah abandoned the couple and joined their peers sitting on quilts across the yard.

While watching the youngsters interact, Cory chuckled. "They're a rowdy bunch. Your brothers fit right in. About the food," he said when Tempia laughed. "I must commend your grandmother's authentic pizza- and-bruschetta-making skills."

"Uh-huh. Thin crust, pureed sauce, sparse toppings, and fantastic seasonings. Gammy would never put pepperoni on a pizza. The bruschetta was exquisitely created. Wait until you taste her lasagna. Magnifico."

Cory glanced around the yard. "The delicious food isn't the only bright spot. This outdoor kitchen surpasses all the ones I've ever seen. Remember when you asked if I might consider moving to a suburb?"

"I do."

"I would definitely consider it for an opportunity to buy this house or one like it. They've put a lot into it."

Tempia studied the outdoor cooking area nestled on a covered platform. "Of course you noticed the aesthetics and functionality. You're quite the outdoor aficionado. Yes, they've done some major things over the years. And they plan to do more."

"Just as I suspected. Too bad my neighbors don't plan to vacate the neighborhood. Regardless of the expense involved, I would snap up their property if the impossible occurred."

Tempia visualized his neighbors' houses on each side and his warm relationship with Evelyn's family. He was probably equally invested in his neighbors on the west side of his house. An Alpine brick duplex and a cherry-brick single-family dwelling. "Why would you demolish either house? You already possess a nice-size backyard."

"I would keep the house intact and connect the back area." He laughed when her nose wrinkled. "A passing thought. I prefer having my current neighbors more than acquiring their backyards."

"Glad to hear it," Tempia said, eating her last bite of pizza.

Cory glanced over his shoulder when Tempia's cousin Billy called his name. "Looks like the basketball players are ready." Holding on to her hand, Cory stood and kissed her cheek. "This won't take long."

Tempia hugged him. "Enjoy the game."

She clocked his steps as he walked to where the men had gathered. Pushing her seat back, she moseyed toward the dessert station. Before long, her grandmother stood beside her.

Wanda removed a plate off the table. "An old friend knows Cory's grandparents quite well. She and her husband have spoken to him on numerous occasions. They hated he never showed an interest in either of their granddaughters. From all accounts, both of those young women consider him a good man."

Tempia faced the grinning woman. "Gammy! You knew how much I wanted to restore a connection with Cory. I would have loved to hear that your friend knew him. Why didn't you tell me?"

"Shush, child. Graham and I agreed not to say one word until we met him for ourselves. This evening, we agreed that he seems like a nice young man. In our opinion, regardless of the outcome, dating him is a splendid idea."

Tempia's shoulders drooped. Why did people commend her for dating Cory yet added the same disclaimer, "regardless of the outcome"?

Wanda changed the subject as her son and daughter-in-law drew near.

Tempia ate French apple cake while the others made small talk. Her thoughts wandered to Cory. She had expected him to mention her text message after everyone had eaten dinner. Perhaps he would bring it up after he had dropped off her brothers at their house.

She moved across the yard and joined her female cousins while the men continued their basketball game.

* * *

Slightly after dusk, Cory parked in front of her parents' house. Turning around, he peered into the back seat. "You guys play a mean hand-off basketball game. How well do you play volleyball?"

Curt glanced at his sister. "I've never played volleyball before, but Tempie said we'll play the next time we visit your house."

"And maybe swim again in your neighbor's swimming pool," Noah piped in, opening the car door.

Cory chuckled. "I enjoyed meeting your family tonight. We'll set up something at my place soon."

Tempia opened the front passenger door and stepped outside the vehicle. "It's after nine. Did either of you bring a door key?"

"You can let us in, or we can ring the doorbell," Curt said, following behind Noah.

Tempia headed after her brothers. "Next time, grab the spare key off the hook inside the laundry room, just in case you need it."

Racing up the steps, Noah called over his shoulder, "Stop acting cranky. Go home and get some sleep. Hope you feel better tomorrow."

"I still like him just like I thought I would," Curt proclaimed as she stood beside him on the porch.

"Me too," Noah mumbled through a yawn.

After unlocking the door, Tempia threw her arms around her brothers. "I love group hugs," she said once the boys hugged her back. "Be sure to share your glowing report with Mom and Dad."

Tempia waved as Curt shut the door. Retracing her steps to Cory's SUV, she slid inside the vehicle.

Cory started the engine. "I think your brothers like me. Did I guess right? Or do I have more work to do to win them over?"

"They like you. A lot," Tempia said, laughing. "They secured the deal last

Saturday."

"Good. I was ready to adopt the motto I had during my school days: 'Onward, rugged soldier.'"

Cory executed a U-turn and headed in the opposite direction. "Speaking of securing the deal, let's discuss that text message. Care to elaborate on your intentions?"

Off the top of my head? Absolutely not.

Tempia had had a great deal to say before he raised the question, and now, nothing. Her mind was blank. The frustration she had felt before firing off the text message had vanished after her finger hit the send button. She had no justification for it, so why make something up when truthfulness was required to further their relationship? Cory might never forgive a fudge, but past occurrences proved he would forgive an honest error. She may as well reveal the insecurities he probably knew she had.

Hindered by the seat belt, she turned her body toward his. Her mouth refused to cooperate as he glanced at her. A trembly smile was all she could muster. Nipping her bottom lip, she cleared her throat several times. "Even though I know better, sometimes I make comparisons between you and Quince." Her hands raised in an "I don't know why" position as she continued her embarrassing confession. "From the first day I met Quince, he and I saw each other every single day. Somehow, his pursuit made me feel better about myself. Knowing his wooing was a gigantic sham dampens the experience, but it hasn't erased how alive I felt. Those genuine feelings embedded themselves inside my soul."

Cory pulled into the parking lot of her complex. "Was Quince your first boyfriend after high school?"

Her fingers fiddled in her hair as she reflected on his question. Tempia had left home because she disagreed with her father's antiquated dating policies, but she missed his firm hand after moving into her apartment. Before meeting Quince, she had never entertained any man at her apartment. "I went on group dates in high school and had fun dates once I graduated. My dad was strict concerning who took me out and gave everyone I brought home the third degree."

"No surprise there. He cares about you."

"With all of that, I never had a serious relationship until Quince. Even though Quince's courtship was a lie, there isn't anyone else I can compare you with."

Cory pulled into a parking spot close to her apartment, walked around the car, and stopped beside the passenger door as he waited for Tempia to step outside the vehicle.

"What cool drink do you have inside?" he asked. The toneless question suggested support but lacked enthusiasm.

"Cold honey, lemon, and ginger tea. I have a full pitcher."

Apparently deep in thought, he followed behind her into the apartment and sat down on the love seat.

Tempia brought in their drinks and took the seat beside him. There was something different about his countenance. Calm, cool, and collected Cory appeared conflicted. "Do you like the tea?" she asked after he downed a swallow. "I hear tea and honey is an acquired taste. Plus, lemon adds tang, and ginger supplies spice."

He drank more of the brew, then sat the cup upon the table. "It's soothing. I'd love the recipe before I leave." He paused. "Ms. Wade, last night I was this close to giving up on us." Raising his right hand, Cory's thumb and forefinger displayed a tiny gap. "I fell asleep on the couch. Starvation, a strained neck, leg cramps, and back spasms woke me up four hours later. I read your message. It didn't sit well."

Tempia avoided looking at Cory. Her mother's painting of Paris grabbed her full attention. The fact that he'd decided to hang in there didn't lessen her regret. She should have known better than to respond like a juvenile. If the roles had been reversed, she would have thrown in the towel.

She counted to ten twice. "Why did you give me a third chance? The night of our first date was the second reprieve," she murmured.

"I've learned the hard way that I need to skip making decisions when I'm angry or exhausted—and especially when I'm both at the same time. But Tempia, you can't make situations easier on yourself by making them difficult for me."

Tempia kneeled on the love seat, grasping Cory's hands. "I have a lot going on inside of me too, but I promise not to second-guess your every move and to tone down my insecurities. A lot."

Cory pulled her body onto his lap. Brushing his lips across her mouth, he whispered in her ear, "Double ditto back to you. This relationship will not blow up by my default. No matter the time or day, please contact me whenever you like." His lips hovered above her mouth. "I will reply as quickly as possible."

That night, Tempia fell asleep muttering Cory's youthful motto. "Onward, rugged soldier" became her battle cry.

* * *

The next evening, her cell phone rang as she stepped onto her parents' porch. After checking the caller ID, she sat on the glider, setting it in motion. "Hey, girl, what's up?"

"Waiting on Rob to arrive home from work. We're eating dinner at my in-laws' house. What's up with you this weekend? Made any plans?"

"Not really, except for eating breakfast at Community Ministries tomorrow morning. After that, I'll probably just loll around my apartment."

"Temp, have you noticed that since you left your parents' house, you've never called the place where you live 'home'? Don't forget that home is where the heart is. Or something like that."

"It's because I didn't and still don't hold any deep affection for either of my apartments, or Quince's house. And don't you dare say, 'You only get as good as you put in,'" the friends exclaimed together. Tempia continued speaking while Gabby laughed. "Cory didn't mention whether he and I were getting together later. Maybe he'll spring a huge surprise this evening."

"If he doesn't pop over or take you out, just remember the marvelous time you spent together last Saturday and yesterday. Where are you now?"

"I'm sitting on the porch at my parents' house. Mom's cooking dinner for me. She wants the lowdown on our outing yesterday."

"So do I. I bet Cory loved their yard and outdoor kitchen. Was he salivating?"

Gabby's awareness concerning minute details about Cory proved amazing. "You truly do understand my boyfriend's personality to a tee. Please clue me in on whatever insight you have. But here's what occurred the night before." Her summary included why she sent the text, Cory's response, their dinner yesterday, plus the couple coming to terms at her apartment. "I've adopted the motto he lived by in his younger years. When feeling neglected, 'onward, rugged soldier' will improve my disposition."

"You have huge expectations Cory will never fulfill. You and he went on your first date just two weeks ago after waiting fourteen months to hear from him again. Don't let nonsense ruin the association before it develops into a relationship."

Tempia removed the cell phone from her ear. *You have a lot of nerve. Cory and I have a relationship now.*

Breathing deeply, she returned the cell phone to her ear. "Maybe you know your husband's cousin better than you do your best friend."

Gabby laughed. "After twenty-three years, we know each other well enough."

"Yeah. We do. Show some compassion, please. I often feel neglected and alone."

"Have you had those feelings this week?"

"I do whenever Cory doesn't contact or visit me even though he could if he wanted to. I fear he might decide that a lifelong relationship between us won't work, even if we end up dating for three years."

"Listen. You and I are best friends because you are a passionate, caring, and dependable person who makes appropriate decisions once you recognize your faults. You are not a rugged soldier but a vibrant woman who wants to marry the man she loves. Do not let present circumstances redefine who you are."

Tempia brushed teardrops off her cheeks. "Thanks, Gabby. I needed wise counsel."

"Just as I needed some the Saturday after Cory dropped by your parents' house. My husband mishandled the situation between you and Cory, but you didn't rant against him. Because of your wise advice, I didn't go home and dump on Rob. I removed my feelings out of the equation and actively listened to his explanations."

"Thanks, friend. I needed to hear that as well. I am much stronger than I sometimes behave."

"So is your boyfriend. Cory kept the date on Thursday. Kudos to him. He handled the problem beyond reproach. Before you glue his feet to a pedestal, just remember, Cory has faults just like we all do. Let's hope he's equal to the task on the next occasion."

Tempia jumped to her feet in a single motion. "I won't disgrace myself a second time, Gabby Stephens."

"Just be sure to forgive Quince, Cory, and Tempia most of all. Otherwise, the same issue will keep happening. Remember to problem solve to cope with difficult situations. Don't live in an alternate reality. Rob's home. Gotta go." Her bestie ended the call.

What drivel. Tempia had forgiven herself and Quince after the divorce became final. Cory hadn't done one thing that required forgiveness. *I'm not stuck in neutral, Gabby. So there.*

She dropped the cell phone into her purse and headed through the front door.

Later on Friday night, Tempia called Cory before she crawled onto the love seat. He answered the cell phone on the first ring.

"What's up, lovebug? I was seconds away from calling you. How goes it tonight?"

Lovebug! Her first pet name. Tempia blushed all over herself.

"I ate dinner at my parents' house and treated the boys to dessert at an ice cream parlor on our way back to my apartment. They're playing an adventure game on the bed, and I'm getting cozy on the love seat. How was your evening?"

"Lazy. My parents treated me to dinner. Home-cooked Meals by Granny Emma had a full house. Now I'm downstairs taking an early night myself. Any weekend plans?"

Optimism for the couple spending this weekend together rose. "We're carrying breakfast to the ministry in the morning around nine, and then my brothers will go home. I'll catch up on my reading here. I've been reading the same novel for three weeks. How about you? Any set plans?"

"Helping Eric tame their front and back yards will steal my entire day. The man should invest in a professional landscaper. Mama's gardener is a phone call away."

The couple continued a leisurely conversation until Cory ended the call.

Tempia set the cell phone on the table. Her boyfriend had made plans that didn't include seeing her. She felt like a one-sided relationship would never reach marriage.

As she inwardly fumed, her prior rebuke from Gabby entered her thoughts and made her pause. She decided to let it go and call him tomorrow night.

* * *

On Saturday morning, Cory left the doughnut shop carrying three boxes filled with assorted doughnuts, muffins, and sweet rolls. He parked in front of Community Ministries five minutes before the Wade family parked behind his SUV.

Grinning, he left the vehicle. "Are you pleasantly surprised?" he asked Tempia as she leaped from her vehicle and hugged his neck in a vise-like grip.

Tempia rolled her forehead across his chest, muttering into his shirt. "You came, Cory. I haven't seen the Pearsons since your parents told them you and I are dating. They are bound to ask difficult questions. Thanks for supporting me."

Cory had recognized the gravity of the moment. The Pearsons might ask questions he didn't want Tempia to field alone. Yet he hadn't envisioned his appearance would arouse such emotions in Tempia. Her brothers' startled expressions lent credence to the compelling notion that his being there deeply touched his girlfriend's heart. Curt and Noah stared at each other, then they flanked their sister's body while Tempia clung onto Cory as if for dear life.

After kissing his shirted chest, Tempia released her hold and flung her arms around her brothers' shoulders, pulling both boys closer. Her lively gaze searched Cory's face. "You should have told me you were joining us today. Or did you make the decision this morning?"

"Either way, your response proves my coming was an excellent choice. My decision was made on the drive home from your apartment Thursday night. Since the Pearsons know we're dating, we should present a united front." Cory handed Tempia his car keys. "I'll help Curt and Noah bring in the heavy stuff. Grab the sweets boxes off the back seat."

Once the food was displayed, the eager families got in lines buffet-style. Chrissy and Lester Pearson took the opportunity to pull Cory and Tempia aside.

Chrissy hugged Tempia and then faced Cory. "Lillie and Tim stopped by here last week and dropped a bombshell."

"That two of our most fervent supporters were dating," Lester added. "How did you two meet each other?"

Chuckling, Cory draped his arm over Tempia's shoulder. "This place has brought me numerous blessings. Seeing this lady here is the greatest one."

"Wait. I'm confused. I didn't know you'd met Tempia at our ministry," Chrissy said.

"I didn't officially, but I saw her here three times while working in the utility closet. The short story is that we met in person six months before her marriage. After her divorce, God let me pursue the relationship I had originally desired." Cory described each visit and meeting Tempia at his cousin's house. He kissed her cheek. "Instead of waiting for the proper moment, I should have made my move sooner and introduced myself on the first day I saw her here."

Deep in thought, Chrissy shook her head. "Tempia got married six months after we met her. Wasn't she already invested in a relationship by then? Would introducing yourself here have stopped her wedding?"

Tears misted in Tempia's eyes. "Had I met Cory sooner, the ill-fated wedding ceremony would've never taken place."

As the couple studied Tempia, Cory cleared his throat. "I'm helping Eric tame the jungle around his house today. We should probably get in on breakfast so I can get over there ASAP."

The women walked away first, with Lester and Cory following behind. Lester touched his hand to Cory's arm. He stared at the younger man with the same intensity he had directed at Tempia. "Tempia was glowing when she walked through the door this morning. I've never seen her this happy." He glanced at the woman who stood behind the table tying an apron around her waist. "Tempia is a kind and dependable person, Cory. She is a true asset in every way that matters. I believe she puts her heart into whatever tasks she undertakes."

Cory nodded. "When she and her brothers visited here the first time, she had a lilting voice, a perky smile, and spoke profound words. I took a quick peek around the utility room door and was awestruck. The total package stood before me: godly, caring, and generous in nature." He glanced across the room. Tempia was doing what she did best. "Before I drove away, the siblings returned bearing gifts. I should have introduced myself instead of driving off."

Lester patted Cory's back. "Just wanted you to know that Chrissy and I think highly of your girlfriend."

Cory released the deep breath he held, shaking the outstretched hand. "Thanks, Mr. Lester. Tempia is a warm and loving person."

Even though Cory had Tempia as a copilot, he couldn't shake the feeling he was flying solo without radar on this flight.

* * *

The next day, Tempia and Candace attended Nikki's women-only meeting. Although she wouldn't join every week, Tempia added monthly visits to her schedule.

Candace voiced the same consensus before she and Tempia parted company. "I really enjoyed all of those women. Their advice was excellent."

"Let's shop on our next outing. I need an updated wardrobe and sensible walking shoes. I'm banning tennis shoes for a while."

"Last summer, I did the same thing. No one needs a closet full of tennis shoes. We'll hit the stores in Illinois. I haven't crossed the river lately. Shawn tightens the leash if I venture too far from home too often."

Tempia laughed. From all accounts, Candace's husband was an easygoing man. "Sounds good to me. Let's get together soon." Tempia opened her car door.

Candace slid inside her vehicle. "Most definitely. I like getting to know you better." She started the car, let down the window, and closed the door. "Tell Cory hi for me."

"I'm seeing him later today. Do the same for me with Shawn."

The women waved again before driving off.

Gabby had said she and Candace enjoyed one another's company whenever the women found themselves together. But neither one had suggested meeting outside of whatever event Cory had planned. Perhaps Candace desired a deeper relationship with Tempia because Cory was Shawn's cousin.

* * *

That evening, Tempia and Cory went on a country drive and ate at a hamburger joint on the way home. Their outing was the perfect culmination of a delightful weekend. The only low spot had been Cory keeping mum about his and Mr. Lester's short chat yesterday. Since Mr. Lester had excluded her from whatever he'd discussed with Cory, she accepted her boyfriend's silence on the matter and chose forward thinking instead.

Tempia had only bitten her tongue twice to keep quiet before Cory dropped her off at home. Gabby had set the correct precedence once again.

Cory and I are perfect together. We're both exiting our comfort zones in numerous ways. We have a romantic alliance that will sustain the long haul.

Chapter Twenty-One

The upcoming months brought an unforeseen whirlwind of activity. The couple incorporated one another into their own personal spheres. For Tempia, redirecting her marriage ambitions proved a laborious task. If Cory experienced challenges balancing the couple's reality, he hid his navigation efforts well. Tempia and Cory supported each other's individual relationships and separate pursuits. Even though seeing Cory every day remained her fervent wish, she revamped her newly acquired social calendar and cultivated a satisfying lifestyle.

These days, Tempia's soul remained peaceful even when alone inside her apartment. She renewed previous friendships and strengthened her existing ties among family and special co-workers. After wavering back and forth, she signed up for another semester of acrylic painting and enrolled in a Spanish Conversation II class.

Without Cory holding her hand during his off-work hours, Tempia's psyche thrived on multiple levels. Why had she thought Quince's nonstop courtship indicated he valued her as a person? She realized he'd just been playing an intricate game of cat and mouse. Cory, however, trusted her choices and didn't seek control over her head space, activities, and friendships. He insisted Tempia engage people in her life other than himself. Also on the upside, her positive attitude and being content when alone ended the need for Gabby's oversight. She no longer gave Tempia motivational tips throughout the week. The new and improved Tempia Wade thrived in her private endeavors and new life experiences.

* * *

One Monday, she and Cathy spent a relaxing evening watching a Cardinals baseball game at Busch Stadium. Cathy, her husband, and Cory's parents were all die-hard Cardinals baseball fans. Why was Cory the only one in the family who didn't care much for baseball?

While talking before the game started, Tempia gained a better understanding of the siblings' relationship. Despite four years separating their ages, Cathy and Cory had always been close.

Cathy stated that Cory hated giving up on anything. In Tempia's mind, that implied that once his heart became fixated on a lady, he would accept her into his life, even despite a poor showing on the lady's part. Cathy's assessment of her brother's mindset didn't compute for Tempia. The fourteen-month Cory brush-off would have lasted forever if not for Quince's unplanned visit.

Most importantly to Tempia, spending the game together had given her time to bond with Cathy. The women planned a monthly get-together before their vehicles drove off the parking lot. Tempia logged another baby step on her and Cory's voyage. In her humble opinion, their relationship would have survived his sister's disapproval, but her endorsement wouldn't hurt the couple's bonding process.

Warmth spread throughout her body as she parked in front of her apartment. Cory sat in his SUV on the other side of the parking lot. Tempia sprang from the car, wound her arms around his neck, then stepped away. "You came to hear about my outing with Cathy. I am pleasantly surprised."

He held up a bag Tempia hadn't noticed. "If you didn't pig out on stadium junk, share dessert with me. No peeking," he said once she reached for the bag. "Be pleasantly surprised again."

Her hands hooking his elbow, she led Cory inside the living area.

Cory placed the dessert box on the counter, then he sat down on the love seat, hitching his right leg over his left thigh. "I hear your team kept up their winning streak. Let's see how well they perform before a hostile crowd. Where is the team headed?"

Tempia carried two plates piled high with apple dumplings. She passed one to Cory and plonked down beside him. "Wrigley Field. The Cubs are advancing toward a certain defeat next weekend. However, the high point was watching the Cardinals win their eighth-straight game with Cathy sitting beside me. I believe she had a good time as well." Tempia beamed when Cory's lips curved into a satisfying grin. She leaned closer. "Here's even better news. We're planning to get together on the first Monday of each month. I like her, Cory."

A light sparkled in each of Cory's eyes. "It's the perfect solution all around. Two remarkable women can only become fast friends."

Tempia planned to make him proud. "Your sister and I didn't murder each other. How's that for taking baby steps?"

Chuckling, Cory placed his empty plate on the end table. "Concerning taking baby steps, I want you and the gang from Rob's games get-together to reunite at my house. What's on your calendar for next Saturday?"

The air circulating in her lungs suddenly felt like it was suffocating her. "Um ... my brain is engineering a way out of meeting your friends. Those people laughed at me."

Compassion lit his eyes. "Not everyone laughed. Besides, that was then, and this is now. Accept they've grown up and will beg for your forgiveness."

Tempia set her plate beside his and held his hands. "Can't we meet my friends first and those friends last?"

"Last? I should continue cutting you out of important aspects of my social life?"

"Okay. So I can't watch you bowl, shoot pool, and play basketball. Surely you have other friends to throw into the mix before I meet that bunch."

Cory held her in his arms and rocked slowly.

Tempia sighed deep within her inner self. She couldn't read minds. What he was thinking was anyone's guess.

"Okay, lovebug," he finally said. "Introduce me to more of your friends. Pronto."

* * *

Cory first met Mia, Kevin, Jasmine, and Marcus at an amusement park. Better to mingle somewhere with activities than spend an afternoon watching Cory deflect open-ended questions. Even though the couples rode stimulating rides, played games, and ate funnel cakes, both Jasmine and Mia proved relentless in their hunt to better know Cory.

On the following Saturday, Sandra and her fiancé, Drew, Pam and her boyfriend, Tuck, Monica, and Nikki hung out at Cory's house along with Gabby, Rob, and the previous Saturday's bunch. Gabby's brother Mac, who had dated Nikki in the past, dropped by and brought along his best bud, Shady. Tempia had always believed the unconventional man and his nickname were made for each other. Monica garnered most of Shady's attention. As in their past encounters, she appeared to like him well enough. Nikki and Mac even managed to hold friction-free conversations throughout the afternoon.

Just as Tempia had suspected, Cory synced with the group like a hand inside a glove. Goodwill spread all around the place, which pleased the woman who now considered Cory's house her second home.

While the other vehicles drove away, Cory whispered into Tempia's ear before Tempia slid into Nikki's Jeep. "I've met your closest friends and most of your family members," he said. "May I please set up a meet and greet with my friends you prefer dismissing from our social life?"

"My boyfriend is a stellar guy in every way that counts. So is his girl-friend," Tempia said, laughing. "Set up something whenever you like. I'll always change my plans for you."

"Aw! How sweet is that? Go on. Give my girl a well-deserved kiss." Nikki coughed into her hand.

Cory laughed. "Sometimes eavesdroppers do hear good news. Although, I can't figure how you heard our discussion from inside the car."

"Some folks talk a lot. Some people listen acutely. I'm all ears."

"Good thing she doesn't gossip," Tempia added.

After Tempia entered the automobile, she and Cory waved at each other as the vehicle drove away.

Temple spun around, facing Nikki, her thumbs in the up position. "Two thumbs up?"

"I would throw in a third thumb if I had a spare one. He's nothing like your psychotic ex-husband. Also, he and Rob know each other inside and out. How did a best friend make those egregious errors in handling the Quince fiasco?"

Tempia shrugged. "Although I still can't figure out what happened, Gabby thinks their close friendship caused the problem, plus saved their relation-ship."

"I agree, and so should you by now," Nikki said.

Tempia laughed. "Perhaps Gab is right. She usually is."

"I observed Cory holding you in his arms after playing volleyball. The man truly likes you, Tempie."

"Everyone always says 'likes' instead of 'loves.' Of course Cory and I are friends, but I want to become his permanent leading lady."

"Slow your roll. You and Cory only started dating two months ago. You dated your ex for six months and divorced him after a five-month marriage. You and Cory are progressing just fine."

All of her friends had voiced the same opinion. If one more person—whether family member, friend, or associate—told Tempia how much her boyfriend liked her, she would … pray that his like developed into an abiding love.

Switching topics, the women discussed Mac and Shady on the rest of the drive home.

Tempia almost fainted when her friend revealed she wanted another chance with Mac. Tempia had assumed their rocky relationship couldn't be resurrected. Yet Gabby's brother wasn't a consummate player and had his strong points. Maybe Nikki and Mac would make a fresh start. And then Nikki said Monica had accepted a movie date with Shady for tomorrow evening.

Turning toward her friend, Tempia frowned. "I can't imagine a relationship between Monica and Shady. Can you?"

"They flirted around the idea while I dated Mac."

Monica and Shady dating each other sounded like a long stretch—but strange happenings were becoming commonplace.

* * *

While blending their lives together, Tempia and Cory spent two weekends per month either watching Westerns with her parents or sitcoms in the Sanderses' living room. They walked Riverfront Trail with Curt and Noah and took Cory's nieces and nephew to the children's zoo.

Tempia and her brothers remained faithful to the boys' overnight visits on the last weekend of each month. True to his word, Cory spent retreat Saturday with the siblings.

Tempia and Cathy got together monthly on Monday evenings while Cory hung out with Curt and Noah on the same day.

The couple visited all of the grandparents on Tempia's family side, ate dinner with Cory's grandparents, and took his great-grandmother to the movies.

* * *

Each day, the couple's burgeoning relationship soared to new heights. Tempia remained calm if she didn't see Cory's face every day or talk to him all night over the phone. He invited her to attend his church and visited her church service in return.

Now her Sundays were thankfully full. On varying Sundays, Tempia ate dinner at her parents' house on her siblings' retreat weekend, joined in on the Sanderses' Sunday dinner, and attended Nikki's women's group. On the fourth and occasionally fifth Sunday, she would cozy up with a romance novel. Tempia commiserated with the couples striving toward their happily ever afters.

* * *

On a June Friday night, tightwad Rob fulfilled his Skyline dinner cruise obligation. The special night commenced on a magnificent cool evening. A light wind fully cooperated. Live music, fine dining, and a captivating view of the St. Louis skyline highlighted the two-hour cruise. Tempia enjoyed a romantic night relaxing on the water with Cory and their best friends. Strolling around the top deck, the couples viewed the city lights from brand-new angles.

Throughout the summer, the couple met up with family and friends for various activities. They attended Candace and Shawn's cookout in July. Cory even attended several Cardinals baseball games with Tempia.

* * *

One late-September evening, Cory entered his living room, dropped his bowling bag by the door, and settled onto the sofa. He was physically and mentally exhausted. This Saturday would become the perfect stay-home day. Even though he and Tempia had dated for six months, most of their events had included other people. It was past time to ditch the crowd and concentrate on each other. Cory was no closer to forming a permanent alliance than he had been before requesting the first date.

One unstated grievance was her ability to brush off his wishes as if his preferences didn't count. Over a twenty-four-week span, he had observed Tempia short shrift his desires if they conflicted with her own. Because the couple had plenty of things in common, she ignored the areas where they disagreed. Years ago, Cory had discovered he enjoyed his own company and preferred spending more than a few evenings a month alone.

In May, Tempia had agreed to meet his friends from Rob's games party. Four months later, Tempia still hadn't settled on a date, accepting exclusion from major events in Cory's life. Cooperation was the key to enduring relationships, and Tempia truly thought she cooperated, yet she weighed their connectivity with her thumb on the scale.

Cory needed some time to himself and had chosen this weekend for his personal vacation. Even though Tempia disapproved of his plans, instead of staging a temper tantrum, she had agreed to not contact him until Sunday night.

Stretching his limbs on the sofa, Cory powered down his cell phone.

* * *

On a Saturday evening in October, Tempia gave Jake his accolades. Cory's cousin had hit it on the head that they would see each other at his grandparents' fifty-fifth wedding anniversary celebration. She and Cory had just stepped into the much-anticipated ballroom setting.

As always, Jake's current date had her gaze glued to her escort while Jake played the gallant role with his usual aplomb. Observing their interactions, Tempia knew this date would suffer the same fate as the women who had preceded her. Jake needed a woman who made him work for her respect.

Leaning closer to Cory, Tempia whispered in his ear. "I think Jake should date women like himself. The women I've met desire more than a few dates."

Cory's brows knitted into a wavy line. "Like himself? Which one of his dating flaws is in your bull's-eye?"

"All of his tactics stink. Every woman Jake has dated has wanted more from the association. They're not allotted enough time to change his direction."

"Women who expect more should date men who offer what they want."

"I never expected a cavalier attitude coming from you."

"After the traumatic experience with your ex, I never expected an 'I can mold him into the man I want him to become' attitude from you."

"Perhaps they view Jake as their dream man."

"Perhaps he doesn't want to be their dream man. Jake doesn't seek anything more than what each woman is ready to give him. Those women should choose their dates more wisely if he doesn't live up to their expectations."

"I disagree," Tempia said as Cory interrupted.

"Look. We came here to celebrate my grandparents' anniversary. Instead of critiquing Jake's social life, focus on ours. I want you to meet my friends who attended Rob's games party."

Tempia recognized a lost cause when she faced one. "Set something up quickly before I change my mind."

"Like you did when I met your friends at my house? What if I can't get everyone together quick enough for you? I'm the only person who aligns his schedule to your becks and calls. Other people pursue lives they enjoy living."

Tempia's heart sank. Now it seemed that, throughout their fantastic spring and summer, Cory had been a participant in name only. Had he set up the rapid-fire activities to lessen her insecurities?

That night, Tempia crawled into bed and dissected her and Cory's argument. He'd jumped down her throat for having a differing viewpoint. Did he harbor a grudge against her for not meeting some of his friends? From taking acrylic painting, brushing up on her Spanish, and hanging around her friends, Cory supported each of her endeavors. Even during his busy season, the couple had spent quality time together.

How hard would it be to properly meet folks who probably despised her? Most people at that party both knew and disliked Tempia's ex-husband. How could any of them have a favorable opinion regarding her when she'd rejected Cory in favor of Quince?

Tempia grabbed her phone off the floor by her bed and sent Gabby a brief message. *SOS. Are you available for lunch tomorrow?*

Gabby sent a swift reply. *Meet you at Capris. Noonish. Or should we talk now?*

Tomorrow is fine. Looking forward to eating a meal with you. It's been awhile. Tempia set her cell phone on the floor, retrieving it when an incoming message pinged.

See you at Capris, Shooting Star.

* * *

On Saturday afternoon, Gabby greeted Tempia inside the restaurant lobby. Their favorite pianist was in full swing as the hostess led the pair to their favorite table.

"Okay, Gab. Talk me down. The stubborn streak you claim I have is gaining fast momentum."

"Still resisting an introduction to the friends Rob and Cory share? If so, get over yourself and graciously give in."

Their regular waiter approached the table, confirming their usual orders. He left as fast as he had arrived. Tempia's mouth gaped on his departure. "How in the world did you know?"

"You sat next to my husband during dinner last night. He overheard the conversation. Cory's mother sat next to him, so she probably got an earful. Relax," Gabby advised when Tempia groaned. "I'm sure she only told her husband, just as Rob only told me. Listen. Surely you knew Cory wouldn't change his mind about you meeting friends he's known for years."

"I've met so many of Cory's friends that I forget about those people until he brings them up."

Gabby sighed. "Remember when I said Cory has faults like all normal folks do? He manages issues unless he believes the other person isn't negotiating in good faith. Then he moves on from that person."

"Like with Quince?"

"Yes, ma'am. Rob said you are the only bridge his cousin has rebuilt. However, I believe the bridge was closed for renovation and never burned. I understand your embarrassment and all that, but only two people made caustic remarks. They're pleasant folks, Temp. Gloria and Bill would've apologized in front of everyone had you returned to the living room. I believe Jaylen was the guy who laughed in the hall. Please understand, he and Cory have been friends since elementary school. Cory had never made an open play for any woman. When he did with you, it had everyone thinking he had fallen hard in a microsecond. They each probably know the truth by now, but back then, the ministry connection was unknown."

"All the more reason why his friends will hate me. They think Cory got rebuffed after he opened his heart. In their place, would you give me a second chance?"

"I would if my friend already had. Besides, he's given them all more details by now and expressed his expectations for when they meet you. Focus on the major point. This situation concerns you and Cory. His friends will agree wherever it's possible for them to comply. Are you happy only sharing a portion of Cory's life? Because you ran Cory ragged for six months, I don't think you comprehend how many events you missed."

"Guess I had too much fun to think about the downside. But I'm thinking now. Why didn't you clue me in?"

"Because you should have accommodated Cory simply because he asked. He does for you."

"Do you think I can make amends? Has Cory taken marriage off the table?"

"Cory has never placed marriage on the table. If he wanted to walk away, he would have done so last night. So far, he's still willing to make the relationship work."

Tempia mustered up a smile when Gabby patted her hand. She had repeatedly blown off the one request Cory had ever made. She would correct her blatant disrespect for the man who deserved her respect.

* * *

When Rob approached the pool table, Cory put his pool stick aside. "Let's grab a drink and talk awhile."

The men ordered slushes then headed toward the farthest table.

"What's going on between you and Tempia?" Rob asked. He continued when his cousin's eyebrows raised. "You and your girlfriend are loud whisperers."

"Does Gabby know?"

"Not only did I tell her, Tempia texted her last night. They're eating lunch together as we speak."

"Tempia's comfort means the world to me. After the heartbreak Quince dealt her, she deserves an enjoyable life." Rotating his shoulders, Cory chuckled. "What's the verdict, cuz? Did I mishandle the situation?"

"Although I commend your patience, you should have kept Tempia on the hook. I'm going to plan a games get-together soon. I want you both there, so be prepared to hold her hand all night."

"What? You don't expect my lady love to rise to the occasion?"

"Do you?" Rob asked, laughing.

* * *

One week later, Tempia dressed for a games get-together at Gabby and Rob's house. The guest list proved identical to the previous one held inside his home. A last-minute renege was not an option. All invitees had RSVP'd they were coming. Cory would pick her up in ten minutes.

She studied her reflection in the bathroom mirror again, then rubbed the back of her neck. Her short, feathered hairstyle emphasized her diamond-shaped face. She had had a professional manicure and pedicure that morning, her open-toe sandals displaying a tiny pearl on each toe. She wore dark-beige cropped pants and a lacey light-beige camisole underneath a sky-blue top. A white knee-length cardigan completed the outfit.

Tempia left the bathroom, slung her purse over her shoulder, and stood in the middle of the combination living and dining area. She should have driven herself to the party or at least to Cory's house. He was coming all the way to pick her up when he lived only three blocks from Rob. Now he had to make an hour round trip and then repeat the process to bring her home. When Cory offered to pick her up, she should have said, "No, thank you. I'll drive myself." Instead, she'd hugged him and whispered, "Thanks, Cory. What time should I be ready?"

It is what it is. Too late to change course.

Chapter Twenty-Two

Her lips downturned, Tempia stepped outside, locked the door, and was standing in front of her apartment building when Cory pulled up. She reached the car before he turned off the engine and slid onto the passenger seat once she heard the door lock pop.

"As beautiful as ever, lovebug. New outfit?"

"Mom and I went shopping this morning. Okay. Tell me about your friends. Likes. Dislikes. Who are these people?"

"A case of an inquiring mind wants to know? Here's the simple low-down. I attended elementary school or high school with most of the guests. Everyone knows that you and I have been dating awhile. Relax."

On the drive into the city, Cory made small talk until he parked the SUV across the street from Rob's house. The couple entered the foyer holding hands. Even though the party was in full swing, a different vibe existed than it had at the last get-together. Excitement and a general sweet feeling tinged the air. Every guest surged toward the couple. Gabby and Rob had come down the hallway and stood beside Tempia. The same man and lady who made the caustic comments on the first go-round greeted the couple first.

The woman wore a cute, short natural hairstyle and hugged Tempia. "Hi, I'm Gloria. My repentant sidekick is my husband, Bill. It's two years too late, but please accept our apologies. During the last party, Cory berated our childish response to the embarrassing accident."

"Forgive my odious comment," Bill said. "I aimed for witty but sounded like a jerk."

So, this was how people humbling themselves looked. Squeezing Cory's hand, Tempia laughed. "No lasting harm was done. I picked up my face off the floor last year."

Instead of laughing, the couple stared at Cory, and then back at Tempia.

Tempia's hand covered her mouth. "Oops. Guess my wit failed just like yours did two years ago."

Tempia glanced at Gabby when her friend gasped. Her equally shocked husband stood beside her.

"Tempie's on a roll tonight," Gabby said, patting her bestie's upper arm.

Rob nodded. "That one-liner was better than one of my knock-knock jokes. Since the shoe is on the other foot, the ice has been sufficiently broken. Who's in for a fun game night?"

Gloria and Bill glanced at each other. "We recognize that a hurt that festered for two years can't be swept away by someone saying sorry," said Gloria. "You'll see. Our apologies are the real deal. We regret disrespecting you."

Holding back tears, Tempia nodded before the rest of the guests passed her, Cory, Gabby, and Rob as if they held court in an official introduction line. Cory made quick work of introducing each person until an auburn-haired man stepped up. "Case Patrick. I acclaimed my buddy's charm that night."

Tempia shook the extended hand. "I remember you used my grandma's favorite applause word, 'bravo.'"

The blonde wet-wipe beauty stood beside him. "Tina Patrick. Your dating Cory is no surprise. His bliss when you entered the room surpassed every reaction I had ever seen him give any woman."

Tempia closed her eyes for a moment, but a lone teardrop trickled down her right cheek. "Thank you both for making me feel like a decent human being that night. Hiding in the foyer while I ate was a fear-based decision I regret making."

"Just like how your boyfriend regrets leaving the party without you." Bill laughed when Cory grunted. "He didn't confide his deepest secrets. I've just known the man since kindergarten."

When the meet and greet continued, Tempia remained at peace until the last man dressed in khakis, a checkerboard T-shirt, and white flip-flops reached the group. His clothes were identical to what he'd worn that night. He spoke before Cory introduced him. "Just wanted to explain my unchivalrous laugh while you and Quince sat in the foyer. That evening, Cory wore his heart on his sleeve. He liked you at first sight, accepted your apology, rejoined the party wearing wet clothing, and blasted everyone—especially Gloria and Bill; yet you chose a swine over a good man. I felt you and Quince deserved each other."

Tempia's slow-burning fuse ignited. "Thank God He doesn't share your judgment. He knows the heart as well as knowing deeds. The laughter and snide remarks, not the man sitting there, sequestered me in the foyer. Only two individuals rose to the occasion besides Gabby. The others didn't offer any sympathy or compassion. They all gawked at the freak. At the end of the day, strangers mocked me. And Cory disappeared. Quince Jones drove me home but then almost destroyed my life."

Tempia recognized she'd crossed the line before Gabby pinched her arm.

"Thanks, Jaylen," Cory said. "The three of us will break bread together a little later. At the first get-together, I left Tempia in the hands of an untrustworthy man. Negative emotions had overridden my brain cells before I left."

Cory and Jaylen locked gazes for a split second before Jaylen faced Tempia. "Looking forward to sharing our meal."

As soon as Jaylen walked away, Cory faced Tempia. He gestured toward the front door. "We need to talk. Let's step outside."

Gabby immediately touched her friend's arm. "Tempie, are you okay? Do you need to lie down?"

Rob grabbed his wife's hand. "Don't interfere, Gabby. Let them speak in private."

* * *

Gabby's tear-filled eyes failed to change Cory's direction. Milestones were recognized whenever he reached one. This was a moment to decide whether to break it off or keep the relationship going. He opened the door, leading Tempia outside. He noted her clenched jaw and rigid stance.

Thinking back to Rob's first game night, Tempia and Quince had suffered Jaylen's disdain in private. Jaylen hadn't spoken one word against Tempia while Cory was within earshot. Although Tina and Case had risen to the occasion, the others hadn't made light of the situation, nor had their fingers pointed. They had simply watched the situation unfold.

Cory realized Tempia's facial expression had changed. Her rapid blinking and trembling lips and chin relayed she was fearful, but fear couldn't exonerate her belittling his friends. She was in a safe place. Why was she afraid?

Taking a deep breath, Cory sighed. "I believe closure is important. We've dated too long without you meeting important people in my life. I'm tired of attending their events alone."

Frowning, her chin rose. "That's because you never asked your girlfriend to accompany you."

"But I did suggest you meet them for the past seven months. You hemmed

213

and hawed each time I broached the topic. You always said you weren't ready to meet any of them yet. The last time you agreed, you wouldn't settle on a date."

"They didn't embarrass you—"

"Nor did they embarrass you," Cory interrupted. "Minor accidents are soon forgotten. Two years ago, two of my friends used poor judgment. The rest simply watched the event unfold. This evening has given you a great way to ease in to the people and feelings, but you dropped the ball."

"Please ... so this fiasco is now my fault?"

"Look. These people are in my mainstay group of friends. Like you and your closest friends, we're all friends for life. Except for your reaction to what Tina and Case did back then, your responses to everyone else were uncalled for."

Tempia shrugged. "Being nice to your friends won't complete me. I don't require new people to enjoy my social life."

"Neither do I. Yet I've hung out with your family, friends, and co-workers on numerous occasions. Some folks I like and some folks I can live without seeing. But I support you favoring them and bit the bullet. Can you do the same for me?"

Her countenance shrank before Cory's eyes. Her head hung while he waited.

While her body shook, tears rolled down Tempia's cheeks. "My whole life fell apart that night. The aftermath almost killed me. I lost you, some friends, plus my self-respect. I'm the one who suffered through untold pain and neglect. Your friends made up their minds about me that night. They don't care whether I live or die."

That declaration proved over the top. How could Cory bring Tempia back to Earth before she crash landed? "Then why did they humble themselves to formally meet you?"

"Because each one likes and respects *you*. Their friend. They couldn't care less about me."

"Is Rob included in that description? Did your heart-to-heart discussion with him mean anything?"

"Of course it did! Earlier, I referenced his actions at the games get-to-gether. Neither do I blame you. However, I would not have dated Quince had you stuck by me. Knowing you were waiting, I would have braved going back into the living room. Jaylen's laughter stripped away what little courage I had built."

Cory barely kept himself from laughing. "In other words, you ate your meal with Quince instead of me because you were afraid of being ridiculed. You let Quince drive you home instead of the friend who brought you because I had left the party. You accepted a date with Quince because you thought I wouldn't ask you out. You disbelieved your best friend's assessment of my dating life because a man you had just met said she was mistaken. You rejected your family and friends' assessment of his character because he treated you well enough. You married him despite the cracks you observed in his shiny armor because he proposed marriage. Did I correctly summarize your logic? If not, correct my errors."

Tempia crumbled on the front steps, crying.

Cory claimed the space beside her, rocking Tempia in his arms.

"Awhile ago ... Gabby ... Gabby predicted ..." Sniffling, she took a deep breath. "Gabby predicted this would happen if I didn't forgive you, Quince, and myself."

"Go on," Cory said when she hesitated.

"Oh, Cory. She made me angry but ended the conversation before I could tell her I had forgiven Quince and myself, and that you hadn't done anything that required forgiveness." Tempia wiped moisture off her cheeks with wet fingers. "That last part was true. You hadn't, Cory. Maybe someplace deep inside, I believed you had. But ... since I no longer compare how you and Quince treat me, and rejected the idea he was a stalker, I assumed the Quince episode had truly ended."

"It hasn't?"

"Maybe. Maybe not. I ... I had believed fear kept me from meeting the get-together crowd. Inside just now, I resented everyone except Tina and Case. During the introductions, my true feelings probably were released." Shaking her head, Tempia's lips drooped. "Do you suppose I need professional counseling?"

Wise advice benefited everyone who listened. Whether Tempia required outside intervention was anyone's guess. He'd witnessed life transformations with only self-correction, yet some people required both methods. Cory stroked her cheek then raised her face toward his. "Godly counsel can equip you to let Jesus slay the dragons in your life."

"So ... you're ... not taking me home? You're giving me another chance?"

"Leaving now would defeat the purpose of you coming. It's better that you give my friends the benefit of your doubts. Just like you forgave the four close friends who didn't accept Quince."

Tempia touched her hair and rubbed her face. "I must look frightful by now. I don't want to embarrass you, Cory."

"Rob's folks live five doors down. You can spruce yourself up at their house."

* * *

Tempia felt no grand transformation as she re-entered Gabby's house. The individuals she disliked before Cory had rushed her outside remained on her bad side upon her return. Thank God that acting proved a beneficial talent she hadn't known she possessed. She ate a meal sitting at the table with Cory and Jaylen without gagging. She did learn that just as life had moved onward and upward for her, so it had for Jaylen. He'd married his longtime girlfriend the weekend before Tempia's wedding. His wife, a nurse, had been working the night of Rob's party and so didn't receive an invite to this one. But the welcoming lady had sent Tempia a message to her via Jaylen's phone. *Tempia, I can't wait to meet you. Please join us for dinner on any night you choose. It's okay to bring Cory along. lol*

A man who married a sympathetic woman must have a few good qualities. Tempia took another look at Jaylen and saw a smile twinkling in his eyes. In Jaylen's defense, he'd laughed at her and Quince in support of his friend. Maybe she needed to reassess her previously held convictions.

* * *

Early Sunday morning, Tempia rang the doorbell then entered her parents' house. "It's me," she spoke in a subdued voice, creeping upstairs. She met her father coming out of the bedroom.

"What's wrong, Tempie? Did something happen at Rob's party?"

Tempia spotted her stepmother standing beside the bed. "Hi, Mom. Dad, I'm fine, but something did occur during Rob's party." She entered the bedroom and sat on the chaise lounge. Once her parents sat on the bed facing her, Tempia relayed the full story.

"Did all the other guests have a positive response when you arrived back at the party?" Blanche asked.

Tempia nodded. "If I accept our interactions as proof, no one seemed to hold my surliness against me."

"Good. Because they treated you horribly on the first go-round."

"Which doesn't demand our daughter respond in kind," Sam reminded. "Tempie, have you decided to seek godly counsel? If so, I recommend Shirley Rutgers from our church."

"I agree," his wife concurred. "She teaches CBT from a biblical perspective."

"Hey, you didn't conjure up that name on a lark. Neither of you are mental-health advocates. Have ... have you both wanted me to go to therapy? What is CBT?" she asked after her parents nodded.

Sam captured his wife's hand in his hands when she glanced his way. Tempia barely discerned her father's brief nod.

Leaning on her husband, Blanche smiled. "Cognitive behavioral therapy, or CBT, proponents believe our thoughts and behaviors influence our feelings. We will feel better once we change our thoughts and reactions concerning situations."

"And ... you ... know this information because ..."

Shaking her head, Blanche sighed. "Ten years ago, I needed assistance navigating my relationship with a daughter I didn't birth: you. In my mind, you have always been the perfect child. But the perfect child always did, and still does, introduce me as her stepmother. I attended counseling sessions to gain a handle on the situation. Your father sat in on the final meeting."

"Mom! I think of you as my mother. I barely remember my real mom."

Blanche's bright eyes sparkled as she laughed. "The words 'real mom' would have triggered heartbreak in the past. I've learned to forget trivialities and focus on the fact that my lovely only daughter calls me Mom every day. Therapy was very beneficial for me. So, if you agree, we'll treat Ms. Rutgers to lunch after church service if she's free. Then you can converse sans commitment."

* * *

Cory picked up his cell phone late into Sunday evening. Last month, he had given up trying to keep up with Quince's previous communication schedule. Cory's contribution to the relationship was trying to understand the person Tempia truly was. He gained pertinent information by mingling with her family, friends, co-workers, and Community Ministries attendees.

In many ways, Tempia was the woman he'd envisioned in his soul. His lovebug was a smart, articulate people person who kept a soft heart regarding other folks. Sometimes she treated strangers better than she treated herself. And then, smack in the middle of something good, she picked the world apart. Her fear of people's negative reactions oftentimes pushed her in the wrong direction. On those occasions, she took the easiest route rather than tackling the messy, tangled path.

Tempia answered the cell phone before the call went to voicemail. "Hey, Cory. Did you have a busy day?"

"I attended church, came home, and stayed here all day. How about you?"

"After church, my family ate lunch with a church member, Shirley Rutgers. She is a cognitive behavioral therapist my parents thought I should meet. I liked her, and she agreed to take me on. I have a morning appointment this Wednesday."

Unwilling to ask questions, Cory waited through a long pause.

"What do you think about me talking with a professional counselor?"

"I believe you will make an appropriate decision by either setting up more counseling sessions or seeking another qualified therapist."

"So, my ... speaking with a mental health worker won't put you off of me?"

"Not taking your mental health seriously will doom our relationship."

A loud knock sounded on Cory's front door.

"Evelyn has an early-evening movie date, so I told her the kids could stay here while she tests the waters. Pray for me."

Her laughter tinkled across the line. "A man that wants six children can handle four. Two of whom are practically teenagers."

"Goodnight, lovebug. We'll talk tomorrow."

Stepping outside, Cory sat on the lower deck. While the kids played a raucous volleyball game, he wrestled with guilt that had developed during his conversation with Tempia. Trying to please her hadn't benefited her much. She might have sought godly counsel earlier had he insisted she meet his friends before yesterday.

* * *

Five weeks later, Tempia mulled the future while driving to her parents' house. Her mother was cooking their family a feast to celebrate her graduation from counseling. She had attended her last counseling session that afternoon. For five weeks, with the help of an unbiased trained facilitator, she had delved into what made herself tick. The sessions had helped her analyze herself. She realized she had never liked Quince but viewed him as an acceptable means to her preferred end: marriage.

After the honeymoon ended, she had effectively led a double life trying to salvage a marriage while hating the man she married. Casting Quince as the grand manipulator allowed her to play the victim and avoid accepting fault. Then she'd accepted her shattered life as retribution for believing her ex's lies. A year later, she still withheld forgiving his deception. Ms. Rutgers suggested an active lifestyle had relegated Tempia's ex-husband to her subconscious mind. Unknown triggers could have revived negatively charged Quince-related emotions—especially if Cory's behavior caused disappointments.

Achieving a significant connection with Cory depended on Tempia taking responsibility for all her choices. In fact, she held a secret grievance against her boyfriend. After she met Cory, he pursued his own dreams and abandoned her. For a man who claimed he liked her on first sight, she felt he had given up on her quickly. Gabby had been right all along: Tempia hated Quince and was angry with Cory. Her observations regarding herself proved complicated. She simultaneously slighted herself and basked in false praise where it wasn't warranted.

These days, Tempia identified and redirected difficult conditions. She trusted her ability to assess situations and select the proper course. Fear had reigned supreme over her life. She realized that introducing Blanche as her stepmother but calling her Mom satisfied misplaced guilt for dearly loving a woman other than her birth mother. From an early age, Tempia had cultivated a full garden of erroneous ideas.

She couldn't redo her past incorrect assumptions but could control her present and future thought process.

Thoughts of the future brought Cory to her mind. Her boyfriend relished being alone and shaping situations to his liking. Tempia did too, in a different way. Compromise proved the key in nurturing dynamic relationships. Going forward, she would split their differences and let Cory win on an equal basis.

When the couple began dating, he adopted most of her plans. Gradually, he ignored her choices and pleased himself. He enjoyed sitting home alone while Tempia wanted constant stimulation and entertainment.

Now, in front of her parents' house, Tempia parked behind her father's truck and hurried inside, hanging her coat on the tree rack.

Noah met her in the foyer. "Behave yourself. Company is in the living room."

"Who's here?" Tempia asked, falling into step behind her brother. She entered the living room, where Cory and her father were deep in conversation. Neither man noticed her standing there.

Cory had won over her reluctant father, who had told her Cory would be welcomed as his son-in-law if the time came. "Don't jump ahead of yourself," Sam had advised in the next breath.

Tempia scurried across the floor and plopped onto Cory's lap.

Laughing, he gave her a gentle squeeze and kissed her cheek. "Your mother invited me to your special celebration. We parked down the street so you could have a greater surprise. I'm proud of you, lovebug."

Their faces close together, the couple's gazes locked. Cory's eyes smoldered with an intensity Tempia had never seen. Voices speaking in the room sounded far away. Tempia felt as if no one else existed in the world besides her and Cory.

As a low voice spoke near her ear, a soft punch hit her arm. "Earth to Tempia," Curt said.

Noah appeared beside Cory. "Ah, man. Don't you two go googly-eyed on us. Dinner is ready. It's time to eat."

"Then head into the kitchen," his father said, studying his daughter. "Tempie, you haven't greeted your other guests."

"Goodness gracious, I didn't see you all." Tempia jumped up and rushed across the floor. "I'm just now deciphering what Cory said about parking. I missed the 'we' in my excitement."

Lillie hugged Tempia. "Congratulations on a job well done. Never look back."

Tim nodded. "Self-control will open many doors. We are proud of you, Tempia."

Wiping her tearful eyes with her fingers, Tempia beamed her gratitude.

"Let's head into the dining room," her father said.

Tempia and Cory entered the kitchen as the group settled around the table.

Tempia hugged Blanche from behind. "Mom, thank you for my wonderful surprise. Eating dinner with Cory and our families completes my day. Do you think it's more likely now that Cory and I will make a trip to the altar?"

"I believe a middle ground exists where you and Cory can thrive. *Can* Tempie, not will. I challenge you to seek common ground."

* * *

After eating a scrumptious pasta dinner, Cory followed Tempia home. Inside her apartment, the couple settled on the couch sipping hot apple cider.

"What are your plans for the holiday?" Tempia asked. "Are you eating dinner with your family?"

"Granny hosts all the major holidays. I was waiting for your counseling sessions to end before bringing up the holiday season. What are your plans?"

"My mother's family joins us for a pre-Thanksgiving meal. I eat dinner with my family on Thanksgiving, Christmas, and New Year's Day. May we spend those holidays together?"

"How about spending Thanksgiving with my family and Christmas with your family. We can split the difference and bring in the new year with both families. However, I've made specific plans for someone's twenty-fourth birthday celebration."

Tempia hugged Cory while blinking back tears. "I'm asking God to make me the perfect woman for my special man."

"So. You're the culprit. The Holy Spirit woke me up one morning with step-by-step instructions. From your mouth to the Father's ears. Keep praying, lovebug. I need His help."

* * *

The Saturday before Thanksgiving Day, Cory joined Tempia's family for a pre-Thanksgiving Day meal. Cory noted how Tempia's stepmother blended within Tempia's mother's family. Tempia's cousins called her stepmother Auntie Blanche. And Blanche called Tempia's grandparents Gammy and Gramps. The entire exhibition made Cory contemplate his family's upcoming celebration.

Five days later, Tempia joined his family's Thanksgiving Day dinner. Tempia's counseling sessions had built the foundation for a well-structured life. She mingled with Cory's family without a care in the world.

Chapter Twenty-Three

On her twenty-fourth birthday, Temple gasped when Cory pulled into the St. Louis Art Museum's parking lot. She knew in a heartbeat that the Festival of Art dinner was her boyfriend's birthday surprise.

"Oh, Cory. I never would've guessed you were bringing me here. Thank you for my marvelous gift. Had I known beforehand, I would've placed one of my mother's paintings on display."

Leaving the car, Cory escorted Tempia inside the building. "See if you approve of the painting your parents chose. *French Tudor-Style Homes* by Tiffany Wade is painting exhibit nineteen."

Tears welled in Tempia's eyes from the depth of Cory's thoughtfulness. "Somehow, saying a simple thank you falls short of your surprise." Brushing off tears, she hugged his neck. She then wrapped her arm around his before he crooked his elbow. Her elation soared when Cory responded with a brief kiss.

While the couple headed toward the banquet hall, the hairs on Tempia's neck and shoulders raised. Skipping a beat, her heart continued beating in a faster rhythm. It felt like somewhere nearby someone was eerily watching her every move. The trepidation she had experienced since entering the building escalated into full-fledged fright.

She took a deep breath and stole an over-the-shoulder peek, locking gazes with her ex-husband. Quince stood aloof. His arms crossed upon his chest, he studied her and Cory. Shock was stamped in each line on his face. Looking straight ahead, she unobtrusively tapped her boyfriend's hand.

"Shh." He tipped her face toward his and stroked her cheek. "I saw him. We have an audience of one." Bending his head, Cory's mouth brushed across her lips.

Her mouth trembled underneath his touch. "The art museum isn't Quince's usual scene. Why is he here?"

"Quince's whereabouts don't concern us. Enjoy the art festival. I certainly will."

Outside the banquet-hall entrance, a hostess led the couple to their table inside the main banquet hall. After being seated, the couple pored over the night's agenda. The artists' painting showcase was the last feature on the live-entertainment lineup.

* * *

Four acts before the artist showcase began, Tempia scooted back her chair and rose from her seat.

Cory reached for her hand. "Where are you headed?"

"Making a restroom run so I won't miss the painting display."

Still holding onto her hand, Cory stood beside her.

Tempia slipped her hand out of his loose grasp. "Please stay seated. I'll be okay."

"There's nothing wrong with me staying near you while your ex is here." He moved closer.

Tempia stamped her foot on the floor. "Yes. There is. Trust I can handle my own problems."

"Of course you can. My discomfort doesn't imply you can't protect yourself against anyone. Look, the man uses intimidation tactics if he feels cornered. I want you to feel safe wherever you are."

"I do feel safe, because I am protected. Gabby always reminds me to trust the God who never fails. The same God goes everywhere I go."

Throwing back his head, Cory chuckled. "Amen to that. A superb belief I must accept because it's true." His voice lowered. "I am here if you need me. See you in a few, lovebug."

The joy displayed in her eyes was worth his stand-down.

"I'll be right back. Do not move one muscle." Wiggling her fingers, Tempia slipped away.

Cory watched her make her way to the farthest corner of the large room. Walking beside walls, Tempia circumvented tables, protecting the diners' privacy. Her respect concerning the little things most people overlooked still amazed Cory.

Cory fiddled with his cell phone while Quince held his rapt attention. He witnessed the precise moment the man realized Tempia was on her own. Through his peripheral vision, Cory noted the quick look Quince gave him before leaving his table. The man's jerky movements didn't jibe with his usual cocky strut.

Instead of following behind his ex-wife, he crossed the room in a straight line. The action guaranteed he would reach the restroom area ahead of Tempia. At the halfway mark, he veered right. The sneak would approach the destination from the right side, blindsiding Tempia, who would advance on the left.

Oh no you don't. Did you forget I've witnessed your unsavory tactics since junior high?

No way would the driven man behave himself.

Dogging Quince's steps, Cory maintained a sufficient distance behind him. He wanted a personal account of what would happen without either party detecting his presence.

Quince passed by the restrooms and peeped around the corner, clocking Tempia's arrival.

Cory slipped into a recessed area behind a decorative column.

Quince adjusted his shirt and tapped his foot.

The foot tapping marked the only instance when Cory had ever witnessed an anxious Quince.

Eyes narrowed, Quince stepped backwards.

Cory knew Tempia had arrived.

Strolling around the corner, she spotted Quince but tempered her shock well. Several emotions flitted upon her face. Eyes averted, she tried sashaying around the man.

Rocking gently on his feet, Quince grabbed her arm.

Biting her bottom lip, she tried to break his hold. "Do ... not ... touch ... me."

His hand dropped, but he closed the gap between them. "I've watched you since you and Cory arrived. You seem happy, content, and well-adjusted." Stroking his chin, he hesitated. "The woman I met was timid. My fiancée fought off apprehension. My wife accepted her fate. This reinvented woman appears vested in future dreams." He paused. "You could at least say a simple hello."

"Hello. Goodbye." She took several steps until Quince blocked her from walking around him. Tempia raised both hands. "Please stop. Leave me alone, Quince."

A tall red-headed woman exiting the restroom hurried beside her. "Are you okay?" She pointed toward a man watching the action from a nearby table. "I can call my husband over here."

Tempia appeared more relaxed as she touched the woman's arm. "Thanks a bunch. I'm fine. Just needed to regroup a bit. He caught me off guard."

"Snakes usually do." The woman eyed Quince. "You sure? We will get involved if needed."

"My boyfriend is around the corner. And probably on his way here."

The woman smiled at Tempia then glared at Quince. "Behave yourself, mister. We're watching you." She glanced at Tempia and Quince as she sat beside her husband, who had turned his seat around, facing them.

"Ignore her intrusion. Here's the deal. Give us a second chance to succeed where we failed. We can make a successful marriage."

While he spoke, Tempia tried circling around Quince.

He cut her off. "Hear me out. I messed up the lifestyle I've admired in respected families. Give me another chance. I promise an abundant future will prevail."

Tempia laughed. "Any association we had died with our marriage. The only regret I have is accepting the first date."

Cory's eyes focused on Quince. The man who couldn't care less about anyone else's feelings recoiled as if he had been attacked.

"I accept all blame for the failure," Quince said. "My boorish, self-serving attitude robbed me of an effective partner willingly working beside me."

Tempia gave Quince side-eye. "I don't welcome being accosted by enemies. Nor do I need to hear pointless information. Happiness surrounds my life on every side. I've moved on."

"Yeah. My supposed friend stole my wife."

Her palms flat on Quince's chest, she shoved him. "Move! This discussion is useless and doesn't serve a credible purpose. My road doesn't lead anywhere near you. My boyfriend is a loyal, kind, and thoughtful man. Nothing like you."

The mulish man hadn't moved one inch. "In other words, I'm deficient in character where Cory isn't?"

"Deficient sums you up. Lacking in decency and missing basic compassion toward other human beings."

Visibly taking deep breaths, Quince flexed his fingers at his side.

Tempia had hit a sore point.

Cory almost left his hiding place, but he remained motionless. There hadn't been any rumors or accusations that Quince physically abused women. Still, his own patience level had reached DEFCON 1.

Lord, help me maintain my peaceful facade. No action would satisfy me more than decking the jerk where he stands.

"I respect Cory's calm, even though his no-drama style doesn't work for me," Quince said. "Neither of us realized our friendship flowed through troubled waters. My angst against him disrupted my inner peace. A way to top him was thrown into my lap. His face lit up when you stepped into the house, and his gaze followed you down the hallway. Cory was excited. The man wanted to meet you."

Tempia's fingers spread into a pleading gesture. "Why are you making a chance meeting more difficult than it should be? The connection you severed no longer exists. I don't choose to communicate with you."

"You've heard his version. Today you get to hear my side." He hesitated, glancing toward where Cory stood.

Too close. Quince almost saw Cory standing there. Good thing Tempia didn't see him. "State your point and leave," Cory murmured under his breath.

As if he had heard the command, Quince tilted his head to one side, studying his ex-wife. "Back to your so-called boyfriend. His excitement raised my antenna. Cory placed his Achilles heel within my grasp."

"A hideous reward to a person who treated you fairly."

"The goal was besting him. It's his fault he got hurt. His understated reaction drove the stakes higher. His nonchalance about our date forced my hand."

"To ruin two lives? Clap yourself on the back if you need applause."

Quince held up two fingers. "Only two?"

"Your life was already a lost cause."

"Those cutting words are beneath you. My aim was topping Cory."

"Asking me out before Cory could wasn't good enough for you?"

"You're right. Past events don't matter. Accept my regrets, and let's make a new start. I'll win you back if given half a chance."

"You're forgiven, but I still don't want you around me. Loving Cory exposed the hatred in my heart you put there. I'm connected to an exceptional man because I vanquished the biggest mistake in my life."

"Defeat isn't an option for me. You and I belong together. Therapy exposed my faulty thinking. Harming you and Cory was an unintentional consequence of wanting to best him."

When two women left the restroom, Tempia edged away from Quince. "Any improvement you've made is a blessing from God. A product inspection won't be required."

"You can prove your forgiveness by accepting me into your life."

"Get real. Either keep your distance or I will lodge a legal complaint. You choose."

His arms hanging at his side, Quince swayed on his feet. "Goodbye, Tempia. I choose to live my life being me, Quince Hightower Jones." He side-stepped his ex-wife then stood still. "Please pass along my apology." Loudly clearing his throat, he stared straight ahead. "We may meet in passing, but I will never contact either you or Cory again."

Walking off, Quince followed Tempia's pathway toward the left.

As if rooted to the spot, Tempia stared after Quince. Compassion high-lighted each feature on her face. A few seconds later, she waved at the couple waving back. Her gaze on the floor, she slipped inside the restroom.

Quince's taking the longer route allowed Cory to reach the table before Quince came into view.

Cory linked his hands on the tabletop. Tempia had held her own when confronting the man who had stolen her self-worth. Charting the proper course demanded nothing less than discernment and conviction.

* * *

Ten minutes later, Tempia reclaimed her seat beside Cory. "Sorry I took so long. I'm amazed you didn't come looking for me. I talked to Quince a few minutes ago. He was coming out of the men's room."

"No, ma'am. Quince followed you when you left the table."

Her eyes squinting, Temple leaned on the chair cushion. "Huh. Imagine that. I thought he took advantage of a chance meeting. Well, let me tell you what happened."

Cory reached across the table and held onto her hand. "He trailed you, and I tracked him. I saw you two talking and heard the entire conversation."

"How, Cory? Where were you standing?"

"Beside the column between the men's and women's restrooms."

"No wonder I got goosebumps," Tempia said, smiling. "My man was nearby and in full protection mode."

"I plan to give it my best shot for the rest of our lives." Cory scooted his chair closer as Tempia gasped. His lips lifted into the grin she loved.

"I don't want to live life without you by my side. I love you, lovebug. Will you honor me by becoming my wife?"

Oh my God! At last. Cory proposed marriage. "I am speechless. Wow! This moment marks the beginning of our happily ever after. At last, Cory and Tempia are getting married."

"Let's spend one year creating a memory scrapbook while combining our lives even more."

"A Christmastime wedding? I like that idea even though twelve months is a mighty long stretch; but I suppose it's well worth the wait. Now I can save my dollars for our dream wedding." Tempia hugged his neck.

Cory pointed toward the stage. "The art exhibit is about to begin. Happy Birthday, Tempie, my beautiful lovebug."

The End

A Note From E. C. Jackson

"The Write Way: A Real Slice of Life" is the slogan on my Facebook author page. If every person reading my book feels connected to the characters, my job is done.

Overflow With Hope is the fifth and final book in the hope-themed series. Many personal and family health issues hindered the writing process, but after three years, I finally wrote "The End." Although I am thankful the promise has been fulfilled, I feel like the characters in each book are old friends and will miss them.

Thank you for hanging in there with me. I am looking forward to writing my next book.

Below, you'll find synopses of my previous hope-themed books. Please give them a read if you have not already.

Book One: *A Gateway to Hope*
Nikhol "Neka" Lacey and James Copley

Twenty-one-year-old Neka is a bit of an introvert, she also happens to be stunningly beautiful. When she discovers her friend James is about to be dumped, she sees the perfect opportunity to escape from her quiet life. Can she summon the courage to leave it all behind?

James Copley comes from a ruthless family. It's rubbed off. Years ago, he disengaged from his brother's smear campaign, but now his father has offered him an ultimatum, "Get married or lose your seat at the table." Plotting to stamp his design on the family business, he proposes to a woman, even though he doesn't love her. But his carefully laid plans start to unravel when she leaves him on the day she's due to meet his family. Could years of planning his comeback vanish with her departure?

A possible solution comes in an unexpected form: Neka. She's not only a friend, but the daughter of his benefactor. And she's right there, offering to support him. But will her support stretch to marriage? He attempts to win her over to his plan but collides with her powerful father who wants to leverage the situation for his own gain.

In their fight for survival and love, they are forced to face some uncomfortable truths. Can they overcome thwarted dreams and missed chances to find true love, or does forcing destiny's hand only lead to misery?

Book Two: *A Living Hope*
Sadie Cummings and Kyle Franklin

It was a match made in heaven. Or so everyone thought. Sadie Mae Cummings is all set to marry her childhood sweetheart, Kyle, when she is assigned to tutor Lincoln, the new college football running back. This sophomore phenomenon has all the girls on campus knocking on his door. But Sadie isn't interested in his advances.

Lincoln's overblown ego doesn't take well to being shunned, and he resolves to make Sadie his own. He pursues her relentlessly, until finally Kyle finds himself shut out of Sadie's life, with their shared future crumbling around him.

After two years, Sadie's relationship with Lincoln ends, and she is left having to put the pieces of her life back together. She desires nothing more than to recapture her relationship with Kyle. He has stayed true to the dreams they had planned together, living the vision even without Sadie by his side.

When she moves back to her hometown, she labors to rekindle their love. But things have changed, and Kyle has moved on. Sadie quickly discovers how hard it is to rebuild burned bridges.

Follow Sadie's story as she fights for a chance to restore broken dreams. Will love endure?

Book Three: *The Certain Hope*
Tara Simpkins and Luke Cassidy

Love at first sight. It's every girl's dream. But Tara Simpkins is finding out it's not as easy as it seems. Is this truly the man God sent to be her husband, or is she just desperate to escape her loneliness? The recent loss of both parents has left her reeling, and close friends don't think she's in any position to make major life decisions. She and her new-found love are convinced they can live happily ever after in the home of their dreams. His family thinks he's moving way too fast and might disappoint the kind-hearted woman he's fallen head over heels for. And then there's Leah. Leah is supposed to be part of his past, but what if she decides she's his future? Tara's match made in Heaven may be over before it truly begins.

Book Four: *The Confident Hope*
Pamela Hayes and Mark Simon

Is there hope for this love between friends?

Pamela Hayes is a smart, successful business owner with a supportive family and a thriving bakery. She should be the happiest girl in the world. But she can't shake the melancholy that accompanies every conversation she has with her best friend, Mark. Pamela doesn't know how much longer she can hide her true feelings.

Why can't Mark see how perfect they would be together? She would make a much better girlfriend than the one he currently has. Pamela prays he'll come to his senses soon and realize he's with the wrong girl. But when her dream comes true, it isn't the fantasy she had envisioned.

There is trouble in paradise from the start, and all the red flags she's been ignoring are starting to threaten her confidence...and her relationship with Mark. She'll have to rely on family and her faith in God to help her secure the hope she so desperately needs

Pajama Party: The Story
Companion book to *A Living Hope*

Pajama Party: The Story is adapted from a play I wrote many years ago.

Most sleepovers are simple. Food, fun, and pillow fights. But sixteen-year-old Karen Duncan has bigger plans for her slumber party. Family troubles have changed her over the past year, and she's no longer the petty, selfish girl she used to be. Now she's ready to shake things up with her friends. The guest list comes as a surprise to some and a slap in the face to others. This popular girl has invited some not-so-popular guests. Even more shocking, she's left out some of the girls she's hung out with since middle school.

Diane and Evette are outsiders, nervous about being stuck in a house with the same girls who tease them at school. Kathy, Lisa, and Joann come to the party with the confidence of the in-crowd, but they're masking inner turmoil that is bound to surface. Sandy and Angela are usually the voices of reason ... usually. And then there's Linda, the friend that got away. She may not ever forgive the girls who abandoned her years ago. Karen hopes to change her mind.

Her agenda is ambitious, and it could spell disaster. But Karen is convinced God will use this party to spark a new beginning for everyone involved. This companion book to *A Living Hope* gives us the inspired story Sadie Cummings wrote for the girls of Shiatown.

About the Author

E. C. Jackson began her writing career with the full-length play *Pajama Party*. Thirty-one years later, she adapted the play into *Pajama Party: The Story*, a companion book to the second book in the five-book standalone Hope series.

Jackson's favorite pastime is reading fiction. She enjoys taking the journey along with the characters in the books. That also led to her unorthodox approach to story writing. Her vision for each book she writes is to immerse readers into the storyline so they become connected with each character.

"The Write Way: A Real Slice of Life" is the slogan on her Facebook author page. She feels that if every person reading her books feels connected to the characters, her job is done.

Made in the USA
Monee, IL
20 December 2023

50098613R00133